THE SPEECH OF ANGELS

Sharon Maas was born in Georgetown, Guyana and studied in England before returning to Guyana where she worked as a journalist. She travelled extensively in South America and spent a number of years living in an ashram in India. She is married with two children and lives in Germany and England.

SHARON MAAS

THE SPEECH OF ANGELS

HarperCollins*Publishers*

HarperCollins*Publishers*
77–85 Fulham Palace Road,
Hammersmith, London W6 8JB

www.harpercollins.co.uk

This paperback edition 2004
1 3 5 7 9 8 6 4 2

This novel is entirely a work of fiction. The names,
characters and incidents portrayed in it are the work of the
author's imagination. Any resemblance to actual persons,
living or dead, events or localities is entirely coincidental.

A catalogue record for this book
is available from the British Library

Drawing of Violin image by Ken Lewis

ISBN 0 00 712386 8

Typeset in Aldus by Palimpsest Book Production Limited,
Polmont, Stirlingshire

Printed and bound in Great Britain by
Clays Ltd, St Ives plc

My thanks to the following for their help in bringing
this book to life:

John Pegler, Simone Clark and Joshua Mehr for
musical advice. Any mistakes I have made are mine,
not theirs. Susan Watt, Sarah Molloy, Sara Fisher
for their help and guidance;

Dennis Austin – he knows what he did!

Mary, Helen, Judy, Joanne, Ewa, Ann, Angelika,
Ulrike, Steve, Marty, Wojtek: Maureen, Manamba,
Fatima, Gloria: for their moral support and inspira-
tion;

Jurgen, Miro and Saskia, for sharing this writer's
life;

Last but not least, Eileen Cox, my mother, without
whom none of this would ever have been.

To R.M.

'Sleeping hearts waken
Dead souls are resurrected
Music brings new life.'

MARTY HANSON-ROSCOE

'And the night shall be filled with music, and the cares,
that infest the day, shall fold their tents, like the Arabs,
And as silently steal away.'

HENRY WADSWORTH LONGFELLOW

'Music is well said to be the speech of angels.'

THOMAS CARLYLE

Prologue

Jyothi's slight form wavered a little as Ma placed the smaller bundle on her head, but she held her head up and gripped it tightly with both hands, and soon found the point of perfect balance. It was bulky rather than heavy, and far easier to carry than water. A single full bucket dragged from the well was back-breaking, down-pulling, stop-and-start work for a girl of five, but she could carry laundry with ease, her arms as props, following Ma with swinging steps and a straight but pliant back, all the way up to the Big House at the top of the hill.

Ma carried a much larger bundle on her head without the help of hands, and she walked briskly, for they were late. Jyothi quickened her pace to keep up. Every now and then she stumbled on the hem of her too-long skirt, stopped to push a fold of fabric into her sagging waistband, and hurried forward to catch up, for Ma would not wait. They reached the top of the hill, turned into the driveway, entered the front courtyard, and walked up the three stairs to the great wooden door at the top.

1

Ma knocked twice with the brass elephant-head knocker. The door swung open silently and Devi Ma let them in, frowning slightly because the sun was already rising above the turrets to the east, and work was waiting.

Jyothi followed Ma who followed Devi Ma; single file they walked along the coloured tiles of a short passageway of fretwork walls into the inner court. Ma lifted the bundle of laundry from her own head, and then Jyothi's bundle, and set both bundles side by side on the marble floor of the inner court. She squatted down herself, and sat back on her haunches, gnarled bare feet firmly planted on the floor, the folds of her sari bunched into a wad between her knees. She untied the knots that held the first bundle, opened the sheet of faded blue cotton, and spread it wide on the blue-mottled marble, revealing a tidy heap of washed and ironed clothes.

Devi Ma squatted down beside Jyothi's ma and together the women began the sorting and the counting: saris in one heap, dhotis in another, blouses and underwear in other, smaller heaps; counting and adding up the prices. Jyothi's ma had lovingly ironed every piece herself and now placed each item with careful, gentle hands on top of the other as if every one was of precious silk, while Devi Ma watched and totted up the prices in her head, rattling off the figures: 'Five, twelve, seventeen, twenty-six . . . This one? Five rupees? No, only four . . . Thirty, thirty-six . . .'

Jyothi's ma could not follow the counting and the calculations but nodded at all of Devi Ma's sums, trusting her. Only occasionally they squabbled over the price of an item, like the big yellow woven bedspread which Jyothi's ma said was so heavy and hard to wash her husband had needed Eldest Son's help in wringing it out, and it was worth fifteen rupees, whereas Devi Ma said it was only worth twelve. But the squabbling was amiable and soon put to rest, and Jyothi's mother got fourteen rupees for the bedspread. After the clean laundry was checked against Devi Ma's list and paid for, the pile of dirty laundry in the corner would have to be sorted, counted and listed. It was a good hour's work, interspersed with good-natured stories of village gossip volunteered by Jyothi's ma in exchange for Great House gossip.

While they did their business Jyothi sat at the edge of the pool in the middle of the courtyard and played with the water-spitting fish. It was an oval pool of turquoise tiles and shallow water which caught the early morning sunlight and played with it in golden concentric circles rippling backwards from the spitting fish. The fish stood upright on his tail-fin at one end of the pool, leaning slightly forward over the surface as if poised to dive in. He spat in a continuous stream that glinted in rainbow colours; but if you put a finger in his mouth, Jyothi discovered, the water turned flat and sprayed out on all sides. You could direct it here and there, and invariably you got your clothes wet; but it didn't matter because soon they dried in the morning sun.

Jyothi wore a red ankle-length cotton skirt and a flowered blouse; her hair was neatly plaited and hung down her back in a thick black rope. She swivelled her body around, lifted her skirt to her knees and put her feet in the pool. She wiggled her toes in the pleasing coolness, then lifted one foot to the fish-mouth and tried to catch the stream of water on her big toe, and laughed as the water ricocheted off the toe and hit her on the forehead. She leaned forward and lifted cups of water out of the pool and let the water fall back through her fingers into itself with a delicious splash. The gurgle of bubbling water was music.

All of a sudden she stopped playing and cocked her head. She had heard a sound, a sweet sound, sweeter even than the water's voice; barely perceptible yet strong, insistent, reminding her of

3

something but she knew not what, calling her somewhere but she knew not where.

If you could turn the first glimpse of the sun rising over the trees at the edge of the village, languidly flinging long arms of light across the meadow where Ranjit's cows grazed, if you could turn that glow and that delight into sound, it would be this. If you could turn the perfume of a rose or the taste of a ripe mango into sound, if you could turn the feel of cool clear water pouring from a fish-mouth and running through your fingers into sound, it would be this.

If you could turn a soul welling with wonder into sound, it would surely be this . . .

Jyothi stood up.

The fretwork passageway led back to the front door in one direction. She had never been in the other direction, had never continued up to its end; always they had left the passage at the arch leading into the inner court.

A last glance at her mother told Jyothi the business of sorting, counting and adding was only halfway through. Her mother had forgotten her presence. The fish with its continuous spitting was oblivious of her, and the spitting itself seemed, now, simply a way of echoing endless, unbroken, unvaried time. But this sweetness . . .

She found herself in a wide room with a wooden herringbone floor, polished to such a shine she could see a faint reflection of herself in the deep brown gloss. A series of arched windows set into one wall let in the early sunlight, casting it in long slanting pools of round-topped light. The room was bare except for a few straight-backed chairs against the walls, and, near the entrance to the passageway, a hat-stand with an oval mirror built into it. Several walking sticks, a black umbrella and a cricket bat leaned against a curved railing at its base. Jyothi was tempted to open and close the umbrella but the heart-stopping sweetness called her on; she crossed the room and followed the sound to an open doorway at the far side. She hesitated just one second before passing the doorway, one second in which she saw again Ma's face and heard as from a far distant time Ma's reprimand, the first time they had entered the Great House: 'Stay by my side, Jyothi, it's a big house and you might get lost in there.'

She found herself in a large hallway, dark, for there were no windows, only several heavy doors of wood, all closed. There was no need to open any of the doors for there was also a staircase, and the sound came from above, from the top of that staircase. Jyothi walked up, her left hand on the banister, looking upwards as if expecting that, any moment now, the glorious sound would take on form and appear as a vision of light before her, a goddess beckoning her on.

Along the upstairs landing there was a wall broken by several more doors, again all closed. As in a trance, Jyothi walked along the landing, arms held out before her as if to feel her way forward, although the landing was not dark like the hallway below, but light, and the light was coming from the far end, as well as the sound. Light and sound merged into a single entity pulling her forward, erasing the memory of Ma and the bundle of clothes downstairs, and even the memory of herself and who she was; wrapping itself around her mind and drawing her into itself.

She felt light-headed, like clear water sparkling with sunlight. As she drew nearer to the source of light a third sense mingled with the light and the sound: a fragrance so pure it hurt. Jyothi arrived at the end of the landing and at the source of light, the arched open doorway out of which the magic drifted. She stopped.

She stood on the threshold of a room which was all light: smooth shining white floor, white bare walls, and, at the far

5

end, opposite to where she stood, an open balustrade broken by a row of slender columns joined by scalloped arches. Beyond the balustrade Jyothi's glance took in the green hills rolling away to the east, and the sun, now well above the hills, brilliant white at its glowing centre, and the entire eastern sky shining white, everywhere a blinding whiteness.

White, too, were the clothes of the two people in the room. It was these two that claimed Jyothi's attention. One of them, she saw at first glance, was the final source of sound. It was a man, sitting cross-legged on a small red carpet that provided the only spot of colour in the entire room. Across his legs rested a sitar; his fingers caressed the strings, and it was the music thus produced which had drawn Jyothi.

Music! This was music! Nothing she had ever heard before was worthy of the name. Not the *filmi* songs her mother played on the tiny radio on the kitchen shelf. Not the blare of the loudspeakers above Chaitnarain's shop which several hours of the day bombarded the entire village with screeching female voices. Sometimes musicians came to the village and there was singing and dancing in the main street, and of course at every festival there was music. She had seen a sitar before; she had even heard one played.

But never before like this. She stood in the doorway, transfixed, staring.

Her gaze included, at the periphery, the second person in the room and now she turned her attention to him. This person was a boy, several years older than herself. Like the musician, he wore two white cloths, one around his hips and one around his shoulders, and he, too, sat cross-legged on the floor, facing the musician, and, it seemed to Jyothi, as transfixed as she herself was.

The musician sat near the back wall, facing the balustrade and the rising sun. Set in the wall beside him was a small arched alcove, in which a shrine had been arranged: a garlanded statue of Krishna, several single hibiscus blossoms, and a rosewood incense-holder with three sticks burned almost halfway down. White filigreed tendrils of fragrance waved softly from the alcove, filling the room to merge with the music and light to form the elusive, insubstantial body of enchantment which had summoned Jyothi.

Spellbound, she remained on the threshold, unable to move or speak, soaking in the sound, light and fragrance.

As if sensing her presence the boy turned his head and looked at her, meeting her gaze and holding it. Jyothi stared back, unsmiling. The thought occurred to her that she should turn, right now, and run back down the hallway, down the stairs, back to Ma. She knew she'd be in trouble if they caught her, if Ma knew she had been caught . . .

And yet . . . she could not move. It was the music that held her, that and the gaze of the boy which even across the room she could see was clear and candid, solemn but not grim, interested but not curious. She stood poised in that gaze for several seconds, then the boy broke the spell by lifting his hand and gesturing for her to come in; and Jyothi timidly crossed the room to where he sat.

He patted the marble floor beside him, and Jyothi sat down, crossing her legs and covering her feet with the hem of her skirt, still looking at him. The boy gestured with his chin towards the musician and Jyothi shifted her gaze in that direction and once again the spell that had been broken by the boy turning his head swept her up and transported her away . . .

Jyothi did not know if she had been sitting there for half a day or only five minutes; all she knew was that the music had stopped and the boy had spoken to her. She shook her head to indicate she had not heard, and he repeated his question.

'What is your name?'

'Jyothi.'

'What are you doing here?'

'My mother brings the laundry . . . I heard the music . . .'

'You like that music?'

'Yes! Oh yes.' Jyothi's eyes glazed over. 'It was the most beautiful thing . . .'

'I think so too,' said the boy. 'This man is my teacher; I am now going to have my music lesson. Every day he plays a morning raga for me and then he gives me my lesson. If you like, you can stay and watch me having my lesson. Not many children like this music; none of my friends do but I love it. I'm going to be a musician when I grow up, like my teacher. What are you going to be?'

But Jyothi's gaze was puzzled; she frowned slightly to show that she did not understand what he was talking about. She was only five but she knew the natural order of things; when she was older she was to marry Harrichand, her father's paternal aunt's brother-in-law's grandson, a boy from the next village who would be a dhobi like her own father. The matter was settled; she knew it and so did everyone else.

She opened her mouth to tell the boy but just at that moment a distant cry startled them and both their heads turned towards the doorway. Jyothi not only turned, she sprang to her feet in guilt for she knew instinctively the cry was because of her.

'I have to go now,' she said hastily, breathlessly, to the boy, and stretched out her hand to him in a gesture of farewell. But instead of doing namaste as would have been polite the boy took the hand in his own and squeezed it, and, not letting go, he, too, stood up.

'Wait! Don't go!' he said. 'I want to talk to you. Won't you—'

But Jyothi pulled her hand away and ran to the doorway.

There, for just a second, she paused and looked back; the boy was still standing on the patch of carpet; he had dropped his hand and now both arms hung at his sides. They looked at each other in silence; simultaneously, as if at an unspoken signal perceptible only to the two of them, they both did namaste. Then Jyothi turned away and ran.

Jyothi was not permitted to return with Ma to the Great House for several days. Ma and Baba were very upset; the Khemraj family was their livelihood, – and a brisk business it was too. Every day there were at least fifty pieces of soiled laundry waiting for Ma when she left the house. Often there were heavy, large pieces: bedspreads and curtains which took long to wash but which paid extremely well, and needed little ironing so that whatever extra time they took at the washing end could be saved at the ironing end. There were eighteen members of that family, the youngest being the baby Arun, the oldest, Great-grandma, ninety-five if she was a day. There were several young maidens who every day wore a different shalwar kameez; three mothers who every day wore a clean sari; as many fathers who dressed themselves in pristine white each day; a handful of wild little boys who dirtied themselves the moment they left the door; and Rabindranath, the dreamer, the musician, he who, they joked, would one day walk one foot above the ground because his soul was so light . . .

Nobody understood what had taken hold of Jyothi, why she had taken it into her little head to disappear. She'd never done a thing like that before.

'It was the music . . .' Jyothi kept repeating, but Ma just shook her head.

'A child doesn't leave her mother's side for *music*,' she scolded. 'Silly child. You will stay home now and sort the dhal.'

So for three days Jyothi stayed home sifting through the dhal with her tiny fingers, fishing out the little pebbles and dead insects and dreaming of music, real music, the music she had heard in the Great House, and the boy who had opened the door to such delight.

On the fourth day, however, Ma relented and took Jyothi with her again; she needed help. There was so much clean laundry today that she had had to make two bundles and Jyothi was to carry the smaller one. Ma loaded it on her head: it was big, but not too heavy, and Jyothi, finding the point of perfect balance, kept her head up and her eyes straight ahead as she walked along beside Ma out of the village and up the hill leading to the Great House.

It was early morning, still dark, though the sky was turning grey in the east and as usual the village was alive with industry – there were women sweeping the forecourts to their houses, sprinkling then with water, and drawing the elaborate chalk kolams. Other women made their way to and from the well with their brass vessels expertly balanced on their heads. In a shed beside the road Kamaraj milked his cow and more women lined up with their battered vessels for the milk. A bullock cart rumbled sleepily through the centre of the main road that cut through the village; a herd of goats, coming from the other direction, broke into two and billowed around the cart like a black wave curling around a boulder. The rumbling and creaking of the cart, the bleating of the goats, the splashing of water and the swishing of broomsticks formed a comfortable background of familiar sound punctuated by the occasional mooing of a cow or the barking of a dog.

A form of music, for Jyothi; sound to wake up into from the oblivion of sleep. There were times, though, when it was different – when it was all drowned out by the loudspeakers, when Chaitnarain decided to do the village a favour by playing one of his cassettes at top volume so that everything you touched vibrated and you had to shout to be heard.

Sookram had started this six months ago, in the wedding season. Then it had been every morning; since then it was only two or three times a week, but Jyothi had never liked it. She put her hands over her ears but Ma pulled them away. Ma wouldn't say if she liked it or not; when Jyothi asked she simply shrugged, 'Where is the question of liking?' she said.

The road was unpaved. Five years ago there had been an attempt at paving: twenty metres leading off from the main road and up to the house had been covered with tarmac, but then left to itself, and now even that small expanse was crumbling away, dissolving into rubble that was painful to walk upon with bare feet. Ma and Jyothi trod carefully along the side of the road where there was a sandy pathway free of pebbles.

As usual, Devi Ma came to receive them but Jyothi noticed at once that something was different: there was not the usual heap of dirty laundry waiting to be counted and bundled and lugged on to Ma's head and carried off to be washed. And, somehow, Devi Ma's smile was different, her attitude more formal.

'Before we begin,' Devi Ma told Ma, 'I want to tell you something. Put down the bundles – we will count later – and come with me.'

She led Ma and Jyothi into the house, through a maze of rooms and hallways to a large, white-tiled room at the back of the house, with an open door leading into a back courtyard.

The room was bare except for one object, a shiny white upright box as tall as Jyothi, against one wall. It seemed to be made of metal. There were the remnants of a puja on top of it: a copper plate with an incense-holder in the middle with the remains of piles of ash and kum-kum, and wilted rose petals, and encircling it a jasmine garland already turning

11

brown around the rims of the little white blossoms, and three small blackening bananas, and half of a coconut. There were the red marks of Shiva on the front of the thing, stains of red against the pristine white; God had been called upon to bless it. Devi Ma walked up to this object and placed one possessive hand upon it.

'This,' Devi Ma proclaimed proudly, 'is a washing machine.'

The washing machine was their ruin. It was a poor village; the housewives did their own washing. The Khemrajs were their only regular customers. Ramkumar, Jyothi's father, was the son and grandson of dhobis who had washed for the Khemraj family in the Great House for generations. The unspoken contract with the Great House was their only means of sustenance. Ramkumar was the eldest son and so he had taken over for his generation; his two brothers had moved to the town and found work there. In the town there were wealthy people, and the wealtheir housewives wouldn't dream of washing their own clothes, and there was work to be had, but not for Ramkumar. The town was not too big and not too small: the dhobis knew the families they worked for and the families knew them, and everything functioned according to an established, pre-ordained pattern. There was no room for a newcomer, an *old* newcomer. Uncles had taken in the brothers when they were still young and they had grown into the work. For Ramkumar, a man nearing fifty, there was no room, no work.

But anyway: Ramkumar had a dream.

Last year his nephew Ganesh had married, and at the wedding Ganesh's grandfather, Ramkumar's maternal uncle Bholanauth, had told him a story which had stayed in Ramkumar's mind.

A year ago this same nephew, Ganesh, had had an accident; he had been knocked over by a motorcycle and had lain in hospital for three weeks hovering between life and death.

'I knew that there was only one way to save my first grandson,' Bholanauth told Ramkumar. 'I had to visit the Ganesh shrine in Bombay. Ganesh is the boy's personal godhead – I knew if I prayed to Him he would intervene and save him. So we sold my wife's gold ornaments and I made the journey to Bombay and went to the shrine.'

Bholanauth described the shrine in glowing detail; he described the city in words of awe and wonder. Listening to him, Ramkumar's mind boggled; he could not imagine a place of such immense proportions; a place of buildings so high you could never see the sunrise; where the streets were so wide and so filled with traffic you had to wait for a light to show green before you even dared cross it; a place where people lived not in huts but in such tall buildings, one family above the other, and hung their washing out of the windows; a place of streets and buildings and swarms of people where you could walk and walk all day and still not reach the other end.

Bholanauth told him of all the miracles he had seen in Bombay, of the shops like palaces and the cars like golden chariots, and the sea that stretched to the sky. But the greatest miracle of all was the Dhobi Ghat.

The Dhobi Ghat, Bholanauth told Ramkumar, was Bombay's vast open-air laundry, the most wondrous place on the face of the earth. He had never seen anything like it, not in all his sixty-one years. Hundreds, no, thousands of dhobis all in one place! The dhobis who worked there were like royalty. They served a city of millions. Each morning the dhobi-wallahs swarmed through the city like ants through a great stone maze. They gathered the soiled clothes and cloths of its citizens and brought them here; they washed, thrashed, twisted, slapped, wrung, rinsed, boiled, and beat the laundry; they strung the garments on pieces of string tied between posts to hang in the windless city heat to dry; they unstrung them

13

and ironed the creases out of them and folded and laid them together and turned them into piles of crisp scented packets of fabric, delivered to the owner's door, on time to the minute, and never a piece lost! Bholanauth had almost drooled with envy at the professionalism of the Bombay dhobis. No beating of cloth on the stone steps of a *tirtha* here; no laying of clothes across a bush to dry. The Bombay ghat was actually made for dhobis; practically laid out in concrete basins and standing cubicles and drainage areas. There were machines to wring the water from the clothes. There was one building, Bholanauth said, with clay ovens lit by fires which heated vats of water which miraculously drove the soil from garments. He spoke of this last building with great awe, as of a temple; it was black and smoky inside from the many fires, he said, and you could hardly see and hardly breathe, and there were half-naked attendants who stood at the edges of the vats stirring the garments in the hot water with long sticks; and there were towers made of garments wrung into long wet snakes and placed in circles on top of each other; and there were hundreds of lines of clothes hanging in the sun to dry; and they used blue to make the white garments whiter, and . . .

Ramkumar's mind reeled at the description; his imagination failed him.

'And how big is the ghat? As big as the Durga Tirtha?'

'Bigger, bigger!' cried Bholanauth. 'Much bigger! Oh you cannot imagine that place! As big as this whole town! And it is laid out in pathways you can walk along to get to the washing cubicles! All day long the dhobis are washing, washing, washing for crores of people – you cannot imagine it, Ramkumar! I have never seen anything like this. Not even the Ganesh temple so impressed me though Ganesh was gracious to me and healed my son – Shiva Shiva Shiva – but the magnitude of this place! And . . .'

And he went on and on, each description of each new feature of the Dhobi Ghat and the people who worked there surpassing the previous so that Ramkumar was easily persuaded that the Dhobi Ghat was the one place on earth he had to see before he died, paradise on earth for a humble dhobi.

And now, out of work, unable to find more work, forced by circumstances to move on to new horizons, Ramkumar remembered Bholanauth's words, and they came to him as an omen.

'To work in the Dhobi Ghat, nephew, is the greatest good fortune that could befall a man of our caste. What must those fortunate dhobis have done in their past lives, to have earned such an auspicious karma! While we stand on the steps of the *tirtha* beating our clothes, those dhobis reign like kings! I can only pray that in my next life I may be born in that great city, and work there among those fortunate laundrymen!'

And Ramkumar, who even as a child had claimed to have visions though no one had believed him, now thought to himself:

This is a sign; it is certainly no chance that Bholanauth told me about the Dhobi Ghat and awakened such urgings in my heart. In my past life I, too, have thus prayed, and lived my life to deserve such good fortune. Losing my work with the Khemrajs was all God's will, to urge me forward to the next phase of my life, to reap the fruits of my deeds in the past life. I will take my family, my wife and sons and daughter, and go to Bombay, and I, too, will work in the Dhobi Ghat!'

Part One

'Music washes away from the soul the dust of everyday life.'

BERTHOLD AUERBACH

Chapter 1

'We should have taken a taxi,' Monika Keller said to her husband Jack. 'I told you we should take a taxi but no, no, Mr Know-it-all thinks it's only a few blocks, we can walk.' She stepped gingerly around a heap of rubble – crumbs of ripped-off tarmac, lumps of dried mud, gravel and sand – that covered half the pavement and extended into the road. On the road next to the rubble was a gaping hole, at least three feet deep and six feet across. Rickety barricades, decorated with warning scraps of red tape, kept the traffic from flowing into the hole; instead, traffic jerked around it in a stop-and-go procedure creating a permanent traffic jam. The hole had been there when they first arrived in Bombay a week ago. Since there were no road-workers digging inside or around it, it was very likely to remain there for another one, two, or three weeks – perhaps indefinitely. The road authorities, Monika assumed, had lost interest. Typical. Chaos. But what else could you expect in India? What could you expect in Bombay?

'Actually it *is* only few blocks,' Jack replied mildly. 'It's this midday sun that makes it seem further. We'll soon be there, just one block more – I know where we are. Come on, give me your bag.'

He placed a gentle hand on her arm to help her around the rubble but Monika shook it off in irritation. 'Don't be patronizing. I can't stand it when you're patronizing. It's not heavy and I'm perfectly capable of carrying it myself.' She shifted the plastic carrier bag from her right to her left hand. 'My God, how I hate this city!'

They had been speaking in German up to now, the language they habitually used when they were alone together. Back home in Germany it was perfectly normal, but here in India they found themselves speaking more and more English together and now it was Jack who, as he often did when taken by surprise, reverted to English. 'Hey, take a look at those kids!'

They had reached the widened area at the corner just before their hotel. Here, two or three lean-to hovels stood against the wall of a building, shacks made up of strips of cloth and plastic and ripped-open cardboard boxes and old planks. Several multi-generational families lived in these hovels – they had seen them before. Women with babies bulging in the fronts of their saris; a wizened old woman who sat muttering with her back to the wall; innumerable ragged children. Jack had glanced at them many times in the days since they'd been in Bombay; Monika made a point of ignoring them.

There were four of them here now on the corner: little girls. Three of them were seated around an old upturned carton. On the carton were leaves of various sizes, arranged like plates around the edge of the 'table', and on the leaves were miniature food arrangements: tiny bits of onions and carrots and banana, cut up fine and delicately laid out to imitate servings at a real meal. It was the work, apparently, of the fourth girl, the oldest, a skinny mite with two long pigtails who was serving the others – mere toddlers – with minute portions of cooked rice, three grains here, four grains there. She held the rice in a screw of paper in her left hand and carefully counted out the grains for each of her 'children' – according, apparently, to a system whereby each child was supplied according to size, the smallest receiving the fewest grains. She herself, the mother, got nothing.

The serving completed, the little mother spoke a word and the chattering, which until now had accompanied the serving of food, stopped; all four children sat stock still and closed their eyes while 'Mother' sang a blessing. That done, they began to eat, each little girl picking up one minute crumb of food at a time with her fingers and placing it gingerly in her mouth, chewing and swallowing before returning for the next mouthful. Beside the roar of traffic and the stench of the gutter, between piles of nasty vermin-infested refuse and crumbling grime-encrusted walls, they ate silently and blissfully, partakers of a heavenly feast.

The little girl-mother must have sensed Jack standing over them and fondly watching. She looked up. Monika, tugging at Jack's shirt and crossly admonishing him to come along, hardened her heart and did her best not to glance in longing at the little urchins. She wagged a stern inner finger at herself and resisted with all her might the urge to gather the four little rag-dolls – for that was what they looked like – into her arms, cart them back to the hotel, plonk them into a warm foam bath and give them a scrubbing, dress them in sweet-smelling new clothes, and pack them all into her luggage to take back home with her. She scowled pointedly. But then the little girl's huge black eyes moved from Jack to her, and caught her gaze, and she melted. The girl's smile was so full of joy and welcome she let go of Jack's shirt and gaped, her jaw hanging loose, foolishly weighed down with unspoken reprimands. Involuntarily, she took a step closer to the feast and joined Jack in what seemed a magic circle in the midst of the filth and pandemonium.

The little girl sat cross-legged at her table, her upturned face bathed in delight. Isn't this all wonderful, her broad smile and beaming eyes seemed to say; isn't this the finest game ever, aren't we having a marvellous feast, and won't you join in? She laughed out loud and jumped to her feet, picked up her own leaf, and offered it to Monika. She spoke some words, which Jack and Monika understood perfectly without knowing a word of the language she spoke.

'Look,' she was saying, 'this delicious food! Help yourself! I cooked it all by myself!'

Monika couldn't help it, she had to smile – that is, she raised the corners of her lip, all the while struggling to keep the surge of motherly sentimentality pressed back into the corner of her mind allotted for such foolish turns. The little girl held the leaf like an offering in her joined palms, and pushed it up nearer to Monika, as if saying, Go on! Take! Eat!

'Take something,' Jack urged. 'Go on! She's offering it to you – it'll be an insult if you refuse!'

'Yes, but . . .' Monika hesitated just one moment before raising her own hands in a gesture of refusal. Sense triumphed over sentimentality. She looked at Jack and wrinkled her nose. 'I mean – from the street! It will be full of germs!'

'Just take a little piece of carrot and pretend to eat it. Like this.' He grinned at the girl, pointed at the leaf and at himself. Immediately, the girl understood and swung her hands to offer the leaf to him. Jack took a tiny square of carrot and placed it on his tongue.

'Mmmm! Delicious!' Jack chewed ostentatiously, contentedly.

The girl tittered and swung her hands back to Monika, prompting her to take and eat with little nudging gestures.

'Jack, you really ate it! You—'

'I really ate it, *you* can pretend. Go on. Have a heart.'

Monika, still hesitating, struggling with the swell of disgust rising in her gorge, looked from Jack to the leaf to the girl's face, met a pair of eager sparkling eyes and couldn't help herself. The feathered lines around her mouth softened, and once more the thin straight line of her lips rose at their corners. Gingerly she hovered her hand above the leaf as if making a careful choice, then quickly pinched up a grain of rice (it had been cooked, she reasoned, so its chances of being germ-free were relatively high) and placed it in her mouth. The muscles on her neck tightened as she chewed, more forcefully than was necessary, for the child's pleasure.

'You really ate it too!' said Jack in delight while Monika clamped the shopping bag under her arm, opened her handbag and took out a paper handkerchief. She wiped her lips, then folded the handkerchief and replaced it in her bag.

'Yes, and if I get diarrhoea tomorrow it's all your fault!' She continued to fumble in her handbag, finally removing a purse.

'What are you doing?'

'Now we have to give her some money.'

'Don't be ridiculous. That would be an insult.'

'What are you talking about? You're the one always giving to beggars. Don't think I don't know you do it behind my back.'

'But she isn't a beggar! We're her *guests*! We can't pay her for—'

But Monika had already removed a one-rupee coin from her purse and was holding it out towards the girl. 'These are poor people. We cannot take from the poor without giving back in return.'

'A crumb of carrot and a grain of rice, for Chrissake!'

'It's the principle,' said Monika primly. She frowned, slightly annoyed that the girl hadn't taken the coin, but had stepped backwards instead, hands behind her back. She tried smiling again, and, holding the coin up between thumb and forefinger, turned it back and forth temptingly. Still the child did not take it. Surprised, Monika took a closer look at her.

She was tiny. Unlike most of the street urchins she had seen (rather, glanced at) till now, the girl's long black hair was neatly combed, not unkempt and caked with grime. Someone had obviously taken the trouble to plait it in the two long ropes that hung forward over her shoulder, tied at the bottom with pieces of red string. The little upturned face was dirt-stained, true – how could it not be, given the constant exposure to exhaust fumes and dust? – yet not grime-encrusted; Monika could actually bear to look at it.

That was not usually the case. More often than not she turned her face in disgust from those miserable sickly creatures that flocked around her legs, it seemed at every street corner, with eyes oozing pus, the bridge between nose and upper lip coated in a slimy green crust, and crooked black stains of grime down their scrawny arms. It hurt too much to look at such human scraps; she could not do it.

Looking at this girl, though, gave pleasure. For the moment Monika forgot about the proffered rupee and lurking emotions and gazed intently at the face. It had a wraithlike beauty to it, a lustre barely veiled by the smudges on the thin cheeks. The eyes shone; the parted lips showed a row of perfect, pearly teeth. The smile was irresistible; Monika returned it, and waved the coin before the girl's upturned face.

'Go on, take it! It's for you!' she said. 'Don't be shy!'

But the girl backed further away, still smiling, and held up a hand in refusal. She spoke, but neither of them could understand. The girl pushed the hand holding the coin away, said something else, then folded the leaf-plate into a little packet and handed it to Monika with two or three more words.

Monika looked helplessly at Jack. 'She's giving it to me! Should I refuse? I can't accept it.'

'You have to,' said Jack. 'I guess it's an honour – if you refuse you might hurt her feelings.'

'Oh,' said Monika. She believed Jack. Jack had an undeniable instinct when dealing with the Indians; he seemed to know what they meant even without understanding their language. They liked him, trusted him automatically. Often Monika had seen Jack engaged in conversation with an off-duty waiter in the hotel lobby; when the room service boy brought their breakfast or the cleaning woman came to tidy their room Jack would end up chatting with them even without a word of a common language. Monika was at once amused and impressed by this unexpected ability, but it annoyed her to be left out of such impromptu conversations. She wished she could be loved as much; in fact, she longed to be loved that way. She envied Jack his universal appeal; she knew that she came across as hard, brittle, unrelenting; she knew it was her fault, for she cultivated that image, but only because she couldn't deal with the reality of her being. For at the core of her was softness. a softness that might overcome her should she once give in to it. And that she could not permit. Being soft made you vulnerable, prey to people who would trample all over you roughshod. But wearing the armour of invulnerability cut you off from people. She wished she could be like Jack: naturally loving and loved by all. Especially, now, loving, and loved by the Indians. She too would like to bask in such a love, to let down her defences and just be. Certainly, such instinctive rapport would be very useful in their enterprise. For she and Jack were no ordinary tourists. They were in Bombay on a Mission.

25

Chapter 2

When Monika had married Jack ten years previously all her friends had said the union wouldn't last. It couldn't: how could Monika, a well-brought-up, well-educated, basically conservative daughter of good middle-class German parents fall in love with a long-haired hippie street musician, drag him home by the seat of his pants, bathe and clothe him, set him on his feet, marry him, and hope for it to last more than a year?

They were called 'the Odd Couple', but they only laughed, and rejoined that no, they were in fact the perfect match! Monika, who laughed much more in those early days of heady love, reminded her mockers that opposites attract: she loved to analyse, she was a head person, a thinker, and Jack was a feeler. Their chemistry was obvious, she insisted; they complemented each other. Jack, with his head up in the air, needed her down-to-earthness and German sense of precision in all matters, practical as well as intellectual.

'And when I get stuck in my head he shows me where my

heart is,' she told her friends with a cocky toss of her hair. 'You can't live on bread alone, and he's my honey! He's a jewel I picked up on the streets!'

Monika wasn't usually given to spontaneous acts of madness. She had been a student at the Evangelical School for Social Work in Freiburg at the time; he, a young Irish-American graduate student of American Literature travelling around Europe on a shoestring, playing the violin on the pavement to earn a bit of extra pocket money.

Monika was captivated by the music Jack played: Mendelssohn's Violin Concerto had always been one of her favourites, and Jack played it with passion and expert ease. She threw a five-Mark coin into his violin case then waited till he finished and the crowd dispersed in order to talk to him. Monika recognized talent when she heard it: she had grown up in a musical family, *Bildungsbürger*, 'educated citizens', a family who made it a habit to play music together every evening after supper. She herself played three instruments adequately but Jack, she heard in an instant, had real talent – that enigmatic, indefinable Factor X. It was no wonder his open violin case held – as she found out later, when he counted – almost twenty Marks.

Monika waited to chat with him, and then invited him home for a meal. He looked as if he hadn't had a good home-cooked meal in a year, she explained afterwards; which was in fact the truth, and Monika was a good cook. The invitation came late in their conversation, of course. First they spoke of music, exchanging opinions, eyeing each other clandestinely while Jack put away his violin.

Perhaps if he had played the guitar Monika would not have stopped. Street musicians playing the guitar were a dime a dozen, especially in Freiburg, a university town with a slight French flair, not too far from the border with the Alsace. But the violin – that showed breeding. And if he had been a misshapen lout, she would not have spoken to him. But Jack was attractive, by no means a dirty stray. Monika had already inspected his feet: they were clean, the toenails clipped. His clothes, too, were clean, if somewhat faded – he did not stink. He wore washed-out jeans, a plain red T-shirt bearing the logo of an American university, and leather sandals, well worn but of good quality. She liked his voice, which was slow, deep and very comforting, and there was something about his American drawl which gave her goose-flesh. He had shoulder-length dark brown – almost black – hair, a moustache and a beard. He had clear black eyes and an engaging, crooked grin – Irish eyes, she thought at once, roguish and full of fun. And it turned out he was, indeed, Irish, or half-Irish. She realized instantly that he too was sizing her up.

Monika, in those days, was generally considered to be quite a beauty. Her red-brown hair was held away from her face by a black velvet band, showing off her high forehead and the classical lines of her face. She too wore jeans, but hers were new and dark blue, and the tailored white blouse she wore over them was crisp and freshly ironed. Her eyes were blue and inquiring, and though her lips were thin they smiled frequently back then. She was a curious girl, always interested in foreign cultures. She hoped to go to America some day, she said. And she *adored* Ireland – the countryside must be quite spectacular.

Jack said he had relatives there and he had recently been to visit them. They were very hospitable: if she ever went to Ireland she must be sure to drop in. And if she ever came to America she was welcome to visit him. She'd be glad to, she replied.

As they strolled over to Monika's student flat in the Stühlinger area in Freiburg, Jack wearing his violin like a rucksack, Monika swinging the plastic bag of new books at her side, they exchanged information, both consciously and more subtly. Occasionally they looked up and their eyes met for a few seconds, questioning and hesitant, exchanging compressed messages in an indecipherable code, then glanced away again, unwilling to expose too much. They both felt it: the chemistry was definitely there.

Jack stayed in Freiburg.

It took some weeks before they had sorted out what they were going to do about each other, and, more importantly, where they would do it. Jack was basically at the end of his European sojourn and ready to settle, and she had known from the start that none of the German boys she had been seeing were fit to tie Jack's shoelaces. They wanted to stay together, but where should they settle, in America or in Germany? Or perhaps, as a compromise, Ireland?

He returned to America; she visited him there. She felt uncomfortable; her English, put into practice, was less than perfect, she found, and Monika was a perfectionist. She felt awkward and disadvantaged, and could not bear the fact that her accent gave her away as a foreigner. Then there was the question of a job: obviously, Monika was going to want to work but what could she do with a German Social Work degree in the USA? Whereas Jack was flexible and could think of a million things to do without being tied to a steady job, which was the one thing he disdained. So Germany it was.

Monika got a coveted government job in the Justice Department, which meant she could join the Civil Service in a year's time: the enviable status offered her lifelong job security, health benefits, guaranteed promotions at regular stages of her career, maternity leave with job guarantee when she had her children (or, if she preferred, a half-time job), and, at the end of the day, a good pension. Jack found employment at the local *Volkshochschule* teaching Adult English in evening classes, two or three classes every day. During the day he read new releases of English books and wrote reviews, which were regularly published in a variety of English and American newspapers and sometimes translated for the German media. He also indulged freely in his one passion: music. Jack was a self-taught guitarist of some ability, and now he went on to learn classical guitar. As a child he had learned to play (besides the violin) the piano and that talent, too, he nourished by at least an hour's practice a day. Monika, who considered herself a musical authority, informed him that he was a born musician with that 'certain something'.

'When we have children,' Monika said (for they had decided to marry), 'we will be a musical family. Each child shall play a different instrument, and in the evening there will be no television – we will have family concerts!'

Their daughter, Monika decided in advance, would play the flute or the violin – she could have a choice – and the boy, definitely, the cello.

It was an ideal set-up, as Monika never failed to emphasize: when children came Jack would be at home during the day, she during the evening, and they could share childcare.

But children never came.

The first few years they didn't want any. Monika was too busy building her career; Jack didn't mind either way. Monika said they could stop birth control after five years. She was paying regularly into a building society and together with what her parents had promised her they could then make the down payment on a three-bedroom house in an idyllic village outside Backnang, near Stuttgart, where they worked. Two children, she thought, two and a half years apart, preferably a boy and a girl but good health was more important.

But children didn't come. Not after five years.

When the fifth year was over Monika and Jack (at Monika's insistence) had themselves tested but the tests showed no medical reason for the failed conception.

'Just keep trying,' said Dr Marx with a leering grin. Monika, offended by his grin, changed doctors. Nature just needed time, she told Jack, her parents, and other impatient family members. Sooner or later, children would come.

But children never came.

Jack was saddened; Monika desolate. With each month her desperation increased; it seemed to her that a child was all that she had ever wanted, all that she would ever ask of life.

In various ways they tried to trick nature into complying with the plan – stopping just short of artificial insemination – but nature refused to comply. And so they proceeded with Plan B.

Plan B was adoption. But, they were told by the blonde hawk-nosed lady at the *Jugendamt*, new-born babies were rare and they would be on a waiting list – they could expect it to be two or three years, probably longer, before Plan B could be realized. Of course, if they were willing to accept an older child, or a disabled one . . . Monika shook her head vigorously.

They left the formidable woman's office and walked down the corridor to the stairs. Jack took Monika's hand in comfort. 'It's all right, honey,' he said. 'We can wait. What's a few years? And we'll just keep on trying . . . We're still young. My mom had me when she was thirty-five! Sooner or later, when we least expect it, it'll happen.'

But it didn't. Their childlessness dulled to a chronic ache in the background of Monika's consciousness, which she tried as best she could to camouflage. 'It's all right for you,' she told Jack accusingly. 'You're a man. Men don't feel these things the way women do.'

After much consideration, she concluded she could best deal

with her childlessness through social activity. Her job as a Court Assistant in the Prosecutor's Office had become a comfortable routine. Prosecutors would send her the files of alleged criminal offenders, and request a personality profile. It was Monika's task to speak to the person concerned, weigh certain variables in his home and work situation, and form an opinion as to any possible future criminal activity. Her written report would then be taken into account when the case came to court, influencing both the prosecutor and the judge when the time came to propose a suitable punishment. It was a job of some responsibility, which Monika fulfilled with great dedication. She was strict but fair, carefully weighing all elements in the case before coming to a conclusion, and never letting her emotions get the better of her. Compassion played no role in this profession. If she sincerely believed that the 68-year-old grandmother who had been caught shoplifting for the tenth time would continue to shoplift then she said this quite clearly, and did not let the grandmother's sobs and pleas for mercy influence her. 'A minimum prison sentence,' Monika would advise, 'would shame and shock her into the desired effect.'

Monika might be a social worker by name, but she was, in effect, a white-collar desk worker whose main task was the management of files and the passing of paper, and therefore highly unsatisfactory. She needed truly to *involve* herself in the lives of others, she decided, and work with her *heart*, which was not allowed to interfere in her Monday-to-Friday nine-to-five routine. Only a properly social activity could absorb the gnawing emptiness left by her unsatisfied maternal urge.

She joined the local chapter of a private charitable organization called A Heart for Children. The main work of the organization was fundraising; it then distributed the money collected to any worthy cause that benefited children. Organizations could apply for help, but so could individuals. The president of the local chapter was a woman married to a top manager of the Mercedes-Benz factory in nearby Sindelfingen. Most of the other lady functionaries (it was, in fact, a ladies' club, a female twin to the Rotary Club) were similarly the wives of managers, bank presidents, entrepreneurs and the like, wealthy and public-minded, with a great deal of time on their hands and the impulse to do good. The club was in the early stages of growth; it had started with a handful of such women five years ago and since then had managed to draw over a hundred members into the fold. Monika was one of the most active. She organized bring-and-buy sales, cake stalls on the local market-place, and a various other fundraising activities. She was responsible for screening applications: visiting the homes of the poor families applying for help to see if their need was genuine. And now, with the chapter's decision to expand and send out feelers to the Third World to see what could be done there, it was Monika who had volunteered to make this pioneering trip. She was to scan the new territory and if possible to set up the structure for the initial project.

They had chosen Bombay for several reasons. One of the women had read an article in *Der Spiegel* that spoke of the deplorable conditions in which the street children lived there. 'We must go where the need is greatest!' she had said at one of the meetings. And then there was Dr Prashad, Mrs Stegmüller's brother-in-law, who now lived and worked in Stuttgart but was from Bombay, and whose cousin in that city was herself involved with charitable work. Dr Prashad's cousin was a *connection*; obviously they would need connections to get started.

Their plans for Bombay were vague. Many of the women thought setting up a home for street children would be the best way to help. Others wanted to start a school for them. Yet others thought it would be better to start an educational fund to support the attendance of these children in a local school. Monika, they all agreed, would have to go and see for herself which option might be possible.

Another young woman, Mrs Thalheimer, agreed to accompany Monika but at the last minute found out she was pregnant and backed out. Jack replaced her. And here they were, now, in Bombay.

Chapter 3

Monika had not imagined, in all of her wildest dreams, the pandemonium she would find here. She had not imagined that every morning she would wake up with all her mind baulking at the mere thought of leaving the cool clean cloistered hotel environment and going forth to brave the bedlam outside.

See no evil, hear no evil, speak no evil . . . and to that, here in this hellhole, add *smell* no evil. Close down all your senses; lock them out and throw away the key. Make yourself immune to the misery, ignore it, for otherwise how could a human heart bear it? That was Monika's policy. So Monika tucked all her outrage and all her horror and all her pity into a convenient little box stowed away in the centre of her heart, stepped into an armour of rational do-gooderism, and performed her mission with a zeal and a perfectionism that permitted not the tiniest chink of sentimentality.

Monika had organized enough second-hand bazaars, written enough appeals and reports for her organization's monthly newsletter, given enough lectures (together with coloured slides and projector) at the local *Volkshochschule* that she could uphold, without a trace of misplaced guilt, the steadfast resolution of never giving a penny to a street beggar.

'It doesn't really help them in the least,' she was never tired of telling her eager flock of helpers back at home. 'Certainly, they might be able to buy a few grams of rice to feed a hungry child, but begging should not be encouraged. We have to help at the *source*. We must remove the very *cause* of poverty. These people must be helped through better organization: better structures – in a word, through better politics. We have to get to the root of the problem! Society itself has to be restructured!'

That was the theory. But then there was Jack. Jack was a constant fly in the ointment of her grand scheme for Upliftment of the Needy. Jack, in his own affable way, managed to circumvent his wife's injunctions by doing it when she wasn't looking – he kept several one-rupee coins in his pocket and had perfected the art of slipping his hand into his jeans pocket, removing a coin, casually placing his hand behind his back, and letting the coin drop in front of a beggar without once looking back. Sometimes she caught him at it and wagged her finger at him, but it was difficult to be displeased with Jack – his sheepdog look and lopsided grin was enough to melt anyone's heart. Moreover, Jack knew her secret, her little wound spot, and poked his finger smack into the middle of it as best and as often he could. That wound spot was children. Monika couldn't resist them; and Jack knew it. If Monika turned away from beggar children it was not out of contempt; it was out of an overabundance of compassion. She could not bear their misery. She longed to gather them all into her arms, bathe, clothe and feed them, settle them all with their parents in homely but clean cottages with running water and pretty front gardens, and generally perform a miracle on their lives.

She glanced now at Jack, who was sitting on the edge of the bed trying out some complicated new finger gymnastics on the guitar. Jack seemed unperturbed by it all. When they walked the streets, Jack looked around him with interest and seemed physically to imbibe the sounds, the smells, the sights, converting them all into some new facet of his being, and revelling at the process. Jack looked at every passer-by, smiling, trying to catch eyes. Jack would stop at anything that interested him, to get a closer look or exchange a few words with the protagonist – or if not words, then gestures. People seemed to understand Jack's gestures, and he theirs.

This attitude irritated Monika no end. She would have liked to exchange notes with Jack over all the things that annoyed her – and most of the time it seemed that *everything* annoyed her. She wanted to murmur things like 'pigsty' or '*kaputt*' or 'slipshod', meet Jack's eyes and nod knowingly with him, partners in disapproval. With Mrs Thalheimer it would have been possible. Jack just laughed off her complaints. 'That's just the way it is,' he'd say, then shrug and grin and get on with life as if this was the norm, adapting his agenda to the circumstances.

Most of all, Monika could not bear to look at the children, and needed all her strength not to grumble to God about the injustice of it all. So many beggar children. So many homeless, so many undernourished children: surely God had made a mistake, giving them to parents who could not afford to keep them – and leaving her own womb empty. The children poked and prodded at the deep wound in her heart and the bleeding she had thought stopped began to ooze again. It was unendurable. The squalor and the misery she saw all around her seemed but a reflection of the mire she was wading through in her own soul.

She looked away. *Why! Why! Why!* she cried to an unfeeling, unhearing God. *Why can't I have my own!*

Jack now packed his guitar into its case, stood up, and slung the strap over his shoulder.

'You're not taking *that* with you, are you?' said Monika, looking up from her open handbag. It was a voluminous thing, which held everything she might need during the day: two packets of paper handkerchiefs; a small bottle of mineral water; two small packets of biscuits, one sweet and one salt; a tube of glucose tablets; hairbrush and comb; a moist flannel in a plastic zipped bag (good for perspiring faces). And, of course, her wallet with a limited amount of hundred-rupee notes and credit card. All other valuables such as travellers' cheques and passport were locked up in the hotel safe. She wore no jewellery; she hardly ever did anyway, and she would not dream of flaunting wealth before the poor. She was dressed simply as a sign of her compassion, yet still managed to look very smart and prosperous: pale blue slacks with a knife-fold down the front, a crisply ironed sparkling-white T-shirt with a bunch of flowers printed on the front and black leather pumps. She was having some trouble with her feet, which seemed to have swollen at the ankles so the pumps pinched, but wearing sandals was out of the question. The first day she had done so she had returned to the hotel with black feet crossed with bars of white skin. So now she wore shoes and thin knee-length nylon socks. If her feet continued to swell, though, she would have to buy a pair of larger shoes. Jack had massaged her feet and ankles the night before. Jack gave good massages.

She locked her handbag with a snap and looked at Jack, who had not yet answered her question. 'Jack! Why take your guitar with you?'

Jack bent his knees, leaned back to look in the mirror and

ran his fingers through his hair, pushing back the black lick that had fallen over his forehead.

'Just an idea,' he replied. 'I thought it'd be nice to sing for the kids. Maybe even get them to sing along with me.'

This morning Mrs Rajpaul was taking them to see the Sri Krishnaji Orphanage, which was one of the children's homes a Heart for Children was considering taking into their financial-support programme. In the last few days they had seen a day-care centre for young children, a school, and the children's ward of a charity hospital.

Every time Monika saw children her heart bled for them. She wanted to help them all, the poor little things! 'Everywhere,' she groaned, 'everywhere the need is so great! I wish we could support them all!'

The thought came to her that they could adopt one of these children. A baby, of course. This was the perfect opportunity: why hadn't they thought of it before! Jack agreed, and they put the matter to Mrs Rajpaul who dismissed it right away. The bureaucracy, she said, was too much for a sane human to overcome and still stay sane.

'I know of one lady, a French lady, who tried to adopt a little girl!' Mrs Rajpaul said sternly. 'And it took her seven years before she got her! Seven years! Do you want to go through that torture!' So they had rejected the idea. But Monika could help in another way, and that she was determined to do.

Monika was stern with herself. She was aware of her own sweet and slightly nauseating sentimentality – an embarrassing flaw in an otherwise perfectly sensible and well-organized mind – and recognized the need to put it firmly in its place in a square white box in a tidy corner of her mind where it could not interfere with the decision that had to be made. One had to be rational about a thing like this, and Monika's rational faculty

– unlike Jack's – was (apart from her one personal little sore point) in good working order.

Now, she said to Jack: 'Jack, remember what Mr Metzger said! We can only maintain our authority if we also maintain a distance! Playing the guitar and singing at an orphanage would be much too familiar – especially at this stage. We should try to maintain an efficient, businesslike atmosphere. Fraternization now could sabotage all our efforts!'

They had dined with Mr Metzger and his wife the night before. Mr Metzger was the president of the German Catholic organization Sacred Heart, which ran the mission hospital they had visited the day before, and which was willing to accept A Heart for Children as a junior – very junior – partner in the charitable venture. The Metzgers had lived in India for ten years and considered themselves old and expert hands, and were more than eager to give Monika and Jack advice on the behind-the-scenes nuances of dealing with Indians. Mr Metzger was absolutely convinced that it was necessary to keep the gulf between foreign donors and Indian beneficiaries as wide as possible, in order to prevent what he called exploitation.

'We foreigners tend to get soft-hearted in the face of so much misery,' Mr Metzger explained. 'It awakens our guilty conscience. The Indians feel this and exploit it. If you give them a little finger they take the whole arm. They are also very sly and will try with various underhand tricks to wheedle more and more out of you. Before coming to Bombay we were in a small town in Andra Pradesh and believe me, some of the beggars there had huge stashes of money hidden in their rags! We couldn't believe it.'

Mrs Metzger nodded vigorously at this point, and seemed to be eager to add a pertinent comment of her own, but her husband continued, leaving her with an open mouth and looking rather silly.

'Some of them make a small fortune from begging and they spend it on women and alcohol and cigarettes. And be wary of beggars with sick or crippled children. Sometimes they do it deliberately to get more money. So you must go about this work very soberly and rationally – don't allow feelings to come into it. We regard it as a sacred mission, a task given us by God which we perform to the best of our abilities and as fairly and as dispassionately as possible. Our motto is: Give generously, but remember you are doing it for Jesus and not for these poor creatures. "Whatever you do for one of these you are doing unto me." Whatever you do, be wary. We made several mistakes in our early years due to inexperience and soft-heartedness – especially my wife. Ulrike, do you remember the story with the leper-woman and how you got taken in? Perhaps you'd like to tell it now?'

Mrs Metzger launched starry-eyed into her story and Monika and Jack listened, Monika drinking in every word. This was the kind of attitude she needed, she realized. With such an attitude she could move mountains! She pushed the little white box of sentimentality further into its corner.

However, Jack had no such little white box, and Jack, as usual, was immune to her sound advice.

Jack patted his guitar lovingly and said, 'Oh, a few songs will cheer 'em up a bit, that can't hurt. You can't call it fraternization. And it's just for the kids.'

'But—'

But Jack and his guitar were gone. He was waiting for Monika at the lift.

When they walked past the lean-to near the hotel the little girl was on the pavement again, playing with a piece of a twig wrapped up in an old rag, obviously an improvised doll, which she held upright and pushed along a crack in the pavement.

41

She was deep in conversation with this little person, and did not notice when Jack came to a stop not a metre away from her. Then Jack said 'Hi!' and she looked up.

Seeing him, her face lit up with a delighted smile of recognition and she jumped to her feet, saluting him, leaving the doll prostrate on the pavement.

'Jack, come along, we'll be *late*!' said Monika, pulling his forearm. Jack ignored her.

'Shall I sing you a song?' he said to the little girl. She answered him in her own language, hopping up and down as if she had understood.

'Jack! We don't have the *time* for this now!' Monika looked at her watch and tugged once again at Jack's shirt.

Jack had removed the guitar from his shoulder. He leaned the case against the wall, opened it and removed the guitar. 'It's OK, Monika, it'll only be five minutes. Just one little song.'

Monika shook her head in frustration. It was what she positively hated about Jack, his lack of a sense of time or of haste. Jack was notoriously late for everything. He never wore a watch, but simply took things in his stride, one event after the other, as the notion took him. They should have taken a taxi. But as the hotel was on one side of a heavily trafficked four-lane highway it would have meant a long detour up one side of the street and then back down the other. It was quicker, more convenient and cheaper to walk the four blocks to the bicycle shop owned by Mrs Rajpaul's husband, where they had arranged to meet this morning.

Jack had slung the strap of his guitar over his head, and let it slip comfortably onto his shoulder. He leaned his buttocks against the wall and began to tune the guitar.

'Jack! That wall is just filthy!' cried Monika, but Jack was busy with the G-string. The little girl stood staring at him, as still as a statue, smiling all the time. She was dressed in rags, pieces of cloth in shades of grey hanging across her shoulders and around her hips, torn and threadbare.

Jack sang 'Puff, the Magic Dragon'. At the end of the first verse the girl was standing right before him, staring now at the strings of his guitar, now at his moving lips, now reaching out to touch the shining chestnut body of the instrument but drawing back at the last moment. Jack's gaze rested on her. Her foot was tapping to the beat; she began to twirl in time to the music. A living dance, longing to be set free, thought Jack.

People were stopping to stare. The old woman who had been here the day before emerged from behind a curtain of rags before the second hovel. A woman with a baby at her breast followed, two little girls – the same ones they had seen the previous day – tugging at her skirt. A weary-looking middle-aged woman came out of the first hovel and placed a hand on the little girl's shoulder as if to tug her back, but the girl reached for her hand and pointed at Jack, smiling, and this woman, too, listened. Two bicyclists paused to listen. A boy carrying an enormous basket of bananas stopped and placed the basket on the pavement.

'Jack, you're creating a *scene*!' hissed Monika, who hated scenes. Jack didn't mind them at all; long ago he had made his way around Europe doing this, and he loved it – bringing music into the streets, he believed, was a service to humanity.

Monika looked around at the gaping people. Quite possibly, she thought, none of them had ever seen a guitar before. There was a fascination in their eyes she had never witnessed even in a concert hall, but the little girl at the front was more than fascinated – she was spellbound.

Jack played a last triumphant chord. The little girl cried out something which he couldn't understand, and then she began to hum, and when he lowered his head to hear better he found she was singing the song he had sung, in perfect pitch but with

43

made-up words. He sang along with her; she stopped, listened, and then tried the correct words, again with perfect pitch.

'Come along, Jack!' nagged Monika.

'Just a minute, this is great!' said Jack, raising a hand that was meant to calm Monika but only fanned her impatience. The little girl ran a finger along one of the guitar strings, and plucked at it.

'Try it,' said Jack, and raised the instrument to remove the strap from around his neck. He handed it to her. It was heavy and she staggered, but then she sat down on the pavement, holding it across her lap, twisting it back and forth, inspecting it, plucking at a string, strumming. She held the neck in her left hand and tried to reach the strings with her tiny fingers, but could not. She gave up, removed her hand, and pressed the strings from above – three strings together, strumming at the same time, and singing.

'Hey, Monika! Just watch that! Christ, that's a C-chord! Just *look* at her! She's playing a C-chord!'

'Jack,' said Monika firmly. 'We can't waste another minute here. We are already half an hour late. Now put your guitar away and let's go! You can come back this evening if you want to but not *now*!'

Recognizing the this-is-the-last-straw tone of voice Jack reluctantly prised the guitar from the little girl's hands, making conciliatory gestures.

'I'll be back later,' he told her while placing it back into its case. 'I'll let you play some more later on today, OK?'

The little girl stood with her hands behind her back, just watching and smiling.

'Me, Jack' said Jack, pointing at himself. 'Jack, Jack. What is your name? You? You?'

He pointed at her. She understood right away.

She pointed to herself. 'Jyothi,' she said.

44

Jack tried to repeat the word. 'Choti?' he said, pointing at her.

She laughed at his pronounciation. Her teeth were even and very white, small like grains of rice pressed flat. 'J-yoti!' she corrected, 'J-yoti!'

'Jyothi,' Jack said. He waved goodbye. 'Hey, Monika!'

But Monika, feigning utter indifference, had turned her back and moved on up the pavement. Jack hurried to catch up with her.

'Her name's Jyothi! Isn't she—'

'We're *late*!' said Monika.

Chapter 4

It was past midday when they returned to the hotel, and they came in a taxi and so did not walk past Jyothi's home. They were both drained, though they had done nothing more than visit the orphanage and talk to Mrs Rajpaul and the orphanage mother about potential future cooperation. Monika was optimistic – it looked as if this was what they were looking for. The orphanage was housed in an abandoned school and occupied only half of the building. With the necessary funding there were a multitude of expansion possibilities. The only fly in the ointment was the fact that it was hitherto run by a Hindu organization, the Sri Satyananda Sangham.

'Many of the ladies at home won't like that,' Monika was saying to Jack as they walked up the stairs to the hotel entrance. A smiling doorman in white livery – narrow-legged trousers, white double-breasted long-sleeved coat with a red sash at the waist and golden buttons, and peaked white cap – held open the swing door for them, and Monika swept past him into the air-conditioned lobby. 'I know for a fact that Mrs Thalheimer is a very strict Catholic and won't agree to affiliation with a heathen organization, and—'

Jack, waving and grinning at the doorman, said casually, 'I thought A Heart for Children is non-denominational?'

'Well, yes, of course,' said Monika, heading for the lifts. 'But only in the Christian, ecumenical sense. I mean, we wouldn't join hands with a Muslim organization in Germany, would we? With all due respect to religious freedom, it would be looking for trouble. Practically speaking non-denominational means Catholic and Evangelical.'

'So that means you'll have to run with the Metzgers,' said Jack. He pressed the button for the fourth floor. The lift door closed and they began their upward glide. 'The Sacred Heart hospital.'

'Yes, but the trouble is, they are *too* Catholic. Many of our Evangelical ladies would object to that as well. And we've already decided the help should go in the direction of education and homelessness. And anyway, the Sacred Heart is so strong on its own, they would dwarf us – they would always have the last word. But if we were to work with Mrs Rajpaul . . .'

Monika's eyes glowed. Mrs Rajpaul had all but gone down on her knees to beg her to adopt the orphanage as Worthy Cause. The orphanage mother, too, had been obsequious in her desire to make a good impression on Monika. As for the children – well. The children had rushed up the moment they had entered the premises, crowded around them laughing and waving, each trying to attract attention, and only a very harsh word from the mother had induced them to be silent and step back. The mother, obviously very embarrassed, had apologized profusely for the display of bad behaviour, and tried to make up for it by fawning.

Monika's little white box had stirred and rattled once or twice at the onslaught but she had pressed it firmly back into position with a silent admonishment: *no sentimentality!* The issue had to be considered along purely rational lines.

'They would be so grateful to us. The orphanage is run on a shoestring; they are desperate for financial assistance. Someone to give them a lift under the arms, so to speak. If we were to step in there now, we would be the primary donors and be highly respected. We would always have the last word in the decision-making process. We could really have some . . . some . . .'

'Power,' suggested Jack. The lift jolted to a stop, and they stepped into the corridor.

'Well, yes, putting it a little crassly,' conceded Monika. 'It's not a bad thing. *Somebody* must hold the reins in an operation like this and you heard what Mr Metzger said. I would not like for us to be controlled by an Indian charity – it has to be the other way around, and this would be perfect. If only they weren't so damned Hindu. All those pictures of Hindu gods all over the place. Dreadful.'

They had arrived at their room and she opened her handbag to take out the key, which was in a zipped-up side pocket. She slid it into the lock and opened the door.

'Mind you, if we were in charge we could insist that they take down the pictures,' she mused, almost to herself.

'And hang up a few crosses around the place instead,' said Jack.

'No, no, we're not missionaries, we . . . Oh, it's supposed to be a joke. Well, you might be laughing now but believe me, it wouldn't be funny at all if they started their Hindu practices in an orphanage run by us. It just wouldn't do. Killing off the girls, and so on.'

'Killing off the . . . where did you get that one from?'

'Well, I read it somewhere, or saw it in a TV programme.

48

Terrible. No, if we decide to take on the orphanage it would have to be according to our own specifications. We would need a German board of directors and someone would have to come over regularly to inspect. Better yet, if one of us were to be actually living here . . . but that's an impossible dream, of course. Although maybe we could find some German living in Bombay who would take on the task on a voluntary basis, as an act of goodwill? Who knows.'

'You sound as if you've practically made up your mind.'

'Well, you know I was quite taken with the Metzgers and it would be nice to work with someone of his experience but I'm afraid he would be just too controlling and we wouldn't have the freedom to develop our own ideas. Quite apart from the Catholic problem, of course. I know you had a good time at the orphanage . . . it's your choice too, I think!'

Monika showered and changed her clothes, and they went down to the hotel restaurant for lunch. After lunch they returned to the room. Monika put on her pyjamas and got into bed, announcing that she would sleep till four after which they had their first planned sightseeing tour.

Jack was restless and could not sleep. He looked through the *Times of India* for the second time, then flicked it aside and switched on the television. He found a German programme and the news in an Indian language, and a host of Indian musical films. He switched it off again, thought for a while, then stood up, grabbed his guitar, and left the room.

Jyothi was not at home, and Jack felt a flicker of disappointment. He mused briefly, and then walked on up the street. After about a block he came to some small shops lining the pavement – a row of shops selling miscellaneous articles and foodstuffs on the right, and various vendors selling cigarettes, sweets, combs, fruit and biscuits on the left. Jack bought a packet of biscuits, several varieties of sweets, three apples, a pound of rice, a pound of dhal, a bunch of bananas and a shopping bag to put it all in. He then returned to Jyothi's home. She was still not there; he called, but no one answered. He wondered about the rest of her family. Apparently there was only a mother; the three little girls he had first seen her with, it seemed, belonged to the neighbour's family. He had seen them clinging to the skirts of a younger woman.

The entrance to Jyothi's lean-to, the hovel he had seen her mother emerging from, was closed by a tattered red cloth which had perhaps once been a shawl. He reached inside with the bag of food and let it down on to the ground, where whoever first entered would be bound to see it. Then he returned to the hotel, went to the bar, drank a beer, met a young Indian businessman, and played cards with him in the hotel lobby till Monika came looking for him at three-thirty.

Monika sent him back to the room to shower and change. After that they went on their tour of Bombay. Jack did not see Jyothi again that day.

During the next few days they often passed Jyothi's home, but saw her only seldom. Whenever they returned to the hotel by taxi they drove past, since the hotel was on a busy thoroughfare and could only be approached from one direction. Occasionally they walked past. Once Jack, returning from a solitary stroll around the area, saw her mother working outside. He smiled at her and spoke a few words of greeting, knowing she would not understand, and she waved back in return. She was a small, skinny woman with an old-young face – eyes still bright with the hope of youth, but weary with the burden of age. She wore a threadbare sari of an unidentifiable non-colour, and was busy hanging bits of damp washing over the filthy wall and along the edge of the lean-to's roof.

On the third day they were returning in the taxi and Jack saw a man holding a squirming Jyothi by one thin little arm and raining blows on her back with a length of thick rope. The mother stood nearby, facing the wall; she seemed bowed over, as if her face was buried in her hands. Two youths stood by, gaping. Jyothi's cries, quite audible above the roar of the city, were those of a child in terror.

'Stop,' said Jack to the taxi-driver, but it was not possible – the roadworks were, at the moment, being carried out and there was a team of men hacking at the street with iron picks. Traffic was reduced to one lane and filed past slowly. The driver explained this to Jack and continued.

'Did you see that?' said Jack to Monika.

'Yes, I saw,' said Monika. 'That awful man beating the poor little girl. That's the kind of thing we— Jack, where are you off to now?'

Even before the taxi could turn into the hotel forecourt Jack had the door open and was out of it.

'Jack, come back! Don't get mixed up in it, it's not your business . . . Jack? Jack!' But Monika's cries went unheard.

When he arrived at the lean-to neither Jyothi nor the man – he assumed it was her father – could be seen. The mother was sweeping the pavement with a broom of reeds, and looked up when he came.

'Where's Jyothi?' said Jack right away, holding his hand out at Jyothi's head level. The woman made a sign, which Jack interpreted to mean she had gone.

'Where has she gone to? Was that her father? Why . . . ?'

But the woman only shrugged and continued with her sweeping. Frustrated, Jack looked around at the pedestrians. One man wearing a white shirt and dark brown trousers looked as if he might speak English and, when Jack stopped and asked him, admitted as much.

51

'Would you ask this woman, please, where her little daughter went to?'

The man spoke to Jyothi's mother, then said, 'The little girl is working, sah. Helping father.'

'What kind of work does the father do?' Once more, the man translated back and forth.

'He is dhobi.'

'What's a dhobi?'

'Washer-man, sah. Dhobi is washer-man.'

'Listen, the man was beating the little girl. Can you ask her why—'

Suddenly the man seemed in a hurry to move on. 'If he was beating her she must have been misbehaving, sah. Excuse me, I have to go now.' He bowed his head slightly and touched the tips of his fingers together, then walked away. Turning around Jack saw that Jyothi's mother had vanished as well. The cloth hanging in the doorway still trembled from her hurried entrance.

Jack walked on down the road, away from the hotel. Twenty minutes later he returned with a bag full of potatoes and a plastic doll. Outside the lean-to he called, and after a minute a small hand drew back the makeshift curtain and Jyothi's mother stood, stooped, in the doorway, looking at him with eyes that concealed more than they revealed, and yet spoke of hurt and fear and suspicion. Jack held out the bag and the doll. He pointed at the doll and said, 'For Jyothi.' The woman nodded and took both without a sign of either surprise or gratitude. Jack took out his wallet, edged out a twenty-rupee note, and gave that to her as well. She took that with the same expression of apathy.

'I'm going now,' said Jack, slowly. 'But I'll be back. See you tomorrow.' The woman bobbed her head slightly but showed no other sign of acknowledgement. Jack returned to the hotel.

He felt heavy and very, very alone. He could not bear to speak to Monika, parry her questions. He went to the hotel bar and ordered a whiskey.

That evening they were invited to supper at Mrs Rajpaul's home. All day long Monika had been mulling over the various possibilities, and more and more the orphanage, and the myriad openings it offered for A Heart for Children to establish themselves in India, jostled itself into first position on her list. The only minus point for the orphanage was the Hindu connection, but, it seemed to her, this could be surely and swiftly overridden once they came down to brass tacks.

And so during dinner they spoke of brass tacks, and by the time they were ready to go home Monika was positively elated. This was it! Mrs Rajpaul was falling over her feet to please and though the subject of Hindu gods had not been brought up (Monika had been tactful on that score – plenty of time for such details later) it was quite obvious that the orphanage was Monika's for the taking. They talked deep into the night.

It was almost midnight when Monika and Jack took a taxi home. About a hundred metres before the hotel the car came to a stop. There was a traffic jam ahead, and it was not possible to proceed.

'Come, we'll walk,' said Jack. He paid the driver and they got out and made their way forward.

As they drew nearer the hotel Jack quickened his pace. Something was wrong. By the light of the streetlamp he could see a small crowd on the pavement ahead, and something else, black and bulky, behind that crowd. There was a police car, and an ambulance, and a babble of voices.

'It's an accident,' said Jack, and ran.

When Monika caught up with him he was elbowing his way through the crowd, which was standing around a black car that

53

stood diagonally across the pavement, the left front fender squashed against the wall behind. There was a policeman taking notes from an excitedly shouting man, and another policeman on the road, directing traffic. The ambulance had parked just before the crashed car, and was wailing its siren and flashing its light, in a hurry to leave, but could not since so many cars had stopped in front of it and were blocking the street, still only one lane wide because of the road-works just ahead.

It was fairly easy to figure out what had happened: the driver of the crashed car had seen the deep pit in the street – from which the traffic was protected only by a single red-and-white strap between two rusty iron posts – next to the pavement too late, and rather than veer to the right and into the other lane, had driven across the pavement and crashed into the wall.

Above the pandemonium Jack could hear something else, a sound on a higher level of perception, and it made him rough in his efforts to navigate the milling crowd. He had to fight past several men – who appeared to be violently angry with someone or something – and jump across the ditch in order to get beyond the stranded car. That was when he saw her. Jyothi. She was in the arms of a man, the same man who had beat her the day before, who held her tightly while she struggled to free herself. She was screaming at the top of her voice and waving her arms at the black car. Her face was a mask of terror and grief, smeared with tears and grime, mouth wide open, eyes wild and staring and seeing nothing. Between the screams she babbled a stream of words. Now and then she turned to the man and pummelled his shoulder, kicked him, tried to get free, but he held her all the more tightly, and seemed unperturbed by her fighting. Behind Jyothi and the man stood a group of older children, silently staring, as if shocked into immobility.

On the pavement was a large dark stain. In the half-light of the streetlamp and the eerie blue flashes coming from the ambulance it glowed darkly red. Blood, Jack knew at once. He looked at Jyothi again and saw that part of her skirt had been ripped away – it lay on the pavement and it, too, was drenched in blood. He moved nearer to the man with the struggling child, who thrashed and writhed in his arms, hysterical with some pain that was not physical. Her body leaned forward, her arms stretched towards the ominous black vehicle.

Jack placed himself in front of her and addressed her by name.

She did not notice him but continued to scream, so he reached up and took hold of one of her wrists, and feeling the resistance she looked down at him, and, for a moment, stopped struggling and stared at him in silence, with eyes so haunted he wanted to reach out and take her from the man holding her, but knew he could not, should not.

'Can someone tell me what happened?' said Jack, addressing the man, but he first shrugged then spoke a few words in his own language. Jyothi started her fighting again, but less frantically, now; she merely wriggled with a grim determination to be let down and so the man stood her on the pavement. At once she lurched towards the black vehicle, but her father held her back.

'Isn't there a doctor around here?' said Jack to no one in particular, and as no-one answered him, he pointed to the police car, which still had not moved off, and to Jyothi.

'Is she wounded? Why isn't she being attended to? Surely there's a doctor in there?' The man made a negative gesture with his hand and said something, and one of the children, a boy of about thirteen, came forward and spoke too, which Jack also could not understand.

'What's the matter, Jack? Oh my goodness!'

Monika, having pushed herself through the crowd, clapped her hand over her mouth as she saw Jyothi, who had now collapsed on to the ground weeping abjectly. She seemed to have lost the strength for hysterics. She sat at the edge of the blood stain, so that it looked as if the blood was hers, but Jack said, 'She doesn't seem to be wounded herself; that's somebody else's blood. Somebody was badly injured or killed, probably her mother. That's why she's shrieking so much. See if you can find someone who speaks English, goddammit!'

Monika knelt down involuntarily and put her arms around Jyothi. The child turned and threw her arms around her. Monika looked helplessly up at Jack, her forehead puckered with concern.

As if on command, someone tapped Jack on the shoulder and said, 'Hello, meester!'

Jack turned around and recognized the face, though the livery had been exchanged for everyday clothes: it was the doorman from the hotel. He was grinning at Jack as if this unexpected meeting were no more serious than a casual bumping into each other on the pavement.

The doorman spoke a little English.

'What's going on here? What happened?' said Jack.

'Child mother getting bad accident,' said the doorman. 'Mother dead. Head bad split open.' He made a graphic gesture with his hands to show just how badly the mother's head was split open.

'But what about the child? She doesn't seem wounded but she's in shock, and needs looking after – they should at least give her a tranquilizer. Why doesn't the police help, why can't she go with the ambulance?'

The doorman shrugged. 'Ambulance taking car driver. Not taking girl, sah, say girl not hurt, child screaming too much. Father say no taking. Too much waiting, waiting hospital.' He lowered his voice, gave Jyothi and her father a sidelong glance, and said, 'Mother head bad bleeding, sah. Mother dead soon.' His face assumed a tragic expression, then he turned to Monika. 'Poor peoples, living street, that place.' He pointed to the lean-to. 'Ambulance not taking girl, madam. Father say not going hospital, too much waiting, staying here. Six children. Poor people, now mother dead. All God's will.'

Jack shook his head in frustration. 'But . . .' He looked down at Jyothi. Now that she was not struggling he noticed a large grazed area on her thigh. He slipped his T-shirt over his head, took his knife out of his pocket, cut a slash into the shirt and tore away a strip of material. As if on cue Monika took the cloth from him and used it to make-shift bandage around Jyothi's leg. In no time it was dark with blood.

'Jack, this child must see a doctor right away,' Monkia said matter-of-factly. The white box had opened and what came out surprised her: not flabby sentimentality but strong clear caring. 'That wound needs stitching. If she doesn't get it dressed it will be infected in no time, the way these people live in the dirt. Poor child.'

She stroked the girl's head. Jyothi had stopped crying, and let go of Monika by now. She sat with stretched-out legs, looking up at Monika with huge moist eyes.

'Oh, look at her. The poor thing . . . Can't somebody get an ambulance to take her to hospital? Has anybody called a doctor?'

'No ambulance taking, madam. No doctor coming this time, all doctor sleeping, child not hurt bad, father not taking hospital, child screaming too much.'

'But she's not screaming now, and— Oh, look, the police car's going . . . Stop, we need a doctor . . . This child . . . Oh, why doesn't anybody . . . I'll go myself.'

Monika jumped to her feet and ran into the street to stop the police car but it had manoeuvred past the roadworks, gathered speed and raced away. Now that the fun was over and no more bodies to be seen the crowd had begun to disperse.

'Oh, the idiots! How could they just . . . Jack? Jack, what are you doing?'

Jack had bent down to pick up Jyothi. He held her across his arms, and walked away with her, striding along in the direction of the hotel. Her father was running beside him, saying something.

'Where are you going, Jack?' Monika called.

'I'm taking her to the hotel. There are always a few taxis there. Come on. We'll take her to the Sacred Heart children's hospital.' He stopped for a moment, and spoke to the doorman, who had caught up. 'Tell that to her father. Not to worry about her, we'll stay with her till her wounds are dressed and bring her back. It's a good hospital, they have two German doctors. She'll get good treatment. Come on, Monika.' He turned and walked off again, Jyothi's ankles bobbing in mid-air. Jyothi, wailing again, dug the fingers of her left hand into the flesh of Jack's upper arm for support and leaned forward, right arm stretched out, fingers spread in the other direction – to wherever they had taken her mother. Jyothi's wail took on a new form. It became a long drawn-out lament, rising and falling to the bounce of Jack's gait, clearly decipherable as a word common to every language.

'Maaaaa . . .' she cried.

Monika ran behind Jack, handbag swinging.

Chapter 5

When Jyothi fell asleep at last Jack and Monika returned to the hotel. They were too exhausted to talk about the accident and its consequences, yet they were strangely united as seldom before, both aware that the part they had played in last night's tragedy would have far-reaching consequences. It had changed their status in and their relationship to the city for ever. They were no longer well-intentioned tourists on an elevated mission. It was as if whatever fate it was that managed the lives of every single person here, no matter how meagre or how lost, had on a sudden whim written in a role for them. As if the hand that moved the strings that caused the fantastic interplay of individuals – lives twisting and turning, touching and moving on – had reached backstage, brought them in and cast them in the limelight, and then left them to figure out the rest themselves. They were together and yet alone.

While she prepared for bed, still in silence, Monika looked across at Jack who was already under the blanket, his head resting on cupped hands, staring at the ceiling with an unaccustomed expression of distress written into every line of his face. Monika felt suddenly alone and abandoned, and knew a desperate need to communicate.

'Jack, do you think that child—'

Her voice was much, much too loud and she stopped, then started again. 'Jack . . .'

Jack did not react, so she raised her voice once more, made the word short and sharp. 'Jack!'

'Huh?' He turned to look at her, then grinned and reached out a hand to her as she climbed into bed.

'Jack, I keep thinking . . . that poor little girl . . . I . . .'

'I know what you're thinking,' Jack said, pulling her to him so that she lay curled up against him. 'I'm thinking the same.'

Monika snuggled into the crook of his arm. 'Jack, if only . . . Do you think . . . I hardly dare . . .'

'Yeah. I know. It's as if putting it into words . . .'

'Oh Jack! It's like – I hardly dare say it – as if Fate somehow . . .'

They lay in stillness, each one enclosed in a separate little world like a bubble; but then the silence was too much to bear and Jack levered himself up onto one elbow and looked down at her. In the half-light given off from the bedside lamp she looked soft, vulnerable, all hard edges erased. There was yearning in her eyes; but it wasn't him she yearned for, not right now; and he knew it, and was content.

'You're sure, Monika? You're really sure? Not a baby?'

'She's the one, Jack.'

'She's the one.'

'I think you saw it before I did. But when I held her on the pavement and I felt her blood on my thighs, and her tears on my fingers . . .'

'I felt it too.'

'Are we being too possessive? She has a father.'

'He doesn't care for her. I can tell.'

'But maybe he does. He's still her father. He has rights. How can we . . .'

'I don't know, Monika. I can't explain it. I just feel it. A certainty. A knowledge.'

'I know. I feel it too. She's . . .'

'Our daughter.'

'Yes.'

'It might be a fight.'

'I know.'

'But if you feel it too, if we both feel it—'

'Then it must be right.'

'Then I'll fight. I'll fight for her.'

'Oh Jack, you know sometimes I think our childlessness has driven us apart. We're so very different . . . But now . . .'

'Now it's going to be all right.'

A minute later Monika heard his slow and heavy breathing, and knew he was asleep. It took her the best part of an hour to fall asleep herself. A quiet elation swelled within her. She had found not only the child she'd been waiting for but – in a new, marvellous, and utterly miraculous dimension they both had yet to explore, hand in hand, together at last – Jack.

Mr Metzger was waiting for them at the Sacred Heart hospital the next morning. They had not met him the night before, of course. When they had brought Jyothi in there was only a skeleton night-shift staff on duty. The nurse had had to call an emergency doctor, and it was he who had looked at Jyothi's wounds, cleaned, stitched and dressed them. They had left a generous donation to cover the cost of the treatment and a bed for the night, and promised to return in the morning to pick her up and take her home.

'But, you see,' said Monika now to Mr Metzger, 'she doesn't really have a home. She has a place to lay her head, yes. But can you call a few pieces of board against a wall on a pavement home? It's – it's a disgrace. Where are the authorities? How can they allow this state of affairs? Don't you have some kind of a – well, some kind of youth service, like we do in Germany, to prevent children living in such abominable circumstances? These children must be taken care of! They . . .'

Mr Metzger smiled smugly and coned his fingers on his slightly protruding belly, pushing his swivel chair back so as to create an authoritative distance between himself and the Kellers.

'One thing you must grasp, Mrs Keller,' he began, 'this is not Germany, this is not the West, and it is absolutely futile to make comparisons. The reality is that these children in such hovels exist, and all we can do is look on without judging and help in a comprehensive way. One needs a realistic vision in order to help and for a realistic vision one needs to maintain a distance. Building a hospital for the poor is a realistic vision which we have been able to bring to fruition. It was well meaning but ill advised of you to get personally involved with this child.'

'But she might have bled to death! Her father wasn't interested in having her treated.'

Mr Metzger shrugged. 'It must seem cold-hearted to you but if you had lived here ten years as I have you would realize there are children dying in this city every day of hunger and abuse and untreated sickness. You cannot save them all. If you want to help you must think it out carefully first and then act. Remember I told you that soft-heartedness is not the correct basis for wide-reaching help. It only breeds dependence and exploitation. What will happen when you take this child back to its father? The father will smell money and beg you for more.

You will feel a personal obligation and the family will sponge on you. These people are parasites. Give them a finger and they'll take the whole arm. Mark my words, if you are not careful they will take you for a ride and you'll go willingly because you will have a bad conscience. That's the bane of Westerners: they feel responsible for the misery they see here and think it is their duty to help personally, instead of in a more comprehensive way – such as by helping to keep this hospital alive. They get a certain ease of conscience by acting in this way, but that is nothing but egoism. I have seen the little girl; she is still asleep. I would advise you to return to the hotel and forget about the incident. Give me the address – tell me where you found her and we will take her back when she wakes up.'

'But her mother was killed! The child lives in atrocious circumstances! We have to at least—'

'Mr Metzger,' said Jack, speaking for the first time, 'we want to adopt this child.'

Monika's mouth, which was open because she had not finished what she was saying, closed again. She swung to look at Jack with a mixture of admiration and admonishment. He had said it out loud. Blurted out their most precious secret to a virtual stranger! Expressing it thus seemed to make the secret at once more real, and at the same time more prone to attack, by laying it bare to criticism. It had all seemed so pure and shining the night before. Now, in the light of day, the whole edifice, made of aspiration and an inner conviction more substantial than brick and mortar, might crumble. Monika wanted to protect it, to keep it inside where no doubt could attack it. For that was what she most feared: doubt, because she was a person who doubted easily.

Her nature, in the normal course of things, would be to go over the pros and cons of adoption and weigh each carefully against the other before coming to a rational decision based on that weighing; to see eye to eye on the subject and clear away every last 'if' and 'but'. Now, however, there was nothing she feared more than the 'ifs' and 'buts'. For she knew there were still far too many of them, too many for her to face, held at bay for the moment as if by a mighty arm, but straining to rush into her soul and destroy every last remnant of hope.

Her only hope was Jack: Jack probably didn't have a single 'if' or 'but'; he never did. Jack would have made up his mind instantaneously and for him it would only be a question of 'how' and 'how soon'. It wasn't right of him to mention it at such an early stage, yet a delicious warmth spread out inside her at hearing their decision so clearly and concisely formulated; as if in merely speaking it out loud Jack had already made any further doubting and faltering superfluous, so that they could swiftly put the 'if/but' stage behind them and go on to the practical side of operations. And there was nothing Monika loved more than operations. So she continued to look at Jack in admonishing and speechless admiration, and waited to hear what Mr Metzger would say.

Unfortunately for her Mr Metzger had quite a bit to say. He covered his eyes with both hands and shook his head as if in the final stage of despair.

'You must be insane!' he moaned, and looked up. The despair was gone, replaced by exasperation. He frowned and fixed his eyes severely on Jack. 'That's exactly what I was telling you about – you tourists have absolutely no grasp of the facts of life! You're soft in the mind! The moment you step off the plane you go berserk; the moment you see a beggar you lose all sense of proportion.' He flung his hands towards Monika and Jack as if writing them off. 'Ach, why should I care? Why should I give you a lecture? All I can say is ...' He glared first at Jack, then at Monika, with beady, glassy eyes. '... don't do it! Don't even consider it! *Es ist wahnsinnig!*

It's crazy! Even to think about it is to open a viper's nest of problems!'

At those words all of Monika's fears came rushing headlong back into her mind and lodged themselves there like silent watchful bats in a dark attic. Anxiety flooded her eyes and she looked uncertainly at Jack. 'Well, we haven't really come to a decision yet. We were just wondering if . . .'

Mr Metzger sensed an ally in Monika. He rolled his chair so near to his desk that its edge cut a ridge into his belly, leaned forward and looked her piercingly in the eye. 'Mrs Keller, I appreciate you as a level-headed woman open to objective arguments. One should not lose objectivity in a serious matter like this. Any kind of fuzzy-headedness at this moment is absolutely out of place. One has to keep a clear mind and look at the facts intelligently without losing one's grip on reason. Perhaps when you brought this child here you felt some sort of . . . some sort of . . .' He waved his hand in dismissal, searching for an adequately pejorative expression. 'Oh, what do I know? Some sort of heart-movement, I suppose. You were blinded to the facts.'

Monika and Jack exchanged glances. Monika had lost all courage; she was once again a cowed bundle of if/but and had already given up the fight as a lost cause. It was Jack who led the way now. He rose, and gestured to her to stand up too.

'The thing is,' he said, his voice amiable as ever and extremely calm, 'the thing is, we love her. She's our daughter. So I guess that'll have to be enough. Come, honey, let's go and see if she's awake.' He turned to leave, nodding perfunctorily at a stunned Mr Metzger. Monika scrambled to her feet, smiled weakly at Mr Metzger, and followed Jack out of the office.

Chapter 6

Jyothi was in a ward with ten beds, in two rows of five down the longer walls. Most of the children were obviously too ill to move or sit up – they lay apathetically in their beds, some of them crying quietly to themselves. Some had visitors. Two were sitting on the bare concrete; glancing down as he passed them, Jack saw they were playing a game with ancient picture cards.

Jyothi was awake. She sat propped up against the headrest of the bed, being spoon-fed by a nurse in a faded blue-and-white-checked uniform, who seemed to be having some problem getting the child to open her mouth.

As they approached Jyothi pushed the spoon away and turned her head to the side, looking beseechingly up at Jack. She did not smile.

The nurse turned around and saw them. She said something in her own language – it seemed to be a complaint concerning Jyothi – stood up, shoved a bowl of cracked enamel unceremoniously into Monika's hands, and walked away.

Monika looked at the bowl and said to Jack, 'Does she expect me to feed her?'

'Looks like it,' said Jack. 'Go ahead.'

Monika sat down on the chair beside Jyothi's head and dipped the spoon into the grey mush in the bowl. It was some kind of vaguely warm cooked grain, like thick porridge, but with a very pungent smell of typical Indian spices. She brought the full spoon up to Jyothi's mouth but, as before, the girl refused to open her lips.

'I don't understand it,' said Monika. 'Why won't she eat? She can't have had a decent meal for ages.'

'She must be too upset,' said Jack. 'Remember, she saw her mother killed. She needs time to get over that.'

As if Jyothi understood Jack's words both of her eyes filled with tears, which flowed over and rolled down her cheeks. She cried silently, her head turned away from her visitors in a half-hearted attempt to conceal a vast private grief.

'But if she doesn't eat . . .'

'She will eventually. Give her time.'

When they had left the previous night Jyothi had still worn the filth of the streets. There had been neither time nor staff to give her the thorough washing she needed. That had been done this morning, before breakfast. It was the first time they had ever seen her without the characteristic black zig-zag lines of grime down her cheek and around her neck, though a faint grey stain, like an ingrained veil of embedded dirt, still spread up from her neck and sank into the rich dark chestnut of her facial skin.

Her eyes were lowered, and though Jack spoke to her in the familiar tone she knew, she would not look at him.

'Maybe she's mad at us because we took her away from her father?' Monika whispered automatically, though she knew Jyothi would not understand. 'He is her father, after all.

Perhaps she needs him now. We should have brought him with us in the taxi. He must be worried sick.'

'That man? I don't believe it. The further away she is from him, the better it is for her,' said Jack decisively. 'He's a scumbag. One look at him and I can tell. We can't let her go back to him.'

'But, Jack, do we have the right? Remember what Mr Metzger said. I don't know if we should interfere.'

'I think we *have* to interfere, Monika. Whether we like it or not we are involved. Call me a meddling foreigner if you like, all I can say is I'm not backing out. I'm not leaving this child to her fate. I'm sticking my nose in and I'm gonna fight to see she gets the best deal. It was bad enough before, living on the street in the middle of a garbage heap, but at least she had a mother. That was a good woman, and she loved her child. The father doesn't give a damn. I intend to see this through, and I don't care what a Mr Metzger says about it. C'mon, let's go. I want to talk to Mrs Rajpaul. She'll give us some real advice.'

He tried to catch Jyothi's attention, to say he was leaving, but she still looked away towards the open window, where the branches of a tree could be seen, and a black bird hopping among the leaves.

The Kellers sought out the doctor on duty – a young Indian – who said it would be better to keep Jyothi one or two days longer to make sure the wound was healing properly, and promised not to discharge her without telling them beforehand. He agreed that something should be done for the child but let them know in no uncertain terms than hardly anything could be done to change the fact that Jyothi was a child of the streets. That was where her destiny lay, and there was nothing he, Jack or Monika could do to change that.

'It is all God's will,' he said at the end of his speech, smiling and shaking his head back and forth.

'Then it's God's will that they should be sick, so why do you work here as a doctor?'

'It is God's will that made me a doctor, sir. It is God's will that I relieve suffering. It is their good destiny and my karma.'

'And maybe it is God's will that I should change this girl's destiny,' said Jack. 'Just maybe it was God's will that placed me in a hotel just down the road from her and God's will that made me come along just after the accident and God's will that moved me to bring her here. Just maybe.'

The doctor smiled amiably. 'Sir, you should have been born a Hindu,' he said graciously. 'Your argument is impeccable.'

As they were leaving the hospital grounds a thin man with a moustache entered. The man looked like millions of other men in this city but Jack recognized him easily as one he had seen twice before, whom he had just five minutes earlier described as a scumbag, Jyothi's father.

Noticing them – Jack and Monika were conspicuous with their white skin – the man glanced over and an unctuous smile of recognition spread across his features. He cried out a word, raised a hand in greeting and hurried over. Monika and Jack exchanged glances as he gushed out some incomprehensible words.

'We'd better go in and find someone to translate,' said Jack. 'I want to know what his plans are.'

The nurse who had been feeding Jyothi agreed to translate.

'This man says he is the father of that little girl,' she said.

'We know that. Tell him she has been looked after and she will be able to go home in a day or two,' said Jack. 'We will pay for the treatment.'

The nurse translated; the man replied. He wore wide khaki shorts from which emerged pathetically thin legs ending in bare feet flattened at the toes like paddles. Over the shorts he wore a faded blue T-shirt bearing the faint imprint of the Indian flag, ragged at the hem. As he spoke he gestured emotionally with his hands, scratched one leg with the toes of the other, and assumed a mien of tragedy.

'He says now that his wife is dead life is going to be very difficult. He wants you to give him a thousand rupees to help . . . Just a moment.' The nurse turned back to Jyothi's father, who looked as if he would any moment burst into tears, and spent a few minutes in what appeared to be a hefty argument with him. She said in English, 'The man is an out-of-work dhobi. He takes on various duties at the Dhobi Ghat. He does not make much money. They have no home. He has six children and this is the youngest. All of the children and the wife have to help in order to supplement the income. The children clean car windows, the eldest son works cleaning tables in a restaurant. The wife is doing some ironing sometimes. Now the wife is gone and he still has the six children to support. He is begging for a thousand rupees. Don't give it to him. The man is a scoundrel.'

'Tell him we want to—' Monika pinched Jack's arm and interrupted.

'Tell him we will help all we can but we can't give him a thousand rupees. We want to help Jyothi.'

The nurse spoke again. The man stood staring in turn at whoever was speaking. His expression of forlorn grief had vanished; once again he wore an ingratiating grin across his face. He bobbed his head as if in agreement with her every word.

'Be careful with this man, he is out to rob you,' said the nurse.

'Acha, acha,' said the man, head nodding and grin widening, and let out a rush of more words, at which the nurse threw him a scathing glare, looked at her watch, nodded at Monika, and strode away. She and Jack were left standing alone in the corridor with Jyothi's father, who was still explaining something to them.

'Perhaps we should ask Mr Metzger,' Monika began, but now it was Jack's turn to interrupt.

'No. We know what his take is. I'm not interested in what he has to say. I want to see how Jyothi reacts to this man. If I were her father I'd have been rushing to her bedside. He was more interested in getting money out of us. Let's go to Jyothi, taking him with us, and see how they react to each other. That's what I want to know.'

Saying that, he smiled and signalled to the man; he led the way down the corridor to Jyothi's ward and up the middle aisle to the cot where she lay with her head turned towards the window, one knee drawn up, her body covered by a thin grey sheet.

'Jyothi!' called Jack. Startled, she turned her head to look at him, and the flicker of a smile played on her lips. But then her father stepped out from behind Monika, arms stretched out and speaking to her.

Jyothi's reaction was swift, an automatic reflex that could not be misinterpreted. The smile fled, panic entered her eyes, and she raised one arm as if to fend off a blow.

Chapter 7

Mrs Rajpaul shook her head. Her eyes were clouded by doubt, and she waved one hand, palm up and outwards, in a gesture of negation.

'It would be very, very difficult,' she said. 'The authorities don't encourage foreign adoptions, especially not if the father is still alive. Even poor people have a right to their children, you know. There was a bit of a scandal with foreigners buying poor babies some years ago and since then the authorities have clamped down. It is very difficult to regulate. If everybody thought they could just come to India and buy a baby from a poor family where would we be?'

'But in this case . . .'

Mrs Rajpaul frowned. 'I know, in this case it seems a bit different. If the father is mistreating her . . . but it would be best if I talk to the father myself. If he can't afford to keep the child or look after her properly she might be able to move into the orphanage.'

'That's what we thought,' said Jack. 'That shack on the pavement is not a home, and—'

'Be careful what you say,' said Mrs Rajpaul. 'Just because they're poor and living on the streets doesn't mean these children don't have a sense of home and parental love.'

'But look, the father has to work, the brothers too. I think even she has to work sometimes. At six years old! How can that possibly be good for her? All the father is capable of doing is leaving her at home alone all day. On the pavement. Do you call that family security?'

'Nevertheless it's the only home she knows.'

'Look, Mrs Rajpaul, we're talking in circles. Isn't the orphanage just for cases like this? Even if we don't adopt her it would be best she came here for a while. She's an orphan, a half-orphan, isn't she? Isn't that what orphanages are for? The orphanage mother is great – she'd be able to help Jyothi over the first shock, give her a bit of security just until . . . until . . . and in the meantime, we could make inquiries about adoption, start the process, whatever.'

'It would be very difficult since the authorities don't approve of foreign adoptions,' said Mrs Rajpaul for the umpteenth time. Jack shook his head in frustration; they had come full circle. It struck him that Mrs Rajpaul's main concern was to lay obstacles in their way because she disapproved on principle of foreign couples coming to India and adopting Indian children. She found the whole idea repugnant, immoral even.

'Look, why don't you speak to the man yourself? I'll try to find him, bring him here, to talk with you. Let him see the orphanage. Get him to see that Jyothi would be well taken care of, that it would be one less mouth to feed.'

'Indian fathers love their children every bit as much as Western fathers,' said Mrs Rajpaul scathingly. 'Westerners

73

think all Indians are just sitting there begging for money. Our children are precious, they are not for sale!'

However, when they finally found him again, coming home from work later that evening with five ragged boys trailing in his wake, Jyothi's father agreed to place her in the orphanage – if they paid him five thousand rupees.

It was as Mrs Rajpaul said: adopting a child was not an easy thing. The accusation of child-buying hung in the air at every interview with every Indian official with whom they had to speak – and there were several. To make matters worse, Jyothi's father made it clear that he was, indeed, extremely interested in child-selling – to the highest bidder. And hinted at all kinds of interested parties who were eager to buy Jyothi for a mind-boggling price.

'It's like he's holding a private auction,' grumbled Jack.

They soon saw the disadvantage of having Mrs Rajpaul as translator; her moral affront came through at every stage of the bargaining process, for a bargaining process it was, and it soon became clear that, notwithstanding the official child-buying prohibition, there would be no other way to get Jyothi; and that if they did not get her goodness knew who would. Jack hadn't liked the father from the beginning and there was nothing he would put past him. Getting Jyothi at whatever price necessary became a matter of moral duty.

Their new translator was a Muslim taxi-driver who spoke perfect Indian-English, a tall thin bearded man named Salim in a white cap and white kurta pyjamas, who during their drives around the city explained to them the intricacies of Islam, Islamic diet, the Islamic stand on sex, alcohol and Middle East politics, Islamic penalties, and the like. Having Salim as translator made sense, since he was readily available, his taxi usually parked outside the hotel, and had appointed himself their personal driver and adviser for the duration of their stay.

It was Salim who alerted them to the possibility that Jyothi's father might be making unsavoury plans for her; Salim who confirmed their assessment of the man as something – putting it mildly – less than honourable.

'He frequents Kamathipura,' he said cryptically.

'What is Kamathipura?' asked Monika, truly interested, but Salim wouldn't say.

Only later, when Monika had gone ahead into the hotel and Jack had lingered to pay him and smoke a *bidi* (which Monika would have forbidden, had she known) did he whisper conspiratorially, 'Kamathipura is bad place, sir. Bad place for ladies,' and made an unmistakable lewd gesture. 'Not good place for mens.' Jack wanted to ask what Salim himself had been doing there, but refrained.

Salim, glancing nervously at the hotel to see if Monika was returning, went on to describe some of the unsavoury practices carried on with young girls, children as young as Jyothi.

'Mens buying girls and training them, sah. Some girls training as temple goddess, big Hindu custom, very bad custom, very small girls selling to Devidasi business. I think Jyothi father talking to one man like this, sah. Now wanting three thousand rupees.'

'What is "Devadasi business"?'

In answer Salim made an ugly face and spat on the ground. He launched into a long explanation but a speech of this length and this complexity was too much for him, his English deteriorated into pidgin, and Jack understood not a word.

Later, though, he asked Mrs Rajpaul, whom they met regularly during their visits to the orphanage. Jyothi, in the meantime, had been discharged from hospital and, with her father's consent, had been taken in temporarily by the orphanage, pending a decision as to her future.

Mrs Rajpaul, too, wrinkled her face in disdain. 'It's a horrible practice,' she said, 'and against the law. Young girls, some as young as two or three, sold to the highest bidder and dedicated to the goddess Yellamma. They end up in the urban brothels.'

She led them up a rickety staircase to the first floor, and the rooms where the children slept. At the end of a long corridor lined with doors was a playroom, where Jyothi spent her days. She was still in a state of mourning; she refused to play with the other children or go outside. She would simply sit, cross-legged, on the floor, leafing through one of the orphanage's tattered picture books, staring at the pictures but, it seemed, seeing nothing.

'We have reason to believe that Jyothi's father is considering such a thing!'

'If that is the case,' said Mrs Rajpaul firmly, 'then you can be certain the authorities will deprive him of custody – that would improve your own chances for adoption. Jyothi!' She swung open the door to the playroom.

Jyothi looked particularly small in the large long room. It was bare of furniture except for three tattered mats; an unpainted plywood bookcase, containing only three more picture books; a toy-box devoid of toys; and a wooden playpen containing a few battered building blocks. Today she was standing with her back to them, gazing out of the window at the triste asphalt playground below, where the other children ran haywire in a game of catch. She did not turn around at their approach. The yard was like an abyss between the grimy rear walls of three massive buildings. At some point, someone charitable had obviously decided to add some playground equipment, for in a corner stood a half-hearted attempt at a swing (supports and crossbar, rings for the ropes, but no swing) and the beginnings of a slide (rickety tower with ladder, but no slide). A pile of dirty sand seemed less of an invitation to play than a sanitary convenience for neighbourhood cats. Two of the surrounding buildings were derelict, with boarded-in windows and crumbling walls. The third seemed to be some sort of an office: several rusty air-conditioning units disturbed the flatness of the bleak concrete surface, and behind a few of the dingy window-panes burned lights. The fourth side of the playground was the orphanage itself, and next to that, the car park. Between the cracks in the asphalt and along the bases of the walls grew tufts of grass, nature fighting a losing battle against civilization's armour. Not a tree, not a flower was visible; the expanse of sky above the roofs was the only respite from concrete, brick and asphalt.

Oblivious to the ugliness of their environment, the children flitted back and forth in gleeful abandonment, and Jack marvelled at the natural ability of children to access some inner wellspring of joy independent of and indifferent to outer circumstances. This ability to overcome, to slide forward into a now with the ease of moving from one room to another was an ability he wished, right now, for Jyothi.

Jyothi continued to gaze, unmoving, unmoved, at the children playing below as they screamed and ran with joy like coloured baubles shaken in a black box. Her own still stance emitted such abject apathy that Monika longed to lift her, hold her, flood her with love until she melted. But she knew Jyothi should not be touched. Not yet.

It had been like this every day. Jyothi did not react. Since that first meeting with her father, in which she had shown fear, she had sunk into a netherworld of sorrow, which left no room for any other emotion. Jack had tried everything: talking to her, singing to her, playing music to her – all to no effect. She was a life-sized mechanical doll in her grief, existing far away from the land of the living, as if she'd died a little death herself. For that reason it had been all too easy to persuade her father to let her live here for the while – there had been no question of him taking her home to the streets. But where to go from here?

The adoption process would take weeks, months maybe, and all was dependent on the father's consent, which he seemed reluctant to give, for he was still looking for the most lucrative deal. One thing was certain: the remaining week they had in Bombay would not be long enough for the complicated transactions involved. Another thing was certain: they wanted this child; Jack wanted her as much as Monika. All of her crusading zeal now seemed focused on this one end: obtaining Jyothi, and possibly saving her from a fate worse than death.

As for the mission on which she had come to Bombay: there was no longer a shred of doubt that the decision had been made: the orphanage had won. The rest would be simply the formalities, and every day, while Jack visited Jyothi and kept her company while trying to find the key that would unlock her spirit, Monika met with Mrs Rajpaul and other members of the Board of Trustees of the orphanage, hammering out the details of the sponsorship.

They would need papers, which would only be available in Germany. Between them they decided that Monika would go home – her job called – and Jack would stay on in Bombay, to keep Jyothi company, to get her used to him, to keep a protective eye on her, to continue the persuasion process with her father, to be on the receiving end of the papers Monika would send, and, most of all, to wrap up the adoption process. His visa was valid for three months; he would take up residence in Mrs Rajpaul's home for that length of time, and if more time was needed get a visa extension.

*   *   *

Monika packed her suitcase and prepared to leave, leave the city she had called hell on earth. From the moment of her arrival she had never ceased to complain: about the dirt, the smells, the noise, the chaos, the misery. And yet, now that it was time to leave, her heart was heavy and not only because of the open question of Jyothi, and not only because of leaving Jack. Somehow, she realized, Bombay had changed her – and for the better. What had happened? Who was she, and what had changed, what was different? Monika looked at herself, and slowly the answers rose up in her mind. Bombay's heartbeat had entered her soul and slowly, lovingly absorbed her own pulse into itself. The squalor that had so repulsed her, she realized, was nothing but a reflection of her own demons, her own inner chaos she had sought to banish beneath a façade of perfection and orderliness. In learning to love one of Bombay's children the fear of those demons had fled, and in its place was a subtle joy, a quickening of the spirit, a lightness of heart! Here was the beginning of a mystery: beauty and joy can be found anywhere, they are in the heart! They do not depend on outer circumstances! She had seen that in the shining eyes of a child, in that child's smile and the joy that lit her steps.

At the airport she hugged Jack as if she would never let go. She knew that it was over; her own world called her back. She had had a glimpse of that other world; and all she would take with her was a sweet nostalgia, and the memory of something as precious as life.

She had come here hoping to do good; but she saw now that she was as much a beggar as the poorest street waif. 'Perhaps,' she thought as she waited to board her plane, 'perhaps all is not lost. Perhaps that is why Jyothi came to me, to us. To help us find that which we have lost.' And she sent up a fervent prayer to the powers that be – Oh, let it all work out! Let her be ours!

Chapter 8

There were statues that moved. Vaguely she remembered that these were people. Vaguely she remembered a time not like this, when there was some connection between her and them. The statues spoke too, but she could not understand them. Did not listen. Hearing is not listening. She could hear their voices, but made no effort to listen. Had no interest. Couldn't care. They were outside. Of no meaning, of no consequence.

Inside her was a solid block. A black block, which never moved. She had seen them building a house once, had seen the workers mixing sand and cement and water which they poured into wooden moulds where it solidified: that was how it felt inside. As if they had poured the concrete into her and it had hardened, so that she was a statue filled with concrete, a statue that could move but not feel.

Sometimes they set a plate of food before her and put her hands in the plate. She felt her fingers on the food. Her fingers knew exactly what to do. Roll the rice into a ball mixed with

*whatever vegetable there was. Her hand and arm knew what
to do too: lift it to her mouth. The hand knew where to find the
mouth, she didn't. The mouth knew to open itself and receive
the food dropped in it by the fingers. Her jaw knew how to
chew, she didn't. Moving was a superficial, exterior thing,
involving no interest or attention on her part. Not-moving
was more important. Not-moving was the solid block.*

*She had a vague memory of the other way of being, but
it was so far away, so long ago. The softness and the light,
the transparency of being. The memory hovered somewhere
beyond her, inaccessible, gone for ever. She feared its treach-
ery. Softness and light were behind her now, locked into the
past. Now was just this: this heaviness, this darkness, this block
of nothingness.*

*There was a white one, a white statue. He seemed to be
there more than the others, hovering in her space. His face
sometimes close to hers, his mouth speaking words that didn't
interest her. When he was there she was aware of something:
an unease that made the concrete shudder. The shuddering
terrified her. When she felt the shuddering she wrapped her
arms around herself to keep herself intact, so that nothing
of her would fall apart, so that the concrete would stay
solid, unmoving. There was comfort in the hardness; there
was safety.*

Reluctantly almost, Jack left the relative coolness of the taxi
and stepped out into the street. It was like leaving the shade
of a heated oven for the inferno of an open fire. It was only
ten in the morning.

'Meet me here in an hour,' he said to Salim through the
open window. Salim touched his forehead and nodded solemnly
before backing the car into the flow of traffic and driving
away. Jack looked around him to orientate himself and noted

a cinema across the road, which would serve as landmark when he returned: it was so easy to lose oneself in this city, to be swallowed by its ravenous bedlam, stripped of all semblance of a thinking apparatus and disgorged again void of all bearings.

Down the stairs from the bridge and he would be there, Salim had said, so Jack stepped down the crumbling steps, past beggars crouching against the wall and urchin children, to the Dhobi Ghat. The Dhobi Ghat was one of the wonders of Bombay, listed among the Places to Visit in Monika's guidebook. Here, Jack had learned, all Bombay's dirty laundry was brought daily, bundled and tied, on the heads of an army of laundry carriers or towered on the backs of bicycles or stacked in handcarts pulled by trotting coolies. Here the bundles were unbundled, distributed among the tens of thousands of washer-men (dhobis, at least in Bombay, are usually male), the clothes scrubbed, beaten and rinsed, dried and ironed, sorted back into appropriate bundles by a mysterious labelling system, and returned to their appropriate owners at the appropriate address with enough organizational efficiency to make a German bureaucrat scratch his head in wonderment and envy.

The guidebook had said the ghat was enormous, but still Jack had harboured hopes of finding Jyothi's father here. The man had disappeared; he had not visited his daughter for three weeks, seemed to have lost all interest in the adoption procedure, could no longer be found on the pavement outside the Hotel Sahil, and had not left a forwarding address with his former neighbours, who when asked simply shrugged and looked blank with the peculiar blankness of deliberate ignorance. He had not once spoken to the official responsible for the adoption process. Youth Authorities had had the hovel where they had once lived searched. The man had gone, taking the boys and anything of use, leaving nothing but rags, garbage and – fortunately – a soiled paper bag full of papers, including, to Jack's relief, Jyothi's birth certificate. But the man himself had vanished.

So Jack had come here, where he, according to all that was known of him, worked. But one look at the chaos before him and Jack's hopes of finding him sank to almost nil. The chances of locating one particular human here were minimal; he might as well look for one particular ant in a swarming anthill. For anthill best described the ghat, with its ordered chaos; ants the faceless masses who milled and mingled, moving with clockwork synchronization, each one with a task, each task an irreplaceable cog in the machinery that laundered Bombay's pitiful rags and splendid robes.

Jack moved up and down the rows of concrete basins where the men worked.

Most of the dhobis seemed to be beating the daylights out of the clothes they held between their hands like pickaxes, lashing them vigorously against the stone slabs that edged the basins. Hardly anyone glanced at him, in spite of his white skin (now quite tanned – perhaps this was the reason. Jack tanned easily and well, and by now was a rich chestnut brown).

After five minutes Jack acknowledged the futility of the search. Salim had warned him; his guidebook had said it was big; but not in his wildest dreams had he imagined that the ghat would be a city within a city.

Jack wandered down the aisles in a state of watchful wonderment, his gaze skimming the faces of the men, hoping for a spark of recognition. The faces all bore a certain similarity of skin colour and bone structure; hair colour, even haircut, seemed identical. Any or all of them could be Jyothi's father, seen from the back or in profile or even face to face. Dark eyes met Jack's and drifted away with what could be interpreted as wile, as if they understood his scrutiny and resented the intrusion into their intimate world, as if closing ranks to protect the sought man, camouflaging him by adaptation, taking on his features deliberately to lead Jack astray. It was a hopeless task; yet still Jack moved on, edging between all these protagonists in the drama of Bombayite daily life in the hope of stumbling by chance on him who was not to be found.

When the hour was over he gave up and returned, drenched in sweat and drained of energy, to the place before the cinema where he sank into Salim's taxi and allowed himself to be whisked back to his own familiar world, that corner of Bombay he now called home.

He had his routine. This little excursion to the ghat was something extraordinary, a break with the structure that helped to keep him sane and hoping. The adoption process was a drawn-out, nerve-racking affair, a matter of two steps forward and one back. He met officials who seemed bent on turning over every stone in their willingness to deliver Jyothi into his safekeeping, and others just as determined to pack him off home empty-handed at the earliest possible occasion, who dragged feet and closed files and mislaid papers in their attempt to break his will.

Jyothi alone kept him going, for with her there was progress, and with every passing day the certainty grew that her place was with him. There were chinks in the fortress of her grief and Jack had found ways to nudge himself through those chinks. His hesitant groping into the darkness of her despair finally bore rewards: like tiny tips of green budding on a withered branch.

Jack spent the best part of the day at the orphanage. The other children went to school every day till mid afternoon, but there was no point sending a little girl to lessons if all she did was stare straight ahead of her, her limbs rigid, neither hearing nor speaking. Jyothi did as she was told and nothing more. She got up and sat down, she ate, she washed herself, she dressed herself, she lay down and fell asleep on command, like a trained doll. At school, she held a pencil; but with that she had reached her limit. So very early Jack volunteered to take over Jyothi's education. Not that she was excused from school – no child in good health was excused and, Mother said, they couldn't start making exceptions now.

So Jyothi had private lessons with Jack.

Mother was not too pleased at the special treatment. 'All of the children here have terrible backgrounds,' she said to Jack when he first put in his request. 'These are all orphans. Some of them we found as babies on rubbish heaps. Some of them were abandoned or mistreated by their parents. Why should this one child be receiving special lessons? She is not the only one.'

'Her mother was run over,' said Jack, 'before her eyes. Her father abused her . . . I'm certain of it. Her mother was all the security she had. Her whole world has collapsed. She needs help.'

'All the children need help. No child is more special than the next.'

'None of them are in her state. Not one. I've watched them.'

'You Westerners think you can just come here and disrupt our programmes,' said Mother. 'All children are to have the same schooling. Just because there is a pending adoption for this child doesn't mean she should have special treatment. The adoption has not come through yet and it may be several months before it is approved, if ever, and till that time she must be treated like all the other children.'

It was not that Mother did not see his point. It was that she did not want to see his point, and it wasn't until Jack realized what she was truly driving at that they arrived at an understanding.

'I was thinking,' Jack said slowly. 'I've noticed the children don't have exercise books . . . they write on the back of used office paper. I was thinking maybe I could supply some books, so that each child would have his or her own . . .'

Mother looked extremely pleased. 'That is very kind of you,' she said to Jack, and the brown mounds of her cheeks moved up to hide her eyes entirely between creases of flesh. 'Extremely kind. You are very generous of your money and your time. And you are quite right about Jyothi, she is emotionally blocked and it is useless putting her in a normal classroom. Her brain, you see, cannot be accessed until the emotional side of her personality is dealt with. I was only this morning talking to Teacher who said . . .'

They climbed the stairs to the room where Jyothi spent lonely hours standing at the window looking out onto the grey courtyard, and while walking up everything was arranged. Jack was to have sole charge of Jyothi's education, from now until further notice. It was as easy as that.

Music, Jack decided, was the key. And so every morning he arrived with his guitar and did nothing more than play and sing for her. He went through his entire repertoire of sixties folk ballads, children's songs, Latin American and Negro spirituals without the least reaction from her. He bought a tape recorder and tried Classical and Western: no reaction. He improvised: composed songs to her, or sang others with changed lyrics, using her name so that, if nothing else, she could understand that. She remained unmoved, her sadness impenetrable.

Yet Jack was convinced that if anything it was music that would melt the icy stillness her mother's death had imposed on her soul. The image he had of Jyothi was of the little girl who had twitched with excitement at the mere touch of a guitar string, whose eyes had sparkled with gaiety and whose feet had tapped the rhythm of his strumming. He had seen a certain quickening of the spirit that indicated another being, one like him, for whom music was the key to all that lay beneath the surface. You and I, we speak the same language, he told her, repeatedly, not in words but in music. But she did not hear.

It was Mother who showed him that, while his premise was basically right, there was a fatal flaw behind his thinking.

'You are wasting your time,' she told him with more than a touch of condescension. 'She isn't listening to you. And she wouldn't like that sort of music. You should play Indian music. Indian people like *filmi* music. I can get you some tapes if you like.' Instantly Jack knew she was right. But it would not be *filmi* music.

'Where can I hear sitar music?' Jack asked Mrs Rajpaul that evening. '*Good* sitar music.'

Mrs Rajpaul, of course, knew when and where. A cousin's father-in-law was a talented sitar player and it was possible for Jack to bring Jyothi to listen to him play. Every evening at six-thirty.

It was not a sudden awakening; rather, a slow dawning, imperceptible, perhaps, to a stranger, for Jyothi sat still and silent all through the playing, her face expressionless, hardly moving except to adjust her ankles, but Jack, who had been with her every day for the past five weeks, felt it. He couldn't say himself what it was. Perhaps the slightest relaxation of the shoulders, or a loosening of the jaw; or maybe it was far more subtle: an inner release of tension which only he, being the closest to her, could feel, an unclenching of the spirit, mirroring itself in him. Whatever it was, it came as gladness, for he knew they had reached a turning point.

The next day Jack arrived at the orphanage with a harmonium and a *sruti* box, and he left them with her, not wanting to intrude on her own private path back to herself. She would have a guide: the tones contained in those two wooden boxes. He entrusted her to music.

To curb his curiosity he left the building and walked the city streets for an hour. When he returned he heard it the moment he came in through the door, growing louder as he walked up the stairs: the resonating hum of the single *sruti* note. He entered the room and there was Jyothi, cross-legged in the middle of the floor, with the little box on her lap working the flap with her fingers. She did not look up as he entered, either because she was so intent on the sound she did not notice his entry, or because she did not care. Whatever it was, it allowed Jack to approach her silently, and when he stood before her he realized that she was humming in unison with the *sruti*, and that was the moment when he knew for sure the battle had been won.

'You must get her here before September,' Monika said on the telephone. 'The new school year starts on the third and I've already registered her but she should come two or three months earlier, so she can start learning German, and . . .'

They had been through this before, umpteen times. But Monika's innate fear that all would not go according to plan caused her to regurgitate all the uncertainties in her life again and again with anyone who would listen, usually Jack.

'She will be the oldest in the class anyway – and not speaking a word of German how will she ever learn anything? I've already spoken to the school principal and he thinks we shouldn't even think of putting her in primary school. He advised me to put her in Special Needs school. Think of it!'

'Sounds OK to me, if you think she'll be disadvantaged in regular school. What's wrong with that!'

'Special Needs school! That's for stupid children! The classes are full of Turks and foreigners!'

'But she *is* a foreigner.'

'No, but I mean . . . You know what I mean! She'll be a German, for goodness' sake! I mean, not disadvantaged in any way. Special Needs schools have such a stigma, we can't possibly send her there. It's just the language that's holding her back, and if she comes earlier she can start learning right away. I've already got a woman lined up who will teach her for an hour a day, and of course living with us she will hear so much she'll learn it in a flash but still she'll be at a disadvantage, and—'

'Monika, cool down, will ya. There's time yet, it's only March. We'll cross that bridge when we get to it. At the moment I'm just happy she seems to have taken a step. Christ, you should have seen, her sitting there in the middle of the room, playing away on that *sruti* box . . .'

'I've got her down for violin classes too, actually. There's a waiting list at the public music school but you remember Mrs Berger, she teaches children privately and she's really good—'

'Don't you think we should wait for violin classes?'

'No, of course not! She should start as early as possible. I would have taught her myself but I don't think it's wise for a mother to teach her own child, or a father for that matter.'

'But first we should get her home.'

'Well, that's *your* business, Jack. I—'

'OK, just leave it to me,' said Jack. 'I'll call you in a day or two, OK, honey?'

'Jack, wait, there's something else. What about—'

But Jack had hung up.

After that Jyothi's progress was a hairbreadth short of miraculous. In a week she progressed from the single tone of the *sruti* box to the two scales of the harmonium. Another week, and she was picking out simple melodies. Sometimes, the phantom of a smile played at the corner of her lips. The opaque dullness had left her eyes; a hollow sadness still hovered like background mist but now there was recognition and communication. Now they spoke, even if only of grief.

Healing comes rapidly to a loved child. Under Jack's protection Jyothi's pain grew visibly less day by day; day by day new areas of her mind awoke to the world.

Jack took her out every day. They took a taxi to the beach, where they went for long walks. Jack bought her snacks, she played in the sand, she waded at the water's edge. He taught her words: 'sea' and 'water' and 'sand' and how to say simple sentences.

When he told Monika she was exasperated. 'That's just like you, Jack, not thinking ahead. You should be speaking German to her; it's German she needs to learn, not English. Really, I thought you'd have the sense to realize that at least!'

'I'll teach her English; she'll need English too. You teach her German. My German's bad, she'll only learn mistakes from me. Don't worry, she'll learn quickly enough when she gets there. Kids are like that. They pick up languages in no time.'

'Jack, don't be ridiculous! *Any* German is better than nothing! You have all this time on your hands, why don't you . . . You could . . .'

But Jack continued to speak English to Jyothi, and Jyothi continued to learn.

Chapter 9

Jack shook his head in amused affection. The photographs were so typically Monika, the letter accompanying them he could have written himself for her, had he been so inclined. He flicked through them quickly. The house from the front and from the back, the forsythia bush in full glorious bloom above the sparkling white garden bench. Another one from the back of the garden, showing the garden pond they had dug and laid out last summer, and which still didn't look as idyllic as in the catalogue. The lounge, with the polished black piano against the wall next to the glass cabinet containing Monika's collection of origami figures.

Monika had cleared out the upstairs room, which all these years had done duty as a guest room, waiting for Monika's pregnancy to be transformed into something else. She had given the furniture to charity, stripped the wallpaper, pulled out the carpet. Now that Monika knew for sure that the new occupant would be a girl, she had gone ahead with the yellow and apricot colour scheme she had had in mind for this eventuality. In the case of a pregnancy she would have had to hold back until the first ultrasound examinations had revealed the sex of the fetus, but now she could proceed at full throttle.

Jack's optimism had rubbed off on her: the positive reports coming from Bombay had only whetted her enthusiasm, and now she too, believed in intuition, and what it told her; that Jyothi would be theirs one day. And now with great zest she had put the entire weight of years of frustrated motherhood into the delightful task of redecoration.

Here, in the photos Jack held in his hands, were the results. The photos of Jyothi's room were at the back of the pile, and he took some time perusing these. It certainly looked good. A mottled apricot carpet, new wallpaper and curtains to match. Solid pine furniture: a single bed, a bedside table, a wardrobe, a desk, two lamps and a bookcase. A special duvet which came in two slices (as Monika explained in the accompanying letter): double for winter and single for summer, and sunny yellow duvet cover, matching sheets, a fluffy pillow.

This time, the shake of his head was not from amusement, but from irritation. This was typical: Monika in action, planning everything in such meticulous detail that nothing was left to chance or spontaneity, and the life crushed out of the future by the controlling hand of Prussian perfectionism.

The guest room had been perfectly presentable. Nothing special: Monika's old bed from her student quarters, plain with pine head and footrests, not new but not old, as was the wardrobe and the sideboard, slightly scratched and weather-beaten. Furniture that was somehow cosy and familiar, for when they had first met they had cuddled together on that very bed in Monika's Freiburg study. When he had moved in with her,

Jack had been delegated his own spaces in the wardrobe and his own drawer in the sideboard, and every piece had been linked to some memory of those times. Monika had thrown it all out, she had written. Not literally, of course; Monika had far too highly developed a sense of social and ecological responsibility to throw out good furniture that someone, somewhere, would be glad to have. She'd have given it to the Red Cross or to Caritas, just as she gave them used clothing that was still in good order.

Everything in the room was new. It looked like something from an Ikea catalogue. Too perfect, too colour-matched, too pristine, but that was Monika all the way. It would have been nice, Jack thought, to have gone furniture shopping with Jyothi . . . but then, what the heck. Jack shoved the photos back into their folder and stood up.

He took Jyothi to the beach as usual and sitting on their favourite bench he showed her the photos, and told her about the things they showed, speaking in the casual tone he would use for any child of her age, whether American or Indian or Inuit.

'See, this is the front door. When summer comes around we'll have big red roses growing up the wall bedside it, and if we're lucky and get home early you'll get to see 'em. This is the room Monika got fixed up for you. Here's your bed, and in that closet there's some stuff waitin' for ya, and you can keep all your junk in those drawers. And put some posters on the wall, whatever you like. Favourite pop stars . . . but I guess you're a little too young for that. Look, she got you a violin. A violin! Ever saw one of those? I bet not. It's in that box; you'll see it when we get there. I'll teach you to play. If you like. A bit smaller than a sitar . . . Remember the sitar, that lady was playing the other night? Remember? The sitar?'

Their eyes met, and Jyothi mouthed the word sitar, and bobbed her head in the manner of Indians saying 'yes', and Jack smiled and showed her more photos. And it didn't matter if Jyothi thought he was showing photos of some splendid palace in a far-off land where milk and honey flowed in the streets, and didn't understand that this was going to be *her* home, *her* room, *her* bed, *her* violin. All that mattered was that she listened: to the timbre of his voice and the faith that all would be well.

It seemed the process was almost over. With any luck the required papers would be his in a week or two, and he would be free to take Jyothi home. He had bought her ticket to Frankfurt, and booked a flight in two weeks' time. Back in Germany Monika had broken into a frenzy of further activity in preparation for the child's coming: no pregnant woman could have done better at providing the complete paraphernalia for a new addition to the family. Down to the last toothbrush and hairgrip, Jyothi could want for nothing.

The telephone call came early on a Friday morning, before Jack had eaten breakfast but after his daily session of yoga, which he had taken up since discovering that it calmed his mind and made the endless waiting for Jyothi less of a walk over burning coals. It was Mother.

'Mr Keller! You must come immediately!' she shouted into the telephone so that Jack had to hold it several inches away from his ears. 'Yes, it is Jyothi! She has gone!'

Jolted out of his calm state of centred attention Jack shouted back: 'Gone! But how! Where to! Has she run away, or what?'

'Mr Keller, just one minute . . .'

There was a minute of cruel silence caused by Mother apparently placing her hand over the receiver to speak to a man, for Jack faintly heard a masculine voice in the background.

In that minute Jack felt he was hanging by the last links of his fingers to a cliff edge above a hundred-metre-deep abyss, ready to drop at any minute but unable to do so till the silence broke and Mother kicked away his clinging fingers with the details.

'Mr Keller? Hello? Are you still there?'

'Yes! What—'

'Mr Keller, I am in a hurry, just come over. The police are here, if you are quick you might meet them. Please come immediately.'

That was it, then. Jack was not to be released from his prison of dread. He was to carry it along with him for the entire three-quarters of an hour it took to pull on his clothes, go down to the street, find a taxi in the early morning chaos, and goad the driver through the gridlocked streets as fast as the creeping metal caterpillar of Bombay rush hour would permit. Rush hour! If ever there was an oxymoron that was it. Never had Bombay's traffic seemed less in a rush than now, never such a dead, stinking, slothful creature.

When he arrived at the orphanage Mother was at the door talking to a policeman. Both turned at his approach, the officer with the blank, deliberately neutral stare of the professionally detached, Mother with a face churning with emotion.

'What happened? Where is she?' Jack cried, and they looked at each other as if each expected the other to break the terrible news. Then Mother spoke.

'Mr Keller, oh my dear, it is just terrible, that man, that awful man came and took her away.'

'Which awful man?' But even as Jack spoke he knew: the man he had sought in the labyrinths of the Dhobi Ghat and in the squalid back streets of Bombay.

'Her father!' cried Mother. 'Her father came to take her away and when I tried to stop him he pushed me. He laid his hand on me! Here!' She patted her sternum. 'He pushed me in the corner, out of the way, and when I ran after him his friends pulled me back by my hair! And the other one gripped me here! Look!'

Quite offended she showed Jack the place on her arm, just below the tight ridge where the sleeve of her sari blouse circled her flesh, where apparently she had been violated. Jack could see no mark, the skin was too dark; but, said Mother, 'It is hurting very much! That thug just grabbed me and flung me against the wall when I tried to block his way!'

'Did they say anything? Where they were going, where they were taking her?'

'He just said he wants his daughter back, he's waited too long and now he has a place for her.'

'And then?'

'She didn't want to go. She was screaming and struggling when he tried to pull her out of the room and holding onto the door but one of the men lifted her up and carried her out. They had a car waiting outside, a taxi, and they threw her in and got in themselves and drove off. That was the last we saw of them!'

'And then you called me?'

'No, first the police. There was uproar in the house at first and several of the children had seen what had happened and needed quieting so it took some time before I rang you and then the police came. This is PC Ashok. He has made a report.'

PC Ashok nodded gravely. 'But unfortunately there is nothing we can do, sah. The father is having custody of his own child; he is having rights to take daughter away.'

'But . . .' Jack had no idea how he managed to speak so calmly, so collectedly, as if this was merely another of the little snags he had encountered along the path to adoption. 'The adoption process is almost complete. Surely this counts as abduction. You must be able to—'

But Ashok gravely shook his head, an expression of infinite sadness on his face as if he were contemplating the sorry state the world had descended into. 'Up to last minute father's rights are valid,' he said mournfully. 'Even if father is poor, he is still having rights over daughter. Very sorry, sah.' His thick shoulders hunched as if in agreement with this sorrow. He now turned to Mother and began, speaking English probably in deference to Jack, 'Madam, there is nothing police can do to help you . . .' then, in mid-sentence, breaking into Hindi, at which point his entire mood picked up. He and Mother launched into a continuation of the animated conversation they had been having on Jack's arrival, which, to judge by the spirited gestures and occasional chuckles which punctuated it, had nothing whatsoever to do with Jyothi's disappearance.

Jack tried to interrupt three times by saying 'But—' until Mother turned to him and said, 'We simply must accept this turn of events, it is God's will. It was not Jyothi's destiny to grow up in the West. The very fact that this has occurred proves it. We must accept God's decision with equanimity, for it is he who pulls the strings and we are mere puppets in the dance of life.'

Having delivered her lecture Mother nodded sternly at Jack, with the same look in her eyes she used on recalcitrant orphans, and turned back to her own conversation.

For the first time since being in India, for the first time, in fact, since he was a wild young boy proving his manhood by ongoing scuffles with the bully from down the road, Jack felt a burning desire to punch someone in the face. Up to this moment he had admired and emulated the Indian attitude of composure in the face of disaster; now all he could feel was a livid upheaval from the depths of his body, so ready to explode into too hasty action that he swiftly turned away. He walked away.

Chapter 10

'What do you mean, she's *gone*?'

'Just that, Monika. Gone, disappeared, vanished. *Verschwunden.*'

'Stop it, Jack, now just stop being so calm and supercilious, don't joke with me about this. Where is she?'

'Madam, believe me, I am not joking. Certainly not. I would never joke about such a matter.'

'But how can you just stand there calmly and tell me that! What have you done to find her! Have you told the police! Jack, where is she?' Monika's shock was palpable across the telephone line; and loud; Jack had to hold the receiver away from his ear. He had regained most of his equanimity during the past six hours. He had waited to telephone home because of the time difference, and used the time to do all that was humanely possible to find his prospective daughter: which, it turned out, was nothing. Neither the adoption agency nor the Indian officials in charge of the case had given him the least hope of finding Jyothi in the teeming city, and even if she should be found, they assured Jack with exasperating self-righteousness, he had no chance of gaining custody of her. He was given one lecture after another on the absolute nature of a father's rights, on the sanctity of the family unit and on the priority of biological ties over all other human bonds, and sent packing.

'If I knew where she was, do you think I'd be standing here telling you this? Anyone would think you've never been to Bombay yourself, to hear you speak,' said Jack. 'Honey, this is a BIG CITY. You get me? BIG, real big. Big as in enormous, gigantic, colossal, humongous, really really big. Big as in an anthill of twenty million swarming ants. You get it? Translate that into hard to find. Real hard to find. Think needle in haystack, think Jack a stranger in big city and no one to help him, and you might get the picture.'

He was in front next to the driver. She saw Him turn around but it was not to look at her. It was to open His hands to the other man, the heavy stinking one at her side, who opened a filthy paper bag and removed a folded wad of paper money which he placed in those greedy open hands. Again He did not look at her but opened the car door and got out and walked away. Now she was alone with the two strangers and though she hated Him she wanted to run after Him, for He was all she knew and better than nothing. She screamed and flung herself against the door but the man next to her grabbed her arm and hauled her back, and then he punched her in the face, after which she was quiet. The car drove off. She looked out of the window and saw rows and rows of houses. She had never seen them before. They were taking her away. She didn't know where to. She felt a freezing over inside her. They were pouring in the cement again. She felt it hardening. She felt fear, more than fear. Terror.

Early every Saturday evening for the past several weeks Jack had held a concert for the orphanage children. The programme consisted of a happy mélange of Indian and Western music. Through his Indian contacts he had organized a small collection of Indian musicians: a sitar-tabla duo, two female singers, a violinist, and he himself with his guitar, and had choreographed a short and lively programme which could be appreciated by a young audience. The children had learned to look forward to these concerts and Jack had persuaded Mother and the musicians concerned to continue with them after his departure. Perhaps it would not run for any length of time. Jack was fairly certain that, without himself as motivating force, the musicians would begin to find more profitable ways of spending their Saturday evenings. But tonight it was fairly certain that the concert *would* take place, since a farewell concert for Jyothi had been planned, and the musicians surely would not have been notified by Mother of the girl's abduction.

Jack was in no mood for music. But at five p.m. a nagging feeling woke him out of the half-sleep he had fallen into in the darkened cubicle that served as his bedroom. He woke, yawned, and rubbed his scalp; he drew back the curtain before the tiny window above his cot and looked at his watch.

The call of duty emerged from behind the sorrow clouding his mind, struggled for a few minutes with the disinclination to do anything but grieve in darkness, and lost. He stood up, wrapped a sheet around his naked body – in this heat what could a man do but sleep naked? – and walked through the cluttered living room to the shower.

Fifteen minutes later, in clean shorts and a crisply ironed white shirt the dhobi had delivered that morning, he was down in the street hailing a taxi. Punctually at six the taxi stopped next to the tamarind tree outside the orphanage. He paid the taxi-driver, stepped out into the dusty street, and crossed the road to the orphanage door.

It was then that he heard the thin, shrill, petrified voice calling his name. He swung around in time to see a slight figure plunging from the branches of the tamarind tree and propelling itself towards him with the speed of a pursued prey; it flung itself into his arms and almost threw him to the ground, and only when he had stopped staggering did he manage to cry out her name.

Jyothi's first garbled words revealed that she feared she had been followed; she had recognized a man who had walked past the orphanage several times in the hour or two – or three or four – she had been hiding in the branches of the tamarind tree, waiting for Jack.

'And your father? Where's your father?' Jack asked.

Jyothi looked nonplussed. 'My father?'

'Yes. Where is he? He took you, didn't he? Jyothi, you have to realize: according to the law you still belong to your father. So we have to be careful, very careful, because he might come back.'

Jyothi shook her head vigorously. 'No, no, no,' she said. 'No!' Tears poured out of her eyes. 'My father never coming back!'

'But he might. So we have to be careful.'

But Jyothi continued to shake her head. 'Never coming back. Not ever, like Ma too not coming back. All dead.' And she began to cry bitterly.

Jack and Mother exchanged worried glances.

'What do you mean, dead?' Jack asked after a while, after the sobbing had grown quieter.

'Dead. Father dead, mother dead.'

'But your father is . . . I mean, he's the man who took you away, isn't he?'

'No, no, no,' Jyothi shouted, shaking her head vigorously, and burst into a torrent of speech. Jack could only marvel at the miracle of hearing her voice. The words came gushing from her lips, as if a great unclogging had taken place and they had finally been set free. Though he could not understand them he exulted; they had crossed another bridge.

'Let me talk to her,' Mother said then, and for five anxious minutes Jack watched as Mother interrogated the girl. Finally she looked up. 'I have the story,' she said.

Jyothi, said Mother, had loved her father, and her father had loved her. He was a kind and loving man. But he was dead. He had died within weeks of the family moving to Bombay, it seemed. Jyothi could not tell how he had died; all she knew was that he had been in a big hospital. Her mother had come home crying one day and said that he was dead.

They had lived by begging for several weeks, or months. And then this man had moved in with them. Jyothi did not know how or why. All of a sudden he had been there, coming and going, sometimes gone for two days, sometimes spending the nights, sometimes not. They still had to beg and to work, helping at the ghat. He said he was their new father but she had never believed him.'

'But . . . what happened last night? How did she find her way back here?'

Mother exchanged a few words with Jyothi, then said, 'When the car stopped she ran away. They could not catch her. She found her way to the beach. From the beach she knew the way back here. She hid in the tree, waiting for you.'

'But what does this all mean? For me, I mean. For the adoption process.'

102

'Jyothi will have to repeat that story for the authorities. They will make investigations. Perhaps we can find the hospital where the father died. Perhaps we can establish that she is indeed a full orphan. If that happens . . .'

She paused. Jack reached out for Jyothi and pulled her towards him. Instinctively she climbed upon his lap.

'Then there should be no more objections to the adoption,' said Mother.

Part Two

'It's easy to play any musical instrument: all you have to do is touch the right key at the right time and the instrument will play itself.'

J.S. BACH

Chapter 11

Travelling with Jyothi was like having a constant shadow. She never left his side, not even for a minute. As they queued at the airport she clutched the bunched hem of his T-shirt in one hand, pulling it tight around his waist, and held onto it as her lifeline in the sea of humans that swarmed towards the check-in counters, using their overflowing trolleys as battering rams to a better position. An entire family materialized in front of Jack: the father, three women (the mother? Mothers?) shrouded from head to foot in chadors, four children and one toddler in a push chair. In ominous silence they thrust away others' luggage and jostled themselves and their own luggage forward into the breach. The women, Jack noticed, were the main actors; the man turned up only after the work was done, sliding in as if oiled, brandishing a thick wad of passports and tickets in his hand as a shield.

The mass of humanity inched forward until at last there was only one person ahead of them, a weary old man in a dhoti who had silently and stoically held his place in the bedlam for one and half hours. There was no question of keeping a distance in this crush; whether he liked it or not, Jack was almost breathing down the old man's neck just as the man behind him pressed uncomfortably close to his own back.

Jack heard the check-in woman say to the old man: 'Sir, you came on the wrong day. You were supposed to take last night's flight.'

The old man spoke in his weary voice. 'The ninth, my flight is on the ninth of May!'

'Yes, that is right,' the woman agreed. 'But very early in the morning. At twenty minutes past midnight. You should have taken the flight then. The next flight is on the tenth.'

'On the ninth,' the man repeated. 'I am flying on the ninth, I told my daughter in London. Today is the ninth . . .'

'Yes, it is still the ninth. But the aircraft flying tonight will actually leave on the *tenth*, in two hours, just after midnight. I'm sorry, sir, you missed your flight this morning.'

'It can't be right! The *ninth* . . . My daughter . . .' the old man wailed, but the woman was already peering over his shoulder, gesturing to Jack to come forward.

The man refused to leave the counter. He was crying profusely now and a scene was brewing, but out of nowhere two security guards appeared and gently but firmly pushed the man back through the crowd. Distracted, Jack watched the extraction of the weeping man and was called back by the matter-of-fact call of 'Your tickets please, sir.'

He laid a comforting hand on Jyothi's shoulder and placed their tickets and passports on the counter. Jyothi still held his T-shirt.

Jyothi had said nothing since leaving the orphanage. It was midnight now; she had not slept, nor eaten since six o'clock supper. She had not gone to the toilet. Perhaps she was too shy to ask.

'Jyothi, you should go to the latrine before we board the plane,' he said after they had successfully passed into the waiting lounge. Latrine was what they called it in the orphanage; Mother's word. Jyothi would have to learn new English words; and new German words. Jack had not taught her a single German word, and already he could hear Monika's recriminations.

'Come,' he said, and took her hand. He led her to the ladies' room. 'This is the latrine. The toilet.' He pointed to the door with the woman's silhouette on the door. '*Das Klo*,' he added. 'You have to go by yourself. No men allowed!'

Jyothi stood staring at him as if she did not understand. He opened the door and gave her a gentle push. 'Go on, Jyothi. It's better if you go now. It's not so comfortable in the plane. The latrines there are very small and you might not be able to go when you want to.'

But Jyothi refused to leave his side. He looked around in despair; she would have to go, sooner or later, and sooner was better than later. He didn't want a similar drama in the confines of the aeroplane. He was certain it was necessary; she had drunk three glasses of water that evening. But he couldn't very well go into the ladies' with her . . . not anywhere in the world, but especially not in India. And he couldn't take her into the men's.

'Excuse me, please.'

They were blocking the doorway. Jack moved aside and gently pulled Jyothi out of the way. A dark-haired European woman in loose green slacks and a short cream blouse smiled and nodded at him, mouthing a thank you, and opened the door. There was something in her smile that encouraged Jack to address her.

'Excuse me, just a minute . . .'

The woman stopped with her hand still on the doorknob, and looked at him, raising her eyebrows in query.

'This little girl is afraid to go in by herself. I wonder if she could go with you, if you could perhaps show her . . . ?' He left the rest of the sentence unspoken; it seemed too private a thing to ask a perfect stranger, yet the woman smiled in understanding. She looked down at Jyothi.

'Yes, of course, come along.' To Jack's surprise, she spoke some words in an Indian language, and stretched out a hand. Jyothi looked at it, then at the woman, then at Jack. Jack smiled and nodded in encouragement.

'Go with this nice lady, Jyothi. She'll help you.'

The woman spoke some more words. Her voice was warm and coaxing. Once more the little girl looked from one to the other.

There was a moment's hesitation in which Jack felt as if Jyothi's entire future hung in the balance. In that glance she seemed to be asking permission: permission not to be afraid, permission to trust, permission to be a person apart from him. And if she could not, here and now, decide to leave him she never would; she would always be bound to him in a web of fear of the world and the damage it could do her. In a split second he saw doubt, fear, panic flicker in her eyes and then, even before he could respond himself and add a word or a smile of encouragement, she had done it: she had taken the woman's offered hand and entered the ladies' room, and Jack stood facing a closed door with a silly smile pasted on his lips and a lift of jubilation in his heart.

'It's not going to be easy,' Rachel said. She blew on the coffee steaming in her hand, and nipped at the edge of the paper cup. 'A cousin of mine adopted a little boy from Peru. His parents

110

had been killed in a bus accident. He was three years old when he came to England and it took him a year to speak a word.'

'Oh, she's speaking already,' Jack said. 'Once she got her first words out she was fine with speaking ... though her English isn't all that good. Our problems have to do with how she'll adapt. And she has to start learning German.' A worried expression crossed his face, which did not escape Rachel's eyes.

'And that's what's worrying you? Learning German? Adapting to the society?'

'Kids learn languages quickly enough. I guess that won't be a problem. And they adapt. I don't see any hassles there either.'

'Then what?' Rachel's eyes, dark as cocoa, were bright and warm, and seemed to notice everything – not just the things he wanted her to see but those little hidden details he preferred not to call to anybody's attention, least of all his own.

Jack had waited for her and Jyothi outside the ladies', and when they appeared he had invited Rachel – after a quick thank you and introduction, and discovering they were waiting for the same flight – to a cup of coffee at the airport restaurant bar. In the fifteen minutes they had been talking he had noticed this uncanny ability of hers to probe without compunction and draw things out of him he'd rather keep concealed. Jack felt he had no defence against the stream of information that he volunteered at the slightest prompting from her. He might have been alarmed had it not been for the unaffected mirth in her eyes and the sincere interest that warmed her queries.

Jack hesitated. 'You ask so many questions,' he said.

'Asking questions is my job!' Rachel laughed, seeing that he was genuinely uneasy. 'I'm a journalist.'

'What do you write about?' Jack asked, but instead of answering she leaned over, unzipped her travelling case, plunged in her hand and removed it with a rag doll, which she handed to Jyothi.

'Here, this is for you,' she said with a smile. She spoke some more, in Jyothi's language, and Jyothi's permission-asking glance at Jack was even shorter this time than before. She took the doll and without even looking at it clasped it to her chest. It was an Indian doll, the 'skin' a brownish-red, in the form of an Indian woman with long black plaits, wearing a blue shiny sari and with a little baby doll sewn to her back.

'No, you can't—' protested Jack, but Rachel stopped him.

'It's fine, I bought several of them to take home for friends, it's not for anyone special. She doesn't seem to have any other toys with her . . . ?'

'No, well . . .' But it hadn't been a reproach, simply an observation. Jyothi sat on Jack's lap, one skinny arm wrapped tightly around the doll and a thumb in her mouth, which she sucked with hollow-cheeked intensity, her eyes fixed solidly on Rachel as if inspecting her for unexpected flaws of character.

'Sorry, it's none of my business.'

'How did you learn to speak . . . what is it, Hindi, Marathi?'

'Hindi,' said Rachel. 'My father was in the Foreign Service. I grew up in Delhi. I forgot it for a few years but at university I took a course to freshen up. It all came back. What about you? And her?' She glanced at Jyothi, who was now snuggled deeply into Jack's arms. She was no longer staring at Rachel. Her eyelids had dropped so that her eyes seemed almost closed; in a few minutes she'd be fast asleep. 'What is she to you?'

That was the signal for Jack to launch into the story of finding Jyothi on a Bombay pavement, and the innate sense of rhythm and melody that had so enthralled him at the very first meeting, of the accident and death of her mother, and the struggle for adoption. Rachel seemed to listen with all her senses; once again Jack had the feeling of needing to place the

112

burden of the last few months on another pair of shoulders stronger than his own.

Rachel was enthusiastic. 'What a wonderful story! She's obviously a very special little girl. Listen, you must keep in touch with me. Here's my card. I'd just love to hear how this continues.'

She whipped a card out of her pocket and held it out to Jack.

Rachel Fitzgerald, the card read, and a London address. 'It's not going to be easy,' Rachel said. There was something in her voice that made Jack look up. An innuendo: as if Rachel knew something he didn't, but of course that was ridiculous. Jack shook away the feeling.

Rachel had a window seat ten rows up from Jack and Jyothi, and managed to exchange it for the aisle seat next to Jack.

'You don't mind, do you?' she asked as the former tenant of the seat, a lanky, long-limbed Indian, probably a student, extracted himself and sloped forward to take the replacement seat.

Jack shook his head, but the question was rhetorical. Rachel had already slipped her case under the seat in front and was now edging herself into the seat next to him.

'You might need help with Jyothi,' said Rachel unnecessarily, and Jack nodded. They looked at each other, smiling in unison and complete agreement. Jyothi, they both knew, was an agreeable excuse to spend the long airborne hours in each other's company.

They talked for most of the night. As it was an overnight flight the cabin was dark and silent; most of the other passengers were sleeping and so they whispered, their faces spotlighted by the overhead lamp, leaning in near to each other, and somewhere over Saudi Arabia Rachel leaned even nearer and kissed Jack gently on the lips, to which he responded with a fair degree of eagerness and a minimum of guilt. They spent about an hour doing nothing but kissing, after which the cabin lights rudely flashed on bathing them both in a highly unwelcome glare. They pulled apart unwillingly.

'You're so pretty,' said Jack, and Rachel nodded and pushed a bunch of dishevelled hair behind her ear. She said nothing but grabbed her handbag and disappeared into the WC.

Jack turned to look at Jyothi. She was curled into her seat, covered by the airline blanket. Jack could see the top of the doll's head where she still clasped it tightly to herself. Her thumb was in her mouth, but her jaw hung slack, and when Jack raised her head slightly to slip a pillow between it and the armrest the hand fell away. She grunted, her lips made a few sucking movements, and then her features relaxed again into the still softness of sleep. Jack stroked a strand of hair away from her cheek and gazed at her fondly, a fount of love welling up within him. He realized with a sharp pang that for the first time in months he had not been thinking of Jyothi. Something else had taken control of him, banishing her. Now, in the harsh light of the cabin, guilt caught up with him.

'Phew!' he said audibly, and shook his head as if to rid himself of a bad dream. He leaned forward almost touching forehead to knees, then sat up and stretched his chin upwards and his neck as long as he could. Muscles tensed and relaxed again; he rubbed his temples and glanced somewhat nervously at the empty seat next to his.

'Hi, you want to go too?' Rachel said, standing in the aisle and beaming at him. She had brushed her hair and washed her face and put on new make-up, a hint of rose lipstick and a trace of blue along her eyelids.

'Yeah, sure,' said Jack, and pulled first one leg then the other from the under-seat shaft that held them captive. He climbed over Rachel's seat into the aisle. As he edged past her she touched his arm and he shuddered involuntarily, and Rachel, misinterpreting his reaction, chuckled suggestively.

Jack spent more time in the WC than was necessary. He splashed his face with cold water, and that helped. Then he sat on the toilet and thought. He thought for fifteen minutes, then got up, opened the door and walked past a disgruntled queue back to his seat. Rachel had changed seats once again; now she was in the middle seat, and the aisle seat was waiting for him. He sat down.

They turned to face each other. This time, she was smiling but he was serious.

'Look, Rache, I'm sorry,' he said right away.

'Sorry? But what *for*?' Her voice rose a trifle hysterically at the 'for'.

'For . . . you know. I'm sorry, I shouldn't have.'

'What do you mean, you shouldn't have! It was lovely!'

'Yeah, well, but you see, in my situation, I . . .'

She was gazing at him and for once she wasn't talking. Her eyes, so bright before, were veiled in hurt. She bit her bottom lip and then looked away, rubbing an eye, and at that moment Jack threw guilt and caution to the wind; this time it was he who leaned over. He hooked a finger around her chin, turned her face back towards him, and this time they did not come up for air until Rachel heard the discreet cough of the stewardess and pulled away.

The stewardess smiled indulgently and held out a little breakfast tray. Jack and Rachel righted themselves, pulled at their clothing, ran fingers through their hair and lowered their food trays. Jyothi was still asleep; they didn't wake her. She could eat later, and besides, once she was awake there could be no more kissing, and neither of them wanted that. Jack looked at his watch. Four hours more till Heathrow. As far as air travel goes, an eternity.

Jyothi stirred and woke up an hour before landing and that was when Jack pulled away from Rachel, asked to change back to the middle seat, and acted as if nothing had passed between them. He helped Jyothi unpack her breakfast, straightened out the muddle of blankets, pillows, clothes and doll she was tangled in, and busied himself with various other tasks which kept his back turned towards the precarious aisle seat. But once Jyothi was eating and everything else was settled to perfection he became aware of an uncanny silence from behind and turned sheepishly to meet Rachel's accusing eyes.

'Everything OK?' He gave her his most winsome grin and placed a hand on hers, but only left it there for a second before withdrawing it, glancing to the side to see if Jyothi, perchance, had noticed.

'No,' said Rachel.

'Huh?' Jack frowned. 'No, what?'

'No, everything is *not* damned OK,' said Rachel. 'Are you ashamed of me, or what? She's only a little girl, for God's sake.'

'Look, Rachel, I'm sorry, I didn't mean . . . I just don't want to confuse her.'

'Confuse her? And what about me? I'm *very* confused. First you kiss me as if I were the last woman on earth and then you pretend you never saw me in your life before.'

'I had to help her with her breakfast! She needed me!'

'Oh, it wasn't *that*. I don't mind you helping her with her breakfast . . . not at all. It was the way you . . . turned the ice on. Immediately. The moment she fluttered her eyelids. You should have seen your face. And then you just *beamed* this ice at me. You literally *beamed* it. Brrrrr.'

116

'Look, it's just that . . .'

'That you're married. Oh, I know. I know. Never get involved with a married man. That's what my best friend told me. She fell into that trap herself: she warned me. Never. And what do I do? Exactly the opposite.'

'Gee, Rache, it was just a—'

'Just a little aeroplane flirt. I know, I know.'

'No, it was more. You know it was more. It was there from the first moment. You know it was.'

'What was there?'

'Rachel.'

They stared at each other. A cloud of unspoken, unspeakable longing hung between them; one false word, Jack felt, would pierce that cloud; one false step and it would break. He could not face the deluge.

'What?'

'The timing is wrong. I'm sorry. I wish it wasn't. I wish I'd met you six months ago. We could have let this happen. Six months ago would have been perfect. But now . . .'

'Now you've got Jyothi. I know, I know.'

'I'm sorry.'

Tears welled in Rachel's eyes and she turned away. 'It's OK. I understand. It's very noble of you.' After which she ignored Jack, leaned across him to Jyothi, who had now finished her breakfast, and spoke to her in Hindi.

'Let her out, please, I'm taking her to the loo,' said Rachel to Jack brusquely, and from then until the landing no further words passed between them.

Chapter 12

The goodbyes at Heathrow were warm between Rachel and Jyothi – at least, warm from Rachel's side – and cooler than ever between Jack and Rachel.

'I'll write you, I have your card,' said Jack.

'Don't bother,' was all she said. She turned then, and walked away. Jack wanted to run after her, hold her back, make an irresponsible and insane decision. But he looked at Jyothi, who stood stiffly at his side patiently waiting for whatever was to come next, clutching the doll to her chest, looking up at him for directions.

He held out his hand to her. 'Come, Jyothi,' he said. 'We have to get a plane to Stuttgart.'

Monika was waiting for them immediately behind the partition leading to the Arrival Hall at Stuttgart. Jack, manoeuvring the luggage trolley with Jyothi perched on the top through the sliding doors, saw her immediately. He waved, because she was waving: a slim, trim figure in perfectly ironed cream linen trousers and a royal blue blazer. Her blonde hair was shorter than she had ever had it. Jack remembered she had always wanted very short hair but he had always begged her not to cut it. Now she had.

But I, too, have done things she would not approve of . . . An image of wild dark curls flickered through his thoughts and was gone before he could name it. He summoned a game smile and touched Jyothi's shoulder.

'There she is,' he said, leaning forward so she could hear him, and pointing. 'There's Mama.'

They had discussed on the telephone what they would like Jyothi to call them. Jack had thought Monika and Jack would be enough, since Jyothi was already old enough to know that they were not her biological parents. Monika was adamantly against that.

'She needs to know us as her parents. It's vital that she should address us as Mutti and Vati.'

Jack conceded the first part of this argument but not the second; Mutti and Vati made him cringe. He wanted Mom and Dad. In India Jyothi had addressed him as Jack if at all – he wondered if she could change to Dad? But Monika did not like 'Dad'. Too American, she thought, and didn't they live in Germany? Wasn't Jyothi to speak German? No, said Jack. He would continue to speak English with her. One parent, one language. That, he had been told, was the best method, and in English Dad would be the right word. They settled on Mama for Monika – stressed, in the German way, on the first syllable – as the easiest and most universally applicable version, and Dad for Jack. This, though, was the first time he had actually used one of these words with Jyothi and the moment the word was spoken it became, for the first time, a reality: they were parents, he and Monika, linked together in an indissoluble bond. He had never questioned the link before this. He and Monika had been together ten years now; their lives had intermeshed so thoroughly he had never even considered there could be any alternative to it. Jack, the eternal drifter, had drifted into marriage and drifted along in marriage, never contemplating drifting out of it since that would have taken too much effort. And now he was a father that door was closed for ever.

Jyothi's appearance into his life had had a disruptive effect; she had been like a tiny plant pushing itself adamantly up through the concrete of his complacency, breaking away old structures, inducing him first to fight and then, more subtly, to open his eyes to the various wastelands of his life. Monika, he saw now in a flash of shocked inspiration, represented a wasteland to him. His inner temperature immediately dropped ten degrees.

There was no time though to contemplate this new insight now. Monika was already bent over Jyothi and had her in her arms, hugging her with an enthusiasm that inspired in Jack once more the very foreign impulse to slug someone. He had no time to reflect on that impulse, though, or carry it out, for there was another person in front of him who had grabbed his hand and was pumping it heftily up and down.

'Oh, hi, Brigitte, I wasn't expecting you!'

He spoke wearily in German, but Brigitte, Monika's sister, didn't hear for she, too, was now gushing over Jyothi: 'She's so small, she's tiny!'

Monika was talking to him, Jack: 'She must be exhausted, poor little thing. Hello, Jack, how are you? Come, let's go to the car.'

Jack and Monika embraced perfunctorily. Brigitte took the trolley out of Jack's hands and pushed it towards the exit. Jyothi still sat stiffly on the topmost suitcase, clutching her doll. She had not smiled at Monika nor shown the least

120

sign of recognition. Monika, walking beside Jack, whispered furiously, '*Sie erkennt mich nicht!* She doesn't recognize me!' in German and English in case Jack didn't understand, and as if it was his fault.

'Give her time,' said Jack. 'Everything is a shock for her. I mean, compare this place to Bombay.'

'Don't be ridiculous, Jack. It's all new, of course, and different, but it can't be a *shock*! A shock is something *negative*! I mean, she must be feeling she fell asleep and woke up in heaven! Don't exaggerate!'

'You call this heaven?' But Jack might well have been speaking to himself for Monika was chatting with Brigitte, having somehow dropped him one pace behind.

Compared to the chaos of Bombay, Jack conceded, Stuttgart Airport might perhaps be mistaken for heaven. There was a bustle in the air, but all contained in an atmosphere of polished civility. The floors were of marble, or something imitating marble; the general impression was of space and cleanliness and light. People were meeting and greeting each other with flowers and hugs, pushing their gleaming luggage trolleys towards the doors or the elevators. Everyone seemed dressed as if for an occasion, and looking down at his own wrinkled shirt and four-days-unwashed, transcontinental-slept-in jeans, Jack suddenly felt like scum. Jyothi, too, he realized, was not dressed for the occasion. She had worn a comfortable cotton skirt and blouse for the journey and he had not thought to change her before disembarking. He had not thought about clothes, either his or hers, at all, in fact. He never thought about clothes. Perhaps, he reflected, that was an instinct reserved for the female gender. He had the guilty feeling he understood why Monika and Brigitte pretended not to know him. He hurried to catch up.

They crossed the road outside the airport, entered the car park and Monika led the way to their green Passat.

Monika had fitted a sophisticated child's seat in the back seat of the car. Briskly she helped Jyothi into the car and buckled her into it. Brigitte opened the rear door to get into the back seat but Jack said, 'No, let me,' and edged in next to Jyothi. Monika drove off. They were zipping along the Autobahn when Monika looked into the rear-view mirror.

Jyothi was sitting on Jack's lap, one arm curled around his neck. She held the rag doll clasped under the other arm and sucked her thumb. Monika's voice could not conceal her irritation.

'Jack, I know it's her first day here and we have to make allowances but it's better if in future we agree that she should always use the car seat, without exception. It's safer and anyway it's the law.'

Jack, who never used his own seat-belt even though it was the law, and safer, hardly raised his eyebrows, and seemed not to have heard. He was lost in thought, a thousand miles away. Monika glanced around.

'Did you hear me, Jack?'

'What? Oh . . . oh yeah, the seat. Sure, sure.'

Brigitte, who had been discussing Jyothi's school career with Monika (she was a secondary school teacher and knew all there was to know about education) turned to glare disapprovingly at Jack.

'I can just see you're going to spoil that child rotten,' she commented.

Jack said nothing, but his lips formed two words that would have caused an accident had they been spoken aloud and had Monika heard. Monika despised four-letter words and would not have them in her home, or her car. Brigitte saw his lips move but could not lip read, especially not in English, and so a minor crisis was averted.

'She should not be sucking her thumb at her age,' said Brigitte.

When they arrived home Jyothi was sleeping in Jack's arms and Jack himself was near collapse, but he didn't know why. He didn't know if this sudden and unexpected aversion to Monika had something to do with meeting Rachel, or if his attraction to Rachel had something to do with his cooled affection for Monika; which, he now realized, had been imperceptibly but slowly and surely growing all through the months of their separation. It was just that the incident with the car seat seemed to exemplify everything in his relationship with Monika that he was unhappy with. He just hadn't been aware of it before. How ironic that it was Jyothi's coming which now seemed to be bringing up all those hidden irritations he had tucked away so conveniently into a dark pocket of his mind. Jyothi was supposed to glue their relationship back into a stable and unassailable fortress. There had been cracks; they both knew that. But the cracks were surely a result of their childlessness; they had both retreated to the two extreme poles of their personalities, had failed to meet in the middle, to reach out to the other for completion, as they had done in the beginning. Jyothi was supposed to be the central light that would melt their differences and fuse them together again. Monika, the analytical one, had explained it all to him. But now her explanation seemed to Jack as dry as Monika herself.

He now realized that in all the years they had tried for a baby they had actually failed to speak of their very disparate attitudes to life and living and what this could mean for the raising of their future children. The car seat incident loomed as a warning of dire things to come.

Don't be silly, he reprimanded himself. Don't exaggerate, don't make a mountain of a molehill. It was only a tiny incident, an insignificant difference of opinion. Monika was right in her own way; she saw the principle of the matter, as always. She's got a good heart, and she really loves Jyothi. Be grateful. Think of all you owe to her.

He had been in the first stages of shipwreck when she had literally lifted him off the street, and God only knew where he would have landed without her support – not financial support, of course, but *moral*, for didn't Jack lack the hard and fast framework of hard and fast principles, a map of inner guidelines to rely on during his journey through life? And wasn't *she* there to provide him with just that, wasn't she the solid root-ball which fixed him firmly on the earth, just as he was the soaring bird of imagination that gave flight to her spirit? But just as it was impossible to map the flight of a bird through the sky, so was it impossible for anyone, least of all for Jack himself, to pin down his stance on any one issue or to predict his behaviour in any one situation.

They needed each other; but whereas she needed him for the little luxuries of life – art, laughter, lightness, inspiration and vision – he needed her for the bare necessities. And just as he might help their mutual child with the creative and artistic aspects of growth, so it would be her task and her duty to provide the basics. This much was obvious. Wasn't it an ongoing joke among their friends that, without her, Jack would be a helium balloon floating far above their heads? And didn't Jack himself grin and accept all this as a given, regarding it all as a compliment?

So why am I so irritated now? Jack asked himself, and found no answer. I'll just forget it, and see what happens, he said to himself. Jack crossed his bridges as he came to them, and that, he thought, was the best way to proceed now.

Jack collapsed onto the leather couch. He had carried the sleeping Jyothi into her room, laid her on the bed and tucked her in with the puffy duvet in its cheerful yellow seersucker cover, and his exhaustion now overpowered him. Monika offered to warm up a plate of soup for him but all he had wanted was a glass of cold milk, which Monika served and which he drank in large, audible gulps, ignoring her frown. There were two things he wanted desperately: a long hot soak in the tub, and bed. The tub could wait.

He yawned and stretched. 'I could sleep for a year. I didn't get a wink last night,' he said. A little tweak of conscience reminded him exactly *why* he had not slept the night before, but he ignored it and set off towards the stairs.

'Take your glass into the kitchen on your way,' said Monika rather ungraciously. Jack turned around, picked up the glass with its wooden place mat, took it into the kitchen, and left it on the dishwasher, instead of putting it away as Monika had taught him. In the bedroom he pulled off his outer clothes and left them strewn across the floor, in violation of house rules: Monika had trained him always to lay them folded neatly on a chair, but he had fallen into his old bad habits in India.

In the final moment before falling into bed, he glanced at the limp tangle of jeans, T-shirt and socks but, after a split-second debate with his better nature, decided that it wasn't worth the effort to turn and pick them up now. Monika would no doubt mention it when he woke up. Then again, she might not. She might have mercy upon him and pick them up herself; but, just before his mind drifted off into the welcoming arms of sleep, Jack doubted Monika knew the meaning of the word mercy. And another little voice said to him: You ungrateful bastard. Then he fell asleep.

Chapter 13

She opened her eyes and it was all dark. There were soft things all around her but she could not see them, because of the dark. Soft things around her head and over her body, and smells she had never known before and could not identify. Jyothi sat up and suddenly she was free of the thing, the soft heavy thing that had been covering her, but it was still dark, blackness all around her such as she had never seen. She couldn't remember. Nothing. She remembered a car speeding along, faster than she had ever been before, a green car, and there had been other cars all like it, all racing in the same direction.

She groped back in time and she remembered a big shiny place with people, and a woman who had kissed her, and Jack who had not been there, but behind, walking behind, and being pushed along on some wheels, and a jumble of other memories. People who looked strange, so many white faces, she had never seen so many and they scared her. She remembered the woman vaguely, she had seen her before *but she couldn't recall where or when and it didn't matter.*

The world had disappeared.

Out of the shadows came her mother. She could smell her, that unmistakable pungent smell that was unique in all the world, the softness as she rested her face in her mother's breast, breathing in her essence. Ma! Her mind screamed, but there was no Ma, only this soft floating heavy thing above her.

She called for Jack, but he didn't come, only darkness closing in so she called louder and he still didn't come. The scream burst out of her before she could think, before she could stop it, before she even knew it was there, a scream that scared her more even than the darkness. There was nothing in the world but screaming. There was nothing of her but a scream.

The scream woke Jack. His hand groped for the switch to the bedside lamp and a moment later he was in the hall outside the bedroom and then in Jyothi's room at her bedside. She was sitting up in bed and crying uncontrollably. He put his arms around her and held her close, speaking words of comfort.

'What's the matter?' Monika stood in the doorway. She wore an ankle-length pale lavender housecoat of a soft, fluffy synthetic material, with matching slippers. Her face without its make-up looked pale and drawn, almost ghostly in the artificial light.

'She must have woken up and not known where she was,' said Jack.

'Oh!' said Monika. 'I should have thought of a night-light! Oh, the poor little thing!'

Jack said nothing but stroked Jyothi's head.

'Shall I bring her something to drink? A glass of milk, maybe.'

'Yes, do that.'

Jyothi gulped down the milk. 'Maybe she's hungry,' Jack

said. Jack looked at his watch. Two a.m. 'It's early morning in India and she hasn't eaten for hours.'

Because of the unfavourable connections from London to Stuttgart they had not come home till early afternoon. Jyothi had been sleeping for eight hours straight, and before disembarking at Heathrow she had also been sleeping constantly. She would most likely be awake for the rest of the night. And she would certainly be hungry. The last meal she'd had had been breakfast the day before, and the last meal before that had been the previous day.

'I'll fix her something,' he said. 'You go back to bed. Guess I'll be up for the rest of the night.'

Monika hesitated, torn between a sense of duty, her desire to be with Jyothi during her first conscious hours at home, and the pull of sleep.

'All right,' she said reluctantly. 'But, Jack, I think you should . . . um . . . put on some clothes.'

Jack looked down at himself and noticed he was wearing nothing but boxer shorts.

'OK,' he said and got up. He tried to let go of Jyothi but she clung to him like a leech. Jack looked at Monika for help.

'I'll go,' she said. She left and returned with a pair of neatly folded jeans and his favourite red T-shirt, smelling of Persil and fabric softener. Jack managed to detach himself from Jyothi enough to dress, in stages. Monika, still reluctant to leave them together, stood watching. She had her hands in the deep pockets of the dressing gown and was biting her bottom lip, a sure signal that she was dying to say something but holding back.

'I put your travelling clothes in the laundry basket,' she said after a while. 'You left them on the floor.'

There was light and there was Jack; dazzling light and he was next to her with his arms around her and it was possible to

128

stop screaming and only tremble next to him. Her eyes were tightly closed, she did not want to see but only feel his nearness and smell his smell and hear his familiar voice.

Where was the world?

Where was everything?

The world had disappeared and all there was left of it was him, Jack.

Jack tried to get up and leave her and she opened her eyes and clung to him. In her field of vision she saw other, strange things she had never seen before and bright colours so she did not look because there was only Jack. That woman was there. Jyothi did not look at her. Then she turned and left, and came back with some clean laundry. Jyothi knew about clean laundry; that was familiar, that was safe. It reminded her of happy, happy times, back in the village. The smell of fresh laundry was the only common thing between this world and her old one. It took her all the way back, back, back, back to Ma, and back to her father. Jack took the little pile of laundry and got dressed while still holding her. She would not let him leave, not ever. Notever notever notever.

He was helping her to her feet. She had never seen a bed like this before. It wasn't like the sharpais she had slept in before. It was thick and there was a thing like a padded cloth on it, not really a blanket. It was soft and yellow and very thick too, and yet light. It was the thing that had been covering her. It was warm where she had been lying. She did not want to come with Jack but he was holding her hand and pulling gently, smiling and saying her name. She stood up.

Her legs felt shaky; she did not think they would carry her. She could not remember walking, nor how to walk. She was wearing a long thin pink dress. He was wrapping something around her: a blanket. He took her hand and smiled, and said come. She tried walking, and it worked. She could walk! At

129

first she thought she would fall but she didn't. She gripped his hand tightly as he led her through this strange new world.

They were in a dark place again but he turned on a switch and it was light. It was a corridor, like in the orphanage, but the walls were pale blue and very clean, and the floor was soft. She had never seen a soft floor before. It was dark blue and fluffy like an animal's fur, like a cat. But blue. It was warm under her bare feet. Her hand was in his and she walked beside him, slowly, swaying a little bit because she was still not sure about her legs. She reached out to touch the wall, to support her. She stumbled, falling over her own feet, but he caught her and set her straight. He was talking to her all the time but she wasn't listening. She heard only the voice and the rising and falling of it, the deep deep music of it, and what it told her about safety, and about him, and about her.

They were in another room now, all of wood, with a long table, and a sink, and around three sides of it there were many doors, big and small. There was another table against the wall, and Jack pulled back a chair and said something, and she sat down. He opened one of the wooden doors and behind the door it was all white and light, and shelves with things on it.

He was talking all the time and now some of the words made sense.

'Hungry,' he kept saying, and, 'Food.'

Those were important words. Words that were always hovering unspoken back in the world she knew, back in time and place before it had come crashing down. Hungry, hungry, hungry; food, food, food. They had lived for these two words. She knew their meaning. She could remember the feelings those words evoked and all of a sudden they were there, living beasts within her: hungry! Food!

And so now she listened to Jack, to the words and not only to their cadence. Let them come alive with her. Her lips moved

*and she tried to speak, but at first no sound came out. It was
as if she had forgotten how to form a sound.*

*But then it happened and it had not been her decision. She
heard the word as it left her lips: 'Hungry.'*

When she spoke he turned to look at her and smiled, and when
he spoke next she understood him perfectly.

'Yeah, I know you're hungry,' he said now, 'but it'll take too
long to cook. What about some . . . aah . . .'

He was opening doors, the small doors up on the wall, and
then he took out a big box and shook it. It made a crackling,
rusting sound.

'Cereal,' he said triumphantly. 'That'll do ya. We'll cook you
a big meal for lunch tomorrow, but now you have cereal, OK?'
He had opened another door and taken out a white bowl, set
it down in front of her. He opened the fridge again, removed
a tall white carton, placed it on the table.

'Milk,' he said.

He went on talking and to her surprise she understood.

'Monika wouldn't touch this stuff with a ten-foot pole,' he
said with a laugh. 'Hates it, but she buys it for me – it's what
I used to eat as a kid and never got out of the habit. She says
it's full of sugar, unhealthy and all that rot. Sugar Puffs, it's
called, that says it all. Who cares? I survived, didn't I? Grew
up big and strong? Bet you never tasted this before. You'll
love it.'

He pulled at the top of the box and then tipped it, and lots
of little brown round things fell out into the bowl. To her they
looked like little pebbles.

'Look, try one!' said Jack, and picked up one of the pebbles
and popped it into his mouth. 'Go on!' He picked another up
and gave it to her. She took it in her fingers and put it to
her mouth. It was sweet! And light, and soft, not hard and

heavy like a pebble. And good, so good. Jack chuckled again and poured milk over the little pebbles.

'She'll kill me if she knows I gave you this,' Jack said. 'She's got a thing about sugar, specially for kids. She bought it for me, not for you. Actually, she probably didn't even buy it. Guess it's been here since before I left; she wouldn't buy this stuff. Never. Yet she can't throw it away either. She can't throw away food, because of the starving kids in India. Now you're here she'll be even stricter with that rule. You're gonna hear that a million times in your life. Think of the starving kids in India, and think how lucky you are, Jyothi! That'll be her theme, I bet. Look, I'll eat with you. Ravenous myself.'

He took out a second bowl and sat down next to her.

'Don't mind if I join in, do you?' he asked, and without waiting for her answer – which wouldn't have come anyway – he filled his own bowl, poured the milk over it, and picked up the spoon.

He grinned across the table at her.

'So, Jyothi, your first meal in Germany. Sugar Puffs and milk, as American as you can get. As they say here: *guten Appetit*!'

Chapter 14

It was a strange new world; to live in it she needed strange new senses. She had to put up a barrier between her and it, to filter the impressions which came flooding in and threatened to sweep her away. Behind the barrier she was safe; she could see out but the world could not see in, and that was the way it had to be. With the new world kept at bay, the old one still surrounded her and kept her safe; though it was physically gone she still had her memories of it and the memories were as real as the world had been. Since you could do what you wanted with memories she chose to keep those of the time before the accident. That way she could have Ma back, make Ma real again, as if Ma had never gone away. The new people, all these pale people who spoke a language she could not understand, had to be kept out.

Not Jack, though. He was an anchor in the midst of it all, a rope from the old familiar world into this one, and she clung to him with all her strength. Jack said she should call him Dad; but she could not. 'Jack' was who he was. Jack was the name of the rope that bound her to the past. There was comfort in 'Jack', none in 'Dad'. She'd do her best, but it would be difficult. She remembered the woman, too, from that old world; the woman who kept pushing her head up close and smiling, and putting her arms around her and squeezing her. The woman felt like an invader. She pressed against Jyothi's barrier trying to come in, but since Jyothi would not let her in, the pressing hurt and Jyothi flinched and stiffened whenever she came near.

The woman kept pointing at herself and saying Mama, and other strange things. Jyothi did not know what she was saying.

The woman would indicate various objects and say a word; things had new names in this world. Sometimes Jack told her the name of the thing in English. Some of the things she had never seen before: strange ones like the noisy object with a long tube the woman pulled around the place, dragged the tube over the floor. *Staubsauger*, said the woman, *Staubsauger*. Then Jack would say: vacuum cleaner. And Jyothi would know that the thing had two names.

It seemed to Jyothi that Jack didn't like her so much any more. Sometimes he played music and sang for her but sometimes he went out, leaving her alone with the woman. And the woman would point to herself again and say Mama, Mama, and smile into her face, that strange empty smile with no echo.

Every morning the woman got Jyothi out of bed. She was usually awake anyway; she was usually awake when it was still pitch black but now she no longer screamed, she simply lay there and waited till the woman came and switched on the light.

She learned to do things the right way. When she got up she had to go to the *Badezimmer*, a sparkling white room, and clean her teeth, have a shower, and put on her clothes. The woman helped her with that. After that it was time to eat but never again was she allowed to have Sugar Puffs; instead, there was bread and butter and jam, and the woman called Mama showed her how to prepare it. There was a mug of hot tea and it always took a long time till she could drink it, for it was hot and burned her lips.

The woman sat at the other side of the table, watching, always. And smiling.

When Jyothi did the right thing she smiled even more, and said, '*Jaaaa!*' in a long-drawn-out kindly voice, and patted her on the back. When Jyothi did wrong she looked at her and frowned, and said '*Nein, nein.*' Jyothi would freeze and stare, waiting to be told what was wrong and what she should do. Like the first day, when they had eaten a meal together at the table. There had been a heap of rice on Jyothi's plate and Jyothi, who was very hungry, had taken some of it in her right hand and was mixing it with the vegetables to eat when the woman said '*Nein, nein!*' and shook her head vigorously. Jyothi had felt like jumping up and running away, but instead she remained frozen to her chair with her fingers still in the rice and stared at the woman.

Her voice had turned softer then. 'No, Jyothi,' she said, and then some words in that funny language. Jyothi turned to Jack, and Jack said, 'Jyothi, in Germany you should not eat with your fingers any more. Look . . .' He held up two metal things. 'This is a knife and a fork. The knife is for cutting things on your plate, the fork is for putting things in your mouth. You have a knife and a fork too . . .'

And then Jyothi had seen that she, too, had those metal things beside her plate. She picked them up and pushed the food around her plate for a while, but Jack said then, 'I think we'll let you eat with a spoon this first time.'

He got up and came back with a spoon, which she took from him. She had used a spoon before.

While she ate Jack and the woman talked to each other in very loud voices. They were angry; Jyothi could recognize that for she knew anger, could feel it like waves of heat encompassing them. She didn't think they were angry with her, though, so she went on eating, but it wasn't so nice to eat when people were shouting over your head. She kept her head lowered so the heat would pass over it. They were not speaking words she could understand so she tried to ignore them. In Bombay she had learned how you could close off the noise so it didn't bother you inside: you could retire into a little bubble where the noise and the heat could not reach you. She could hear but she did not listen. Then Jack said, loudly, 'Goddammit, woman, if you wanted a perfect little German girl you should have got yourself one!' And he stood up suddenly so that his chair fell over, and hurried from the table.

Jyothi wanted to go after him but the woman looked at her and smiled, and handed her the knife and fork across the table. Jyothi knew she had to stay seated. She finished her meal using the knife and fork, but only because she was so hungry. She did not taste it. She found it very hard to eat that way, but the woman seemed pleased. '*Jaaaa!*' she said, and smiled, and then Jyothi knew it was all right. She felt a slight softening of the barrier. She looked at the woman, and smiled back, just faintly. To her surprise, the woman began to cry.

'Oh, Jyothi!' she said, and got up and hurried around the table to Jyothi, lifted her out of her chair, and squeezed her so hard she could hardly breathe, and all the time she was sobbing like a small child. Jyothi did not know what to do, so she did nothing. She let herself be hugged.

That night Jack took her upstairs and helped her prepare for bed. He spoke in English and Jyothi understood every word.

'It's a hard time for all of us, Jyothi,' he said softly. The sun was still shining outside and sloping in through the windows but Jack pulled a thick yellow cloth in front of the window to block out the sunlight, and then he sat on her bed and spoke to her. 'See, we're a family now, you belong to us. To both of us, not just to me. So I have to stand back and let Mama get to know you as much as I do, and teach you things. She can teach you things better than I can. I know she's a bit strict at times and she looks as if she's mad but she's not, she loves you, and even if she's mad it's usually not at you it's at me.'

Jyothi wanted to speak but she couldn't, she didn't know what to say. So she simply looked at Jack and listened to what he had to say.

'God, I hate it when you look at me that way,' Jack said. 'Makes me feel I ought to . . . take you away from all this. You don't really fit in here, Jyothi. Neither do I. Funny I didn't think of that before I brought you here, I just assumed you'd be fine once you had a home. You'd just grow up normal, like the other kids born here. But I don't think it'll be that way at all.

'But, you know, it's just your first day. Things'll get better. I promise. You'll find friends; you'll learn German. You'll get to like Monika and then love her. Her bark is worse than her bite. She can't help being the way she is. And I'll try not to fight with her. We never used to before but where you're concerned I guess we have different ideas. But we'll sort 'em out and give you a good home. I promise.'

He leaned over and kissed her on the forehead. Her hand was in his, and she squeezed it to show she understood, and then Jack sighed. 'I just hope you start speaking soon. Kind of spooky, the way you just look out of those big brown eyes of yours. You were speaking fine in Bombay, I didn't realize that coming here would be such a big shock for you. But, hell, take your time. Take all the time you want.'

Monika had bought a huge, fluffy Steiff bear for Jyothi, and when Jack left the room she pulled it to herself, turned over to face the wall, and curled herself up into a warm round ball.

She burrowed down so that the goose-down duvet covered her completely, leaving only a small slit at the top for air. She clasped the bear tightly to herself, almost ceasing to breathe in the effort. Here beneath the duvet was the one sure place in her life right now, the one place that was reliable and always the same. Everything else was a jumble.

Chapter 15

The next day, Saturday, Brigitte came to visit, with her
own daughters Sabine and Tanya. Sabine was twelve and
Tanya eight. They had been given strict instructions to
'be nice to Jyothi and play with her', and they were sent
out into the garden with her to give them the chance to
do this.

Jack and Monika had built their home five years previously,
when they had first started making plans for a child. It was
a house of average proportions for an average family: three
bedrooms and a bathroom upstairs beneath the eaves, and a
large kitchen, living room, dining room, study and lavatory
downstairs. There was a strip of garden in the front and a
well-manicured patch of emerald lawn, surrounded by rose
bushes, delphiniums, lilies and rhododendrons at the back.
Last summer Monika had started with the excavation of a
garden pond and this year she intended to finish it. Behind
the sliding glass terrace doors from the living room was

a large patio covered by a blue and white striped awning, which extended and retracted automatically with the sunlight. In summer there was a set of wooden garden furniture on the terrace, covered with plastic protections when not in use.

Brigitte pressed badminton racquets into the children's hands and chased them onto the lawn.

'You can show Jyothi how to play,' she said to Sabine. 'Don't make such an ugly face. She's your cousin, you know you always wanted a cousin, now go and play with her.'

'But, Mum, I wanted to watch Suderof this afternoon. You know I always watch.'

'Not today. Go on now, play!'

Nothing kills the desire to play in a child as much as the command 'Play'.

Sabine and Tanya listlessly hit the shuttlecock back and forth, missing more than they were hitting. Jyothi made the third point of a triangle but simply stood there with the racquet dangling from her hand, looking lost.

'Sabine!' called Brigitte who came out to see how far the friendship had developed. 'You must include Jyothi in the game!'

Tanya's and Sabine's voices rose in offended protest.

'She doesn't want to play!'

'She doesn't know how to hit the ball!'

'She didn't even *try*!'

'Well then, you must teach her, for heaven's sake!' cried out Brigitte, and disappeared once again into the house. She was helping Monika prepare a Black Forest gâteau and coffee and they still had not decided whether or not it was warm enough to eat outside, on the terrace, or inside, at the coffee table in the sitting room.

'If we sit outside we can keep an eye on the children,' Monika

140

said, meaning she could keep an eye on Jyothi and see how quickly the friend-making process developed. She explained this to Brigitte.

'That's exactly what we *shouldn't* be doing,' countered Brigitte. 'We should let them get to know each other by themselves, and not interfere. That's the best way. You'll see. I'm not even certain you weren't too hasty in inviting the Schmidts, Monika. Too many children all at once might be too much.'

'I just wanted to . . .' but what Monika just wanted to do was would be for ever a secret for at that moment the doorbell rang.

'That will be Mrs Schmidt and Andrea,' said Monika.

'I'm supposed to play with you,' said Andrea with a scowl.

'Well, you can play with *her*,' said Tanya, pointing towards Jyothi, who was still standing with a dangling racquet. '*We're* playing with each other.'

'But I don't want to! She doesn't speak German!'

'Well, you don't need to speak, you just have to play! Hey, Sabine! Watch out!'

Tanya whacked the shuttlecock high up in to the air. All four girls watched as it slowly fluttered to the earth, and then Sabine slammed into it with such force it went spinning straight into the branches of Monika's peach tree, where it lodged itself firmly between the leaves.

'*Scheisse!*' shrieked Tanya.

'*Please* let me play with you!'

'No! It wouldn't be fair if one of us has another person.'

'But if *she* plays too, we could have two teams of two.'

'She isn't moving. I don't think she knows how to play.'

'Well, I'm not too good myself so it wouldn't matter.'

141

'Yes it would, she doesn't even lift the racquet. Go and ask her and you'll see. You'd have to teach her first.'

Andrea glanced at Jyothi and said, 'I don't think she wants to play or she wouldn't just stand there so stupidly.'

'She doesn't even speak, she hasn't spoken one word. She just stands there. It's so stupid.'

The three girls moved closer together. Andrea and Tanya eyed each other, badminton forgotten. Andrea said, 'You're her relatives, right?'

Tanya replied, 'Not really, she's not a blood relative, you can see that. My aunt adopted her. I think she's a dummy.'

'Ssssh, not so loud.'

'It doesn't matter if we speak in loud voices about her because she can't understand a word.'

Sabine said, 'Well, if you two only want to gossip I'm going inside to watch Suderhof. Bye.' She walked towards the terrace, twirling her badminton racquet nonchalantly.

Andrea and Tanya moved yet nearer to each other and Andrea lowered her voice. 'My mum said she's going to be in my class and I should make friends with her. But I don't want to. She doesn't say a word.'

'Well, you can't anyway, she doesn't speak German. We're supposed to be friends with her too because she's our cousin. What a pain.'

'And if we don't play with her we'll get into trouble.'

'I mean, what does she expect if she just *stands* there like a dummy. It really gets on my nerves.'

'It's creepy. I have a feeling she's watching us and under-stands every word.'

'No, she doesn't. She only understands English and Indian. I know it for a fact. If they had to adopt someone they should have adopted a baby, now we're saddled with having to be nice to her.'

142

Andrea, recognizing a kindred spirit, giggled, glanced again at Jyothi, stood on tiptoe and whispered something into Tanya's ear. Tanya covered her mouth with her hands and tittered, hunching her shoulders. Encouraged, Andrea put her hand on Tanya's arm and whispered some more, giggling loudly and leaning in so far she tottered. Both girls stumbled, dissolved in laughter.

'Andrea! Tanya! Jyothi!' Brigitte called from the terrace. 'Come on in, it's time for cake!' Andrea and Tanya catapulted themselves towards her, breathless, enthusiastic, and still giggling.

'Where's Jyothi?'

Tanya turned and pointed, sniggering wildly. Jyothi was still standing on the lawn, the raquet dangling from her hands. She had not moved an inch.

Chapter 16

Sometimes, Jyothi simply lay on her bed when the music played. She could stare at the ceiling for hours, so that occasionally even Jack had his doubts. What went on in that little head of hers? What did she dream, what did she think? She seemed unwilling or unable to express herself; though she could communicate on a general level, talk about the little practical things of life, she was absolutely silent about herself and there was no way of knowing what moved her, or what she cared about. She was an unknown continent. Once she had learned the secret of playing the cassette recorder, it had become the centre of her life; but she also pored over the picture books Monika had provided for her, sitting cross-legged studying each picture, sometimes frowning with concentration, sometimes biting her bottom lip. She had the gift of immobility, a thing Jack had never seen before in a child of this age.

Often, he worried. Though she obviously loved music she had lost something: a certain sparkle, the dynamism that had made her a being of light in the midst of Bombay's squalor. Now she had an evanescence to her; she seemed to him to be a wraith who could, at the bat of an eyelid, dissolve into thin air, leaving nothing but the pain of her absence in his life. He felt the need to approach her with delicacy, as if she were made of the finest filigree, fragile and easily destroyed.

He longed for the little Bombay girl, the child who had danced in the streets, unable to contain her joy, the waif with the seraphic smile and the midnight-black eyes that had shone with delight. Was she lost for ever? Was she permanently broken by the loss of her mother? Had it been wrong to take her from her own familiar world – however foul and chaotic that had seemed – and transplant her into the ordered, clean, yet somehow sterile domain of middle-class Europe? There are some plants that grow best among stones, others that flourish in the mud . . . was Jyothi one of those, a plant that could only develop in its own particular soil, and would wither when removed? His intention had been good, but sometimes the way to hell is paved with good intentions.

At the beginning it had seemed possible to reach her through the senses: through a square of chocolate melting on her tongue; or through music, when their eyes would suddenly meet in complete understanding; reading a book together; or simply by holding her on his lap, through a hug or a squeeze of the hand. And even now, there were moments of deep warmth and intimacy between them. But for the greater part of the day Jyothi was wrapped in her own little world, and closed the door to him. Perhaps, Jack thought as he entered her room, he was expecting too much, too soon. Patience, he reminded himself as he went upstairs to join her. More patience.

To his surprise Jyothi was not lying on her bed but standing at the little blackboard Monika had provided for her. The blackboard was covered with marks. Jack grinned in pleasure. But on closer perusal he realized that the marks were complete

145

gibberish: random collections of letters grouped together as words, but gibberish none the less. He was nevertheless surprised that Jyothi could write the individual letters, for she had not been taught, and went forward to praise her for this.

She was still writing as he approached. She placed a comma after one of the 'words', and started a new 'word' with the confidence and intensity of a person taking down dictation, not pausing between the letters or the words. She had her back to him so he could not see her facial expression but from the alert self-assurance of her posture he could imagine it: the very same intensity and concentration as when she was 'reading', biting her bottom lip, slightly frowning in the effort. There was something uncanny about it; Jack felt a shiver down his spine as he watched. She had not noticed his entry, and continued to write, now starting the fourth line.

'Jyothi,' he said quietly.

She looked up. In a split second he saw it: the frown and the lip-biting swept away to be replaced by a glorious beam of exultation, such as he had never seen since her arrival in this country.

He knelt down and put one arm around her waist.

'What are you writing, Jyothi?' he asked.

'From that book,' said Jyothi, pointing.

Jack saw that one of her favourite bedtime books lay open on the bed, the cover up. It was 'Goodnight Moon', a simple story that was actually more for a three- or four-year-old, but Jyothi loved 'reading' it with him and looking for the little white mouse hidden on each one of the pictures. She knew it almost by heart, he believed.

And now, looking closer at what she had written, he saw that she did know it by heart. She had written, word for word, and without a mistake, 'goodnight to the old lady whispering hush'.

But she had written it backwards.

Jack sat on the carpet, Jyothi opposite him, between them

146

the little violin case. Jack opened the fasteners, slowly lifted the lid. The half-violin lay cushioned in thick blue velvet, its wood glossy like a newly peeled chestnut, graciously curved and pleading to be given a voice. Jyothi's eyes were on it. Jack glanced at her, then slid the bow out of its holder, tightened it and rubbed it with rosin; he did this silently, aware of Jyothi's eyes on him. He laid the bow on the floor, removed the violin from its bed, adjusted the strings, took the bow, tuned the violin. Jyothi, cross-legged on the floor, watched.

Finally, Jack handed her the violin. She hesitated, glanced at him, then took it – gingerly as if it were a delicate orchid. Again her eyes rose to him as if asking what to do next. But she knew – she had watched him play so many times. Jack made the gestures, and she understood. She placed it under her chin, took the bow with gentle fingers. She knew how to hold it, where to place it. She drew the bow back across the E string. It was just one note, long drawn out like an endless outbreath. It was perfect. It was round and rich and exquisite; a keen pure spear of sound that entered the heart at its pinpoint core, the very source of all emotion. The hairs on the nape of Jack's neck stood on end. His eyes were wet.

Jack lay on a deckchair on the lawn, reading the novel he intended to review next. He hated it; it was one of those experimental works where the author seemed more intent on showing off his brilliant and unexpected use of language and his lack of taboos than in telling a story. The sun was nearing its zenith; the sunshade needed to be adjusted; and he needed a drink; and maybe . . . He stood up lazily. He had been getting a good deal of sun recently, and his skin was now a dark, glowing bronze. He and Jyothi went to the local swimming pool every day; he was teaching her how to swim. He walked across the terrace and glanced at Monika and Jyothi.

147

Monika's hobby was origami, and she was teaching Jyothi how to make a few simple animals. They sat across the garden table from each other, Jyothi's little dark head lowered and quite still in concentration. Monika's blonde head was also bowed, and she was speaking to Jyothi in calm, slow language as she demonstrated the folds on a square of paper. Jyothi imitated the folds on her own paper. The animals they had already created sat in a line across the table, watching their moving fingers in blithe indifference.

Jack entered the coolness of the house and slid back the terrace door. Before entering the kitchen he glanced at the hall telephone, hesitated just a second, closed the door to the living room as an extra precaution, lifted the receiver, and dialled.

Chapter 17

'We believe she may be dyslexic,' said Mrs Fuchs. 'I'm being very cautious, I don't want to label her . . . but you will have seen yourself . . . this last dictation . . .'

She pushed the page of writing across the desk towards Monika. Half of the page was covered with Jyothi's spidery scrawl. Almost every other word was slashed through with red ink, and there were numerous little marks, one mark for each mistake, all down the margin.

'More than fifty mistakes,' said Mrs Fuchs. 'And not just simple mistakes. She tends to write words backwards. She writes them more often backwards than forwards! She even writes the letters backwards. That is normal at the beginning; many children do it until their sense of perception has righted itself. But at this stage – end of the second form – she should at least be showing signs of understanding the difference between backwards and forwards.'

'We noticed that,' Monika said. Something inside her seemed

turned to stone. She looked at Jack, squatting next to her on the tiny chair in the classroom, his long legs clad in faded jeans splayed out before him.

'The funny thing is,' Jack said, picking up the piece of paper and inspecting it carefully, 'she gets the backwards words perfectly right. I mean, in the right order, only backwards. It's the ones she tries to spell forwards that are wrong.'

'Mr Keller, backwards is *wrong*. I understand you looking for mitigating circumstances but really there's nothing to change that fact. That's why I asked you to come today. I would advise you to get her tested, and in the long run it would be better for her to go into Special Needs Education. Even if she isn't dyslexic. She's just too far behind the others. She'll never catch up.'

'What about math?' Jack said. 'She doesn't seem to have any problem there.'

'Oh, she's fine with the actual *mechanics* of mathematics. She's actually very good at mental arithmetic, better than most of her age. But again we have the same problem: she writes the numbers backwards more often than not. She just seems to have problems translating words and numbers into understandable signs on paper. And even if she can work out the right answers in her head, she can't show her *steps*. We need to see the *steps*! She can't just write the answer next to the problem, and hope for the best! And I can't give her the attention she needs with twenty-eight other children in the class.'

Jack and Monika were both silent. They looked at each other, and away. They had discussed this at home. They had seen the signs. They had talked to Brigitte, who had gone over Jyothi's work. They had practised at home with Jyothi, going over each word ten, fifteen, twenty times with her, speaking it out slowly while she carefully copied the letters onto the paper, explaining to her the difference between 't' and 'd' and between the long and the short 'a'. Then they learned the next word, and the one they'd so painstakingly learned the previous day was gone. Vanished into thin air. The only thing Jyothi could do right was spell words backwards.

'Also, Jyothi is particularly difficult to get to know. She is so quiet and never speaks first. That's not the way to make friends.'

Jack opened his mouth to speak but Monika pinched his thigh as Mrs Fuchs continued.

'I notice she does have one friend, little Sarah in the First Form, but Sarah is something of an outsider too: maybe that's the reason they found each other. I believe they are friends outside of school too. But the point I am trying to make is that Jyothi would be far happier among children of her own level of learning. That's why I asked you to come today, to discuss a transfer to a Sonderschule. It's for her own good.'

'Couldn't she just repeat the class?' Monika's question harboured despair. There was a definite stigma attached to the Sonderschule, and Jyothi had enough to deal with already.

'Well, that's another possibility but I wouldn't advise it. I think the smaller classes in the Sonderschule would help her develop at her own pace, and—'

'No way,' said Jack adamantly. 'You don't get it; this kid isn't dumb, she's gifted, brighter than most. She can do mental arithmetic like a pro, she reads books above her age level, and as for music . . .'

Mrs Fuchs brightened; Jack had offered the perfect diversion. 'Oh, yes, I heard she plays the violin very well! That's one thing to be grateful for. I think you should really build on that and accept the fact that she's not going to be an academic . . . but music, now . . .'

Jack relaxed palpably and leaned back in the chair. He said with some satisfaction, 'She's a born musician.'

They could be sure of it now, though it didn't seem obvious at the beginning. Jyothi had started her violin lessons the first week after she had started school, and though she mastered the technicalities of her instrument very soon, it became clear that she had absolutely no relationship with the little marks on paper which were supposed to represent music. She had battled on for a year until Jack put an abrupt stop to it. From then on, he was her teacher, and from then on there was no paper.

Jyothi had perfect musical memory, and once she had learned the various notes she could play almost everything after hearing it but once. Learning in this way, first listening and then repeating, sometimes improvizing, even composing, she progressed at the speed of light, and in only a few weeks Jack and Monika realized that they had a musical prodigy in their care.

Chapter 18

Above all, Monika had hoped for them to be a perfectly normal family. In the beginning, she simply refused to believe that Jyothi's presence in their midst could make a difference: other people adopted children; adopted children belonged as much to the parents as biological children, it was the love and attention that children received that made them an integral part of the family or not and, God be her witness, Jyothi could not possibly receive an iota more love and caring. This was the theory.

Certainly, Jyothi arrived with a real deficit on account of her lack of German, and her socialization in the Bombay slums. She had a lot to catch up with. But that's what Monika and Jack were there for, for goodness' sake: to help her with that effort, and the final goal of that combined effort was to assimilate Jyothi completely into their lives, to eradicate all traces of her unhappy past, and to be a living example to all the world of what a *gelungene Integration* could be, a 'successful integration'.

Monika had harboured images of a happy, laughing little

girl who just happened to be Indian playing in the midst of a throng of German neighbourhood children – how much more normal could you get? The joyful little girl they had met in Bombay, reproduced on the streets of Frankenthal, walking to school with her satchel bobbing on her back, chattering away with her best little friend. Herself with the other mothers, waiting for their daughters after ballet class, fretting about this and that – the lack of adequate parking space outside the building, for instance. Monika knew that this was a major issue among the ballet mothers and would have loved to add her voice to the complaints. Or, had it been riding that caught Jyothi's interest, grumbling about muddy boots and hairs on jodhpurs and the stealing of sugar cubes: all that would have been so normal . . . so everyday . . . Monika longed for such trivial problems, becuase they were what life, a normal life, was all about.

So it was greatly to Monika's chagrin when it became obvious to them and to the world at large that they were anything but a normal family. It just wasn't working according to plan.

By the time she was ten Jyothi certainly understood German perfectly; she spoke it perfectly, too. But she did not communicate. She did not chatter in the light-hearted, amiable manner of ten-year-olds, discussing this and that with the blitheness of an unencumbered mind. She was much too still, too serious; she thought about matters that should not concern her, and instead of prattling on at the dinner table as would have been normal, Jyothi liked to reserve these serious topics for bedtime, and then unload them on her or on Jack, and she had no answers. And Jyothi had no friends, except for Sarah, who didn't seem to mind Jyothi's speechlessness.

It was as if the more Jyothi mastered the intricacies of the language, the more she retreated into the silences of her own mind where spoken language would not be called for. She had virtually no social contacts. She walked to school alone, and returned home alone, head slightly bowed, shoulders slightly hunched. But, worst of all, her performance at school was atrocious.

Monika wore her pain internally, sharing it with no one but Jack. Her love for the child grew like a protective shield fielding off the contempt of a world that viewed external success as the measure of a person's worth, and academic achievement as a reflection of a parent's skill.

Jyothi opened the violin case and carefully, lovingly, removed her instrument, holding it as she would a doll of finest porcelain. It was her second violin; the first had been replaced by an older, bigger, better, more expensive one which produced tones of such richness it sent a shiver down Monika's spine.

Monika had replaced Jack as Jyothi's teacher. Jack had been too undisciplined in his methods. Jack could not keep to a timetable, or when he did, he let his feelings of the moment dictate the procedure. Jyothi's progress, under Jack's tutelage, had been erratic and subject to her own moods and whims; on a sunny day she preferred, like Jack, to sit on a blanket on the lawn staring at the sky or reading a book. In winter, she and Jack went for long walks in the nearby woods, where they would gather dry twigs for kindling, and later Jack would light a fire and they would sit on the thick Chinese carpet, Jack leaning against the couch, Jyothi cuddled in the crook of his arm, while Jack read to her. They both preferred such pleasant, snug and effortless activities to the hard work of learning the violin. For though Jyothi was highly talented, and respectful of her instrument and the magic it could produce, Jyothi's relationship to the violin had been, with Jack, precarious.

Now she fixed the chin-rest to the violin, placed it onto her shoulder, nestled her chin onto the instrument, picked up the bow. One minute later the bow was dancing across the strings, Jyothi's fingers moved with supple grace, her shoulders swayed to the rythym, her eyes closed the better to let the music itself take possession of her. Monika, sitting on the wicker chair next to Jack's piano, watched in elated wonder.

When the session was over Monika praised Jyothi effusively, clapped her affectionately on the back, and replaced the violin in its case as if in gratitude for the gift of perfect music it had graced her with. But Jyothi's face was unsmiling.

Life was much better now. She had worked things out with Jack and Monika. Jack was for comfort, near to her heart and full of understanding. Jack she could tell secrets to, if she ever had any, and Jack was the one who made her smile.

Monika made her work. Monika gathered the scattered ends of her personality, the ones Jack left sprawling on the carpet, lined them up and coaxed them into effort. Monika was the trellis to a drooping vine; Monika gave support and coaxed her on and up; filled her with encouragement and gave her vision. Monika placed music at the centre of her life, and having a centre she could breathe again and live again, and all that was good. She just didn't like the violin.

She liked the sounds it produced, she liked the act of producing such sounds, she liked the purity and ease with which they emerged, as if through magic. It intrigued her to weave those sounds into tonal tapestries of great beauty. She regarded her gift with a certain amazement, unsure of how it came to be, astounded at the incredulity she produced in others, and perplexed at the discovery that what came so easily to her was a rare ability, setting her apart.

But there was no joy in her playing. And Jack, sensing her lack of joy, and not knowing how to create it, had lacked joy in teaching, and the two of them conspired to evade the timetable Monika wrote to keep them both on their toes.

So it was that Monika, though a mediocre violinist herself, took over, after which everything changed.

Monika had the discipline and the drive that Jack lacked, and the spark of excitement at Jyothi's gift. The gift had remained with her: simply to hear a piece of music once, or, if it was more complex, twice, in order to reproduce it almost note-for-note with dancing fingers, strings and bow. It was as if the music entered Jyothi through the ear, invaded her blood, coursed through her body, and re-emerged through the remarkable co-ordination of fingers, arms, head, chin, shoulders; almost, not quite, exactly as it had been, only the tiniest variations showing it up to be the fake and not the original.

Jack had at first marvelled, but then taken it for granted. He let it be, to grow as it would, not recognizing the fact that a gift is like a garden, needing attention if it is not to grow into a wild tangle of weeds where beauty cannot breathe. But Monika knew, and so it finally became Monika who supported, pushed and praised Jyothi, and entered her for her first concert at the age of twelve.

Getting to this point had been difficult. In the musical tradition there seemed a definite bias against a little girl who could not read music but yet could play so sublimely. At first, Monika was strongly advised to promote her pupil through the regular channels; the stumbling block was ever Jyothi's complete inability to read musical scores. It reached the stage that the moment Jyothi even saw a page of written music panic would grip her and she'd be unable to play, making a fool of herself at the various auditions Monika dragged her to. Professional teachers refused to take her on; they had their established teaching methods and were not about to adapt for Jyothi's sake. And so Monika was forced to rise to the challenge, and this proved to be the turning point for her relationship with Jyothi, for Jyothi's musical education, and, finally, for Jyothi's emergence from the slough of inferiority and into the light of her own personality.

'I'm going to make her a star,' Monika told Jack. 'That will be our revenge.'

'Revenge? What revenge?' Jack asked dreamily.

'Well, you know what I mean, Jack. You can sense it. We're outsiders. Have you see the way people's eyes narrow when they look at us?'

'Hmmmm,' said Jack.

'Jack, you're not *listening*.'

'What?'

'Pay attention! Put down that book for one minute, will you! Listen!'

Jack glanced at the ceiling and closed his book around his finger. 'What?' he said.

'Sometimes I get the impression you've lost interest in Jyothi!'

'Bull!' said Jack. 'I'm the one she spends her free time with.'

'But if I left it up to you she'd just sink into the same idle cocoon you live in, and she'd never get anywhere!'

'Well, those are nice words! Just because I'm not into a twenty-four-hour military regime . . .'

'Jack, this is no time to quarrel. It's not a military regime and you know that.'

'Sure is a lot of drill, though. Good she has me to loosen up with.'

Monika sighed. 'That's as may be. But you haven't even bothered to comment on her progress for ages and you didn't hear what I said a moment ago.'

'About revenge? Sure I did.'

'No, what I said before that.'

'What'd you say, then?'

'I said I'm going to make her a star. She's got the right stuff.'

'Oh, yeah, great, do so,' said Jack, and opened his book. But Monika would not be put off.

There had been quite some trouble in registering Jyothi for the concert, because usually only pupils put forward through the official channels – the government-sponsored Music School, and private schools and teachers – could be registered and Monika was not such a teacher. However, her sister Brigitte managed to arrange for special permission, and Jyothi was added – reluctantly – to the programme.

Monika was eager to show off Jyothi's talent. She had been for years. Her gift was such that she could easily have thrilled an audience at the age of seven, after only a year of lessons. But it had been obvious that Jyothi was not capable of performing publicly. She was still excruciatingly shy; it didn't take a degree in psychology to know that she would rather have died than face a public and play. Whenever Monika had asked her to play for guests she had frozen into immobility, and again and again made a fool of herself. Now, though, the time was right.

Jyothi was still shy, but Monika had been, as ever, efficient in her handling of the matter. All it had really taken were five simple words; 'Do it for me, Jyothi.'

In the last few months they had discovered together that *that* was the secret. If Jyothi could manage to block out the entire world and hold Monika alone in her heart, and play for that adoring audience of one, everything was all right. She could play.

'Do you think you can do that in public too?' Monika had asked. And Jyothi, finally, had said yes.

Now, as she sat in the audience wringing a handkerchief in anxiety, Monika's nerves were like jagged bits of barbed wire twisting inside her heart. Jack, sitting next to her, placed a hand on hers to calm her down.

Monika shook her head and dug her fingernails into Jack's hand. 'Oh Jack, maybe it's too soon . . . What if she panics – that would put an end to anything! She'd never be able to overcome a failure now!'

'Don't even think of failure,' said Jack. He stroked her hand. 'It's going to be all right, honey. She can do it.'

Monika squeezed her eyes tightly shut and whispered: 'Do it for me, Jyothi. Oh, please: do it for me!'

And Jyothi walked on the stage and did it. Accompanied by Brigitte on the piano Jyothi played her very best, for Monika, for Mama. She blanked out the world, did not even glance at the sea of faces before her. She knew where Monika was seated – Monika had told her in advance – fixed her heart on Monika, and played for her as if she were the only person in the world. She had chosen a piece Jack had often played for her – Elgar's 'Salut d'amour' – and played it with all the love in her heart and with all the fervour of her soul, and Monika listened with tears streaming down her cheeks.

Jack glanced at her and finally he understood: Monika had usurped his place in Jyothi's life. He was assigned the role of mere onlooker, and bystander; he who, after all, had initially discovered Jyothi, who had recognized her gift and vowed to nourish it and allow it to grow to fullness and fruition. Monika had succeeded where he had failed. He felt once again – as so often in the last few years – the gnawing, nagging resentment that he tried so hard to disguise and suppress. But it was there, relentlessly nibbling at the substance of their relationship.

'I'm jealous,' he said to himself with some alarm, but the moment the thought came he rejected it; it could not be! He was as proud as Monika of Jyothi . . .

There she stood, in the spotlight; a slight little thing, insignificant to look at, filling the hall with music of such beauty, so much innocence and sweet sincerity; such melancholy and nostalgia, such truth, that the audience was nothing but a single rapt body gazing awestruck at her. Those who had played before her – the Music School star pupils – had been adequate and even competent: but this! This was magic; it filled the heart with joy and gladness, with some indefinable element beyond the mere sum of musical elements. It was divine. It was the Speech of Angels. Jyothi had found her voice.

Chapter 19

She liked being with Jack. Jack made her laugh. But Mama always said Jack couldn't be taken seriously, so she didn't. Mama was like a wave carrying her forward. She made her practise the violin, day after day, relentlessly. At first Jyothi had objected because it was hard work and she preferred being with Jack, and having fun, and laughing. But after a while when she did what Mama wanted she felt as if Mama's strength were seeping through into her, as if she could really build on that strength and become somebody, through her. So she practised harder and harder, for Mama, and she was good! Everyone said she was good. It was so easy to be good. She never understood why other people thought it was so difficult to make beautiful music on the violin. To her it always came easily. She only had to take the instrument and the bow in her hands, and imagine the music she was going to play, and an energy coursed through her moving her hands just the way it – the music – wanted to so that it came out through the instrument. She had nothing to do with it. So when people praised her and said how clever she was, Jyothi could only look down and shake her head, as she knew she wasn't clever. There was something in her beyond herself that made it happen. That's what other people could not understand! Mama didn't understand either. She praised her all the time – she said praise gave confidence. But that wasn't true. The confidence came because the music was so perfect, and when she played she too was perfect.

Mama wanted to make her famous. At first Jyothi didn't think it was necessary. But Mama goaded her on, and she did become sort of famous, and then she found it kind of nice that she could do something that everybody else couldn't. Even though she didn't know how, or why – it really wasn't fair for her to take credit for an ability she had not made, but there it was, and people were giving her credit, so why shouldn't she accept it? Jyothi was basically shy but after a while she began to like the applause. Mama thought the more famous she became the more confident she would become.

Jyothi was too shy, too quiet, Mama always said. She didn't like her shyness and her quietness. She wanted her to be strong – that's what she told her again and again. And that's why she wished success for Jyothi. To help her become strong.

How could Jyothi tell her that she didn't need success to become strong? When she played music she felt strength taking possession of her, so that all that existed was music, music, music . . . did it matter then, whether the world acclaimed her, or not?

But it's a funny thing with success. Jyothi didn't seek it for herself. She did what Mama wanted, to make her happy: and success came uninvited. But once Jyothi had it, something changed. A sort of headiness took over. She felt a heightened sense of 'me' – something growing inside that relished the success, that basked in the limelight, not only enjoyed but nourished itself on applause. That something grew and grew. She won another competition, and another. The applause increased, and so did that new Me whom she had not known before. It was like a stranger living inside her; and gradually that stranger became a ruling entity within her. She was a demanding and rather temperamental mistress, something of a prima donna. Jyothi was not sure she liked her, for often she found her frowning and thorny when things did not go her way. Sometimes she was at war with her, she was so strong, and always fighting for supremacy!

This new person stood by her bedside each night, and whispered in her ear. She put thoughts into her mind – thoughts of the future, of more success, and what she could do to ensure it, and what she would do when it was fully hers. Ultimate success! The best violinist in the world! They said she could do it. Only believe, Mama said, and you can make it come true. So Jyothi believed she could do it. She practised and practised and practised. Her technique improved from day to day – she was quick – oh, how quick she was, and the quicker she was the more they marvelled. The applause was deafening, she was called for one encore after the other – and she learned to love it. The first time she was scared but after a while it became second nature to step out onto the stage and smile broadly all around, violin in one hand and bow in the other, and the thunderous applause swept a her up, and up, and up, to the skies.

I will make you a star! Mama had said. And now it was happening. The sky's the limit, said Mama! And Jyothi believed. She believed because she wanted to believe. And she wanted to believe, because . . .

It is power to be applauded, to be admired, to see your face in the newspapers, and to appear on television! To be wanted, to be loved, and not just by your parents, who have the duty to love you, but by all the world! It nourished this new Jyothi, the self-assured, powerful Jyothi who could look around and see only admiring faces and hear only words of praise! That was power, something to feed on and to fill her hunger. That hunger swelled, lifting her up with it; the new Jyothi, not the poor little girl from the slums, who couldn't read and write! And the more that other Jyothi grew inside the more she needed it and the more she needed it the more it grew. Merely by thinking she could add brick to brick, till finally she could conjure up images of the new Jyothi at will, sparkling, radiant images, Jyothi in the spotlight revered and applauded, and the more those images grow the more the old little slum-baby receded.

Chapter 20

They planned to spend the summer holidays in the Alsatian hills, as they always did. Monika's grandmother was from the Alsace – as they called it – and had left her and her sister the pretty stone farmhouse in a village a few kilometres south of Munster. The house had been refurbished and modernized, and was now a very comfortable three-bedroom holiday home; Monika and Brigitte each spent three weeks there in summer. For the rest of the year it was rented out to other holidaymakers – mostly to Germans, but the occasional French, Dutch or British family also dropped in for a week or two each year. The rent was a welcome source of extra income.

But this year, two weeks before they were due to leave, Jack announced that he wouldn't be going with them. He was going to America, he said. His parents wished to see him.

'I thought they had disowned you?'

'Well, we've made up . . . partly,' said Jack evasively. 'I've been corresponding with them now and again and Mom's health isn't too good, so I thought . . .' his words petered out, and Monika didn't ask for more details. Actually, she thought, it wasn't a bad idea to establish contact with Jack's American family. She had great plans for Jyothi, and a foothold in America . . .

'So I booked a flight two weeks before the Alsace thing.' Jack said.

'Two weeks before! When are you coming back? If you're leaving two weeks earlier you'll be back in time . . . ?'

'No, I'll be staying till the end. Actually, I return on the same day as you do.'

'Jack! You *aren't*! We could have discussed this in advance; you can't just go ahead and book things . . .'

'Why not?'

'Well, for instance, maybe we'd have liked to go with you! I'm sure Jyothi would like to meet your parents, and I—'

'No, no way, not this time,' Jack said quickly. 'I have to do this slowly, there's a lot of stuff we have to go through, me and my folks, and . . . Well, maybe next year we can all go. There's lots of time!'

'Well, Jack, I don't think . . . The holiday won't be the same without you.'

'Oh, you'll manage!' Jack flashed his infectious grin. 'Say, why don't you take someone along with you! A friend or something. There's room enough, and it won't cost them anything.'

'Thanks for the suggestion,' said Monika scathingly. 'And thanks for telling me now, in June, when everybody's already booked their summer holidays!'

'Oh, I'm sure you'll find someone. Just ask around. Or you could take a kid, one of Jyothi's friends.'

'Jyothi hasn't *got* any friends,' snapped Monika, 'unless you count those snivelling little hypocrites whose mothers all of a sudden seem to have recalled a deep relationship to us. You'd think they'd all taken a course in Public Relations, the way people smile at us these days. Anyway, forget it.'

'There's always Sarah,' said Jack. 'Bet they're not going anywhere.'

Jack was right; Sarah's parents were staying at home for the summer and they were only to glad for their daughter to spend two weeks – Monika had decided to shorten the holiday – in the Alsace with Monika and Jyothi. For Monika it was a relief. Without Jack she had no idea how to entertain Jyothi, and she couldn't have her practising the violin all day, not on holiday. This way, Jyothi and Sarah could occupy each other, relieving her of the chore, and while they did so she could unwind, do all the things there was no time for at home: read novels, listen to music, sunbathe on the terrace. She began to look forward to August, and lengthened the holiday back to the original three weeks.

They drove Jack to the airport and at the moment of parting Jyothi grabbed hold of him and did not want to let go; it would be the first long separation for either of them since her coming to Germany seven years earlier. She had now lived half her life here; the first half was quietly fading into oblivion: Yet loss was an experience that had imprinted itself indelibly on her mind so that now, just before Jack disappeared behind the Immigration counter, she broke down.

'I'll be back in a few weeks, honey. You'll see: before you know it I'll be back.'

'No, you won't.'

'I will!'

'Not before I know it!'

'Honey, don't take everything so literally! You know what I mean.'

'But I'll miss you.'

'I'll miss you too.'

'Then why are you going?'

Jack, his arms around Jyothi, tilted his wrist and looked surreptitiously at his watch. He glanced at Monika who took her cue immediately.

'Come on, Jyothi, we've been through this before. There's no need to cry, you're only holding Jack up.' She spoke briskly and as she spoke peeled Jyothi gently away from Jack. Jyothi let herself be peeled but could not control her tears. Jack held her face in both hands and kissed her on both cheeks, then turned to leave. Monika and Jyothi watched until the very last moment, and Jack looked back and waved as he walked; they could see him behind the barriers, still looking and waving, and finally there was no more Jack and a Jyothi weeping like a child of four.

Monika placed her arm around the girl's shoulder and led her away, out of the building and into the car.

On the way home Jyothi was silent, but she no longer cried. 'What do we do now?' she said at last as the car turned into the driveway. She said it in such a tragic tone she could have been lamenting a dear one's death, and Monika looked at her with eyebrows raised in astonishment.

'Why,' she said, 'nothing has changed, Jyothi, except that Dad's not here. We'll do everything we did before, just as usual!'

'Everything's changed, without Jack!' is all Jyothi said to that. They got out of the car, walked to the front door. Monika stuck the key in the latch, turned it, and they walked in.

The house felt empty, forlorn; to Jyothi it was as if the voice of one instrument was missing from a familiar symphony: one listened for it but its absence was so palpable

169

one had to switch it off. But Jack's absence could not be switched off.

'Promise me,' she said to Monika that night, 'that you'll stay with me for ever.'

'Not for ever,' Monika said. 'I can't promise that, and you wouldn't want that either. One day you'll grow up and want to leave home. You'll see!'

'No, I won't! I don't want things to change, ever. I don't want you to go away, ever. Or Jack. Why did he have to go? I want things to stay the same, always.'

'Things don't stay the same, Jyothi. Life is always changing. That's what life is all about. Otherwise nothing would ever happen.'

'But if things change, what will happen to me?'

Jyothi's face was half in shadow, half shining in the dull glow given off from her bedside lamp. Her eyes, large and dark, glistened with unshed tears and an unspoken plea of such poignant distress Monika leaned forward and closed her in a warm embrace – a rare enough occurrence.

'Oh Jyothi! Things change but usually when they do, we change too, and we get used to the changes and see that they were good. Listen, when you came here from India a long time ago you were terrified, because it was such a huge change for you, but you see what happened? You learned to love Dad and me, you learned to like living here, and you got used to the change. You'll get used to Jack not being here. It's only for a few weeks.'

Jyothi, though thirteen years old, looked much younger; small and slight, she could easily be mistaken for a child of ten. At times she displayed a wisdom far beyond her years, yet at others, times like this, the lost child in her came to the forefront and demanded to be comforted, and that was when Monika knew that the tragedy of her childhood – the loss of

170

her mother and her whole familiar world – would never be completely erased.

'Jyothi, do you know where Dad put the negatives of you winning the Youth Plays Music competition?'

'No, Mama.'

Monika clicked with her tongue.

'I promised Barbara and Gerd that I'd bring them along – I need to make some more prints. Now where could he have left them? Why can't he keep them in the photo drawer, with all the albums? He never uses the negative folder I bought. Typical Jack!'

Monika always complained about Jack losing thing. He was the one who took the photos, but once he got them back he had no system for keeping the negatives. Monika organized the best photos into albums, but Jack stuffed the negatives into drawers, and then he couldn't find them. 'Typical Jack!' Monika always said, but she said it fondly, as if she liked him for it. So when she couldn't find those negatives she looked for them in his desk. But now Monika was in stress, and her 'Typical Jack!' had more than a nuance of annoyance in it.

Jack's study was full of open suitcases – Monika was packing them a little every day. She'd been doing that ever since he left, so as not to have any kind of last-minute stress. Jack's desk was always a mess. It had five drawers down one side of it and an electric typewriter on the top, and piles of paper here and there. He always told Monika not to try and tidy it up because he knew exactly where everything was. Everything had its place in the chaos, Jack said, but he and he alone could find things. And Monika never touched his things normally.

'Look at this mess!' she said now. 'I'll never find them here.'

She opened one drawer after the other and flipped through the piles of papers she found.

Letters, and bills, and pages torn from magazines, all in unorganised heaps in the drawers, haphazardly stuffed in and forgotten.

'Who can find anything in this mess! I don't care what he says. I'm going to tidy it up. Jyothi!'

Jyothi appeared at the door.

'Yes, Mama?'

'I'm going to clean Jack's desk. Go to my desk, will you, and get me some folders.'

Jyothi did as she was told, and didn't say anything because there was nothing to be said ... she knew Jack wouldn't like it but when Monika decided to do something there was nothing in the world she could say to keep her from doing it. She watched when Monika removed a whole drawer from its socket and tipped it upside down on the floor. And then she sat down on the carpet herself which is a thing Monika almost never did.

Monika began making little heaps of her own. She was happy doing things like that. Jyothi could tell she had waited a long time to do this. She had even forgotten the negatives.

She finished one drawer and started on the next. It was more of the same. But when she tipped that drawer upside down a big manila envelope was on the top.

'What's this?' Mama said, and looked inside.

That seemed to be the moment of her undoing. She took out a letter and some photos, looked at them, turned a deathly white, and put them back. After that she put everything back into the drawer just the way it was, the manila envelope on the bottom, and stopped looking for the negatives. She hadn't been the same since then.

'Mama,' Jyothi whispered that night. 'Are you all right?'

Monika, who had been watering the plants on the windowsill, looked around, startled.

'What . . . why, why do you ask? Yes, yes I'm fine!'

'Oh.'

Monika moved over to the bed and sat down on the bed-side.

'Jyothi, I just wanted to ask you something. I hope you don't mind. About Jack.'

'Yes? What?'

'Did you ever . . . have you ever seen . . . or did he ever say . . .'

'Say what? What's the matter, mama?'

'Oh, nothing, never mind. It's not fair to burden you. Don't worry, Jyothi. It's nothing.'

And Monika smiled her broadest everything's-just-wonderful smile, tucked Jyothi in, kissed her, turned off the light and left the room. Jyothi was left to ponder in her bed.

Jyothi turned over and put the worrying thoughts of Monika away. Tomorrow they were leaving for France, and Monika would be all right again. She was always all right in France, so free of care. And then Jack was coming, and everything would be righter than ever.

Chapter 21

The dark blue Passat, loaded so full it was impossible to see out of the rear-view mirror, nudged out of the driveway and into the street. As always before the holidays Monika went through all the last-minute details that might have been forgotten: traveller's cheques, cooker off, iron switched off, fridge off and door open, plants watered, back door locked, but knew with fatalistic certainty that if she had forgotten something it would only occur to her when they had crossed the border into France, at least four hours from now.

Relax, she told herself. Relax. You need to relax to make this work. Jack's not here to share the driving and it's going to be a long, long journey. She flexed her shoulders as if gathering strength and pressed the accelerator.

Sarah was waiting on her driverway, standing beside a red suitcase. When she saw the car she ran to the house and pressed the doorbell and seconds later her mother bustled out of the door with a plastic bag in her hands.

'Chocolate for the journey,' she said to Monika, 'and crisps . . . and some Coke.' She turned to her daughter and so did not notice the slight curling of Monika's lips as she took the bag.

'Have a good journey, dear, and remember to . . .' The usual parental counsel followed. 'And thank you so much for taking her along, she's really been looking forward to it, so kind of you. Ring me the moment you get there, do you hear? And . . .' More advice followed. Monika pushed the suitcase into the last empty slot above their own pile of luggage and slammed down the hatchback door. And at last they were off.

The autobahn was an immobile line of coloured metal. There had been an accident an hour earlier; traffic was jammed in both directions. Monika cursed herself for not taking the diagonal country road across to Freiburg; she decided to take the next exit, but so, apparently, had several other motorists: traffic there was at a standstill. Monika stayed on the autobahn, where at least she could creep a few inches further every quarter of an hour. Radio reports informed her that the accident was still several kilometres away, and that traffic would be creeping along for at least another half an hour. The sun blazed down; the heat collected in the car. There was no air-conditioning; their clothes stuck to them like extra sticky skins. The girls peeled off their blouses and giggled at their half-nakedness, fanning each other with their girls' magazines. Every so often Monika wiped her sweating palms on her trouser leg, or wiped her face with a paper handkerchief, and muttered to herself using the words Jyothi was not allowed to hear under any circumstances. Now and then when there was no movement at all she opened the car door but the heat outside rivalled the heat inside. Once she walked around to the boot and removed the icebox, and the cool mineral water lent them a few minutes of respite. The girls took out the ice packets and pressed them to their foreheads, and Jyothi leaned forward and slid one along Monika's hairline. It brought another few seconds of relief.

Finally they reached the accident spot. The girls gaped at the overturned lorry and the car, completely crushed, beneath it, but then they were past and the road was free, and Monika was never so happy to press the accelerator down to the floor. They raced forward.

Their own accident took place just after Freiburg.

By this time Monika's nerves were frayed to breaking point; she was hungry, thirsty, tired and desperate for a toilet. She had eaten a sandwich three hours ago, and an apple a short while later, and now and then she had stopped at a lay-by to stretch her legs and drink some water. But she wasn't a long-distance driver, as Jack was, and not for the first time she regretted bitterly not having taken the train, or split the journey into two stages. There was the pressure, too, of having to meet her sister at the cottage before nightfall; Brigitte was going to hand over the keys and the house and then, with her family, proceed to Freiburg, spend the night there, visit a friend the next day, and proceed home leisurely the day after that. Which was exactly what Monika should have done, the other way around.

Just before Freiburg she had contemplated doing just that. She could ring up Brigitte, suggest that *she*, Monika, check into the reserved hotel instead, spend a restful night there, and drive on to France the next morning.

But the cottage was just a jump from Freiburg. Brigitte would be inconvenienced. And Monika just wanted to be there, home, the tedious journey behind her.

So that might be why she pressed a little harder on the accelerator, applied a little less of her precision and care to her driving, and why, leaving the main street to search for a petrol station where she could fulfil the entire variety of her needs (except the most pressing one, the need for rest), she plunged into a roundabout without looking.

The Mercedes slammed into the driver's door like a long white bullet streaking out of nowhere. To Jyothi, afterwards, it seemed there had been a split second of utter silence before the deafening crash, and the sickening crunch of metal on metal, and the heart-stopping screech of brakes, and the splintering of glass, and the screams that seemed to go on for ever, the screams she was screaming at to *stop* until she realized they were her own. And after that there was silence again.

When she woke up she was on a narrow bed in a white room, and there was a man, holding her wrist gently between his fingers. Her eyelids fluttered; she took a deep breath.

'So, now you're awake!' said the man. He was young, perhaps in his early twenties, and his eyes were bright and friendly and he was smiling down at her. 'How are you feeling?'

'Mama!'

He seemed not to have heard her. 'I think you're going to be fine. All you've got is a bit of a bump on your head. You see how important it is to use a seat-belt! If you hadn't . . . Are you thirsty? Hungry?'

'Where am I?'

'You're in a hospital in Freiburg. In a little while your aunt is going to be here. You're going to be just fine!'

'Mama . . .'

'I'll just go and get the doctor,' said the nurse quickly, and left the room.

Jyothi closed her eyes and tried to recall, but all that came to mind was pandemonium caught in the red-hot net of her own terror, and after that, blackness. A tear seeped out from

177

under her closed eyelids. She remembered Sarah . . . where was Sarah? And most of all, where was Mama? She had to find Mama.

She sat up, and the sheet that covered her fell away. She could feel the bandage around her head, and there was another bandage around her upper arm. There was pain, but the mental anguish was greater so that the pain receded to a dull thud in the background of her consciousness. She rose unsteadily to her feet and stumbled rather than walked to the door, and out into the corridor.

'Mama,' she cried as she reached for the wall for support, and the word seemed to break open a dam because now the tears began to flow, and she gulped for air because now she was crying, blubbering, calling for Mama.

Steady arms closed around her. 'Come on, it's all right. Back to your room. It's going to be all right.' The voice was deep and soothing; it was the man in white, the nurse, again, and she felt she knew him: he was the only familiar face in a strange white empty world, so she let herself be led back into the room.

A woman, also in white, holding a thin sheaf of paper, stepped in front of the man, and like him smiled at her.

'I'm Dr Baumeister,' she said. 'How are you feeling? You banged your head up quite a bit, and there's that cut on your arm, but other than that no injuries. You're lucky! You're—'

'Where's my mother?' Jyothi's voice, even to herself, was little more then a squeak – lost, forlorn, the voice of a waif alone in the world.

'Your *aunt* is on her way,' said Dr Baumeister.

'But I want Mama!' She saw the glance the doctor and the nurse exchanged. She said it again, and this time it came out as a wail: 'I want Mama!'

At that moment a sort of madness gripped her and she tried to scurry to the door but the nurse held her back, clamping her arms to her sides; she struggled, and now the doctor was holding her too and speaking to her in that calm pathetic voice she despised, telling her everything was all right when she knew – she *knew* – it wasn't.

'Where's Mama! Where's Mama! I want Mama!' she cried, and out of the corner of her eye she saw Dr Baumeister break away and hold up a syringe to the light, staring at it; she felt strong steady hands, too strong for her to fight, rubbing something cool on her upper arm and then the prick as the needle entered. Then came surrender into the delicious black oblivion of sleep.

Aunt Brigitte was at her bedside when she next awoke. A face she barely recognized at first, leaning over her far too closely, with a smile that was false. It was not a smile of joy but a smile of deception. Jyothi could tell the difference immediately, and scowled.

Jyothi tried to speak but her mouth was dry and all that came out was a croak. She raised herself onto an elbow and reached for the glass of water on the bedside table. Aunt Brigitte was quicker than she, placing the glass into her hand with eager haste. She was speaking, but Jyothi could not hear the words because her own thoughts were louder.

'Where's Mama?' she said when she had swallowed a few gulps of water.

'Darling . . . Jyothi . . . your mama . . .'

'Tell me,' begged Jyothi. 'Where is she? Why isn't she here? There was an accident . . .'

And then the memories came crowding in once more. She pressed her two fists to her mouth and her face crumpled.

'What happened to Mama! Tell me! Don't lie to me! Why isn't she here!'

Brigitte tried to hug her but Jyothi beat her away. 'Don't!

Don't come near me! Just tell me where she is! Something happened to her. I remember . . . I saw her, there was . . . blood . . .'

Hysterics overcame her, because in her heart she knew; she had seen her mother catapulted across the driver's and the passenger seat, head first into the opposite window like a rag doll; she had heard the splintering of glass on impact, for the darkness had come a split second too late, and she had seen, heard, smelled and felt the horror. And the horror of that split second had conjured up out of some deep pocket of oblivion other scenes, other horrors, another crash, more blood, louder screams; and the memory of an earlier loss so devastating it had crushed her down for years, and from whose shadow she had only recently escaped.

Brigitte was spared the awful duty of telling her by the sheer frenzy of Jyothi's grief; grief born of sure knowledge, knowledge born of intuition. Her hysterical weeping was terrible to watch and impossible to calm. All Brigitte could do was sit and wait, until finally Jyothi herself was tired out and slumped back on the bed with open, empty eyes.

Only then did Brigitte speak. 'Jyothi?' she said hesitantly.

Jyothi turned a listless face towards her. 'Huh?'

'Jyothi, I need to talk to you about your dad. About Jack.'

'I want him to come here.'

'I know; that's what I mean. We have to let him know so that he can come back as quickly as possible. But, the thing is, we don't know where he is.'

'He's in America. With his parents.'

'Well, that's just it . . . he's not! We found a phone number in Monika's address book and we spoke to his mother but he's not there! He *was* there, it seems, but he left two days ago and his parents have no idea where he could be. He told them he

180

was coming home. So I was wondering . . . do you know where he was going to?'

Jyothi shook her head listlessly, and said nothing. Thinking was just too wearying.

'Come on now, Jyothi, you have to think . . . you want him here, you need him. Where could he have gone to?'

Jyothi shook her head again, but her face wrinkled in anguish and tears leaked from under her closed lashes. She pushed the edge of the sheet up to wipe the tears, covering her face, and then turned over to bury it even deeper into the pillow. She longed for a place to hide, to disappear into and never return. She longed for sleep and forgetting, but even now she could hear Brigitte's prying voice. 'Jyothi, we must find out. Think, think. Where could Jack be?'

But Jyothi would not answer. She placed her hands over her ears so as not to hear Brigitte's voice, and then pretended to fall asleep, and it was then, lying limp on the bed, that she heard feet enter the room and the exchange of greetings between Brigitte and an unknown man's voice.

'Good morning, Mrs Reinhard. Have you spoken to her?'

'Good morning, officer. I'm afraid I didn't get very far. She refused to speak. All she does is cry . . . I think she's asleep now but . . .' She lowered her voice.

'It's understandable. It's the shock. So you still don't know where to find the father?'

'I'm sorry, I have no idea. Did you speak to the other girl's mother?'

'Yes. She says she has no idea either. Apparently she wasn't very close to Mrs Keller, they were little more than neighbours; only the two girls are friends.'

'So they are back home already?'

'Yes. The girl's parents came as soon as they could and drove back immediately; it was best under the circumstances, since she

181

had no more than a few scratches. But as I said, they can't help. Perhaps your sister has a close friend who might know?'

'You could try Susanne . . . or Karin. But I doubt if they would know Jack's plans. I . . . I actually doubt if Monika herself knew. She told me that Jack was staying for the entire five weeks with his parents. I remember very well, because I was surprised he'd stay so long, after not having visited them for so many years.'

'Aha . . . he could have gone to visit an old friend perhaps, in the USA? Is that likely?'

'It's possible, of course . . . But there's no point asking Monika's friends. Ask Jack's friends. They're more likely to know.'

'And can you give me a name . . . ?'

Brigitte shook her head slowly. She was fatigued, grieving, confused and, she had to admit, irritated at Jyothi for her lack of co-operation.

'Officer, please, when can she go home? Surely she's fit to leave. She can come to our home till we find her father, it's no problem whatsoever. All she has are a few scratches.'

'From our viewpoint she can go whenever you want to take her. She's in no condition to make a witness statement anyway. It's up to the doctor.'

'I'll ask. I'd like to leave as soon as possible. I've got my own family to think of.'

The police officer shrugged. 'We won't stand in your way. But let us or your local police know as soon as you establish contact with the father.'

'Yes.'

'And . . . you must go to the morgue . . . uh . . . to identify the corpse.'

The moment the word 'corpse' was spoken Jyothi broke into another fit of uncontrollable weeping, still face down in her pillow, her little body quivering beneath the sheet as the sobs shuddered through it in wave after wave of shock and despair. Brigitte and the policeman looked at each other, both embarrassed by the emotion of the moment and the tactlessness that had brought it on; both blushed and nodded, and moved towards the door.

In the end it was Sarah's mother who found Jack.

He had telephoned the cottage in Alsace on the evening of the accident, and no one answered. He tried repeatedly the next morning until finally, at midday, he rang Sarah's parents to find out why they had not yet arrived. Thus Jack found out that overnight he had become a widower.

It took Brigitte and Jack approximately the same amount of time to get home. Brigitte was only home for half an hour when Jack turned up on her doorstep.

'How did you get here so quickly?'

'I flew. I took the first plane!'

'From Philadelphia? Impossible! You didn't even know this morning, we couldn't get hold of you, and now it's five p.m. and you're back home already! Did you come on Concorde, or what?'

Jack blushed. 'Actually, I didn't come from America. I flew from England.'

'England! What on earth were you doing in England!'

Brigitte was not known for her tact, and Jack was not above blushing. 'Visiting someone,' he answered, a trifle too quickly.

Brigitte lowered her eyebrows in suspicion, but this was no time for prying questions and Jack pushed her gently aside and entered the house. 'Where is she?'

'Upstairs, sleeping. She had another sedative.'

'Sedative? What for?'

'Whenever she wakes up she gets hysterical.'

'Jee-zus,' said Jack, and took the stairs two at a time. 'Which bedroom?' he called on his way up.

'Ours,' Brigitte called back.

Jyothi was not sleeping. She was still standing at the window when Jack entered the room, but the moment he stood at the threshold she ran across the room and flung herself into his arms.

'Oh baby,' Jack stammered. 'Baby baby baby. It happened again. But I'm here for you. Now it's just the two of us.'

But only when he had spoken the words did Jack realize that they were, strictly speaking, not entirely true.

Part Three

'*Music expresses that which cannot be put into words and that which cannot remain silent.*'

VICTOR HUGO

Chapter 22

When Mama died I went into my hole, because there seemed to be nothing much else to live for. I didn't have much of a life because everything I'd been doing up to then was for Mama's sake.

Without Mama the edifice of myself was deflated. I had thought it to be built of bricks and mortar but found instead it was nothing but a balloon, filled with hot air. It was Mama who had constantly fanned the wind of greatness into me, I'd been just her accomplice, and I could not do it on my own. I had no will to continue on the path she had set for me, and no strength. Mama had given me both, and with Mama gone I lost both the art and the craft.

There were outpourings of sympathy from all around. There were stories of my tragedy in the local and national media. They asked Jack if I could pick up the pieces Mama had left and build a new life for myself. Since Jack gave them nothing, they speculated themselves and came to the conclusion – rightly –

that I could not. Mama had built my career; the talent had been my own but the motivation had been hers. They picked apart my story once again. It was Mama, they said, who had rescued me, discovered my aptitude and carried me forward on a wave of success. Without her I was nothing. Oh, they didn't put it as crudely as that. They were tactful; they were polite. But finally, they concluded, who was I? Had it not been for her where would I have been? It's a pity she had to die now, before I had reached maturity. I was too young to progress on my own, and Jack (they assumed) could offer me nothing.

Then the media – and the public – forgot me. It took them all of two weeks to do so. Once more I was a nobody, fallen from the crest of success.

Jack tried to speak to me. He told me of somebody called Rachel, whom I knew and who thought we should go and stay with her for a while. He said we had met before. Rachel had given me a rag doll once. It didn't take me long to figure out that Rachel was his mistress, and that he'd been with her at the time of Mama's accident. Did Jack think I didn't know about mistresses? Of course I did. I also knew that Mama had known. That Mama had been very upset at finding out, so upset that she wasn't as careful and concentrated as usual on that drive down to France. And that . . . but then I stopped thinking.

Actually, I was beyond caring. I let Jack make the decisions; I nodded at all he said. Yes, Rachel. Yes, England. Yes, a new school. Yes, a new beginning. There was only one no in my life, but a big one, an insurmountable one. No violin.

Rachel was at the airport, waiting for us. When I saw her face for the first time at Gatwick Airport, I felt a slight tremor of recognition. Some vague memory I couldn't place, but no more than that. Apparently she had been kind to me on the plane to Germany – that's what Jack kept telling me. I was supposed to like her, because of that long-ago kindness. But of course I did not remember her. How could I? Seven remarkable years had passed since the flight to Germany; my whole world had been turned upside down and inside out since then.

Nevertheless Rachel greeted me with a heartiness which might have been reassuring if there had been a single thin crack in my curtain of grief – which there wasn't. I could see the heartiness but not partake of it.

Rachel hugged Jack, but not for long. She turned to me, and said, 'Welcome to England, Jyothi! I hope you'll be very happy here!'

But perhaps it wasn't just my armour of grief that keep me closed off from Rachel. Perhaps I felt, even through that barrier, that her heartiness was not all it seemed? Perhaps I knew, vaguely, with the fuzziness with which children grasp the daunting world of adults, that Rachel, in some mysterious way, was at the root of my grief? Though her words were friendly, and welcoming, could they be just a mask? Whatever it was, I gave her my hand but I did not even smile. I could not. I had forgotten how to smile.

I looked out of the window on the way to Rachel's house and I liked the countryside. It seemed wilder than Germany, less cultivated, and the villages we passed through were like those in a storybook. After a while I felt tired, and nestled into the back seat of the car. Jack and Rachel were talking in the front seat, and the drone of their speech finally lulled me into sleep. When I awoke we were there, at Rachel's home in Kent. It turned out to be an old barn, restored and refurbished, nestling in a sleepy village and so overgrown with vines and creepers that the grey of its thick stone walls was barely visible beneath the tangle of green. The building was set back from the main road and hidden from public view by towering shrubs;

a narrow gravel driveway curved up to a small wrought-iron gate and narrowed to a pathway that wound through beds of marigolds and wild roses growing with little sense of order or plan. It was the antithesis of Mama's perfectly laid out and meticulously tended garden. Mama would have set to work immediately, pulling out weeds and snipping at the overgrown plants. I ached for Mama.

'I'm glad we're hidden away back here,' Rachel laughed as she opened the gate and led us in, 'the neighbours would be shocked at the amount of weeds I have among the flowers. The secret is . . . they're not weeds. They're herbs. Every one of those little plants down there has some medicinal property or other.'

Jack carried one bag on his shoulder and another in his hand. I pulled my little roller case behind me, and we followed Rachel down the path to the front door.

'Here we are,' said Rachel, and stepped in before us.

Jack placed his free hand on my shoulder and guided me into the entrance hall, a small square room with a shoe rack along one side and a row of wooden hooks along the other. There was one pair of battered gardening shoes and some sturdy leather boots on the shoe-stand, and a pair of muddy Wellingtons before it, together with three pairs of well-worn slippers in varying sizes. The coats and jackets that hung from the hooks were equally old and shabby, and like the boots were of excellent make.

A volley of enthusiastic barks emerged from the house's interior, and Jack smiled down me. 'Do you hear? That's the dog I told you about: Sheba.'

I nodded. Jack and Rachel seemed pleased. Rachel said, 'Come, Jyothi, take off your shoes and try on these slippers. They're much too big for you, I know, but never mind. Jack, those are for you.' She pointed to the larger pair. She edged off her own shoes, slipped her feet into the third pair of slippers, and opened the door. Immediately a creature like a huge sleek panther – but which turned out to be a Labrador – flung itself against her, almost knocking her over, whimpering and quivering as if unable to contain its delight.

'Yes, that's Sheba, how are you, old girl!' Rachel patted and stroked the animal heartily with both hands, and laughingly let her face be licked. Satisfied, the dog came squirming up to inspect the two newcomers, tail wagging so furiously her entire hindquarters writhed and wriggled to its rhythm. Jack patted the sleek black head. I wanted to myself but held back. One of my hands was still clasped tightly on the handle of my roller bag and the other was stuck into the pocket of my jeans. I felt safe that way. I merely glanced at the dog, and when he came to sniff me I let him and resisted the urge to pat his head. I stared straight ahead of me, waiting for instructions.

Jack and Rachel exchanged another glance, and this time Rachel's brow creased slightly, but only momentarily, for then she said, 'Jyothi, I bet you're famished! I've got a wonderful apple pie I made especially for you, with apples from our own tree. I made it this morning and it'll be just right now! Or would you prefer to go up and see your room first? Freshen up? Have a rest?'

I nodded because I didn't care either way, and nodding was neither rude nor polite, and how was Rachel to know if that meant, yes, apple pie, or yes, see my room, or yes, freshen up, or yes, rest? But my vagueness was convenient for Jack, who made up my mind for me and said, 'I bet she'd like to see her room and feel at home first, right, Jyothi? She ate on the plane.'

Rachel seemed about to say something but Jack caught her eye and shook his head slightly. I noticed all these things; they had no idea how much I noticed! What she actually said was,

'Right. Follow me then. Or . . . Jack, you know the way. Show her up to the room, and I'll go into the kitchen and make some tea for us all. Jyothi can come down when she feels like it?' She smiled again at me, patted me encouragingly on the back, and disappeared into the kitchen. Jack picked up my two suitcases, lugged one onto his shoulder, and took the other in his hand. 'This way, m'lady!' he said. 'Bring your other stuff.'

My other stuff consisted of my little roller case and my violin case, with violin in it. I had not wanted to bring it but Jack had insisted. I picked up the roller case and left the violin where it was, sitting against a wall in the hallway, and followed Jack across the carpet towards a staircase.

Jack joined Rachel in the kitchen. Rachel looked at him and there was no mistaking the accusation in her eyes.

'Jack, you shouldn't have. It's too early. Far too early. You should have given her more time. Heavens, it's been only three weeks since her mother . . .'

'Rache, we've been through this before. We couldn't possibly have stayed at home. She'll recover far more quickly if she's out of the home atmosphere. Monika seems to be in every atom of that house, she seems to fill all the rooms, like some kind of a . . . of a . . .' The word he was looking for failed to arrive so he continued: 'She can't get over it in that house and neither can I. Better a complete break and a new beginning, and as soon as possible. Better for her and for me. It's as if she's hovering in the very air there, accusing, nagging . . .'

'That's your guilty conscience speaking there, my friend. Nobody's accusing or nagging except your guilt.'

'Oh, give me a break. All this psychology stuff . . .'

'But it's true, isn't it, Jack? You have to admit it to yourself.'

'Admit what?'

192

'That you feel guilty.'

'I said, give me a break. You're laying a guilt trip on me.'

'No, you're laying a guilt trip on yourself.'

Jack's voice rose, both in volume and in pitch. 'Now why would I want to do that? OK, so I was cheating on her, but—'

'But if you hadn't been cheating on her, if you'd been at home, you'd have shared the driving with her and she wouldn't have been so tired and she wouldn't have—'

'Monika was never a good driver, she was always nervous. It could have happened any time, whether I was at home or not.'

'That's what your head tells you but your conscience tells you something else. And it didn't happen any time, it happened when you were here, with me, instead of with her on your holiday.'

'Look, if I'm guilty then you're just as guilty.'

'Oh, I share in the guilt, you can be sure of that, but the thing is, I'm willing to admit it. You're not.'

'I don't see what good wallowing in guilt is going to do. It happened, it's over, nothing's gonna bring her back, no amount of wailing and gnashing of teeth and beating of breasts. It's over. I'm sorry, but it's over!'

'Yes, and that's another thing, isn't it, Jack?'

'What's another thing?'

'Being sorry. Are you really all that sorry?'

'Hey, what are you accusing me of now? D'you think I'm *glad* she's dead? Look, this woman was my wife, for goodness' sake, I lived with her for almost twenty years. Of course I didn't want her dead!'

'Still, you have to admit it was bloody convenient. Her dying like that. Almost on cue. Just when—'

'Get off my back, will you!'

Jack, shouting? Jack never shouted. It was one of the myths

of his disastrous marriage that Jack, cool, easy Jack, never shouted. Jack never got angry; Jack never had arguments. Jack never lost his cool – *that* was Monika, the uptight, nervous, quick-to-anger Monika. But now Jack sat there at Rachel's table glaring at her and shouting, and it wasn't Jack, it was a stranger in Jack's skin and with Jack's voice. But then the stranger collapsed into himself.

Jack lowered his head and pressed the heels of his hands into his eye-sockets. His elbows rested on the table; his shoulders heaved. 'Next thing you're gonna be saying I murdered her, because I have a motive. Get off my back, Rache, will you? Just get off. I've got enough stuff to work through without that crap.'

Rachel was at his side in a second, bending over him, her cheek against the back of his head. She rubbed his arm soothingly, but pulled away as Jyothi entered.

Jack reached out for Jyothi, placed an arm around her skinny form and drew her gently to the table. 'Slide yourself in there.'

He showed her the corner bench and eased the table out a few inches so that Jyothi could climb over and settle in. Rachel said nothing; she smiled kindly at the girl and placed a wedge of apple pie on her plate. Jyothi sat stiffly with both hands on her lap. Her eyes were unfocused, her whole expression was one of remote passivity, as if she couldn't care less where she was or who she was with, indifferent to whether it was apple pie on her plate or sauerkraut.

Chapter 23

Jyothi's return to the land of the living was neither speedy nor simple. The loss of a mother for the second time, and in circumstances that duplicated the first loss so many years ago, had shattered the reserves of confidence built up over the previous years. Those reserves had themselves always been fragile, since their very foundation was unstable: the unquestioning trust of a child in the world she knows and the mother she loves had been permanently destroyed, permanently haunted by the shadow of fear.

If only she could cry, Jack thought. Tears held a healing power, and if Jyothi could only once let go, then, perhaps, the healing could truly begin. He had no idea how to reach her. She had lost interest in all the little things she had so enjoyed: books, and nature, and most of all, music. She had not once picked up her violin since Monika's death. Nor had she picked up a book, and when, later that afternoon, Rachel took her into the garden to show her the apple trees and raspberry canes laden with fruit her face had regained the stolid expression of utter indifference.

'Try one, Jyothi, they're delicious,' coaxed Rachel, and Jyothi obeyed, picking a plump berry and placing it into her mouth with as much enthusiasm as if she were trying out dentures. They moved on. Rachel tried again.

'Smell these roses, Jyothi, they're heaven,' and Jyothi pushed her nose up to sniff at a flower willingly enough, but with the mien of a Buckingham Palace guard.

At the very end of the garden was a heap of garden waste: branches and twigs thrown together in a haphazard tangle of leaves and rotting wood.

'We have a hedgehog living in here,' said Rachel almost desperately. 'She's had babies . . . I saw one the other day. If you're lucky and wait here quietly you might see one too. You can feed her if you like. That'll be fun for you.'

But Jyothi looked as if nothing would ever be fun ever again.

One of the reasons Jack had come to Rachel so soon after Monika's death was the no small matter of Jyothi's education, which had been a worry for several years. It had become eminently obvious to both him and Monika, more so than ever since her genius had been made public, that the local Special Needs School was completely the wrong place for her. Yet there was no other school, public or private, that would take her; her academic deficiencies were too great. Whereas Rachel, to help him make up his mind, had described in glowing colours the excellent independent schools in the South of England where Jyothi would receive help with her academic problems and at the same time enjoy an outstanding musical education. She could be a boarder . . .

'No question of that,' said Jack firmly. 'Jyothi's not the boarding type.'

'. . . or a weekly boarder, coming home at the weekends. But the school I'm thinking of mostly is near enough for her to be a day pupil – it's about half an hour's drive away. It's the one my nephew attends.'

'Oh. The Indian nephew you told me about?'

'That's the one, Dean. He's been there for two years, and seems quite happy. He's a weekly boarder. He started there under similar circumstances . . . hmmm, I'm only just realizing *how* similar.'

She paused, thinking.

'What are you thinking about?'

'About Dean. It's quite uncannily similar. His father, my brother, was killed in a climbing accident three years ago. Afterwards his mother brought him back from India where they'd been living. It was a big change for him, too, and he's not the easiest of children – well, he's hardly a child, of course, but he was a bit of a handful when he first came. He goes to his mother in the holidays, and during the term he's a weekly boarder.'

'How old is he?'

'He's about fifteen now. A bit too old for them to be friends but we could at least introduce them. He might like to play the part of big brother to her at school – he's a bit of a wild thing but he's got a good heart and if he knows what her problem is it might waken his protective instinct. He was her age when he first came to England: he'd sympathize. Goodness knows she needs a friend.'

'Another thing, Rache, you said it's a private school?'

'Yes, of course. Why?'

'Well, I guess it'll be pretty expensive . . .'

'But you told me you wanted to spend the life insurance money on Jyothi? On her education?'

'Yes, that's true. It's just that I haven't seen any of the

197

insurance money yet. It'll take some time. I was wondering if . . .'

'Yes, of course. I can tide you over till you get your money. Don't worry about a thing.'

'I just hope . . .' said Jack, and paused. He reached across the table and took Rachel's hand. 'I just hope that she finds her music again. Because if she loses music she's really lost everything.'

'She'll find music in time. I'm positive.'

'You're positive about everything, Rache. But remember: Monika was her teacher. Not only that, she played for Monika. It was incredible that a child with so much talent played only because her mother loved to hear her play. She has absolutely no motivation of her own.'

'Then it's your job to help her find her way back to music.'

The following Wednesday Rachel took them to Sevenoaks to meet her parents and her nephew Dean. During the drive she warned Jack that there were certain matters that must not be discussed in her parents' company, and one of these was Dean's mother.

'They were always against the marriage,' she explained. 'They thought she was not good enough for their beloved son and more or less cut him out of their will. At least, they threatened to do so, claimed they *had* done so, but I don't know if they actually went through with it or if it was all hot air. They were always against Will's fascination with India and his going to work there.

'You know, they had both lived in India for a long time. My mother in fact was born there. So were we, and we spent our childhood there. But they couldn't take the changes that came after Independence, and wanted to cut all ties. And wanted *us* to cut all ties. But Will was always strong-headed and of course did exactly as he pleased.

'And then Will died on them. They were berserk with grief: they hadn't seen him for fourteen years and hadn't had a chance to make up with him so it was a terrible time for all of us. He was a great brother to have. When he died I offered to take Dean. It was all planned. I knew him, of course; I'd visited India many times. I shared Will's fascination but never thought of actually living there, so for my parents that was tolerable. But Dean's my only nephew – of course I'd take him! I even checked out schools nearby – that's how I heard of Roxby Manor, which seemed just right for him. But then my parents took it into their dear heads that *they* should have Dean, that he would be a substitute for Will, and, after all, what did I know about raising boys? And then there was my job, which requires a lot of travelling. I was willing to change jobs, of course, but there's not much in the way of office jobs available to me, especially not around here, and, well, it really wasn't very convenient having Dean stay with me. Not that it would have mattered if there wasn't any alternative, of course, but there *was* an alternative, and my parents really wanted him and so . . . well, we did the obvious.'

'But what about Dean's mother? Where is she? Why wasn't she good enough for your parents?'

'I told you, they didn't like the changes in India. They were of the old school, you see, and for them the English and the Indians were two separate species. They couldn't take the insubordination of Indians. Will choosing an Indian bride was a slap in the face for them.'

'But why didn't Dean stay with his mother after his father's death?'

'Well, she wanted him to, but finally had little choice. Will

199

was awfully incompetent: there was no insurance money, no security, no widow's pension. They didn't even own their own house. She found she couldn't pay the rent on her little secretary's salary. So she moved in with her parents and three brothers, their wives and about a dozen children . . . well, half a dozen, at least. They had to sleep on the veranda, there was no room for them inside, and her sisters-in-law treated her like dirt, especially the eldest, who's like a matriarch ruling the nest with an iron hand.

'So she decided to leave India. She asked my parents for help in coming to England. She wanted to come here and work so the two of them, she and Dean, could be together. As the widow of an Englishman there was no problem getting a work permit.

'But my parents wouldn't help. They said she was only going to scrounge on them. So I offered. She could have lived here with me, she and Dean. That was actually my first offer. But then . . .'

'Then what?'

'She got an offer of marriage. From a fine Indian man, a professor, a faculty member of the university where Will had worked. It was an offer she couldn't refuse. She just isn't really the type, you see, to set off on her own to a different country, a different continent, and struggle as a single mother. Not even with my help. She really liked the man, and he was courting her as if his life depended on it. My sister-in-law is a very pretty woman, and good-natured besides. The kind of woman men love to marry. It was pretty obvious she wouldn't stay single for long.'

'But the man didn't want Dean?' Jack guessed.

'Well, I don't think he put it that way. He just persuaded her to pack him off to England. The schooling would be better, he said. And Dean could come home in the holidays. Sort of a boarding school situation, except that he spends the weekends

200

at my parents' home. But they have long holidays and Dean always returns to India in that time, and sees his mother. He's acquired a half-sister in the meantime.'

'But if your parents resent India and Indians, what about Jyothi? How'll they react to her?'

'Oh, they've mellowed a bit since Dean's been with them. And she's just a kid. They won't be nasty to her. I told them all about her and my mother actually feels sorry for her. They're not really dragons, you know. They just have these misconceptions. But they're angry at Dean's mother for marrying again, and so quickly: they think she should have remained true to Will's memory. They're like that. They couldn't appreciate the fact that, as an Indian widow – well, half-Indian – she was really lucky to find a man – an Indian man – willing to marry her at all. And a professor at that! Very well situated. She did the obvious thing and I think it was for the best.'

'But is Dean happy about it?'

'Dean . . . happy?' Rachel stopped speaking to ponder the question. 'He seems happy enough. Dean's the sort of person who can be happy anywhere, as long as he has the things he loves, and what Dean loves most is his camera. He's always taking photos. You'll see. They encourage it a lot at Roxby Manor. He won a prize last prizegiving, and another amateur prize in a magazine, and had some photos published. That's not bad for a fifteen-year-old. Dean's the kind of boy who keeps his inner thoughts to himself, and adjusts to the outer world with the greatest of ease. He's an extroverted, outdoors type – he carries his own world around with him so at least he appears fine. He doesn't seem to make any close friends, though. That's what I mean about him keeping his inner world to himself. None of us really knows what goes on in his head. It'll be interesting to see how he reacts to Jyothi.'

Jack glanced behind him to the back seat, where Jyothi sat in the corner staring out of the window. How much had she heard? he wondered. Had she followed the conversation? Did she wonder about Dean, his story – almost as tragic as hers – and did she even care? And when she stared out of the window, was she interested in the landscape, the rolling emerald green hills, the picturesque villages they passed through? Was she even seeing anything, as opposed to looking; was she taking anything in, as opposed to merely resting her eyes on the world passing by?

He glanced back again, and his eyes lingered a little longer, taking in the rigid profile, the stony expression on the girl's face, and came to the conclusion that the answer to all those questions was a very emphatic no.

Chapter 24

The Fitzgeralds lived in a stately Edwardian house in the leafy outskirts of Sevenoaks. Rachel parked the car on the driveway and the three of them stepped out onto the pavement. There was a short flight of stairs leading up to the massive oak front door; Rachel led the way up. Jyothi hung back as if she wanted to go up last but Jack waved her past and reluctantly she followed Rachel. Rachel pressed the doorbell, and even before the gong had completed its double peal the door swung open.

'Well, hello, Dean! That was quick! Seems like you were expecting us!'

The young man who grinned at them from the doorway stepped back to let them enter. 'Sort of. I was coming downstairs just as you were coming up. Nice to see you again!'

Dean was tall for his fifteen years, and skinny, with the long, rangy body of a teenager who had just made a growth spurt. His generous mouth seemed too wide for his long face, but the promise was there of future symmetry. His skin was of a creamy light-olive quality whose source – together with the heavy black hair worn in a long page, the thick black eyebrows and the large dark eyes set wide apart – could have been as much Middle-eastern or Italian or Turkish or Greek as Anglo-Indian. He wore an open-necked blue denim shirt loose over jeans of a darker shade, and his feet were bare; all of which seemed incongruous in the formal atmosphere of the entrance hall. Behind him a dark staircase laid out with a thick maroon carpet sloped up into even darker upper regions, while the hall itself seemed designed more to strike fear into the heart of the unprepared visitor than to welcome. He switched on a light and immediately the hall seemed a friendlier place.

'I see Mum still hasn't convinced you to wear slippers in the house,' laughed Rachel as she hugged him, and Dean chuckled.

'I have duck's feet – paddles,' he said when she let him go, and stuck out one foot, wriggling his toes. 'Comes from running barefoot most of my life. So I have the excuse that shoes don't fit me – I get blisters. And I can't stand slippers. At the most, socks. But barefoot is best, inside or out. Hi. You must be Jyothi. Pleased to meet you. And Jack.'

He briefly touched his chest with his right hand in greeting, but when Jyothi and Jack – trained in German politeness – both stretched out their right hands he reconsidered and took the proffered hands, barely touching them before letting go again, the kind of limp handshake that Germans call 'washcloth', and which Monika rigorously trained out of Jack.

A maid in a blue dress and a frilly-edged white apron scurried into the hall from a back room – presumably the kitchen – followed by an older woman.

'Rachel! There you are! My goodness, I must be going deaf, I was listening to the news and didn't hear the gong, how are you, dear!'

Mother and daughter embraced. It was a swift, unemotional

clasp, born of lifelong habit rather than of genuine warmth and closeness.

Mrs Fitzgerald was meticulously dressed in a pale pleated skirt and long-sleeved silky ivory blouse with some sort of a bow structure at the neck which was held in place by an amethyst clasp. Her hair was of an even russet which, considering her age, was most likely dyed, and combed away from her face in short stiff waves. The pallor of her face together with the sharpness of her features – a ridge-like nose, prominent cheekbones which must once have been considered regal, thin, straight lips and a severe jawline – completed the impression of a woman who held herself in high esteem and demanded that same high estimation from others. And woe betide him who failed to bend the knee, thought Jack, resisting the slight quivering in his own knees. It was hard to believe that this woman could be Rachel's mother – as well as Will's, who, according to Rachel's description, had been the epitome of an absent-minded professor.

Mrs Fitzgerald's eyes met Jack's over her daughter's shoulder and, abruptly letting go of Rachel, she stepped towards Jack with outstretched hand and a shrewd, probing expression in her eyes to greet him formally. Jack had to make a conscious effort not to recoil, and to adjust his features into the polite smile suitable for this fist crucial encounter.

The look she gave him over the brisk handshake was cool and calculating, but did not linger. She moved on to Jyothi.

After Dean's handshake, Jyothi had retreated to stand against the wall in the shadow of a great grandfather clock, which, though not offering much protection, was at least tall and straight and statuesque, all the things she was not. Its loud rhythmic ticking offered a sort of comfort, and just listening to it her erratic breathing seemed to swing into a rhythm of its own and her feelings became quieter.

*　　　*　　　*

After facing the bag of nails that was Rachel's mother, I was glad when the boy called Dean asked me if I wanted to come up to his room. Dean was two years older than me and as he was a boy he was much taller, of course. I could tell at once that Dean was benign. There was nothing to fear.

The trouble with most people is that they construct an image of how they would like you to be, or how they think you are, and they see that image and not you yourself. I was only thirteen but I knew that this was how people approached each other. When I was a young child they saw me as a poor little girl from the slums. So whenever they spoke to me they were speaking to that slum-child, and not to *me*. Later they saw me as a musician, and a brilliant one at that, and again they spoke to that image, and not to *me*. Dean was the first person in years who did not speak to an image when he saw me. He spoke to ME. That was the difference.

Dean's room was right at the top of the house. It was small and it had a sloping roof, with a little alcove in the slope containing a window and a window seat. I went to sit there straight away. There was a cosy, light feeling to it. It was covered in cushions. Dean sat on the bed, which was under one of the slopes.

'Don't let my grandparents upset you,' he said at once. 'They always act like that with people they don't know. Very formal and upright. If you're not afraid of them you'll be OK. Look, do you mind if I take your photo?'

That was Dean, right from the start. Absolutely direct. I let him take my photo, of course. Dean didn't mind my not talking. Dean was never afraid of silence, least of all my silences, and I never felt pressured into having to talk. Not with Dean. First he told me why he had wanted to photograph me. He told me there was something unearthly in my expression. My eyes, he said, were extraordinary: veiled on the surface but beyond the veil, if one cared to look, was a whole universe, and he'd only seen eyes like that once before in his life, in his gardener's old mother back in India.

'An old woman?' I said, and those were the first words I'd spoken since arriving in England. But Dean couldn't know that and so he didn't act astonished or make a big fuss. But I was interested. I was only thirteen! Why should I be like an old woman!

'Yes. I hope you don't feel insulted. It's just that . . . well, some people have flat eyes. You look into them and you get to see the colour, but no dimension, no depth. You can't get behind the surface. And their eyes don't speak. But this old woman I'm telling you about . . . I'll show you her photo, in a minute. It won a prize. Just a minute.'

He took five photos of me while speaking, from various angles. Then he stopped speaking and took a few more. He had a quiet intensity to him, which I felt I ought to respect; as if he had sunk his consciousness into himself, and was no longer available either for a superficial comment, or for conversation. Then suddenly he re-emerged, and gave me a broad grin like sunshine. At least, it felt like sunshine. He radiated warmth and well-being and I could not help but smile back. Smiling at him gave me a feeling like spreading wings, or the opening of a flower. I took a deep breath.

When he had finished he put away the camera and opened a cupboard, and searched through an unruly pile of magazines and papers. He came up with an old issue of *Photography Today*. The magazine opened almost of its own accord to a page that had obviously been viewed many times, and there was the photo he had spoken of. It was a colour portrait of a woman balancing a battered tin pan on her head, supporting it with one thin arm from which the skin hung in loose loops. Her face was of a deep chocolate colour, crisply wrinkled, her neck a series of leathery folds. She seemed to be wearing nothing but a strip of cloth across her upper body, for one shoulder was bare. She stared unsmiling out of the page, and I saw at once what Dean meant about her eyes: set deep beneath the thick black eyebrows, they were open windows and it seemed possible to read a thousand emotions into them, joy as well as sorrow, dignity as well as humility, youth as well as age. It hurt to look at her and I quickly closed the magazine.

I felt like asking more about this woman but I hadn't spoken for a long time and before I could summon up the words Dean himself had spoken. Returning the magazine to its pile and closing the cupboard door, he said, 'That's Nirmala, I photographed her hundreds of times and each time she looks different. Would you like to go for a walk?'

The change of subject came so suddenly that at first I did not hear him, I was still dwelling on the enigmatic Nirmala, and he had to repeat his question.

Of course I agreed! So he led the way downstairs and out the front door, down the street and up a narrow lane that led to the open country, without saying another word. I did not mind the silence; in fact, it was a relief because most of the time people seem to be under an obligation to spout words, no matter how meaningless, just so that there is no gap in the conversation. I never feel such a duty, which makes them uncomfortable in my presence. That's when they start asking all sorts of questions, and I know they are just speaking for the sake of speaking and don't really want to know anything, so I keep silent, which makes them even more uncomfortable. Mama used to hate silence. Jack was better but since Mama's death Jack thought I had to be made to speak at any cost. But Dean didn't mind silence, so we walked companionably together, and when he did start speaking on the little lane it was no problem for me to respond because in the silence before our minds had mingled and harmonized themselves, so that now conversation was an effortless flow. Dean was the second – the first was Sarah – person I'd ever met who understood that two minds must first meet and adjust in silence, before they can meet comfortably in speech.

He asked me about India. And when he asked it seemed the most natural question in the world, and I found I had lost my shyness, and wanted to reply. But I wasn't sure if I had anything to say.

'I don't remember too much about India,' I said, almost questioningly. 'It was so long ago. I was a small child.'

'But it's still there,' said Dean. 'If you dig deep enough you will find the memories.'

'They're buried so deeply . . .'

'But experiences never really disappear,' Dean said. 'They're like stamps on the mind – like a photographic image. I bet if you try you'll find something.'

I stopped, and started again, and said quietly, 'And they're not all good memories. Most are painful.'

'But some are beautiful?'

I was silent, thinking. I became aware of something inside, a swirling dark mass, like billowing clouds. And it seemed to me I could raise a hand and stop them, or let them come, swelling up into the light of awareness.

Memories, I discovered then, are like a chest a grandmother has kept closed in the attic for years and years. It has gathered dust and cobwebs on the outside, and the lock is rusty with age and moisture, and it is completely forgotten; but then the grandchildren come and throw open the attic window and find the chest and sweep away the cobwebs and break open the lock and swing back the lid, and inside they find the past preserved in dazzling colours and tantalizing scents.

'I lived in Bombay,' I said, finally. 'Jack and Mama used

to speak of Bombay as the ugliest and dirtiest city in the world.'

'Hellish' was Mama's word for the city, and even tolerant Jack could find no better praise for it than 'chaotic'. So I was hesitant to open that lid and look.

'Yes, but they were strangers there. People say the same about Delhi. But I loved Delhi.'

'You didn't grow up in the slums,' I said, and was silent again.

'And you loved nothing from your childhood? Nothing at all?'

I thought. And strained my mind to think back, beyond those last terrible weeks when the bottom fell out of my world. They did not count. But what came before . . . now the memories came tumbling out, and they were good. I looked at Dean, and smiled.

'I had three friends,' I said. 'Our neighbours' daughters, Chandra, Rookmini and Priya – much younger than I was. We all lived on the street . . . on the pavement. It was quite busy, and we lived against the wall in little huts our fathers had built of slabs of wood and pieces of cloth. There were six of us, children I mean. The girls had a bigger brother. He didn't like to play with us, he used to go begging. As for my older brothers – they had no use for me.

'I cooked for them: little pebbles and tiny pieces of left-over onion skin and chopped up banana peel, but sometimes Ma gave me some real food to play with and then we could eat properly. I cooked on a red brick pretend fire. I was like a little mother. They adored me!'

I found myself talking with Dean as easily as if he were Sarah, except that I had never told Sarah about Bombay. It was as if my past had been hidden away behind some dark wall labelled 'dirty' and I wasn't allowed to look, not without shame and

210

revulsion. But here was Dean encouraging me to look and to drag out the memories and find them worth preserving, like old photographs. I chattered on as I had never chattered before, unselfconsciously, not aware of the countryside nor of him at my side, digging up the relics of the past and showing them all to him.

I found memories of an earlier time rising – before Bombay, of life in our village, when all was whole and good. But those memories were vague, as if crushed by the city's giant footstep, and I found I had no words to conjure them up. I returned to Bombay.

'My father died,' I told Dean. 'It was terrible. And then another man came . . . he was cruel,' I stopped, and then I started again: 'He hit us a lot. Ma said we had to bear it because we had no protector otherwise. He made me go begging. But it didn't matter because Ma loved me.'

I stopped, because I suddenly saw Ma's face as vividly as if she were standing in front of me. I stopped laughing and fell back into a pit of silence. But Dean did not let me stay there.

'That's where they found you, right? Those people who took you to Germany? Your parents?'

'Yes. Jack played the guitar for me. And I danced.'

Dean said nothing. Neither did I. And suddenly I no longer wanted to talk about myself; it seemed I had discovered a vital part of myself but I knew I could only continue to explore it when I was alone, and that I would have hours and hours to do so . . . later. We walked along in silence for about five minutes, and again it was a companionable silence, each of us comfortable with our own thoughts and yet aware of the other's presence – at least, I was now aware of him and glad that he was there.

We came to a stream, flowing down from a tree-covered hill in bouncing, splashing abandon. Our path continued across a small bridge, but Dean pointed to a tiny footpath leading up through the bracken flanking the stream, and that was the way we went. I followed him up the hill; after a while we came to a flat, stony place on the hillside and Dean sat down, still not speaking, and smiled at me.

I found a large rock at the water's edge a little above him, and sat down too. The stream here fell in a small waterfall from a higher level and it seemed someone had helped nature by placing the rocks in a circle to form a pool a little more than a metre across. Just below me the water collected in a second, tiny pool, whirled around as if in search of an exit, and left by eddying out of a tiny space between two rocks to join the larger pool.

'This is where I come sometimes,' Dean said then, 'when I want to be completely alone. It's gloomy and oppressive at home and I get the feeling there are ghosts hanging around, all the people who have lived there before me. You know what I mean?'

I knew exactly what he meant. Once again I marvelled at how well he understood me, even before I had put things into words for him. I'd never met a person like this before and I'd not realized how glad, and how grateful I could be just to meet someone like me. I was so tired of having to speak, and ask, and be questioned, and having people wondering about me, about what's the matter with me, what's wrong with me. Always something wrong, wrong, wrong just because you can't articulate your feelings. And here was Dean who already knew even without words. It was a miracle. I turned to him and smiled my widest smile; it felt like a shifting away of the thick curtain of clouds blotting the radiant sky.

'Stop! Hold it!' Dean whipped his camera to his eye. I was so startled by the movement I frowned, the moment was lost and the clouds fell back into place. Dean dropped the camera; guilt and embarrassment flickered across his features.

212

'Oh shit. Shit, I'm sorry. I shouldn't have done that. I'm such an oaf. I'm sorry.'

'It's OK,' I said, but the moment of magic had passed. However, I felt it was up to me to relieve Dean's discomfiture so I slipped off my sandals and dangled my feet in the swirling water, and it was so cold I cried out in shock, and laughed again. Dean's uncertainty vanished and he laughed too, and then all was well between us again.

'It's not deep enough or big enough to swim in,' he said, 'but when it gets really hot it's nice. Not that it ever gets really hot in England.'

'It feels good on my feet,' I said. 'I'm going to wade.'

I rolled up my jeans and stepped into the pool, making a face so as to endure the cold.

Dean groaned. 'I'm just itching to photograph you,' he said. 'I'm sorry. I'm addicted. I can't see an interesting face without trying to capture it for ever. I'd better sit on my hands.'

I laughed heartily at that, suddenly freed again from the clouds. 'Go ahead,' I said. 'If you want to. You just surprised me the first time, that's all.'

Dean didn't wait for second invitation. As if afraid I'd change my mind he swiftly raised his camera and began clicking away as I played with the water. I bent over to plunge my hands in and wet my face, and my neck: that felt good. By this time my feet were used to the cold and I felt an irresistible urge to be naughty. I kicked some water in his direction, not enough to wet him but quite enough to warn him, and he got the message. He removed the camera from around his neck and laid it away carefully, out of danger's reach, and a moment later he too was in the water.

'OK, if it's war you want!' He laughed, and so did I. I held up my hands to keep him away, but he took hold of my wrists. His grip was strong, and yet gentle, and as I tried to free myself

I could feel exactly how it adjusted to me, applying enough force to keep me at bay, but not enough to hurt. I relaxed, and so did he. And that's when I attacked: I grabbed hold of *his* wrists and pulled in the split second when his attention was distracted, and next thing Dean was on his bottom in the pool.

'You little . . .' he spluttered as I tried to escape. He caught hold of one of my ankles and tugged, and I too was in the pool, laughing and struggling to get up.

Now that we were both wet through there seemed no need to be careful and we both started acting like children: two overgrown water-babies splashing and trying to duck the other, crying in delight. The stones beneath my feet were slippery and more than once I fell, and more than once I managed to pull Dean down beside me; we struggled laughing to our feet, and in a moment we were both on the ground again. I screamed as Dean grabbed my ankle again; I had to hop, and stumbled back to the ground; when I managed to pull myself up I scrambled up the rocks at the far side of the pool and plunged into the undergrowth. Dean was behind me in a trice. He chased me, roaring, but I was faster and if I hadn't trodden on a thorn I might have escaped. As it was the pain shot through my foot and, screaming for mercy, I sat down and held up my foot to inspect the sole. Dean skidded to a halt and crouched down beside me.

'What's the matter?'

'A thorn,' I said.

Dean took the foot in his hands and gently turned it to look. 'I see it. Just a sec.'

His hands were steady and his fingers deft. He secured the tiny sliver between his nails and pulled it out. 'You should be OK now,' he said. 'I'm good at thorns. In India we always ran around barefoot and we always got them. You OK?'

I nodded, testing the foot by pressing it against the ground. 'Thanks. Hadn't we better be going back now?'

'Yes. C'mon. Can you walk?'

'Mmmmhmmm.'

'You go on down. I'll get our shoes and the camera.'

I made my way down the hillside, skidding on the layers of leaves and humus. When Dean joined me I stopped and we both put on our sandals, again not talking. It was as if we both knew instinctively when to speak and when not to, an interplay of silence and sound that seemed only natural, and yet was so rare that it appeared to me remarkable.

We were both soaked through; my clothes clung to me and my hair, though dry on the scalp, hung in limp tendrils down my back. As we walked I combed it through with my fingers and plaited it into a clumsy rope.

When we passed the first buildings on our way into town Dean said, 'Will your dad be angry at you for getting wet?'

I shook my head. 'Jack's never angry. It's one of the best things about him. But what about your grandparents? They won't think well of me, coming home like this.'

'Don't worry about them. I'll sneak you in through the kitchen and then you can put on some of my clothes. Nobody'll know the difference.'

Chapter 25

In the bathroom I pulled on the jeans Dean had given me.
They were too small for him and too big for me, but with a
belt to cinch the waist, turned-up legs and a wide blue T-shirt
I looked fairly respectable, except for the soggy plait. I looked
around and saw a hairdryer on a shelf. I plugged it in, pulled
the plait loose, and aimed the hot air at it; it fanned out around
me, sailing in long feathery strands that framed my face like
living, moving spokes. That face looked incredibly small, and
incredibly childlike. For the first time I wished I looked not
younger, but older than my years.

Dean was waiting for me outside the bathroom, leaning against
the banisters with his long legs stretched across the corridor.
There was approval in his eyes as they met mine.

'Ready?' he said. I nodded, and we exchanged a smile and
went downstairs.

Everyone was gathered in the drawing room: Jack and Rachel

on the plush green sofa, Rachel's mother sunk in a deep armchair, and her father still in the wheelchair.

'There you are,' said Rachel as we entered. 'We were beginning to wonder where you were.'

Jack looked at me, surprised 'Jyothi, what are you—' but caught my look of warning and stopped in mid-sentence.

Rachel's father looked at his watch and frowned. 'Five past five,' he said. He was a bony man with a thick thatch of silver hair and a beaked nose. He wore thick tortoiseshell spectacles, which magnified his eyes, and there was no mistaking the hostility in their pale blue-grey stare. He assessed me with cold precision, as if I were a microbe he was studying through a microscope and found unsavoury. I could read him like a book: I knew that closing of a mental door, which said: you have nothing to do with me. I had encountered it before, many times. From the time I was six I had known and absorbed such glances, and I had developed my own particular brand of indifference towards them.

'I'll just tell Dora to serve tea,' said Rachel's mother then and bustled out of the room.

Rachel said, 'We're going to have tea on the terrace, it's such lovely weather.'

So we all went out onto the terrace, Rachel pushing the wheelchair, and took our seats around a heavy wooden table. The table was already decked with china and silver on a heavy white brocade tablecloth.

The maid arrived with a trolley and placed a teapot, milk, sugar and a plate of sandwiches on the table.

Rachel's mother poured tea in all the cups and for a few moments nothing could be heard but the chink of spoons in cups and the glub of pouring milk. Rachel tried to get the conversation going.

'Dean, you must tell Jack about Roxby Manor,' she began. 'Jyothi will probably be going there next term.'

'Really? You didn't tell me that!' Dean gave me an accusing glare, but the softness in his eyes told me he was joking.

'It's a good school, isn't it?'

'Oh, as far as schools go it's probably OK,' said Dean. 'Better than the one I went to in India, that's for sure. You just have to watch out for Killer.'

'Killer?'

'Mr Killingley. Deputy headmaster. He's a monster. Mr Ellis is OK though. He's the headmaster. What form will she be in?'

'We've no idea yet. She's two years younger than you. What form are you in?'

'I'll be in Lower Fifth. So she'll be in the Lower Fourth first year.'

'Schools are not what they used to be!' said Rachel's father. 'I would never have chosen that school. They have a reputation for leniency and indiscipline.'

'Daddy, that's not true!' said Rachel. Her eyes blazed and I knew at once they had had this conversation time and time again. 'It's a liberal school, that's true, but liberal doesn't necessarily mean lacking in discipline! Just because they don't cane the pupils—'

'Spare the rod and spoil the child!' grumbled the old man.

'A child needs to know limits!' said Rachel's mother. 'Limits! If you don't set limits it will—'

'Mummy, we've been through this before! They do have limits! But I recommended this school to Soona because they are so well known for their arts programme. In fact they have quite a reputation! Look at the way Dean has been able to develop his photography!'

'But who's footing the bill! Tell me that!'

'Her husband, and you. We all know that, Daddy. But she is his mother after all and she does have the last word!'

'What does that woman know about British education?

Born and bred in India ... all she got to see was a glossy brochure that went on about how proud it is of its international character and its generous scholarships for non-subject subjects like Art and Drama and Sport! Not a word about academics!'

'Daddy, it did say more than a few words about academics, but if you see what you want to see what can you expect? They actually have quite good exam results, but you simply refuse to—'

'Whoever heard of Roxby Manor? What a ridiculous name anyway! Some fantast's idea of a modern institution ... If you ask me you should have stuck with tradition, chosen a good solid school like Rugby or—'

'Eton and Harrow, we know, we know. Why don't you change the record?'

'Mind your manners, girl!' He was red as a lobster by this time, and so was Rachel. I saw Jack drop his hand from the table and so did she, and I knew they were holding hands. I could see her make a conscious effort to calm down.

'Sorry, Daddy. But we'll never agree on this subject. Let's leave it at that: Dean's mother liked the idea; Dean is happy there; they've got an excellent photography department. What more can you demand?'

'He should be aiming for Cambridge, like his father!' spluttered the old man. 'Or at least Oxford.'

'But I want to be a photographer, Grandpa, I don't need Oxford or Cambridge for that!'

'A good all-round education, that's what a child needs,' the old man continued, tapping his plate with his knife. 'Hard work, strict masters, sport, discipline and religion. That's what builds character. Not this namby-pamby nonsense.'

'I think Dean's doing well,' said Rachel.

'Balderdash! You mean he's being spoilt silly, mollycoddled by a pack of soggy-brained nursemaids who . . .'

I can't possibly remember all he said about the failings of modern British education and the glory of the Old Ways. He blustered on about the virtues of the Stiff Upper Lip, the development of character through cold baths, morning runs and open windows, the inculcation of the Christian values of modesty and forbearance, the spiritual upliftment implicit in the singing of 'Onward Christian Soldiers', 'Land of Hope and Glory' and 'Rule Britannia'. Before we knew how we got there the subject had turned from education to patriotism.

'And how do you expect *her* to get along there? How's her English? Does she speak a word of it?' The change was swift and indirect, he indicated me with his knife, not looking in my direction.

'Well, that's why I think they'll be good for her too. They take lots of children from overseas and they have special classes for English as a Foreign Language. They do take her language deficit into consideration—' Rachel spoke calmly but I could hear the exasperation smouldering beneath the surface. I kept my eyes lowered to my plate but out of the corner of my eyes I glanced at Dean, who seemed to be only waiting for Rachel to finish before he had his say. But his grandfather was quicker on the uptake.

'Balderdash! If you ask me that's exactly the point! How can they take in hordes of foreign children who can't speak a word of English and hope to be competitive? Ridiculous! All they do is drag themselves down into the mud! Any halfwit can see that! But that's typical for this country these days – What is England coming to? Walk down a London street and you might as well be in Timbuktu or the Black Hole of Calcutta! And if you open your ears you might as well be in the Tower of Babel!'

I looked up now, to see how people were taking this. Jack seemed petrified and Rachel's mother must have agreed with her husband because she said nothing. Dean got up suddenly and walked indoors without a word. It was Rachel again who rose to the occasion!

'Daddy, I won't have it! I won't have you insulting my guests with your mean-spirited tirades! I've had enough of it to last a lifetime. You already lost one son through your bloody-mindedness and if you lose the rest of your family – that's me and Dean, you've got no one else, let me remind you – it's your own bloody fault! You'd better get used to the fact that we don't live in your closed-up little prison because if you don't you'll find yourself alone in your dotage! Sorry, Mummy. Jack, let's go.'

'Rache, please . . .'

'Don't bother with good manners, Jack, he isn't worth it. Jyothi, that goes for you to, come along. You may only be a child but you still deserve respect. We're going.'

What could we do but follow? I was terribly embarrassed. As I rose I nodded at the old lady who smiled stiffly but I couldn't bring myself to glance at the man. I followed Rachel through the patio doors. Jack was right behind me.

In the hall Rachel stopped and turned to us.

'I'm awfully sorry about that. Listen, I want to have a word with Dean. You go on out to the car, I'll be with you in a sec.'

'Rache, listen, it wasn't necessary—'

'Oh, it was. You believe me, it certainly was! Run along now. Don't worry about good manners, if he can't show any he doesn't deserve any.'

She sprinted up the stairs. Jack looked at me, shrugged, and said, 'I suppose we'd better go out to the car.

'I'm sorry about that,' Jack went on, echoing Rachel's words.

I found it strange that they both felt they had to apologize to me. Did they think I was shocked by the old man's words? I wasn't. Not in the least. I guess some people are only shocked when things get put into words, but I knew for a fact that the old man was only saying what a lot of people thought inside. I suppose I was lucky because I knew these things even if people didn't say them out loud; and not for the first time I realized how different I was from most people. Was it worse if people expressed what they thought, or if they kept it to themselves, and pretended, for the sake of appearances and politeness? Well, I knew it was good manners not to say certain things but at my age I was past caring; I had known for years that people judged me because of my origins and because of how I looked. They didn't think I knew but I did, and that was my advantage.

You can't fight these people; you can only shield yourself from them, and that was what I had been doing for the last seven years. By now I was an expert; and that's why the old man's words shocked me far less that they did Rachel, or Jack. I didn't need their apologies. I smiled at Jack to reassure him, and shrugged. 'It's OK.'

Those were my first words to Jack since coming to England, and he acknowledged them with a smile and a squeeze of my hand.

We waited for Rachel.

'Why's she taking so long?' he said after a while, and he looked at his watch. The waiting didn't bother me. I settled into the car and reminisced about the wonderful time I had had. I thought of Dean, far and away the most marvellous person I had met in my life, and I wished I could have said goodbye properly. I was just thinking that when Dean's face appeared in the window.

'Bye, Jyothi!' he called. I jumped, and then I grinned all over my face, rolled down the window and offered him my hand. He seemed a little startled; later I learned that people in England don't shake hands as often as they do in Germany. Dean took my hand and squeezed rather than shook it. 'I'll be seeing you,' he said, and then he said goodbye to Jack, and hugged Rachel before she climbed into the driver's seat.

'Think about it Dean, OK?' said Rachel.

'I will,' he replied, 'and thanks!' He patted the car on the flank as we drove off as if sending us on our way, and waved. He was still standing there, waving, as we turned the corner. I stuck my head out of the window and waved back; and then he was gone.

'Listen,' said Rachel when we were well on our way. 'I don't know why this didn't occur to me before, but I didn't really realize how intolerable Dean's position in that house is. They accept him because when all is said and done he's their grandchild, the only one, and he's so good-natured he has no problem getting along fine with a would-be far-right demagogue. But it's a scandal. And only today I realized how much my position has changed now that the two of you are living with me. So I invited Dean to come and live with us too. If you don't mind, that is.'

Chapter 26

I had been dreading school but now I looked forward to it with all my being . . . Dean would be there!

The week after that disastrous, wonderful visit to Rachel's parents Jack and I paid a visit to the school and spoke to the headmaster to discuss the finer points of my education: my musicality and its loss; my lack of English skills; my dyslexia.

Mr Ellis exuded an extraordinary confidence that all these worries were actually not problems at all, or at least none that could not be solved under his supervision.

They talked about my music. The moment they mentioned the word I interrupted. 'I can't play the violin any more.'

Jack looked helplessly at Mr Ellis. 'She hasn't touched the violin since . . .'

'Oh, we'll take care of that,' Mr Ellis boomed. 'We'll soon have her back in form.'

'No,' I said, pitting my stubbornness against his enthusiasm. 'You don't understand. I can't play. I only ever played for

Mama. And now she's gone . . .' I don't know where I found the courage to say such personal words to a stranger. They seemed to leap out of me without my commanding them to, and when I realized it I stopped, startled.

'Well, all the more reason for you to play!' Mr Ellis exclaimed without a pause. 'D'you think she'd have wanted you to drop it? Don't you think that the right thing to do for your mum is to continue to play?'

I had no answer for that so simply stood there, looking at the floor.

'See, Jyothi,' said Mr Ellis, and his voice was quieter now, 'when people die life continues; if we were all to stop doing the things we can do just because somebody died then soon the world would come to a complete standstill. And that's wrong. She wanted you to play because she recognized that that is where your talent lies. The thing that you were meant to do in life. She wanted it for you, for your own good. And now she's gone the best thing you can do for the sake of her memory is to go on. That's the best way to show your gratitude and your love for her. Just as if she were still here.'

His words hit the mark. I found myself nodding. And for the second time since coming to England I knew that I had come to the right place. The first time was when I met Dean.

My violin was still sitting in the hallway where I had left it at my first arrival. Nobody had touched it. Now, as we entered the hallway on our return home, it was the first thing I saw. It seemed to vibrate with authority; so small, and yet it filled the room. I stared at it. So did Jack. Then he walked across the room, picked it up, and handed it to me. His smile as he did so was kind, and almost apologetic. I sighed audibly, took it from him, and walked upstairs. I laid the case on the table and opened it slowly. Looking at it reminded me of Monika; I remembered how she had chosen it for me, how she had stroked its polished wood, smiling at me in the music shop, handed it to me and said, Play it, Jyothi! And when I had played she had said, That's the one! And forked out the money for it. My eyes grew moist. I wanted to touch it, but could not. But then I remembered Mr Ellis's words, and it was as if Monika were standing right there beside me. I caressed it, and lifted it tenderly, like a tiny, fragile young bird. I would play for Monika's memory.

I spent the morning of my first day at school pining for Dean, for just a glimpse of him. I looked and looked but he was nowhere: not at the Chapel service and not in any of the corridors and not anywhere. Everything was so strange, so new, that clinging to the thought of him was like holding onto a life-raft in a turbulent sea. The thought that somewhere under the same roof he was alive, moving, walking, talking, laughing, and that at some unexpected moment I might see him, kept me from falling into an abyss of self which I knew all too well.

At lunchtime I at last caught a faraway glimpse of him. He was leaving the dining hall by one door just as I was entering by another, and so engrossed in conversation with a very pretty blonde girl that he did not see me. There was a bit of congestion at the doorway so I was able to watch him for a full minute before the door was unblocked and traffic was restored to a steady flow and Dean streamed out into the corridor, to disappear for I knew not how long.

After lunch there were games; once again I was swept off by a tide of girls, this time wielding hockey sticks, and carried along to the games field where I spent some time learning to bash a ball, and there was no Dean anywhere in sight. A girl called Lynne by this time had taken me under her wing and I was grateful for her attention since it gave me an orientation; back in the classroom she arranged for us to sit next to each other.

After games there were two more periods; one was my extra

English class for which I had to disappear up a flight of stairs into an attic classroom. When I returned to my classroom there was a sudden hush as I entered and they all turned to stare at me.

'Somebody came looking for you,' Lynne declared breathlessly. 'A boy from Lower Fifth: Dean Fitzgerald. A real stunner, tall, dark and handsome. Wow, I didn't know you had a boyfriend here, and Dean of all people! I had no idea you knew him!'

'My dad's girlfriend's his aunt,' I explained.

Those five little words changed everything. They changed me from eminently uncool to Somebody Worth Knowing in the seconds it took to pronounce them. So simple are the politics of popularity.

But what did I care! I didn't care about anything except that Dean had come looking for me, and no doubt would come again, and that my heart had taken a direct flight into the stratosphere.

Dean did come again, just after the bell at the end of the last lesson had rung. He was waiting for me in the corridor. He looked grown up and dashing in his uniform, and he stood in the corridor whipping slightly on his toes with both hands stuck in his pockets, his hair falling over his forehead, and a bag slung over his shoulder. I could feel the stares as people left the classroom after me, and I just stood there with my bag of books dangling to the floor and felt as if I would dissolve with love into a pool around his feet.

'So, how was the first day?'

I beamed up at him. 'Fine! Great!' I lied. 'I think I'm going to like it.'

'Good,' said Dean. 'You know I came looking for you? I didn't get a chance earlier. I've got a tight timetable this term and on the first day everybody seems to grab hold of you and not let go. But I thought of you and wondered how you were.'

'Thanks a lot,' I said shyly and wondered what else to say to keep him from dashing off to all the other people who might not want to let go. But I remembered the blonde girl I'd seen him chatting with and that memory strangled any light banter that might have eased the situation. I grabbed a strand of hair and wrapped it around a finger, floundering about for words to say to keep him here with me. But I had nothing to say.

'Isn't it great that I'm coming to stay with you at the weekend!' Dean said then and it was as if he'd switched on a light inside me, turning on the joy and the gratitude, but just two seconds later the smile froze on my face as a ravishing girl with long chestnut hair tumbling about her shoulders sidled up to him from behind, slid an arm through his, and leered up at him.

'See, I found you!' She crooned. 'Go on, say your goodbyes quickly, the gang is waiting for us at the tuck shop. Is this the little girl you had to rush off to? Hi, I'm Natalie.' She gave me a steely smile and tugged at his arm. 'Come on, Dean, they're all waiting.'

Dean let himself be tugged. 'OK then, see you around,' he said, waved casually and turned his back on me. I stared after him as he sauntered off, arm in arm with this Natalie, and now I understood exactly what was meant when people talked of hearts breaking. Mine didn't just break, it crumbled into the dust. I might have stood there for ever staring at the place where they finally vanished from my view if Lynne had not come up behind me, taken my own arm in hers, and dragged me away.

'That's Natalie Littleton, the school vamp,' she said disapprovingly. 'She thinks she's the bee's knees and her father's . . .' She chattered away as we walked down the stairs, but I hardly listened; I preferred to listen to my dreams, for a dream is as real as you let it be, and it gives no space to Natalies or other foreign bodies. At the bottom of the stairs we parted company. Lynne walked off to the dining hall for tea, and I joined the crush of day pupils streaming out through the side entrance, where the bus to take me back home would be waiting. I had survived the first day.

I went on to survive the first week. I saw little of Dean but my connection to him had raised my status in the eyes of my classmates no end. I suppose any other girl would have been grateful for the new attention, but not I. I had had my taste of fame and my fill of fawning. I felt adrift and alone and the only person I knew who could lift me out from my swamp of alienation was Dean. But Dean was far too popular in his own right, and far too engaged with his Natalie and his Lucy and his Emily – which, I learned, were the names of the girls in his fan club – to have much time left over for me. I never saw him without one or other of them, each one more beautiful than the next, and by the time Friday arrived I had lost most of my optimism and my dreams most of their shine.

I had my first music lesson.

My teacher, Mrs Abbot, declared her delight, but I had heard such praise before, and it left me cold. My virtuosity of old was back in place; but the magic was missing, and I was the only one in the world who knew it. And I grieved for that magic as I grieved for Mama. Without the magic music was as dead as she was; it lay lifeless in the centre of my being, without the sparkle of love or joy.

But I was young, and longed for life, and love, and joy!

Dean was all that to me, and Dean was coming home with me that weekend. There'd be no Natalie, no Lucy, no Emily, just Dean and me. I pined for him as a young plant longs for sunlight, and my whole being strained forward to Friday evening when at last he'd be all mine.

Dean was the antidote to grief.

Chapter 27

I was the first to board the bus that Friday evening but I couldn't bear sitting there waiting for him; I descended again to wait in the car park. It seemed the whole school was going home that weekend; everyone but Dean swarmed past me chattering with sports bags and backpacks banging against their bodies, boarding buses or getting into cars while I stood there foolishly shifting from one foot to the next. 'Come on, Jyothi, the bus'll be off in a minute!' yelled a girl out of the window. I smiled back at her and gestured that'd I'd be there in a sec.

Dean was the last to burst through the door into the car park. He lugged a small soft suitcase in one hand and a collection of plastic carrier bags in the other and grinned from ear to ear when he saw me, just as if he was as eager as I was that we were together at last.

It was like the sun coming through a thick curtain of cloud. I had waited all week for this moment. From now on he was mine. For the whole weekend.

When the bus stopped in our home village half an hour later Rachel's car was waiting for us, with Jack and Rachel in it. Dean's luggage was plopped into the trunk and seconds later we were off.

I was sitting next to Dean on the back seat. I grinned across at him but he was listening to Rachel, who was one of those people who feel constantly compelled to initiate conversations. I could have wrung her neck . . . but on the other hand, I had no idea what I should say myself and I couldn't be certain that, if I'd been silent, Dean would have said anything.

I wished with all my being I could be like Natalie, oozing self-confidence and sophistication out of every pore, every strand of hair in place and saying all kinds of witty, charming, perky things that would impress him no end. But I wasn't; I was just me, charmless Jyothi from Bombay, with nothing to offer him but a heart brimming over with love, and still a child.

When we got home there was a quiche waiting for us: Rachel had timed it so that it was ready five minutes after our arrival. The table was laid and all we had to do was eat. Again, Rachel seemed to have no end of small talk and plied Dean with questions on school life. I listened, of course, because everything about Dean interested me, but still I wished we were alone and that it was me putting all those intelligent questions to him, and me he was talking to about his life with such enthusiasm.

The talk was mostly about photography. I knew nothing about photography but Rachel knew so much. I could never, ever grab Dean's attention in that way. He would never, ever . . . I was just indulging in such morose defeatist thoughts when Dean turned to me and said, as easily as if he had noticed I'd been crashing around like a blindfolded sheep on a bed of hot coals, 'Oh, by the way, Jyothi, I've got a surprise for you!

Excuse me one minute.' He scraped back his chair and made a beeline for the door leading into the hall. He was back next minute holding a small yellow folder, which I immediately recognized as one of those packets they give you in a photo shop when you get back your prints.

'Your photos!' he said, radiating excitement at me, and a moment later he had removed the sheaf of photographs, had dragged his chair up next to mine, and was laying the photographs one by one on the table in front of me. I could only stare; from the start of the meal no sound had left my lips and now I was more speechless than ever.

Jack and Rachel, sitting on the opposite side of the table from me, were craning their necks to see, but the photos were upside down for them. So when I had looked at each one I passed it over the table to them, and the praise and admiration that they expressed was music to my ears. A delicious warmth spread through my being.

He had made me look marvellous. That wasn't me in those photos; that was some other girl, much older, much more mature, much wiser than me, yet still young, as fresh and as graceful as a newly opened rose. There was a special quality, at once ethereal and earthy, about her; she looked a stranger to me and yet I knew she really was me, and I knew that Dean had captured something in me that had to be there or else he could not have captured it, and that meant he had to have seen that special quality before he had captured it, and that meant . . . I could not even begin to conjecture what that meant, what inner sight Dean possessed that could make of a foolish clumsy awkward colt like me such a . . . princess. One photo after the other landed on the table, I gazed at each one in awe, and passed it on, and let Jack and Rachel do the gushing for me. Once more, I was speechless, but when I looked up at Dean after I had passed over the last photo I knew I was no longer the inarticulate tongue-tied fool but had been transformed, in real life, to the girl in those photographs. I felt it. I *was* her, she lived in me, and she lived in me right *now*, and she would never ever have to hide from Dean again.

After tea was my designated time for violin practice. I had been hoping that tonight of all nights I would be relieved of this duty but no such luck. Jack would have been merciful, that much I knew, but as ever Jack was incapable of authority and by this time he was completely under Rachel's thumb; from the start it had been Rachel who had insisted on this schedule and there was no respite today. Not for the first time I wished a little more machismo on Jack; all the women I ever met were always going on about women's lib and how men ruled the world but I couldn't agree. Jack was more than happy to let himself be ruled, and it wasn't always right because I knew that Jack's decisions would often have coincided with my own desires. I would have been happy to let Jack rule. But no such luck.

I went up to my room to practise, and went through the required motions, knowing the magic was missing. As ever, the sounds that came from my instrument were wooden and lifeless; I played quickly and fluently, making no technical mistakes, and I knew my playing would impress a non-musical listener. But I could tell the difference, and that's what mattered.

I played one of Mama's favourites: Mendelssohn's Violin Concerto. I found my Music Minus One cassette, on which the orchestra plays without the violin. I pressed the 'start' button, and as the great music swelled out around me I closed my eyes, thought of Mama and played.

But there was no joy in it. I did it for Mama, as I always had; but now it was for her memory. The sounds might be flawless, but they did not touch me. It was like an energy flowing through me, through a network of nerves which did all the work, and I remained for ever apart from that liquid, flowing essence. I was just a passive onlooker, allowing it to control my body, granting it full rein over my fingers, not by doing, but by doing nothing; nothing, that is, but standing aside. Standing outside, beyond the joy. The music was so warm; but I was cold. I could feel the warmth as through a pane of glass, like a waif shivering in the snow, gazing through a window onto a Christmas scene, a glowing fire with a family gathered around, unable to enter, perpetually cut off.

I played the last note. Silence engulfed me and for a moment I simply stood there, the violin still at my chin, my right hand with the bow at my side, listening to the last echoes of the music reverberating through my nerves, as if they were the strings of the instrument and my body was the resonating soundbox.

And then the silence was broken: somebody was clapping. I swung around and saw Dean. He had entered the room silently and remained standing behind me, listening as I played. How long had he been there?

'How long have you been here?' I said shyly as he continued to clap. To hide my embarrassment I turned away before he could answer and made a big fuss about loosening the strings and stowing my violin back into its case.

'That was fantastic!' said Dean. 'I don't know much about music but I know what I like and you're really good.'

'No, I'm not! Not at all!' I said. I wanted to sink into the ground, disappear.

'Don't be so modest! Of course you're good, even my untrained ears can tell that! And I just heard you were pretty famous in Germany. Rachel just told me.'

'I'm quick, that's all. It's nothing special.'

'Oh yes it is, and it's more than quick. That was *music*. *Real* music.'

I could do no more than shake my head in denial, and keep my eyes lowered so that they wouldn't meet his, so that he wouldn't know just how deeply his words touched me. Real music! To me those words were like the echo of paradise, constantly withheld. *Real music*, the equivalent of *true love* and *perfect happiness*, all synonyms for the same thing and each other, for ever out of reach. States that I knew existed, without ever being able to experience them. What he had heard was no more *real music* than our relationship was *true love* or our playful repartee of a week ago *perfect happiness*. I could not lower the threshold of definition just for his sake.

I glanced up at him, enough to see without being seen, shook my head again and mouthed the word, 'No.' And just so he understood me properly, I added, 'Real music is something else.' I walked over to the window and stared out just to give my eyes a focus point, but he walked over and stood beside me.

'You're a strange one,' he said. 'Anybody else would be pleased and proud to play an instrument as well as that. I once started to learn the piano but I gave up after a year. No aptitude for it.'

I started: 'It's just that . . .' and stopped. I had never articulated it before and I didn't know if I could find the right language. But then the words simply came.

'It's just that it's all so *mechanical*, it's merely something that happens to me and I can feel it happening and I can hear the notes and feel the rhythm and the melody but it's all as if someone else is playing, not me, as if I'm far away looking down on my body playing but I can't get inside it, I can't get inside the music, and yet it *seems* to sound good, everyone else says it sounds good and they applaud me for it and say how wonderful it is, and I can only cringe when I hear that. It's not false modesty. I cringe because I know music is really music when you're one with it, when there is no me and music, there's just one steady flow of it like oil and I am music and music is me, and it's just not happening, it never happened to me but I know it should, I know it must, and I'll never be happy unless it happens but it's as if I'm enclosed in glass or something, I can see it happening and it's all so far away and I hate it when people say it's good because it isn't, it isn't at all! It's . . . it's like that children's champagne my mother used to give me. It looks like real champagne, it even tastes like real champagne but it's not, there's something missing, and you long for the real thing, except I never *longed* for real champagne the way I long for real music, because champagne is just champagne, you don't need it really, but music is everything, it's love and happiness and God and I just . . .'

I had spoken in a rush of desperation, gazing into Dean's eyes as a drowning person will cling to a safety-ring but I must have seen something there that brought me to my senses. Something snapped and I stopped in mid-sentence. I looked out of the window again, over the top of an elderberry hedge to the meadows beyond. I saw a black horse grazing in the distance and kept my attention fixed on it, and so was able to pull my mind back from wherever it had gone gallivanting and down to this earth.

'I'm sorry,' I said, not looking at him.

'For what?'

'I got carried away. It didn't make sense.'

'It made perfect sense,' said Dean.

'But then why did you—' I broke off.

'Stop listening? You noticed? Can you read minds?'

I wasn't sure if he expected an answer to that question and so remained silent, and Dean continued.

'It's when you compared it to champagne. And it suddenly occurred to me: I know what you mean. It's exactly the same. With my photography, I mean. Sometimes I look at a photo and I know something's missing. A special ingredient X. A sort of . . . life. A soul. The photograph is flat; technically perfect, maybe, but one-dimensional, soulless. And I'm the only one who can tell. It's so frustrating when a photo like that wins a competition. I could tear it up; and I feel a fake when I don't but I know that others won't notice the missing ingredient, they'll go on about it anyway, and so I let it go.'

'That's like me and my concerts,' I said. 'I hated giving concerts! But I did it to please Mama. And now . . . and now . . .' I felt the tears glistening in my eyes and looked away.

I could tell that Dean was at a loss what to say to that, which made it even more embarrassing, but he was older and more sophisticated than me and he said, 'Shall we go down again now?' and I nodded. He led the way back downstairs and we spent the rest of that evening watching a romantic comedy on television with Jack and Rachel.

Chapter 28

The next day was Saturday. After breakfast Dean and I went with Rachel to Tesco, where she stocked up groceries for the week. After that we went to a house and garden centre where we bought paint, brushes, a bucket and various tools; then to a carpet shop where Dean chose a carpet. When we returned home Rachel set us the task of putting Dean's room together; there'd been no time for this in the past week, and last night he had slept on the living-room couch.

His room was to be next to mine; it was smaller but somehow cosier, owing to the two small windows set in the eaves and a sloping ceiling panelled in wood. It had one brick wall containing a neat little fireplace, and the three remaining walls had to be painted. Because of the sloping ceiling the entire surface to be painted was finally quite small, and Dean, Jack and I, working together, were finished by lunchtime.

Rachel in the meantime had prepared a delicious pasta salad, which we ate on the terrace in the shade of an apple tree. It was still early September and warm enough for us to wear T-shirts and shorts. Sheba dozed on a folded tartan blanket against the wall of the house, and one of the cats sat licking her paw on a windowsill. Rachel laughed and pointed up into the branches of the tree. A red hen perched there, almost unmoving.

'That's Miranda,' she said. 'Miranda doesn't much care for the company of her sisters and prefers to roost in the apple tree. She's quite a character.'

'Like all the animals around here,' said Jack.

'Speaking of which,' said Rachel, 'would the two of you like to take Sheba for a walk after lunch?' She looked from Dean to me.

Dean smiled at me. 'I'd like to. What about you, Jyothi?'

Was there any question? I beamed at him and nodded; at last, alone with Dean! And so, after we'd taken in the dishes and placed them in the dishwasher, we set off.

There was a path just outside the back hedge to Rachel's property, which led straight across a meadow where Sheba could run free, up the hill behind the house, down the other side and into a small wood, and that was the way we took. I had walked this way two weeks ago with Jack and Rachel, but then I had still been burning up inside. Then I had been a completely different person . . . what a difference time can make! Or rather, not time itself, but the incidents within time which can turn you around, change your perspective with a snap. One minute you're gazing through a telescope at a landscape ravaged by war; the next minute, simply by turning around, the telescope has gone and you're in an English country garden, complete with roses, marigolds, lark song, and a hero on a shining white steed.

As always when we were alone together I was painfully shy at first, and as ever, he broke down my shyness by simply not noticing it. This time he chatted about ordinary things – school life, and how I was getting on, and which teachers I had, and who was my favourite mistress, and what was my favourite subject, and whether I had a friend yet. My replies developed from monosyllabic, to detailed, to intimate; within ten minutes I was telling him about my deepest shame. Apart from my parents I had never spoken of it to a single human being, and even then it had only been with a sense of guilt, of letting them down. Normally I found it hard even to say the word.

'Dyslexia.'

There. It was out. We were walking through the woods by this time, Sheba scampering ahead of us. It was cool here in the shade and as I said the word I shivered, but I knew it was more in anticipation of his reaction than of physical cold. I looked up at him anxiously.

'Oh, that's common enough,' he said easily. 'And you've come to the right place.'

'The right place?' I could hardly believe my ears.

'Quite a few Roxby Manor kids are dyslexic,' Dean said. He said it as artlessly as if he were saying they were left-handed, or even blue-eyed. I could hardly believe it.

'Really? But I thought . . .'

'What did you think?'

'I thought it was a school specializing in the arts. That's why Rachel was so keen to send me there, you know. They have this great music department, she said, and—'

'Well, there's a connection,' Dean said. 'A lot of dyslexic people are gifted – creative, artistic, what have you. It's the way their brains work. It's normal.'

'Normal!' I almost cried the word, so great was my shock.

'Yes, normal. I mean, look at you! You may be dyslexic but you're also a musical genius just about.'

'No,' I said. 'Not a genius. It's just an . . . an ability. I don't know how it got there.'

Dean made a swatting gesture with his hand. 'Ability ...
genius ... gift ... whatever you choose to call it.'

'Yes, but that has nothing to do with being dyslexic! I mean,
I'm just glad there's something I can do right otherwise I'd
be a complete failure. Being dyslexic I could never succeed in
school the way my parents wanted me to. They'd have liked
me to go to university but there was no chance, and so at least
I could—'

Dean interrupted. 'You never thought you're a musical
genius *because* you're dyslexic? That somehow your brain is
wired in such a way that makes you unable to read and write
and deal with letters and numbers efficiently, but opens you
up to music in a way other people can't? You never thought
about it that way?'

'No,' I admitted.

'Well, it's about time you did.'

I thought. We walked along in silence while I thought. Sheba
came prancing up with a stick in her mouth; Dean threw it
far up the path, and she galloped off to fetch it. The ritual
repeated itself. Dean ran off with Sheba dancing all around
him to grab the stick he held tantalizingly above her head, out
of her reach.

I quickened my pace to catch up with him.

Sheba was delighted; she obviously thought I had come to
join in the fun. She jumped up at me, yelped, and flung herself
into the air again in a desperate attempt to regain her stick. I
laughed, bent down to pick up another one, and threw it as far
as I could. Immediately she hurtled away in a smooth streak of
sleek black suppleness.

Dean and I looked at each other. I beamed at him, overcome
with gratitude.

'Dean, you're not just saying that to make me feel good, are
you? Do you really *know* it's true? Is it, somehow, *proven*?'

Dean clasped his hands and raised them to the sky in a mock gesture of supplication. 'Lord, help me! What shall I do with her! Here we have a musical child prodigy who can play Mendelssohn as if it were a nursery rhyme and what does she do? Cry her heart out and beat her chest and tear out her hair because she keeps forgetting her eight times table!'

'You *need* maths to be a success,' I retorted. My elation was somewhat dampened by his mockery, and Dean must have caught the slight quiver in my voice because he apologized.

'Sorry, but you exasperate me, you know! You *are* a success. A musical success. And anyway, it's not so important to be a success as to be *you*, and that means doing what you love. And you love music.'

I didn't answer. Sheba returned with the stick in her mouth and dropped it at my feet. Picking it up and throwing it again gave me a welcome excuse not to say anything.

'You love music!' Dean repeated, and this time I had to say something.

'I'm good at it,' I said blandly. 'For some reason,' I added. After another pause I said, 'That's what people think anyway.'

'You don't sound very convinced.'

'I told you last night.' And I couldn't help but add, almost under my breath, 'Sometimes I hate it.' I hoped he hadn't heard.

But he had.

'Hate it? You hate music?'

I nodded miserably.

'But how can you be so good at something you hate?'

I knew the answer to that one.

'Because I had to be good at *something*, didn't I? I had to make a success at *something* after I was such a failure at school! I was such a disappointment to my parents, my mother especially. They did so much for me, bringing me to

242

Germany and adopting me. What would my life have been, Dean? I was living in the slums, in the most terrible situation, and they rescued me! I had this stepfather, he tried to sell me after my mother died! Can you imagine! I owe *everything* to Jack and Mama, everything! And then it turned out I was so stupid at school and I couldn't learn anything, I couldn't write, I couldn't read, I tried so hard but somehow I just couldn't and I felt terrible, but then it turned out that I was good at music, that I had this talent, and they were both so delighted and so proud of me and so determined to make a success of me in spite of me being a failure, and so . . .'

'And so you did it to please them.'

I nodded. Dean was silent then, and so was I. After that emotional outburst I felt frayed and close to tears, unable to speak a further word. We walked along for several minutes, occasionally stooping to pick up the stick that Sheba so faithfully returned and dropped at out feet. Sometimes Dean picked it up, sometimes I did, and the game took on a clockwork regularity that had a soothing effect on my nerves. I took an inner step back and wished, not for the first time, for a thicker skin and the ability to stay cool and calm under all circumstances, not to give in to these fits of self-pity and self-denigration, and *especially* not in Dean's presence. How could he ever respect and care for me now, seeing how weak and prone to hysterics I was! I longed for sophistication; I longed for maturity. I longed to be a cool femme fatale like Natalie. Anything but me.

He had been so admiring of my music, I should have left it at that. Admiration of my music would have turned to admiration of me, and that, finally, was what I wanted. But all I was was a snivelling little child worried about her eight times table.

'Jyothi,' Dean said suddenly, and his voice cut through the layers of self-immolation. I swung to face him.

'Yes?'

'You met Mrs Ellis, didn't you? You must have, she takes care of all the new pupils when they first arrive. The headmaster's wife.'

'Yes,' I replied, grateful that he seemed to have changed the subject. 'I remember I met her on my first day.'

'Well, what I told you just now, about dyslexia ... you know?'

When I heard that dreaded word all the nervousness came back. I cringed, and regretted with all my heart that I had ever mentioned it. But he was waiting for some response. 'Yes?' I said.

'Well, she's dyslexic. She talks about it a lot, that's how I know so much. And you know what? She's proud of it.'

'*Proud?*' In disbelief I raised my voice, and it came out as an embarrassing squeak.

'Yes, proud. She says that if she weren't dyslexic she wouldn't have been such a great sculptress.'

'*Sculptress?*'

'Yes. You didn't know? Those figures all over the school, in glass cases, they're all by her. She's the pottery teacher and she also has a studio in town, where you can go and see her best work, and you can buy some of it. You should see her prices!'

'I didn't know that!'

'Well, it's true. I guess she's been too busy this week getting things organized but sooner or later she goes to the special needs department and talks to the kids with learning difficulties and gives them pep talks and tries to see if they have some hidden talent. She says that all dyslexics have a hidden talent and it's just a matter of discovering it – *un*covering it. She says that's the way their brains are made – not for letters and figures but for greater things. That they've all got a special gift buried

244

in them somewhere. She says you can't have it both ways: either you have little squiggles on paper, or you have a special gift. Like two sides of the coin. I bet that sooner or later she'll hook into you about your music.'

'Did she really say that? Little squiggles on paper?'

'That's what she calls letters and numbers.'

I had to laugh. 'That's what I always called the musical notes on paper. I was never able to make sense of them and I got into a lot of trouble with my music teachers for that. I used to say they were little squiggles on paper. I was never able to read music. But I had perfect hearing, perfect pitch, perfect recall, and somehow I was able to play from memory. But it made me an oddball. Different.'

'Well, that makes two of us.'

'You, an oddball? No way.'

'You don't believe me? Ask my mother. Well, ask Rachel.'

'You're the most sane person I ever met!' I cried. 'And the nicest!' It came out before I could stop myself.

'It seems like that. Most of the time, I'm normal, or I seem normal. My oddness . . . well, OK, call it something else. Call it eccentricity. It's a sort of addiction I've got.'

'Addiction?'

'Not drugs or anything like that,' Dean was quick to explain. 'But almost as dangerous. Luckily I don't get to give in to my addiction too often. But, you see, I'm addicted to heights. Mountains. Cliff faces. Rock walls. The higher the better. And steeper. It's a sort of craziness all right and I manage to rein it in for most of the year but if you let me loose in the mountains . . . I nearly drove my mother mad with despair. That's how my dad died, you see. Climbing in the Himalayas. I guess I got it from him – the madness. Even when I was a toddler, I was climbing. Up trees, up drainpipes, up walls. When they gave me a camera I finally found a nice safe hobby which kept me earthbound and they breathed out in relief. But photography's only a temporary relief, a sort of placebo, if you like, for the mountain madness. That's what she calls it, my mother. Madness. The other side of the coin. The moment I get the chance . . .'

He stopped. We had been walking side by side, he loping along in his loose, casual manner, and I had kept my gaze glued to him as he spoke. Now I could see that his profile had taken on an almost statuesque stillness, and though I could not see the expression in his eyes I could sense that some other entity had taken hold of him and held him in its thrall. I shivered, and again it was not from the cold.

When we returned home we found that Rachel and Jack had laid the carpet in Dean's room, and the paint was dry. The walls were now a pale green colour, which blended well with the russet carpet; the room looked warm and glowing and eager for occupation. But it was empty. 'All I can offer you for the time being is this inflatable mattress,' Rachel told Dean. 'And you'll have to live out of your suitcase. But I imagine you can manage that all right, you're young.'

'No problem,' said Dean.

'Next Saturday we'll go to Ikea and look for furniture,' Rachel continued. 'You can choose what you like, of course.'

'Oh, any old stuff will do,' Dean replied. He was busy attaching the nozzle of the mattress pump to the valve and appeared uninterested in interior decoration.

'Really?' said Rachel. She looked keenly at him as if to ascertain whether he was serious or just being polite. 'In that case, I could buy some things during the week, and have the room ready for you by next weekend. If you're not fussy . . .'

'I'm not fussy,' said Dean. 'Just the basics: bed, cupboard, desk. That's all.'

'Whew,' Rachel said. She grinned broadly. 'I was thinking of Amy, my friend. She has two teenagers and they insisted they could only have this bed and that desk and those curtains and that carpet . . . it was a nightmare getting their rooms together. What a relief to have two such easy young people in the house. No, I do appreciate it, Dean – and you too, Jyothi – adolescents have such a terrible reputation and I remember my own youth and I can only say it's a pleasure to have you both . . .'

'Don't count your chickens,' said Dean. He pressed rhythmically on the pump and the mattress moved sluggishly as it slowly filled with air. 'For all you know we only need time and in a month or two you'll have a couple of hellions screaming at you and throwing things at each other.'

'Could be, but I don't believe it,' said Rachel smugly, and, patting Dean on the shoulder, added, 'So, shall I leave you to it? Dinner's in half an hour.' She turned and rattled off down the stairs.

'She's great,' said Dean to me.

'Um,' I replied.

Rachel was soon to eat those words. Over the next few weeks Dean began to show his true colours. Perhaps he had hid them while staying at her parents, and only now allowed them to show. Maybe it was turning sixteen that did it. Neither Rachel nor I approved of those new colours.

Dean had friends in town and now that he lived so near he developed the habit of meeting them in Farnleigh after lunch on Saturdays and staying out till late at night. Sometimes they went to parties. Rachel tried to come on as a strict parent, doing what she thought strict parents should do. She didn't like not knowing exactly what he was up to, but there was nothing she could do: she knew very well that at Dean's age the more you tell them what not to do the more they'll do it. That's what she said to Jack at supper when they discussed Dean's new habits. Jack advised her to leave well alone, and even drive into town on Saturday nights to pick him up, which she didn't like at all. She did it nevertheless. As for me, for once I sided with Rachel. I knew there were girls among those friends. And then the shock: it was not just girls, plural. It was a girl. Singular. A steady one.

I didn't notice it at first; perhaps I didn't want to notice it, but anyway, how could I? Then circumstances forced me to take note.

It happened on a Saturday evening, November of that first term. Bonfire night at school.

Dean, as usual, was not at home. This Saturday he had been gone since the morning, and there was only Jack, Rachel and myself in the car.

I was excited as anything; I had never seen a live firework exhibition in my life before this. Monika had strongly disapproved of fireworks. 'A terrible waste of money!' she used to say. 'Millions and millions just for a few coloured lights in the sky! Think of all the starving children in India that money could save!' And so I had never been allowed to watch the New Year's Eve fireworks displays in Germany.

The school courtyard was swarming with people: students as well as their parents and family friends. We queued up to buy our tickets, then queued up again to get our boxes of chicken and chips and our drinks. After that we proceeded to the back of the school where the bonfire and display were to be held. There was half an hour to go. Rachel met some old friends of hers and she and Jack stopped to chat with them. Dean was nowhere to be seen, of course. But I hadn't expected it to be otherwise.

I sat down on a low wall by myself to eat and drink; I watched the people, young and old, milling around, chatting, laughing, and felt apart from it all, as apart as I had ever been. Would there ever come a time when I would feel perfectly at home, perfectly in the right place at the right time? Always tiny fleeting glimpses of happiness, and always I stood outside of it, looking through a window at a cosy family scene.

As usual when I was at school, a part of me automatically, tiredly, scanned the faces around me for Dean's. As far as I could tell he hadn't yet met up with Jack and Rachel either. He'd be somewhere with his friends, with Natalie, not even aware that I was somewhere here nearby, and not caring; I was family, taken for granted. How I longed to be special . . .

The back courtyard curved around the playing field where the bonfire stood ready to be lit. A loudspeaker from one of the games rooms blared out grotesque dance music and some of the younger pupils were hopping around like bunnies. The air seemed to sizzle with anticipation, and even I, who had no idea of what was awaiting me, felt touched by the spirit of excitement. I finished my food and drink and sidled into the crowd in the hopes of maybe finding Dean. It would be nice to stand next to him during the exhibition. Maybe Natalie's parents would be here and she would be with them.

But Dean was still elusive, and soon the music stopped and a disembodied voice announced that the countdown was about to begin.

The crowd chanted in unison: 'Ten! Nine! Eight! Seven! Six! Five! Four! Three! Two! One! ZERO!' And at the shout of 'ZERO!' the loudspeaker blasted forth with the bombastic opening to 'Thus Spake Zarathustra' and the first firework shot high into the sky and burst into a million red, blue and yellow stars which covered the entire night sky.

I gasped aloud in amazement. I craned my neck back as far as I could, gazed upwards and marvelled, for I had never seen such unspeakable glory! This is what God must be like, I thought, beyond anything one could ever imagine. *A few coloured lights in the sky!* Oh Monika, how you have deceived me!

The loudspeakers changed tune, bursting into the triumphant chords of 'Land of Hope and Glory'. The entire sky became a glowing, sparkling, crackling mass of exploding stars. Carried away with the magnificence of it all I forgot Dean, forgot Rachel, forgot myself even, and my heart swelled with exhilaration.

My neck hurt from craning and I lowered my head to rest it for one moment. And then my eyes widened. Across the courtyard from me stood Dean. Natalie was next to him. Rather, she was pressed against him. Pressed *close* against him. He was quite oblivious of the spectacle above our heads, and so was she. He and Natalie were alone in a world in which all other eyes were fixed on the sky, and there, in the middle of the crowd, in full public view, they were doing *it*. He held her in a strong embrace and he was kissing her, long and passionately, just like in the movies. I had never once imagined that Dean – my Dean! – could do a thing like that.

I looked away and back up at the sky, misty-eyed. All my elation had vanished. It was as if my own heart too had soared so high that all it could do was first explode into a million stars, and finally fizzle into nothingness, all its fire spent.

Chapter 29

The rest of that school year brought new changes. Perhaps it was the shock that brought me ultimately to my senses. Whatever it was, my life swivelled around on its axis and, like someone turning a telescope to find a new view, the landscape of my life took on a new profile.

Dean, Jack and Rachel, not to mention Mrs Ellis and Miss Jordan, convinced me that my best – and only – hope lay in music and so I channelled my lost dreams and fizzled hopes into that one avenue. My performance improved dramatically.

I played for Dean.

Dean was dazzled. That was enough for me. I made it my goal to dazzle him out of his mind. That dazzlement was the beginning of a whole new way of life. I threw myself into my music with new energy and new motivation. Music became the underpinnings to a more stable personality, as they call it. It was as Monika predicted, though back then I had been too young to understand: the more applause I earned, the more my self-estimation grew. I began to revel in applause, to hunger for it; but most of all for Dean's.

I played at school concerts and won standing ovations. Sometimes there were inter-school musical competitions, and I shone there as well, more often than not winning the first prize as solo violinist.

I still couldn't read music adequately, but instead of this being a handicap it became merely the negligible side-effect of a skill which enthralled all those around me. They might be able to read music, but I only had to hear a piece of music once in order to reproduce it immediately with virtuosity, for which I won chin-dropping admiration. I relished that admiration, and made the effort to earn more.

When I came home from school I would immediately retire to my room and practise for hours. Musical self-improvement became my only goal in life. The truth of Mrs Ellis's words opened up to me: being true to myself meant developing the talent I was born with. I did so now to the exclusion of almost everything else in my life.

I was granted a full musical scholarship. I won prizes, all the ones available to me except the one prize I wanted, Dean. I consoled myself with the reminder that I was too young for Dean, but, I vowed, one day he would be mine. I would dazzle him into loving me as a woman, as a wife.

Jack was once more proud of me, and Dean was in thrall. Often he came to my room just to hear me play, and that was when I was at my best. When I played for Dean I put all my heart into it and I knew that his heart heard, and responded, and that I was building an invisible bond, a cord, fibre by fibre, between us which he could not be aware of yet but which all the time was growing stronger and stronger beneath all the other distracting layers of his life; and that one day he would capitulate.

I clung to that cord. And hungered for his applause. And received it.

As I gained confidence in music so I gained confidence in myself. I was no longer the shy, self-effacing girl in the background. I learned to speak up and say what I thought, to laugh and joke with others. I was popular; I was a part of it all! At last! But all the time I waited and watched for Dean, hungered for his approval. And all the time my music failed to fill me with joy.

The summer term came and went, and the long holidays were upon us. Dean was due to return to India to see his mother. He had been there for two weeks in December (returning before Christmas, which his mother and stepfather, being Hindus, did not celebrate) and two weeks at Easter; now he was due to spend eight whole weeks there, three of which he would spend climbing with his friends in the Himalayas.

This time, though, we were going with him.

Jack and Rachel had both always had a deep connection to India and over the past year had started to learn yoga. This summer they had enrolled themselves in a yoga retreat in Rishikesh, and I was to accompany them. We were to fly to Delhi, where we would first visit Dean's mother and her new family, and then travel on to Rishikesh for a week, followed by a week's holiday in the Himalayas.

When the trip had still been at the planning stage Jack had asked me if I cared to go to Bombay to look for my family: the brothers who had cared nothing for me and done nothing to protect me when I was a child. I had replied with an adamant no. I could not remember Bombay without dread. All happy memories had vanished; all that remained was the vague memory of the horror of my mother's death. Coupled with the appalling accounts of the city brought back to us through the media, Bombay seemed the last place on earth I cared to visit.

I wasn't even sure I wanted to go to India at all. Wouldn't it be better to cut that connection entirely? My roots were there, certainly; but Monika had always insisted that my best hope of happiness in the West was to put aside those roots and the unhappy memories of the past and start completely afresh. I was a Westerner. Yet my indifference to this journey back to India gradually turned to curiosity, and I found myself looking forward to it more and more.

What was it about the very sound of the word 'India'? Was it the fact that it was the country of my birth, of my blood, of my spirit, and that the feeling had gradually begun to grow within me that there I should finally discover what it meant to feel at home in myself? I could not tell. All I knew was that as the time drew near the mere thought of the coming journey was enough to set some unseen, hidden part of me humming like a lightly plucked violin string, resonating within me in a thousand brilliant inner sights and sounds and smells conjured by my imagination.

As a result my first few days in Delhi were deeply disappointing. None of the magic I had imagined: instead, a sterile town mansion made of concrete, with furnishings more modern that any I had ever lived in before, a TV set that flickered unceasingly, and Dean's two little half-siblings, Sunil and Lata, who seemed to be constantly underfoot or screaming their heads off for sweets – scuttling servants bearing glasses of cold *nimbu pani* and plastic flowers in all the vases.

Dean's mother was friendly but cool at one and the same time. I had the distinct feeling she did not approve of me, which could have been merely my overactive imagination coupled with the guilt that in spite of all my efforts I still had not uprooted my crush on her son. She smothered Dean with a love which he seemed to accept with indulgent patience, smiling angelically when she hugged him out of the blue and accepting her kisses with grace.

She was a very buxom, matronly woman with light milky skin, which I learned was because she herself was a half-caste; her father, too, had been English. Her husband, on the other hand, was extremely dark and extremely fat, and spoke English with an exaggerated upper-class accent, which was due to the fact that he had studied at Cambridge. He was a talkative, jovial man and I imagined that if he had indeed been an Englishman he would have been florid and constantly wiping his face with a handkerchief (unnecessary here, as the house was air-conditioned). As it was he gave the impression of an Englishman living in the wrong skin. He was friendly enough and seemed very fond of Dean.

We spent a week with them in Delhi, during which we saw all the usual Delhi sights and took a day trip to Agra to see the Taj Mahal, enclosed in a little bubble of sterile luxury. Uncle Ravi (Dean's stepfather asked me to call him this but I avoided calling him anything at all) had a sparkling white air-conditioned limousine and a chauffeur and we glided from one sight to the next, never so much as setting foot on a dirty street.

On our third day in Delhi Aunt Soona (Dean's mother) took Rachel and me shopping. I had never shopped this way before. The chauffeur would stop outside the particular shop Aunt Soona wanted to show us, blocking the traffic, which would continue to swarm around us like a flowing river temporarily obstructed by a rock. The chauffeur would step out, open the rear door to allow us out, drive away, and circle the block a few times to find a parking spot, or not, as the case might be. The chauffeur seemed to have a second sense, knowing exactly when Aunt Soona would be finished with her shopping, for when we left the chilly opulence of the shop there he would be, waiting for us in the second row of traffic. These luxury shops all seemed to have annexed and repaved the length of pavement outside their gorgeous showcase windows, peopled by tall, slim, sleek mannequins, draped in the finest silk saris, frozen at a moment of high drama. As far as we were concerned the pavements of Delhi were all of pristine white or polished black marble.

The car windows were tinted so that everything beyond them appeared as in shadow, veiled, a dark and unreal world, which did not touch us demi-goddesses in our cool white universe. We could slide through the most stinking shantytown and not know it existed, for we could (and Dean's mother did) pull the curtains of the windows and thus doubly ensure that whatever unseemly sight loomed outside, it would not offend our eyes. But the front windscreen was not smoked, and I saw the world.

I saw the hot dusty streets and the ragged people; I saw the old lined faces of the beggars and the grimy cheeks and matted manes of the street urchins. I could not smell those streets, nor could I hear the din, but seeing was enough. I remembered.

First of all I remembered one of Jack's favourite songs, something which had been popular in his youth and which, he had once told me laughingly, suited me. It was about a ragged little girl from the back streets of Naples, who had made good and forgotten her roots. 'Where do you go to, my lovely?' her childhood friend asks; and wonders if she remembers those days.

The song did not suit me at all, of course; I never went back there, to those back streets of Bombay. Not when I was alone, and not when I heard that song. But now I did.

Memory is the strangest phenomenon. Entire scenes, in intricate detail, smells, sounds, the rip on a piece of tarpaulin or a rat scuttling into a hole in the wall, can be stored for years, decades even, without causing even the slightest ripple in the sea of consciousness, yet, suddenly, some small trigger can act as a pull-rope, hauling the entire conglomerate of a buried past to the surface.

So it was with me now. I sat in the middle of the rear seat, which meant that there was not much I could see at the best of times. But while waiting at the traffic lights I saw a face at the front window, the face of a young girl, perhaps five, her face streaked with black grime, a naked baby on her hip. I saw the gesture she made: the fingers of her right hand bunched together and gesturing at the baby's mouth. The imploring lips as she mouthed some words we could not hear in our protective sheath of shining metal and glass. The blandness of the baby's expression, completely indifferent to its plight.

I had done that myself. I had waited at traffic lights till the luxurious white cars stopped; I had borrowed our neighbour's baby and lugged it around the grimy streets as an asset to my begging forays. *I was that little girl.* A chill settled on my soul.

The chauffeur stared poker-faced in front of him. The girl gave up and wandered off to find another victim. The memories erupted into my mind, pouring out their swill and flooding me with the perfect recall of a cinematic film: my entire childhood before arriving in Germany passed before my inner mind, the agony of hunger as well as the comfort of my mother's arms – my real, my first mother – and the comfort was greater than the agony, and I could not bear it. I slammed the door shut on the memory, and buried my face in my hands.

'What's the matter, Jyothi?' Soona's voice showed concern, and the hand she placed on my back helped to restore my equilibrium.

'Nothing,' I murmured. 'I just have a bit of a headache, that's all.'

'Here, have some water,' said Soona, and poured me a beaker from the silver flask she took everywhere with her in a wicker basket full of essentials one might need when away from the house for any time.

'Thanks.' I swallowed the water in four huge gulps, and simultaneously pushed the image of the little girl at the window and the world she had conjured up back into the furthermost recesses of my mind. That was over. That world had nothing to do with me. I was a different person now in a sumptuous world of white leather and Benares silk, a talented and successful young woman on her way up. I had been rescued from *that* world; *this* here was where I belonged.

Yet I did not feel much at home in the sterile, over-modernized palace that Aunt Soona and Uncle Ravi called their own, and I was glad when the next day we all – Rachel, Jack, Dean and I – left Delhi for Hardwar at the foot of the Himalayas.

We went by train: club class in the legendary Rajdhani Express. Rachel and Jack were delighted to find that the entire journey in the air-conditioned coach, including all meals, would cost less than ten pounds each, and indeed it was a pleasant journey made even pleasanter by the fact that Dean and I sat side by side and spent the entire journey doing a crossword puzzle together. I was good at finding words and he was good at spelling them, and so, metaphorically speaking, we licked the platter clean, after which Dean drifted off into sleep and I gazed out of the window at the monotonous plains, parched yellow by a monsoon that this year never arrived, slipping past beyond the window. Every half-hour a smiling waiter edged down the middle aisle, offering cold drinks, hot drinks, biscuits, samosas, a hot meal, a cold snack . . . until, well nourished and rested but stiff and bedraggled, we emerged into the bustle of Hardwar station.

India, the true India, closed in on us. In less than a minute we were surrounded.

They came from all directions. A ragged, grimy, evil-smelling, bawling horde of people: men, women, children, pushing each other away in their efforts to draw near; shouting at us; holding open clawlike leathery hands black with dirt; grabbing at our pieces of luggage; each one screaming for attention.

Each one was relentlessly prying open those parts of me I had closed and nailed shut. I could not bear it! I felt faint; I wanted to escape, but we were locked in. I clapped my hands over my eyes, shutting out the sight.

I heard Dean's voice, then. He spoke Hindi. I had not heard this language for eight years; in Delhi we had spoken exclusively English, even with the servants. But now it all came back. I remembered; I understood each word! He was telling them to go away, just as I had been chased away in my begging forays! He spoke in that commanding voice the rich use against the poor, the voice of authority that brooks no insolence. It all came flooding back: the streets, the smells, the dirt, the gnawing hunger . . . I grabbed Dean's arm.

'Dean, stop it, stop it, please stop it! Let's go! Let's get out of here!'

'Hey, what's up with you, Jyothi? That's what I'm trying to do . . . Hey, you!' He spoke firmly to a man in khaki shorts; by now the crowd, recognizing from Dean's voice that this was no greenhorn tourist, had dispersed and only a few of the more serious taxi-drivers were left. Several arms grabbed at the various pieces of our luggage, and a few minutes later we were piled into a taxi, all except Dean, who was walking to his hotel to meet his friends.

259

'Thanks, Dean! I always forget how to deal with that sort of situation!' said Rachel, and then she spoke to the taxi-driver in Hindi herself; and again I understood each word. I was flabbergasted. Rachel and I had never spoken Hindi together; I had forgotten that she had a good working knowledge of the language. But mostly I had forgotten that I had once been fluent in it. And now, I realized, I was fluent again. I was no longer a European. In the space of a few hours, since leaving our cloistered existence in Delhi, I had undergone a transformation, and now the metamorphosis was complete. I had become an Indian. I could no longer deny it. But I could fight it.

Looking out of the taxi window as we drove through the town I regained some of my composure, and most of my senses. Here in India all of life is played out in the open for all the world to see: women peeling vegetables and washing clothes and bathing children and folding saris; men repairing bicycles and counting money and writing things in exercise books. A group of schoolchildren on their way home, barefooted, laughing, satchels swinging on their shoulders; girls with long black pigtails, boys with spindly bare legs emerging from the short trousers of their uniforms. A youth on a bicycle, one hand on the handlebars and the other holding a battered radio up to his ear. We came to traffic lights and halted.

'Look!' said Rachel suddenly, and pointed excitedly out of the rear window. I turned around to see, and stared: it was an elephant, standing behind us in the lane of traffic, on whose head a thin, turbaned man sat cross-legged. The car moved off and so did the elephant, slowly lumbering forward, seemingly on a verbal command of its master, for there were no reins, nor any other sign of guidance.

Outside of town we passed a slum of lean-tos and primitive shacks where ragged children played in the caked mud and once again I shuddered inwardly and whispered to myself, There but for the grace of God . . .

Never let it be said that I was ungrateful. I knew where I came from. And I knew that it was only a miracle that had hauled me out of the pit and placed me among the select few. The violin had transformed me. The violin was the proof of my identity: I was European.

My violin, I reflected, was in fact my closest friend in all the world. No one person had done as much for me as it had; it had opened the door that led from the world of the beggar girl in the car window – the beggar children out there, playing outside their hovels, just metres away from us as we drove past. I shuddered again and shook off the grim reflection.

No. Actually, it was Jack and Monika who had physically saved me from that world; but that ragged beggar girl had lived on inside me until the violin – not this one, of course, but the little half-violin that had been its predecessor – had given me the wings into a higher universe. I stroked the case again in complacency, and grim gratitude.

I was the only one of us with no set purpose for this Indian trip, and I would dedicate my stay to music. I had two uninterrupted weeks to do almost nothing but practise. I had a recital early in September and I was determined to be perfect. I had not been able to play much in Delhi because of the rigorous programme of sightseeing Soona and Ravi had subjected us to, but now I would have all the time in the world.

Chapter 30

The ashram was situated on the River Ganges just above the town of Rishikesh. It turned out that Jack had always wanted to come here, ever since he had emulated the guitar expertise of George Harrison in his youth and had followed the youngest Beatle's career with admiration and fascination. Finally, decades later, he had made it.

The taxi drove into the wide, sandy ashram grounds and came to a halt. We lugged our cases out of the boot, Jack paid the driver, and the three of us dragged our luggage to the first and largest of several white buildings of varying shapes and sizes. This one, facing the entrance and the road, had a veranda along the front and a veneer of officialdom; sure enough, as we drew near a bronze sign with the cursive letters 'Reception' became visible.

The smaller cottages in the background were the living quarters, it turned out: simple semi-detached cabins placed back to back. When making reservations Jack and Rachel had actually thought of my needs and asked for a cottage as far away from the others as possible, so that I could practise the violin without fear of the other residents disturbing me. That's how Jack put it, but of course I was aware that he meant something else: he meant that others should not be disturbed by me.

At the moment though I could not think of playing. My room was nothing more than a cubby-hole next to the bigger bedsit that Jack and Rachel would share. I had a narrow bed, a simple wardrobe, and a table: that was it. The floor was laid with some rather worn and faded linoleum; the window had no curtains. On the wall hung a photo of an old, white-bearded Indian man. There was a candle stump on the table, sitting in a mass of wax on a small white saucer, and next to it a box of matches. That was the entire furnishing of my room. But it was clean, and as I slung my bag onto the table and carefully laid my violin case on the seat of the chair I found myself looking forward again to fourteen days when I could play my violin to my heart's content. That thought cheered me up. I opened the case, removed my violin and stroked its rich shining curves. As if to draw strength from its beauty I lay down on the bed for a moment, hugging it to my chest like a baby on its mother after birth, the tangible symbol of all my dreams and hopes.

The thought of the expertise I could achieve within the coming space of uncluttered time filled me with glee. I was tempted to spring to my feet and begin playing right now, but I restrained myself. That would have to wait till tomorrow. It was already dusk and presumably there would be some sort of evening meal awaiting us. Reluctantly I left my violin and went out on to the veranda.

It was a beautiful place. At the centre of the compound were the two-storey administration and other main buildings, surrounded by the smaller cube-like living quarters sprinkled like dice thrown carelessly from a giant hand. The low white cottages were spaced apart at respectable intervals so that one was neither too near or too far from one's neighbours. Between the two nearest buildings I could see the swiftly flowing brown waters of the Ganges. Beyond the river the far bank rose steeply into an incline covered with what looked like deep jungle, and indeed, the atmosphere here was not the temperate mountain air I had expected but rather the close, humid feeling of the tropics; though it was no longer hot at this time of day there was the lingering mood of sunlight trapped by encroaching evening, and I returned into my room to decide what to wear. I pulled various shalwar kameez combinations out of my bag: Aunt Soona had forced Rachel and me to buy a huge collection of these garments, some of them of such fine quality I knew I would never have the opportunity to wear them. For this first evening I chose the one I liked best – of a rich green colour, with golden embroidery inlaid with tiny mirrors down the front, and a matching shawl.

I left my room again and knocked on the next door, which was a small bathroom between Jack and Rachel's room and mine. When no answer came I entered, showered quickly – there was running hot water, which I had not expected – dressed, and re-emerged on to the veranda. Jack was just locking their door; Rachel was already waiting for him on the sand beneath the veranda.

'Oh, hi, Jyothi,' said Jack when he saw me. 'That colour really suits you!'

'Yes, you look really smart!' Rachel stretched out her arms and twirled for me, showing off her own outfit. 'How do you like mine?' She was wearing a shalwar kameez of what looked like heavy silk, pale mauve and very elegant – but rather insipid.

'Lovely,' I said.

Supper was held in a plain room in one of the central buildings. It was a simple meal of rice and spicy vegetables but well cooked and quite delicious. We sat around a large rectangular table with the other guests: two Indian men, one other Western couple, and five single Westerners, men and women.

I was the only hanger-on, meaning, child-dragged-along-with-parent, though of course at fourteen I no longer considered myself a child. Not for the first time I thanked the heavens – or whoever was responsible up there, if anyone – for my violin, which would keep me delightful company for the next couple of weeks. All the talk was of meditation and God, which didn't interest me, so I thought about the things that did; and since there was no point whatsoever thinking about Dean I thought about music and the recital coming up in less than five weeks.

After supper I went for a short stroll around the compound, ending up on the wide concrete steps leading down into the river. There was an area within the water sectioned off by some strong metal barriers, presumably to prevent people being swept out into the middle of the river. I stayed on the steps, and dunked my toes into the cool water.

I listened to the river. Its voice was hushed; I had to tune my hearing to a different, finer wavelength to hear it, but it was there, a constant unwavering whisper which seemed to send a steady flow of coolness through my soul, mesmerizing and soothing at once. When I finally stood up to return to my room I felt refreshed and energized; the thought came to use that energy to practise for two or three hours but a spontaneous protest rose up in me with a vigorous NO, which surprised me; the days were long gone when I was too lazy and too unmotivated to practise! I toyed with the two alternatives

– to play or not to play – for some time before making up my mind not to. It was too late, and I remembered Jack's words about not disturbing other people. Instead I returned to my room, got ready for bed, turned on the overhead fan, lay down, and within a minute of my head touching the pillow I was asleep.

The next day everything went wrong; it was as if my fingers were made of clay. I had started out with such eagerness immediately after breakfast, but what emerged from my instrument was something worse than the amateur attempts of some over-ambitious Roxby Manor scholarship candidate.

Not only that, I felt as if internally paralysed. The music was dead within me. I combed my inner recesses but all I found was silence.

It terrified me.

I struggled against that silence. And it defeated me. In anger I railed against it, kicking and screaming. What if it lasted! What if my gift, my music, had vanished into thin air, as inexplicably as it had come, as if I had never been singled out for a special and extraordinary gift, as if I were not one of the Chosen?

I fought all day, to no avail. It was as if someone had poured liquid cement into my soul where it had solidified, destroying the music that was at once the nourishment of my spirit and its fruit.

I was devastated. I tried to imagine a life without music and it was impossible. I would be a nothing, a *nobody*! I could still remember what existence without music had been, those sterile days spent in brooding alienation or spinning fairy-tale dreams of Dean!

I had invested all I had in my music. If that were to go . . .

I tried again and again. I placed my instrument beneath my chin, held the bow poised above the strings, and waited.

Normally, all I would have to do was remember the sound of the music I was about to play, call it to my mind, hum the first two bars silently, and then it would all happen: my body would come alive with the music, bow and violin would be extra limbs, doing as they were told. There was never any conscious direction from me; I was a marionette, not playing but *being played* by the music. Today there was nothing.

'What's the matter, Jyothi?'

I looked up at Jack. It was lunchtime, and I was grateful for the break because it meant I could stop the battle for the time being, gather my resources, and try again afterwards.

I smiled across the table at Jack. 'Nothing, why?'

'You look a bit glum. How did you pass the morning?'

He and Rachel, of course, had gone off to their yoga and meditation class immediately after breakfast. They had heard nothing of my pathetic efforts – at least I had been spared that ignominy.

'Oh, I was practising, of course. How did your class go?'

Nothing like asking a counter-question to divert the attention from oneself. Because if Jack began to probe to deeply . . . but he had taken the bait. He groaned and made a long face.

'I always thought I was in such good shape but I've realized just how stiff I am. I couldn't get my head anywhere near my knees. Rachel's better than me. She even managed a headstand.'

Rachel, who had been chatting with her table neighbour, Nicola, heard her name and beamed over at me. Just as Jack never missed an opportunity to bring her name into a conversation, so she never missed the chance to jump in, feet first.

'Oh Jyothi, you really should join us! At least for the morning sessions! You've got such a lithe young body, I'm sure you could show us old fogies a thing or two about flexibility! As for the headstand, I think I must have done something wrong. Pulled a muscle, or something.'

'Jyothi would be a natural,' Jack said. 'She's been doing headstands since she was five.'

'I've got some Tiger Balm,' said Nicola, 'you can rub it on your neck.'

'There's also an excellent ayurvedic doctor in Rishikesh,' said Stephen, at Rachel's other elbow. 'I was having the most terrible diarrhoea – had it for weeks – and he cleared it up in a day.'

'Really?' Richard, at my right elbow, pricked his ears at the word 'diarrhoea'. 'I've been taking this stuff that does no bloody good.'

'Well, you should change your diet,' said Nicola. 'This food is so fatty, you shouldn't be eating meals here at all. You should stick to dry rusks and Coke. I thought your diarrhoea had cleared up. You haven't mentioned it for some time.'

'Don't like to complain,' said Richard. 'It's a bit better but it comes and goes. I suppose it's chronic.'

Ulrike, who sat next to Jack, said, 'I have got the perfect remedy for diarrhoea! *Heilerde*! Healing earth! I brought it from Germany. I never come to India without it. It is indispensable against diarrhoea. And I have several packets of – how you say it? Crunchy bread?'

'Crispbread,' said her husband Jörg. 'You should be eating only crispbread or *Zwieback*. No milk products, nothing cooked in oil. These vegetables are poison to your system. Come to our room afterwards and we will give you some packets.'

'But don't you need it yourself?' Richard-of-the-chronic-diarrhoea asked.

Ulrike and Jörg both grinned triumphantly. 'No! We are

returning to Germany next week! We did not have any upsets this visit!' said Ulrike.

Meanwhile Stephen was talking to Rachel about her head-stand technique. '. . . careful when you return to earth,' I heard him say. 'Never jump up afterwards. Take everything slowly. Give the blood time to flow out of the head. Everything must flow. No sudden movements.'

'. . . a little bit every day,' Nicola said across the table to Jack. 'Just bend over till you feel you've reached your limit, relax those muscles, isolate them mentally and relax them consciously. Every day a little. And watch your breathing. By the time you leave here your head'll be right down on your knees. Guaranteed! It's all a matter of . . .'

'Lufthansa,' said Ulrike. 'Non-stop to Frankfurt.'

'. . . inner harmony,' said Stephen.

'Rajdhani Express . . .'

'Hari-ki-Pauri . . .'

'Brings out our latent talents . . .'

'Club class.'

Snippets of their conversations fluttered around my ears like butterflies. I alone sat still and silent in the middle, mechanically moving my fork to my mouth, not having a word to add. I noticed that all the people around us were India experts, while the two Indian men, presumably the real experts, ate in silence. I glanced clandestinely at them. They seemed remarkably alike to me; perhaps they were brothers, or perhaps it was because they were, if not dressed alike, at least dressed in Western clothes, unlike the foreigners, who all went native: the men in either white dhotis wrapped around their hips, or in white cotton drawstring trousers, and white kurtas. The women, including Rachel and myself, all wore shalwar kameez.

In the midst of all this two words sailed out from the fluttering mass and froze before me.

'. . . brilliant violinist . . .'

I looked up. Jack was smiling fondly across at me. Nicola, who had practically ignored me previously, now gazed at me in interest. The others seemed to have taken note of the little swirl of attention around me and they all gradually stopped talking to perk their ears.

'She won England's highest prize for her age group,' Jack was saying.

'Oh yes, she's quite brilliant!' Rachel, of course.

Involuntarily my shoulders hunched and I kept my eyes fixed on my plate and on my knife and fork shoving the food around. I closed a door on the chatter; the butterflies returned to their flutter.

'Wunderkind.'

'. . . can't read notation . . .'

'. . . standing ovation!'

I longed to melt into a puddle that would slip down to the floor and trickle into the woodwork, vanishing without a trace, just as my music had done that morning.

'But that's marvellous!'

'She must . . .'

'Yes, this evening!'

'. . . play for us all!'

'Do you play?'

'As a child, I hated . . .'

'. . . actually, I'm tone deaf, but . . .'

'Tchaikovsky . . .'

'Oh, I adore his violin concerto.'

'But Vivaldi . . .'

'She can play anything. Anything! She only has to . . .'

'So amazing!'

'Tonight.'

'Yes, it must be tonight as we are going . . .'

And so, over my head and virtually behind my back, it was all arranged. I was to give an impromptu recital that evening. And I was the only one who knew that I could not do it; that I had lost the magic. For my own self-esteem I wanted to keep it that way for as long as possible. I could not risk discovery, but neither did I know how to refuse.

'Oh, please, please,' I prayed to whichever God had given me music, who held sway over the strings, 'please let it come back! Give me back my music!'

I felt eyes on me, and glanced up to the right. One of the Indians was looking at me with an interested expression. Not the same kind of overawed interest as the others; it was as if he alone saw my deep embarrassment, and that this, and not the talk of my prowess, interested him. Our eyes met. He smiled. I smiled back.

And then I murmured an excuse, pushed back my chair, picked up my dirty plate to bring it to the kitchen, and left the room.

Maybe it's not true. It was just this morning. I'll go to my room, have a rest, and later this afternoon it will be all right. I'll give the recital. I need it; I need to know I still have the magic! I have to do it! This is just a temporary thing. I'll get over it; the magic is still there. All I have to do is will it back.

But deep down inside I wasn't so sure any more.

The rot had set in.

It was as I had feared. The moment I picked up my bow and held it above the strings, it was as if something inside me froze. The music had vanished, and I had no means to call it forth. Where was it?

I stood there as if petrified, violin clamped under my chin, and I could not play a note. Not a single note. I had planned Mendelssohn's Violin Concerto but I could not recall a single note of it. Instead of the delicious music tumbling forth in a golden stream: sheer emptiness.

We were on the veranda of the main building; my audience sat cross-legged and eager on the floor before me, waiting. When nothing happened I could sense their impatience: the slight shuffling of bodies, an embarrassed cough, and the veiled exchange of worried glances. I could see it all on the periphery of my vision, but all I could do was stare at a single spot on the tiled floor, a tiny stain that was all I had to hold onto in this moment of undiluted panic.

'Jyothi?'

The voice penetrated the cloud of confusion surrounding my consciousness. I looked up and met Jack's anxious eyes.

'Yes?' My voice was small and hardly recognizable.

'Is something wrong, honey?'

'I . . . I . . . I'm not feeling too well . . . I'd better go and . . . lie down.'

My arm with the bow dropped. I carefully removed the violin from under my chin and held it uncertainly before me; what was I to do with this useless thing? Jack sprang to his feet and took it from me, passing it to Rachel who was herself attempting to rise, and put his arms around me to support me.

'It's all right, honey, come with me. I'll take you home.'

He glanced at the still seated audience; I saw his apologetic grin and cringed at the shame I had brought on him and Rachel.

'Sorry!' I heard him say. 'Another time, perhaps.'

But I knew there would never be another time.

Chapter 31

I hardly slept that night, and I woke up early next morning; it was still dark but there were sounds outside my open window that alerted me to the fact people were preparing for the new day. In the distance I heard the sound of temple bells, and footsteps walked past my room accompanied by the sort of creaking sound that comes from a swinging bucket: a pleasant and entirely comforting sound which reminded me of something I couldn't place.

I sat up and, stretched; it was hot and sticky in spite of the open window so I got up to turn on the overhead fan and to drink a glass of water from the flask on my table. I walked out onto the veranda and the air outside was fresh, as if carrying the vapour of the Ganges. I breathed deeply and rubbed my upper arms, then stretched again. For some reason I felt rejuvenated, as if the night had dissolved the humiliation of the previous evening and given me a whole new being. My music was gone. I had no idea what I would do without it; yet for some reason I did not care. I felt free, carefree, like the young girl that I was yet without the burden of fame and a golden future, as if the failure of yesterday had restored to me the power of the present moment, the magic of now.

I slipped on a shalwar kameez and left my room. I walked in the direction of the river. There were wide stone steps leading down to it and as I approached I saw that I was not the first, in spite of the early hour. Several Indians, men and women, were taking their baths. Some had descended to the lowest steps; one man had submerged himself entirely beneath the surface of the water. I had to hold my breath as I watched him, and was relieved as he very slowly rose again from the depths. A matronly woman whose sodden cotton sari clung to her like a second skin slowly poured a metal cup of water over her head; her eyes were closed and she was murmuring a prayer as she did so. A younger man seemed to be filling a row of plastic bottles with the holy water. And as I stood there the man with the buckets, now empty, returned and walked slowly down the steps to refill them. I sat down on one of the upper steps, my bare feet in the water, which lapped around my trouser hems and crept up the thin cotton to my knees. It was cool and deliciously fresh. Did the Ganges really possess divine powers? I had no idea; but at this moment I could believe it.

The pre-dawn sky was of a brilliant navy blue, still sprinkled with stars. Against a backdrop of silence the tinkling water sounds were like music; gentle soothing splashing noises as bodies rose from the river or sank into it, as vessels were filled or hands cupped to splash faces. I watched the ceremonies of ablution for some time; they imparted to me a deep sense of peace and belonging – as if I were part of an ancient rhythm beating an unseen and unacknowledged undercurrent to the world's pandemonium. I felt far removed from my life in England. It was as if it had never existed. My musical career was in shambles, but what had seemed like a major catastrophe yesterday was just a minor blip, no concern of mine. It was a feeling of reconnection . . . a realignment with something that always was and always had been, a silent river flowing steadily in the backdrop of my life. Through all the turbulence there had always been this silent current like a silver thread that had no end and no beginning, a lifeline that had always been mine yet hidden in the depths of my soul, not seen and not heard above the everyday fray; and now, with the peeling back of the outer layers that formed the crust of self, it was here again, revealed to me as my mainstay and my home.

I was aware of someone who had taken a seat beside me. I turned and recognized the Indian who had been at the dinner table last night. I recognized him furthermore as one of the men who had just emerged from the water after taking a bath. He was dry; I had not noticed but he must have walked up the steps, dried himself, put on some fresh clothes, and returned to sit beside me. I smiled, and through the pre-dawn light I saw that he smiled back. Up to now none of the bathers had spoken a word and I had assumed that silence was prescribed for this time but my companion said, 'Good morning.'

I returned the greeting. Our words were barely whispered, yet still they seemed incongruous, like the noisy clanging of a cymbal at a moment of piety. He must have realized this too, for he said no more.

We sat in silence for some five minutes. Dawn's approach was now imminent; I felt rather than heard him rise to his feet, and turned to look at him. He gestured with his hand, signalling for me to follow him. We walked away from the ghat.

When we were a few paces away he spoke again. 'Would you like to come with me to hear some music?'

'Music? Now?' I was faintly surprised; it wasn't a question I had been prepared for. But in fact I was not prepared for any question. My mind seemed to be free of any sort of expectation whatsoever. He could have said, 'Would you like to come with me to climb Everest?' My reaction would have been similar. Time and place seemed to have met at a point where anything could happen; certainly, I was in a state of mind where the future seems disconnected from present and past, poised to take a fresh and unanticipated turn. And I myself was ready. Before he could answer my question I hastened to answer it myself with a quick, 'Yes. Where?'

I was in the mood for music. My mind had been made receptive by the silvery flowing of the river, as if the current had swept away the sediments of care and long-ingrained sadness, and made of me an open vessel. He said nothing but smiled at me, gestured to me to follow, and quickened his pace.

I followed. We left the ashram compound and walked down a small path between the trees of a thinly planted wood. A small herd of sheep driven by a boy of about ten trotted towards us and parted to flow around us; even the cacophony of their forlorn bleating did not jar on the atmosphere of bucolic early morning peace, but completed it. They swept past and I was alone with my companion. The thought came to me: What on earth are you doing? Following a strange man, a man you've hardly spoken a word to, into a lonely wood! Yet the very idea that his intentions could be malevolent was immediately rejected by overwhelming peace and a sense of *rightness* ... as if I were at one with myself, and anything that now happened was all a part of that oneness, and thus no evil could befall me.

We walked for some ten minutes, without speaking; silence the obvious and purest medium for communication. Morning was by now fast approaching, heralded by the flutter of unseen birds in the trees above us and the grey light that filtered through the filigree of leaves overhead. Sunlight itself, I assumed, would be late to reach us as the mountains on either side of the valley would delay the sunrise, but the half-light that surrounded us tingled with the miracle of a new day. There was a nip in the air and I hugged myself, drawing the shawl of my shalwar kameez tightly around my shoulders.

Our pace was brisk, and soon we arrived at a one-storey cottage set back between the trees, surrounded by a rudimentary hedge made of thorny branches stuck between rows of wire. It had a thatched roof; its front door was painted bright green and approached by a wide low front veranda. The man – it was now that I realized I didn't even know his name – held open a small gate in the fence for me and closed it as I passed by.

I waited for him and together we walked down the short path – nothing but a well-trodden trail across a sandy patch before the house – crossed the veranda, and stood at the door. He knocked once and entered without waiting for a summons.

It was darker inside the cottage than outside. It took my eyes some time to adjust to the dimness, and as they were immediately drawn to the flickering flame of a candle at the back of the room I did not see the dark figure sitting in the shadows of one corner. It was only when the figure spoke that I turned sharply and saw the man with the sitar.

He sat cross-legged and as still as a statue, and he spoke only one word: 'Rabin!' It was a statement, not a question.

'Yes,' said my companion in English, and added a few words in Hindi. He repeated the words in English. 'I have brought a friend. She speaks English.'

I felt compelled to speak; the words came unasked from me. 'I speak Hindi too!' I said, in that language. Both men smiled.

'Ah. I see her now. A young lady. Let her come forward; sit down, sit down, my dear. Any friend of Rabin's is a friend of mine.

'Do you like music? Did you come to listen?'

I wanted to speak but could not. I nodded, and he seemed not a bit perturbed by my apparent rudeness, but then, he probably didn't consider it rudeness. I had already grasped the fact that in India silence between people is not the social faux pas it is in the West, and carries neither the same weight of embarrassment nor the crushing obligation to break it at any cost. Indeed, it seemed to me that to lurch into a torrent of small talk at this moment would be not only inappropriate but highly discourteous; as it was I felt like a bull in a china shop, inept and clumsy with my careering thoughts. The contemplative mood which had been with me since awakening had fled the moment I walked in the door, as if an invisible Godzilla had taken my mind in its hands and given it a robust shake, so that its entire contents scuttled like millions of ants in as many directions.

I could not see him clearly. In the flickering glow of candle-light I could barely make out his silhouette; but I could see that he wore a white cloth around his hips and another around his shoulders, and I could make out a long thin beard. His skin was dark, but I could see the whites of his eyes shining through the darkness and knew he was looking at me. The thought made me tremble; I felt he could see all of me, every thought I had ever had, every nuance of feeling I had ever known. One part of me wanted to flee and the other wanted . . . the opposite. To open the Pandora's Box of my soul and lay it all before him, as if in doing so I would at last find the ease and the solace and the sense of homecoming that had eluded me all my conscious life. I felt tears budding in my eyes.

The burning incense spread fragrance into every last crevice of space, and with every in-breath its enchantment became a part of me, and I too felt like dissolving into the air, ethereal and finally free. I was aware of my friend, the man called Rabin, sitting at my side, but only vaguely for all my attention was absorbed by the still dark figure in the shadows before me.

I don't know how long we sat that way; Rabin and I cross-legged on the straw mat in the middle of the room, the other unmoving in the corner, vague in form but so palpable in spirit. Sometimes my eyes were closed, at other times they opened involuntarily to gaze and then to close again.

I only felt a stream of tears along my cheeks. I did nothing to wipe them away; they seemed only right and proper, and they carried with them the entire turmoil that had so suddenly risen in me on entering this room, and just as suddenly dissolved. Everything was right. I was at peace and complete, and there was nothing more I needed but this living moment.

At some point the man in the shadows – I still did not know his name but all names by now were superfluous – must have taken up the sitar and laid it across his thighs, for I heard a first tentative sound, just one plucked string but it reverberated for an eternity and I thought my hair would stand on end; it was as if every cell of my body was filled with the echo of that one sound so perfect it could only have originated in heaven.

He began to play.

My body no longer existed, not as physical mass. It was created of sound, a delicious stream that dissolved the boundaries between body, mind and soul. This was me. This was all I was and all I would ever be and all I ever wanted to be. Life was nothing but glorious sound and now it had found me there could be no letting go. Such exquisite beauty was the culmination of every desire that had ever groped and scratched within me, craving fulfilment and always starved of it.

The music rippled on. Sometimes I opened my eyes to gaze at the musician, and watched his long graceful fingers as they glided over the strings of the instrument, moving as if guided by a divine puppeteer. How long did he play? I have no idea.

I only know that suddenly it was over, and again I possessed a body of flesh and blood, sitting on a straw mat in a dark little cottage.

We sat in silence for about ten minutes in which I made new acquaintance with myself and with all the rearrangements that had taken place inside me on this strangest of mornings. After a while the first pangs of hunger, which had been held at bay by sheer wonder, made themselves known, and I shifted my legs and leaned forward to massage the slight cramp out of my left calf. As if he could read my mind the musician, who had set aside his instrument and now made the motions of rising, said, 'You have not had breakfast I think. Can I offer you some tea and biscuits?'

Rabin glanced at me; I nodded, and he said yes for both of us. The musician left the room through a doorway that must have led into the kitchen, for I heard the sounds of a match being scratched and the splash of running water, then the clatter of crockery and the chink of spoons. Rabin got up and joined him in the kitchen and a few minutes later reappeared with a tray on which stood two cups and saucers, a jug of milky tea and a plate of Milk Bikis. The musician did not join us again; he seemed to have left the house. Rabin and I partook of this simple breakfast – which was as delicious as a feast – in silence; the music still reverberated within me and I had no need of speech. When we had finished we both stood up. Together we washed and dried the wares.

Rabin said to me, 'Let's go.' There was no need to say goodbye to our host; he had vanished without a trace.

On the way home I could hardly walk straight. A kind of intoxication overcame me: my feet wanted to dance rather than walk, as if infected with the joy that tingled all up and down my spine. I was aglow with it, a huge grin spread across my face, and it was all I could do to contain it and not grab hold of Rabin and dance a mad polka down the forest lane. Something told me that Rabin was not the type for polkas, but I longed to fling my arms around him and embrace him for what he had done: brought me to this magic place, this magic person, this magic music. The music was over but its rush was still with me, as love that welled up in me, up and up, and I longed to embrace all the world. Nothing at all like the love I had for Dean but rounder and fuller and freer, and so full of gladness I could burst.

The path was too narrow to walk side by side. On the way there he had led the way but now I was in front, and I wondered: did he notice the lightness of my steps? The swaying motion of my body as it tried not to dance? When I lifted my arms as if they were wings – oh, how I longed to fly – did he think I was mad? But then, what did it matter! I *was* mad, mad with elation! And I had a right to be mad. I had found IT!

IT: the elusive something I had been looking for all my life. No wonder my music, so gratifying to others, had been, to me, so unfulfilling, so unfulfilled! I had not yet known IT: the central element, this joy that was the essence and the goal and the source of all music; without which all music was but a series of notes. All my life, I saw now, I had been trying to find this joy in my music, and always I had failed. And now it was in me and I knew I could do it: play out of this joy, let it flow into my music, let it dance through my fingers.

Yet there was one other thing, a tiny little issue compared to this new knowledge. A thing I would have to deal with later; perhaps when I returned to England.

I had been playing the wrong instrument. I wanted a sitar.

I put away the thought the moment it came as I sensed it spelled Trouble and I would not let Trouble spoil the Now. So it was a welcome distraction when the path widened and Rabin quickened his pace to walk beside me. I turned to look at him and the smile that lit my face was the warmest I had ever given anyone in all my life. He returned the smile, but said nothing, and we walked on in silence as we had done earlier that morning.

By now the day had properly broken, and the sun had climbed high enough to peek into the valley. The rays of light that slanted through the foliage above us etched a filigree pattern of light and shadow on the sandy lane at our feet; tiny drops of dew pearled on every single leaf and blade of grass that bordered our path. I felt as if we were walking through paradise. One of our school hymns, 'Morning had Broken', came into my mind; I felt like bursting into song and could barely keep back the joyous words:

> *Praise for the singing!*
> *Praise for the morning!* . . .
> *God's recreation*
> *Of the new day!*

I think I would have taken his hand if I were not so shy and if this had not been India, where such things are not done.

Certainly, he did not seem a stranger to me. I felt as if I had known him all my life, as if he were a twin soul, though we had exchanged little more than a sentence or two. As I glanced at him again he even seemed physically familiar. His looks only confirmed my feeling of inner rightness, for his eyes and smile were warm and welcoming – like those of a long-lost brother. His age was hard to guess, but I placed him in his early twenties, with thick black hair so long he wore it tucked behind his ears. He was of medium height and lean, and he walked with a buoyant swing and tell-tale languid grace – music was in him, as it was in me. I should have seen that right away. Perhaps he had recognized it in me, last night at dinner; I certainly had been too lost in muddied self-pity to recognize it in him but the talk had been of my music and that had given him the clue. Which was why he had addressed me this morning. Had he been at the aborted recital last night? Had he seen my shame? I couldn't remember. For just one second the thought that he had been a witness to my failure embarrassed me, but only one second for between friends there is no such thing as shame. I knew I had to speak.

'Thank you so much for bringing me there!' I said, in English this time. 'It was – out of this world. But you know that.'

'I knew you'd like it,' he said. 'Swami is a very gifted musician. It's a great privilege to listen to him.'

'Can I go with you again? The next time you go?'

'Well . . . I won't be going back,' he said. 'Not this time. I'm leaving this afternoon, you see. I'm returning to Delhi – that's where I study music. I've been in Rishikesh for two weeks and this is my last day.'

I couldn't keep the disappointment out of my voice.

'You're leaving . . . but . . . oh, what a shame.'

'But you can visit him by yourself. Why not? I am sure he would not mind. He will know how the music affected you.'

'But I couldn't! I wouldn't like to barge in on him . . . disturb him . . . I can't just . . .'

'It's all right. He won't mind, I promise you. His doors are always open. Not many people know about him – if they did his room would be full all day, I'm sure. He likes his seclusion but he is not at all hostile towards visitors, as long as they are quiet. Why don't you just drop by? This evening or tomorrow, or whenever you feel like it.'

'I would feel like an intruder. I don't even know his name!'

'Swami Satyananda. And you are not an intruder. Take my word for it. I think you could learn a great deal from him.'

I nodded in acquiescence. 'I can hardly put it into words . . . I never knew music could be like that. You know I play the violin?'

It was a statement more than a question. I glanced at him to gauge his reaction.

He nodded. 'Yes. I couldn't resist coming to your little recital last night!'

'Oh! I . . .'

'It's all right, no need to make excuses! There was some commotion going on inside you and you could not play. The atmosphere was not conducive anyway. Music should not be put on display like a prize cow.'

'Oh,' I repeated. I could think of nothing else to say. All my life I had been putting music on display like a prize cow.

There was a moment of silence, and then I whispered, 'How, then?'

'How then what?'

'If we are not to display music then what? Should a musician just play for himself, like Swami? Never for an audience?'

'No,' said Rabin. 'Beautiful music is to be shared. It is perfect communication, as you felt with Swami this morning. The error comes from drawing from the music, instead of giving to it.'

'I don't understand.'

'It's simple. If you use music to enhance yourself: if you use it to build up your notion of who you are; if you suck on it like a parasite, using it for your own fame and glory: that is drawing from it.'

The elation that had been buoying me up seemed suddenly to have a puncture; my feet touched ground. I wanted to hear more but a vague sense of guilt kept me from asking. Was he talking specifically about me? It felt like it.

'For music to live the musician must give him- or herself

entirely into it and merge with it. If you take from the music, on the other hand, you are trying to become great *through* the music. You are using it to enhance your ego, to gain the applause of the world. Not the music, but *you* are the focus of your playing. And as a result the music is dead. Stillborn.'

'But how can I . . . I don't know how!'

We had reached the gates of the compound and turned in. Slowly we walked down the path towards my cottage, engrossed in our talk.

'The true musician is humble,' said Rabin. 'His ego has dissolved in the music. His life-force lives in the music and so the music can live. In India you will find most of the great artists of the past were anonymous – that is as it should be. The less there is of the artist, the greater the art.'

'Oh!' My third exclamation was one of shock, for what he was saying was revolutionary: destroying every notion Monika, and every audience I had ever had, had planted in my brain. 'But then . . .'

'You are afraid that when you dissolve you will be a nothing, but no. You will not be a nothing. You will be filled with the ineffable grandeur of your music. Just as you live in it, so it will live in you. You will grow into the full beauty of who you really are – just as Swami did. This is Swami's teaching to me and it is what I am trying to live in my own life.'

We had reached the steps leading up to the veranda of my cottage. Rabin stopped and turned to face me. The blacks of his eyes shone with an inner fire, and his expression was serious and all the joy of that dawn was gone.

'Jyothi!' he said urgently. 'Yes, I know your name is Jyothi – light. You must let music be your light! That is the only way! I can tell that music is your being but it is trapped inside you like a bird desperate to escape from a golden cage. The golden cage is your mastery of your trade. Yes, I heard them talking about you, about how brilliantly you play your instrument. But believe me, that is not all! You can be the most skilled violinist in your country without being a true musician. A musician is a different being altogether; a musician is divine – because music is divine. If you subjugate your music to your ego you cease to let it live and it is a dead thing – a caged bird denied free flight. You may impress crowds with your expertise – for they see the gold of the cage and the beauty of the bird – but if your music does not live you will be forever miserable, because you know you have killed the inner fire that elevates it from a craft to an art, from mortal expertise to a divine gift. Jyothi, I have not yet heard you play but I saw, I felt, that you too are a musician. I beg of you: go to Swami. He can show you the way. Go to him every day as long as you are here and learn to access your own divinity!'

Up to now I had felt defeated, a sham of a musician. But at these last words I felt the straightening of my back and the lift to my shoulders and a quickening of my spirit, and I looked him in the eyes and I said, 'I will, Rabin! I promise!'

I did not know it yet but at that very moment capricious Fate, skipping along behind me with mischief in her mind, decided that this was enough nonsense for one day. I worked it out later: it must have been at this very moment that Dean, on a sheer rock face not too distant from here, slipped, and fell five metres. I know this because it was now precisely eight o'clock and a bell pealed out calling the devoted to morning puja. The time of Dean's fall, as recorded.

Oblivious to Fate's invisible games, I had eyes and ears only for Rabin. 'Would you give me your address?' I said. It was so clear to me that Rabin was the one who would open up a whole new universe of music for me. My life was about to surge forward in an entirely new direction and Rabin would show the way; I was overwhelmed with gratitude.

Rabin smiled. 'Of course!' he said. 'We should certainly keep in contact. I would stay another day, if it were not for . . . Listen: I don't want to be late for puja, and then I am going to see a friend in Rishikesh. I will see you later. I also have to pack and leave for Hardwar. I'm travelling on the Rajdhani Express this afternoon; I'll see you after lunch. Is that all right?'

I nodded enthusiastically. But Fate was already knocking at my door, in a few hours she would be wiping the smile of joy from my face and all the gladness from my heart.

Chapter 32

The news of Dean's accident reached us just before lunch. Dean's mother put through a call to the ashram office and, because it was so urgent, Rachel was called out of her yoga class to take it. Dean was to be flown by helicopter to Delhi, and we were all to return post haste. Dean had a broken arm, broken leg, broken ribs and head injuries; he was still unconscious. We would learn the worst when the Delhi doctors – the best – had seen him.

Dean's mother had given Rachel a garbled report which reduced to frenzied cries of 'Hurry, hurry, hurry back, he might die before you come!' This solitary account of Dean's state would have to carry us for the entire nine-hour drive to the capital.

There is nothing as debilitating as uncertainty. If Dean had been killed outright it would have been horrendous. But the dread of *not knowing* – amplified by the frustration of a never-ending taxi drive – was simply unbearable. Delays that in the course of a normal drive would have been amusing episodes, worthy of a photograph, turned into crises of devastating magnitude, driving us all to the far edge of anguish. In the first village we were intercepted by a herd of cows that leisurely meandered forward and swarmed around the taxi for a dawdling eternity. Several villages later, school had just finished and as we drove by hordes of barefooted uniformed children, bulging satchels bouncing at their sides and on their backs, rushed into the street in gay abandon and, seeing us, peered laughingly into the taxi windows and tried out their few words of English. 'Good morning, meesta! Pen, pen, pen giving! How do you do! Where do you come from!' On the level stretches of road there was no question of racing as the potholes needed to be circumvented. At every single level crossing the light turned red in the minute before our arrival. This must have been a deliberate ploy of Fate. One red light might have been normal, two coincidence, but *three*! In each case it involved a wait of at least half an hour, then a thirty-second rush as the train sped by, followed by another fifteen minutes till the gate opened.

We arrived in Delhi in the middle of the worst rush hour, which lasts until deep into the night – or so it seemed to me that night. Total gridlock or stop-and-go traffic until the last few blocks before the hospital. It was the longest day of my life: starting in elation, and ending in agonizing fear.

Not once in all the long hours since I heard of Dean's accident did I think of the magnificent morning, of Rabin, or of music. Not for one second. It might never have been, so traceless was its erasure from my mind. The light and the insight that had seemed so indelible had been wiped out in an instant and I did not care. Nor did I regret it. All that I had ever felt for Dean overwhelmed me and left me floundering in misery. Dean was my hero, my brother, my best friend. He had encouraged me, pushed me forward, and allowed me to lean on him when I thought I could not walk myself. Though I knew my adoration was one-sided it had never lapsed; in the last months it had merely receded. Dean's social life had taken him ever more out of my reach and I had developed what adults describe as a realistic approach towards him: knowing he could never be mine and would never look on me as other than a little sister, I had humbly accepted a secondary role on his life, successfully fought my jealousy, and concentrated on another love which promised more than Dean ever could – my music.

But now Dean might be dying. The very idea filled me with dread. My love for him surged forward, driving every other thought from my mind except the fervent prayer to the powers that be: 'Oh, let him live! Oh dear God, oh sweet Lord, please let him live! I will do anything you want but *let him live!*'

I had already lost two mothers whom I had loved to death. To lose Dean would be the end.

The next morning the telephone rang and Jack was there in a second. It was Rachel; she and Soona had spent the night in the hospital. Dean had been operated on the night before, but could not immediately be declared out of danger. The nurses had tried to send them home but they had both adamantly refused to leave until they had news, one way or the other.

I watched Jack's face with bated breath; concentrating on the vow I had taken that if only Dean lived I would never again be unfaithful to him.

All night I had been unable to sleep; my thoughts had spun out of control and woven the most intricate web of causality so that in the end I had convinced myself that I alone was responsible for his accident and – unless I recanted one hundred per cent – for his death.

I had been unfaithful to him! Only in thought, it is true,

but I had to admit it. That damned Rabin had taken possession of me for one whole morning, and Dean's soul, so closely connected to my own – *Dean*, not Rabin, was my twin soul! How could I have ever thought otherwise! – had felt it, and that disloyalty had catapulted him from the rock face. I thought along these lines for so long that I finally convinced myself that this must be it. My love for Dean might be hidden but his soul surely *knew*, somewhere deep inside! And it had felt my betrayal! And if Dean's soul could react to a spiritual adultery with such vehemence, that must mean that it was waiting for me . . . that Dean was waiting for me . . . that all I had to do was love him with all the power of my heart and my mind and my soul; and that would bring him through. So I stayed awake and concentrated on loving him that night, and in the morning I knew that my vigil had worked because I saw immediately from the way Jack looked at me with a huge smile that Dean would live. I cried my heart out with gratitude.

Dean was in Delhi's best hospital, in the hands of Delhi's best doctor – a friend of his stepfather – and would remain there to convalesce for several weeks. I was allowed to visit him once before we left, in the second week after the accident; when I saw his familiar schoolboyish mischievous grin I melted, sank into the chair next to his bed, and took his hand.

'Hey, Jyothi, why the tears? I'm fine!'

'I know, but – but – oh Dean, I can't tell you how happy I am to see you! I never knew . . .'

He placed a hand on my head and rumpled my hair in the fond brotherly way he always did. His touch – so real, so palpable – brought tears to my eyes. I didn't want him to see me cry so I turned away, but he had seen and he wiped them away with a corner of the sheet.

'Come here, you!' he said. He had been half sitting, resting back against a puffed-up pillow on the raised backrest, but now he leaned forward, put an arm around me, drew me to him and gave me a long hug. He had never done that before. I was delirious with happiness; I closed my eyes the better to savour the moment, to make it last for ever.

Then it was over, and Dean was back against the pillow. His head was encased in a bandage, and his left arm was still in a cast, as well as his left leg. He had never looked so much the hero.

I didn't know what to say but Dean spoke for me. 'I feel terrible about cutting short your holiday in Rishikesh,' he said. 'I was a damned fool.'

'No, no. It doesn't matter. It was more Jack and Rachel that wanted to be there, not me. I'd have liked to go climbing with you.

'You would? Really?'

I nodded. That was another conclusion I had made last night. If I loved Dean I would have to share his life, his interests – men liked that, and expected it. It had been wrong to try to woo him with my music. Instead I had to follow in his footsteps. If I could just prove my willingness to do that for him, maybe next year he would let me go with him into the mountains. Maybe he would teach me to climb. Maybe he would notice me . . . and no longer as a sister. Next year I would be fifteen. That seemed incredibly grown up. At that age Dean could surely see me as a woman! Perhaps . . .

'Perhaps Jack would let you come with me next year. That'd be great. You'd love it!'

'I wouldn't want to cramp your style . . .'

'No, to tell you the truth I'd enjoy teaching you a thing or two. And . . . well . . . I promised Mum and Rachel that I won't do any dangerous climbing again – for a while. They think I'm a little boy . . . but maybe it's wise. Maybe I tend to overestimate

292

my abilities. Maybe it would be better to slow down a bit. I got some great photos, though! Look, I'll show them to you . . .'

He turned to the bedside table at his other side, his face scrunching with pain at the effort, and removed a yellow Kodak envelope from the drawer. He showed me the photos of fantastic snow-capped mountains but I was hardly looking; I was listening to the cadence of his voice and looking at his long supple hands and dedicating my entire being to loving him, and him alone, for the rest of my life.

Chapter 33

Jack and I returned to England without Rachel and Dean. Once back home I had a huge mountain to climb. I had to lift my violin again; raise it to my chin; take the bow in my hand; and see what would happen. Would my music return to me, or was it gone for ever? I was terrified of that moment and delayed it for as long as I could.

Sometimes the memory came unbidden to my mind: of standing there before that small but eager audience when the music refused to flow. That's the difference between being a musician who plays by ear and one who reads the written notes: at a moment such as that there is no guideline to conduct you further. I cringed at that memory. And merely to think 'violin' brought it all back: the failure, the shame, the fear of a repeat.

Then there was another memory, a far more dangerous one, hovering at the periphery of my awareness like a delicious dream you can only half remember and yearn to summon but when you do, refuses your invitation, as stubborn as a shy child.

In my heart I knew that that child, once summoned and given the freedom to play, would become a goddess, glorious, powerful, shining. And I feared she might destroy all that I had built for myself, destroy me entirely. I knew that the child was shy only because I refused to summon it with the love it needed to grow.

I stood between fears: the fear of a failure too crushing to contemplate, and the fear of a beauty too dazzling to behold.

Once Jack and I returned to England I did not remove my violin from its case for a week. At first Jack didn't notice. But then: 'I haven't heard you practise for some time, Jyothi,' he said casually one morning as we took Sheba for her walk. 'In fact, not since we were in India. You'd better start again soon – you shouldn't let it lapse for so long. Professional violinists have to practise every day. But you know that. And don't you have a concert coming up soon?'

That was the way Jack said things: diplomatically, always considerate of feelings that might be hurt, giving you the chance to back off. Monika had been the opposite. Monika would have noticed the second day, given me one of her stern, eyebrows-pulled-together glares and said in a tone that brooked no contradiction: 'Jyothi, it's time for practice!'

Sometimes I needed Monika's blunt approach. Someone to stick my nose in the mess of my cowardice and say: Get on with it and make your decision. Life is too short for dithering.

But I welcomed Jack's question for it gave me the chance finally to talk about what had happened. And Jack and I had not talked seriously for an eternity – not since before Monika's death, for Rachel had usurped all his attention. Now at last I had him to myself. The opportunity was not to be wasted on the small talk which was all that was left of our relationship.

'The thing is,' I began slowly, 'I've been thinking . . .'

'Yes? Sheba, come here! Leave those sheep alone! Sheba!'

It took at least five minutes to rescue Sheba from the sheep; Sheba was drawn to them by some irresistible urge – Rachel always said she must have a sheepdog ancestor, some gene that never failed to catapult her full-tilt in the direction of a flock of sheep, scattering them like ants.

When Sheba had been successfully leashed Jack picked up the threads of our discussion.

'Yes, you were saying . . . Um, what were you saying? Ah, yes. About your violin practice. Remember you've got that concert coming up. I don't think I've heard you practising. You shouldn't slacken off, you know.'

'I know,' I said. 'The thing is . . .'

'When I was your age I had to. My dad forced me to. You know I'm not the type to force but I must say daily practice honed my skills. I had the talent, just like you, but it's the practice that really makes perfect. But you know that. I know you'll get back to it when you feel like it.'

'No,' I said.

'No? What do you mean, no?'

'I mean, I don't know if my gift is really for the violin,' I said. It was time to grab the bull by the horns; I simply could no longer stand being torn in two.

That brought Jack up short; we both stopped walking and looked at each other from either side of the grassy lane. Sheba tugged at the leash, trying to return to the sheep, but then gave up and began digging furiously at a rabbit hole.

There: I'd said it. I'd formulated the thing into words and spoken them, and somebody, Jack, had heard. Whatever came now would be fate; would have to be fate. I was incapable of making a decision.

Jack's brow was wrinkled with concern; the expression in his eyes was of bewilderment. 'Not the violin? But of course it is! If not the violin, then what?'

'When I was in India,' I said slowly and softly, 'the second day in Rishikesh – you remember, the day after . . . that recital?'

Jack's face lightened immediately. 'Ahhh, the botched recital – I'd completely forgotten. Look, if that's what's preying on your mind, just forget it. It must have been a shock for you at the time but it's nothing to be concerned about. It's like my occasional bouts of writer's block, just more public. You simply had an attack of nerves. It's never happened before and it won't happen again and there's no need at all for you to think—'

The glory of that morning came back to me; as if in simply speaking of it I had opened the door to that shy little girl and let her in, and even as I talked I could feel her blossoming into her full glory, feel the delicious warmth as I drew her to me and let her be mine . . . be me. Jack would understand. He would *have* to.

Jack didn't understand. He let me ramble on for a while about my feelings and my joy and how much I longed to play that way; he listened, just as a good father should, and let me have my say. And then, just as a good father should, he put an end to my dithering, and brought me down from my fuzzy-edged cloud with a few short, sharp words. There were times when Jack knew what he wanted and that was not a Jack to contend with.

'There's no question of you changing to the sitar,' he said, and that was the end of it. The end of my dithering, and the end of my vision.

I have to say this for Jack: when he means business he's as tough as nails. And, yes, I needed that. The Monika touch . . . perhaps he had learned it from her. The very tone of his voice withered the goddess and drove the shy little girl back out into the darkness, where she crouched low, drew her rags about her, and buried her face in her elbow. Another girl took her place.

'You can have a sitar – learn to play it as a hobby. But the violin is your instrument. Jyothi, when you play you are a queen! You are a magician, weaving a magic spell. We all know that. A gift like that should not be wasted, and in your case especially not.'

'In my case?'

'It's the raft that is carrying you through school,' Jack said, not noticing how cruel those words were, or the ones that followed them. 'We live in a world where education is everything. That's a simple fact of life, like it or not. Not being a scholar, you'd have been doomed to failure if it weren't for your music. You've got GCSE exams in a couple at years – how many passes do you think you'll get? How many grades above a C? Music will be your only A. And it's the same for your A levels. Do you think you'd even have a *chance* at A levels it weren't for music? And when I say music, I mean violin. Not sitar. We just happen to live in Europe and you can't escape from reality by wandering off into some pleasant dream of sitar-strumming in the Himalayas with some bearded master!

'This great talent, this wonderful gift, has been thrown into your lap. You can't even *think* of ditching it in favour of some half-baked pipe-dream!'

I stood before him with hanging head, silenced and mortified.

Jack noticed my chagrin; it calmed him down. He took my hands in his. 'Jyothi, you're great. You are going to be even greater. There's no question. I know what brought this on: that damned recital. We should never have even thought of it – but we couldn't know. It gave you doubts about yourself, and your ability. That's why you were so taken with this sitar thing. But listen, your talent is beyond words and you should not let one little mishap like that throw you off course. Come. We're going home now. And you're going to play for me. Play for me as never before.'

He felt my shock because he gripped my hands even tighter. 'Don't be afraid. It's going to work. What were you going to play that evening?'

A still small voice said, 'Mendelssohn's Concerto. Dean's favourite.'

'Then that's what you'll play for me now. Let's go home. Come, Sheba.'

We returned home; reluctance dragged at my feet. Jack led the way up the stairs; I led the way into my room. I stood before the table where my violin lay. I opened the case, lifted it gingerly, tenderly stroked its glossy wood. Jack watched, a smile playing on his lips as I looked up to him for encouragement. I smiled back; tuned my instrument.

I placed it under my chin, held the bow poised in position. Closed my eyes and spoke a small prayer. And played.

Not Mendelssohn's violin concerto: Tchaikovsky's. I don't know who made the last-minute decision. It wasn't me.

I played as never before. The music took hold of me. I was possessed by it and played as one possessed, with all the elation, the dread, the questions, the longing, and, yes, the rage at a fate that had placed me between two alternatives, both so glorious that to relinquish one would tear me apart. Rebellion rose up in me and translated itself into pure musical passion that coursed through my body and into the instrument and out again in a glorious fountain of pure expression.

At the end of it I replaced my violin carefully in its case. I sat down on the edge of my bed savouring the silence that had descended on the room, for Jack had neither applauded nor spoken a word. Jack sat down beside me. He placed an arm around me and drew me close to him and for a while we sat together in the darkness. There was really nothing left to say and we both knew it, and we both knew that the other knew it. Finally Jack stood up and silently as a cat left the room, closing the door behind him.

That's when it overcame me. I threw myself down onto my pillow and cried for everything exquisite in life that I had lost, and everything exquisite that had been given to me.

Finally there was no decision to make. It had been made for me. Perhaps it had been made for me long before my birth. The episode in India belonged in the unwritten mythology of my life; the future that might have happened, but never would. The door closed on the shy little girl for ever.

I stood up then, and placed a Music Minus One cassette in the player. I was overwhelmed by sadness and a sweet nostalgia for something that could never be. Only Beethoven could echo that mood; his 'Romance in F'. As I played, silent tears ran down my cheeks, because I had to face the truth, heartbreaking and glorious at once.

I was a violinist.

Part Four

'The goal and final purpose of all music should be, for none other than, the glory and praise of God.'

J.S. BACH

Chapter 34

I was a violinist.

Once I had made that decision the rest was easy. Over the next ten years the world would discover what I already knew. It was as if, in burying the sitar for ever in the past, the violinist in me grew new muscles, and new determination. New ambition. When I first started playing I had done it for Monika. Then I had played for Dean. Now, for the first time, I played for myself.

So much happened in those ten years; and yet they can be covered with so few words.

It began with the concert at Wigmore Hall. The following Saturday Jack woke me up waving a newspaper at me in triumph. 'Read this!' is all he said. I read the review:

> . . . Jyothi Keller is a musician to watch: she combines impeccable technique with music that flows as naturally from her as breathing, music that soars and shimmers with intensity, warmth, and even a touch of the divine. She

combines the spontaneity, romantic fervour, passion and exuberance of youth with a remarkably mature reflection and serenity. While her virtuosity astonishes, Keller expresses herself with great charm, and without a trace of sentimentality; her musical sensitivity is sincere and totally lacking in external flamboyance.

The following weekend there was another concert, a small one in the school gymnasium. At the end of it I was approached by a certain Mr Adrian Harvey. Mr Harvey, after reading the review, had contacted my violin teacher, whom he knew, and who had invited him without my knowledge.

Mr Harvey was an agent. He spoke to me, and to Jack, and my future was decided. I was to have a solo career, and that career would be shaped and moulded by Mr Harvey. I was to have the best: the best teacher, who happened to live in Berlin; I was to fly to Berlin once a month for my violin lesson with him. And the best violin, a Stradivarius, financed by a bank. I sailed through school on the wings of music. The rest would be arranged by Mr Harvey. I had been Discovered.

Mr Harvey wanted me to leave school at the end of my GCSEs but Jack put his foot down there; he wanted me to get the most out of a conventional education just in case, and so I moved on to the sixth form. Of course even then my subjects were tailored to my talents and my abilities. I took Theatre Studies and Home Economics as well as Music, but everyone knew where I was heading and nobody cared about the two extra subjects.

Of course, before I took A level Music I had to learn to read music and that was a bit of a bother; also, my music teacher in Berlin insisted that I make the effort. However, I learned the trick by playing what I knew and at the same time following the written music, and thus I was able to imprint the meaning of the notes on my mind. I've heard of children teaching themselves to read by following the words of a story they know by heart in a book; that's how it was with me.

I was accepted into the Royal College of Music, but Mr Harvey had other, more ambitious plans for me and this time Jack did not object.

The sound of applause became a second music to my ears, and always I could imagine Monika there in the front room, clapping furiously, her eyes moist, fighting against the urge to give in to tears of pride. I could see Dean, gazing at me with adoration in his eyes. I swelled with pride; now at last I understood the meaning of the word. I was heading straight for the stars. Monika had done it; Dean had done it; I had done it.

Jack and Rachel were duly proud of me and all I had achieved at such a young age, and in fact instead of Monika it was they sitting in the audience and leading the standing ovations, and the calls for encore! I loved those curtain calls. I loved my audiences; what a thrill to step out there and hear the roar, as of a great ocean, and all for my benefit!

My agent had decided that the name Jyothi was rather unsuitable for the career he had planned for me, too unwieldy, too foreign. I changed it to Jade. Jade Keller had a touch of the exotic, yet was not too outlandish, easy to pronounce and to remember.

I had grown out of my silly resentment of Rachel, and my jealousy. If one had music, where is resentment, where jealousy? I had all that I could ever have dreamed of. Who would have thought that a little girl from the Bombay streets could rise to such heights? The media made much of my background, of course, just as they had done in Germany. It was a classic 'rags to riches' story, and I never failed, when driving in my chauffer-driven limousine from some concert hall in Paris or Prague back to my luxury hotel, to look out of the window at some of the miserable creatures I shared the planet with and think, There but for the grace of God go I. And sometimes I thought, Why me? and gave thanks for the fate that had led Jack and Monika to the Hotel Sahil so long ago.

But then again, I reasoned, I had reached this place by my own hard work. I had in fact dragged myself up by my own fingertips. Luck, or coincidence, or karma may have played a role in the first instance but had I not made every effort to triumph over the overwhelming difficulties that had surrounded me from the moment I set foot in the West? I certainly had every right to be proud of myself. And even those events that had seemed so tragic when they happened had all turned out for the better – even Monika's death, so shattering at the time, had triggered my coming to England, where I had progressed so startlingly

Jack and Rachel were happy; they were made for each other and it was hard to imagine how Jack had ever found his way into Monika's life. (But if he hadn't, where would I be now?) They were so well suited: both writers, of different yet complementary temperaments. Jack continued to write his reviews, but now that he lived in England there were more books at his fingertips and his own career began to take off. Rachel, in the meantime, continued as a journalist and travelled abroad several times a year, leaving Jack in charge. She and I would never be close, but she was good enough as a stepmother.

Jack was less enthusiastic about my success than I had expected; he thought that I was too 'ambitious'; but I put that down to his laid-back nature and that Irish-Celtic frame of mind so hostile to the solid Protestant ethos of moving forward in life, which Monika had passed on to me. (Monika, of course, must have been turning cartwheels up in heaven.)

But perhaps I'm being too harsh on Jack. Of course he was proud of my musical abilities and only occasionally cautioned me to 'relax' and 'enjoy it more' and 'not to get carried away by success'.

Once a year he and Rachel returned to Rishikesh; that first aborted retreat had been made up for long ago, and now they were both deeply involved in some obscure spiritual practice. I lived in London, but I visited them often and they came to my concerts whenever they could – not often, but also not seldom. I still had my little room in Rachel's house and I often felt that it was there that I played my best, and not on the concert stage; alone with myself, the window flung open, looking out on the splendid countryside, I relaxed palpably. Perhaps it was the memory of youth and serendipity, but there I could play without the pressure to be perfect – which, I had to admit, was at times a strain. Strain, however, was the price I had to pay for success, and it was right that way. In London, that pressure was constant; and I needed it as I needed air.

I made no excuses. I was determined to be the best violinist in the world, and I was prepared to work hard to achieve my goal. I aimed for nothing less than perfection; and perfection depended on absolute precision and flawless timing. It demanded discipline: music had to come first in my life. There was no room for any social life, and certainly pleasure had to take a back seat. What greater joy is there than a perfectly presented piece of music? The philistine pleasures pursued by others meant nothing to me. Who would want millet when they had a sumptuous feast spread out before them?

Music was my lifeline and I needed nothing more. Eating and drinking were merely inconvenient requisites for keeping the body alive; clothes were for modesty and keeping warm; I had my formal wear for concerts and casual wear for home, and that was it. I had a rather nice flat in Kensington with all modern conveniences. I liked bothersome household matters to be carried out with a minimum of fuss and attention, and developed quite a taste for microwave dinners; though my friend Fran – who loved cooking! – quite frequently came over on

Friday evenings and cooked for us both. I could afford to eat out several times a week, and did so. However, the bottom line was that when I was with my music I even forgot to eat and drink, and that was as it should be.

Certainly, I had friends – very good ones, even – but they were all musicians. I've already mentioned Fran, a cellist in her mid forties who early in my career had taken me under her wing and who now worried about what she called the exclusivity of my life. Then there was Simone, another young violinist, arguably as talented as I was, who had attended the Royal College – co-incidentally, she was also half-Indian, and we had a covert rivalry going on, though neither of us mentioned it.

I could name any number of talented musicians: pianists, flautists, oboists, clarinettists, even singers, and they were all my friends; but all we did when we were together was play music, and when we talked it was music talk.

I had a large number of admirers, of course. That is to be expected. Any talented young woman who finds herself in the limelight is bound to gather a doting male following. And I have to concede I wasn't bad looking . . . quite beautiful, in fact, especially when I dressed up for a concert! Had I been interested in looks I might have become quite vain; as it was, I had to contend with numerous love letters, bunches of flowers and little presents from these young men, not to mention several offers of marriage – but what was I to do? I threw away most of the letters, kept the flowers, returned gifts with a return address and passed on the others to the make-up ladies and other stage helpers.

As for love, and romance, I considered myself above it. I thought I had escaped the tender trap I had seen so many of my musician friends fall into, not realizing at first that it was a trap. It began with falling in love; that part of their heart which was given to music reaching out, at first hesitantly, reluctantly even, to enfold another human; and then, before they knew it, WHAM! They were married, and music relegated to second place in their lives. It had happened to Vicky, a flautist friend. Since she had married four months ago the chamber orchestra she played in was slowly but surely disintegrating, for husbands demand their share of time. Fran didn't count – she and her husband Julian were as devoted to music as they were to each other, and that makes all the difference. They had been married for a couple of years and were more like one person than two. Music was the hub of their marriage. They had wooed each other with the fluid beauty of Saint-Saëns' 'Swan', and their life had continued along that vein. Now, *that* was a different story: a doting husband with a never-ending supply of Chopin nocturnes. If I were ever to marry it could only be to such a man: he and I, priest and priestess at the altar of music. But I would never marry.

There had only ever been one man in my life and he had shown me in no uncertain terms that he had no interest in me except as a sister. Since then I had made myself immune to romantic love. I had failed to win Dean with my music, and if I could not have him I wanted no other.

In the end I began not only to accept but to appreciate this fact. When would I have had the time for music, where would I have ended up, if I had won Dean! As a housewife in suburbia, or, worse yet, following him around like a groupie on all his exotic photographic adventures! For Dean was almost – but not quite – as successful as I was in his own chosen field.

Dean did not kept his promise to me to take me climbing the year following his accident. In fact, I had not seen much of him at all after that ill-fated trip to India, the trip I much preferred to pretend had never happened. Because of his ongoing conflict with Rachel he had decided to stay on at Roxby Manor as a weekly boarder, and managed to charm his grandfather into continuing to pay school fees. He still came at the weekends; but we saw little of him as he spent most of his time with friends in Farnleigh.

For our remaining school years together under Rachel's roof Dean had an active social life in which I played no part; but I never once showed him that I cared. I could see his interest in me was negligible, and though it hurt at first I found a way to obliterate the pain of rejection. For there was one area in which I still held sway over Dean's heart: with my music. I still played for him; that is, he still came to my room to hear me play. I knew that I impressed and amazed him, and this was enough. His favourite was still the Mendelssohn Concerto and so I played this for him, again and again, and learned to derive a peculiar sort of satisfaction in pleasing him in this way. It was my secret, delicious delight: to see the admiration and sheer wonder light his eyes. And over time I learned that true union is only in the spirit. It was infinitely superior to the antics normal men and women partake of in bed, the very idea of which disgusted me.

In time Dean drifted out of my life, and I played for him no more. He went on to study photography in America, at the world's best school, and went on to win as many awards as I had done.

I heard of all this second hand from Jack and Rachel, for Dean did not write to me; when they spoke of him I tried not to show any undue interest, neither distress when they told me he had become engaged to an American woman, nor delight when, two months later, they told me that the wedding was off. I would not have attended anyway. I could not – my engagement calendar was full. Sometimes Rachel read out one of his rare letters; I accepted his warm greetings graciously, and asked them to send him my love – an entirely sisterly love of course!

By the time I was twenty-four Dean had drifted so far out of my orbit that my feelings for him had faded into a platonic long-distance friendship, and I knew I had conquered the mawkish puppy love that had so long stood between my music and me. But our paths never crossed; I had not seen him for six years.

Chapter 35

And then, out of the blue, there he was. Before every concert I liked to look out and see the audience, scan the faces, take in the collective atmosphere of joyful anticipation that preceded a performance; I felt it helped calm the stage fright that invariably set in the half-hour before I was due to play. And there he was.

I saw him immediately. He was sitting in the fifth row, near the centre. It must have been his eyes that caused me to single him out, drawing mine to him as a magnet. Alone of all the hundreds in the audience I saw his face, one single familiar face in a sea of strangers. Jack and Rachel had said they were coming tonight and this was where they usually sat. I had to assume that for some reason they could not, and had given away their tickets to Dean.

I played, with my usual brilliance, Beethoven's 'Spring' Sonata, and I must admit that the thought of Dean there in the audience gave me a little shot of adrenaline that enhanced my performance to the nearest I had ever been to perfection. At the curtain call I was pleased to see Dean clapping enthusiastically. However, just as I was stepping back into the curtains I saw him turn to the person next to him. It was a young blonde woman, and from the way they smiled and looked at each other I immediately knew everything.

There were the usual people waiting for me backstage and in the wardrobe there was an enormous bunch of red roses, with a note attached, which read:

Hello, Jyothi!

I'm in London tonight with a friend. Jack and Rachel couldn't make it. I'm staying at the Hotel Rembrandt. Can you come there for dinner after the concert? I've booked a table for three in the hope that you can! It's been a long time and it's not often I'm in London when you are so I'm keeping my fingers crossed. Julia and I'll be there waiting. If you can't come it would be nice if you called this mobile number, otherwise I'll be expecting you.

Love, Dean

By the time I had read it all I was seething. I was furious with them all: with Jack and Rachel for giving him their tickets, and for letting him know that we had planned dinner together after the concert, depriving me of an excuse; with Dean for assuming I'd be available to meet him for dinner, and for the absolute gall of bringing along some girlfriend; with the girlfriend for being the girlfriend; and with myself for not regarding all of this with absolute calm and indifference.

I pushed the bunch of roses into the arms of one of the wardrobe girls and stormed off to change my clothes. There were two girls to help me get undressed but they were so clumsy and slow I hissed at them to go away and let me do it myself. However, the zip at the back of my dress had caught – part of the clumsiness. 'What are you two gaping at? Get it open!' I yelled and they both scooted to my back and began some more ineffectual fumbling. 'Oh, just rip the damn thing off,' I fumed. I saw a pair of scissors on the dressing table, grabbed it and whipped around to push it into their hands – just in time to catch one of them making a throat-cutting gesture, right hand against her neck.

I glared at the girl and ordered her to disappear and never reappear, then commanded the other one to cut the dress from my body, which she did so gingerly – obviously hoping somehow to save it for herself – that I grabbed the scissors back from her and did it myself.

In the background I heard someone whisper, 'What's she on about this time?' but I didn't bother to find out who it was. People love to take out their inferiority on us celebrities and the best thing to do is ignore the slights. I was able to change in half the time it would have taken with those ineffectual girls, and after a few words with Mr Harvey I was out in the street getting into my taxi.

I had made up my mind to go straight home and simply ignore Dean's request, but curiosity got the better of me and I found myself telling the driver to head for the Rembrandt. Because the fact of the matter was if I didn't turn up Dean might suspect I was jealous – which of course I wasn't, but I couldn't allow him to suspect that I was anything more than his dear little sister-friend from way back when, just dying to meet him and whoever-she-was. I had changed, naturally, but how was he to know that? I wanted him to meet the other Jyothi, the sophisticated Jyothi who was no longer the sweet little sister, but a grown woman, confident and successful. I wanted him to meet Jade. The new me.

Having made this calculation I realized I was much too early.

If I went directly to the restaurant I would arrive at exactly the time Dean had asked me to appear and I couldn't possibly do that, it would seem much too eager. And anyway, I was in too much of a flurry. I had to calm down. I had to appear regal, show him that though we were still friends I really was now in a different league. I wanted his admiration. No. I realized it now. I wanted his *adoration*.

For so many years I had been the little girl gazing up at *him* in unrequited adoration, and it was really only now I realized what a humiliating position that is for a woman. Rejection makes you feel inferior, and the only way to overcome it is to turn the tables. And I had just the means to do so. Dean, though not musical himself, had always worshipped at the altar of music. For him I had always been the ministrant at that altar. Now I would be the High Priestess.

I ordered the taxi-driver to park somewhere and wait twenty minutes before going on to the restaurant; this would give me time to lose the anger. I pressed my back into the seat of the car and took some deep calming breaths. Eyes closed, with great effort I aligned my thoughts and feelings. A musician needs enormous discipline to reach the higher echelons and in less than five minutes I had arrived at the state of inner composure I had sought. A High Priestess is never flurried. She is mistress of her emotions, mistress of her self.

I was ten minutes late, which was reasonable, though still a bit too early. I had also gathered all the loose threads of my reawakened and rampant infatuation, bundled them nicely together and tucked them into place where they would not disturb the polished cool of my outward image.

'Dean! How marvellous to see you again! How long has it been – seven? Eight years?'

'Six,' said Dean.

He and I embraced and kissed cheeks as always. I then moved back, still holding his upper arms, and, wearing the most generous and warmest of smiles, I said, 'Let me look at you ... Dean, you haven't aged a day! How do you do it, manage to look so young! Must be that rugged lifestyle of yours! And this is ... ?' I turned to his companion, beaming benevolence and interest.

'Julia,' he said, but his eyes were still on me. I could feel it.

Julia and I shook hands; our eyes met and I could see her sizing me up, calculating the competition, and cowering away. She was petite, blonde, blue-eyed and pretty – from head to toe Dean's type, the kind of girl who formerly had sent my self-esteem plunging. Success had changed all that. Now I knew my strengths and was proud of them. How could a pleasantly shaped body and a striking face ever triumph over music? In sixty years that body would have lost all its appeal and in eighty years would be mere dust: how could it possibly compete with the ineffable grandeur of music, which was for all time? My initial jealousy fled in the light of absolute knowledge of who I was and what I could do, and she couldn't. I smiled at her with genuine benevolence.

'Pleased to meet you,' she said in a very small voice. I sensed her insecurity, and immediately felt sorry for her.

'Julia and I are old friends,' Dean said almost dismissively. I was embarrassed for her and when we sat down I deliberately asked her a few questions about herself to make up for his rudeness.

'So where did you two meet?' I asked.

'Oh, we've known each other for simply ages,' said Dean, answering for her. 'Since I was at school. Her dad's a climber too and we met in Switzerland when I was about seventeen or eighteen – she's Swiss and she's been running up and down mountains since she was a little girl. Whenever I'm in Switzerland we manage a peak or two. She's now doing a graduate degree in England. That's why we met here. I told her she just had to hear you. She was quite bowled over. Jyothi, you were so—'

'Oh, and what is your degree in?' I asked politely, once again focusing the conversation on her. Dean really had no manners. As for Julia, I suspected she was the very girl he had met the summer after out India adventure, the Swiss girl for whom he had broken his promise to me. If I remembered correctly, her name had also been Julia.

'English Literature,' she said, and now I heard the thick accent that told me German was her native accent. She had turned scarlet, and I suspected it was because of my unexpected attention.

It amused me no end to see how far the tables had turned. Now it was Dean looking up to me, and his girl who felt inadequate; I was the star of the evening, and we all knew it, and it was simple for me to be gracious and warm to them both. Dean's eyes were fixed on me, moist with adoration, and I noticed that, since I had joined them, he had not once looked at Julia. Men can be so impolite, so disrespectful of the feelings of others. I parried his compliments and his attempts to flirt with ease; I had grown used to the fawning attentions of men and I knew how to keep them in their place without bruising their egos too much.

Not that I wanted Dean. I made that perfectly clear to myself. *I did not want Dean.* All I wanted was to be liberated from my calf love. And that was what happened in the course of that evening. Yes, the tables had truly turned. I was his High Priestess; he was hungry for my blessing, and it was up to me to bestow it, or refuse it. Mine was the power, and the key to the kingdom of music. Dean knelt outside the door.

Chapter 36

Looking back, there's a feeling of inevitability about it all, of predestination even. As if Dean and I had been unconsciously and inexorably led towards the moment when the timing was just right; the moment when I would be ripe for him, and he for me.

We could not see each other again for several weeks as Dean had only been visiting England. His home base was New York City but in fact the whole world was his playground and he moved from one country to the next, on this commission or another, with remarkable ease. Both of us had ended up with careers that demanded much travel, but whereas he was immediately at home in any new country and thrived on changing landscapes and new sights, much of which he captured with the exacting eye of his camera, I loathed travelling.

I hated those anonymous hotel rooms, luxurious though they were. It was always with relief that I turned the key in the lock to my cosy little Kensington flat after an exhausting visit to some foreign stage. I loved the familiarity of my own four walls and furnishings, the rich fabrics and thick carpets, all carefully selected to fit into a warm apricot colour scheme. My sofa was one of those huge enveloping things that closes around you when you throw yourself onto it; soft and rust-coloured with several large cushions casually thrown against the back. I spent many hours lying here, my head against one of the armrests, eyes closed, listening to the most delicious music; and now I spent hours here dreaming of Dean.

Of course, it took only one telephone call from him to win me over. So much for being inaccessible, my infatuation over and done with. In fact, it was just beginning.

Dean rang me that very evening, to thank me again for the concert and 'just for being you'. He told me had to fly to Ecuador the next day on an assignment to photograph some volcano that might or might not be on the verge of eruption.

'I'll call you again,' he promised and I had to take three deep breaths to stop the palpitations of my heart.

He rang me again next morning, from the airport. 'I can't tell you how much I enjoyed being with you last night,' he told me this time. 'I just wanted to let you know that. It was like seeing my nearest and dearest friend again, and finding out that she's even more than a friend.' At those words I felt a sort of softening around the contours of my High Priestess image, like a statue of ice sweating in a warm summer breeze. I began to mutter something in reply, but Dean interrupted. 'Look, I can't hear you. It's too loud here. And anyway, I have to go now, they're boarding. I'll ring you from Ecuador. And see you again soon. Bye.'

I did not hear from him again for weeks.

It wasn't his fault; it was our inexorable timetables. A day after he left for Ecuador I left for Prague; when I returned there were several messages from him on my answering machine.

The first was from Ecuador:

'Christ, I'm sorry it took so long to call – you can't imagine how difficult it is to get a working telephone here. I'm sorry you're out; I'll call again.'

The second was from New York:

'Jyothi! I can't believe I've missed you again! Listen, I have to speak to you. I hope you're just out, and not out of the country! I'll call you back this evening.'

That same evening:

'Jyothi! Right, I'll just keep it short. I have to tell you . . . I love you! I always have! Give me a call when you get back, my number is . . . Listen, I'll be in London next week . . . I'll call you then.'

The next three were short and sweet:

'Jyothi, hello, I'm in London now. I'll call again.'

'Jyothi? Rachel tells me you're in Prague and coming back in a day or two. I'm *leaving* in a day or two so ring me immediately when you get back, OK?'

'Jyothi! Christ, I only have one more day in this damned city, ring me back for goodness' sake!'

I rang him back.

'Jade?' I heard Fran close the door behind her as she entered the flat. 'Jade! Hey, where are you? We're late! Aren't you ready yet? What's the matter?'

Of all the musical friends I had made in the last few years Fran was the closest. She was a tall, thin woman who looked as if she had been put together with spare parts from other people's bodies, since nothing seemed to match: her legs and arms were too long, her forehead too high, her bosom too flat, her hips too wide, her torso too short. But little did Fran care; like me, she lived for music and she was one of the best cellists

I knew. She had an extremely powerful bow arm, producing vast, rounded tones even in virtuoso passages, and in her hands the cello spoke in a warm, rich, almost human voice. She had a warm, rich, cello-like personality as well, dependable under all circumstances and always there for her friends.

Fran was Head of Music in an exclusive girls' school with a very strong Arts Department, a profession which was perfect for her because, unlike me, she was the quintessential People Person. Much as she loved music it would never have sufficed for her; she loved the interaction with other people, and playing music for her was not so much self-expression as communication. Fran's mission was to make the world a better place through music; and, if necessary, through counselling, a slap on the wrist, hot chicken soup, or a wagging finger. If you won a prize Fran would be the first on your doorstep with roses and champagne, and if you were ill Fran would be there serving you endless cups of tea. I'd always known that if I ever had a problem Fran would be the one I would turn to, but up till now the only problems I had ever had were musical ones, of technique or pitch or tone, which could be solved by playing a few bars together.

I heard her walk to the bedroom and then the bathroom looking for me before she finally found me on the sofa. 'Oh my God, Jade,' she cried, 'what's the matter? Are you ill?' She sank down to the carpet and laid a hand on the back of my head. By this time I was lying face down with my face buried in the cushion, and feeling her touch I turned to look at her.

'Jade, what on earth! Darling, what's happened! Gosh you look terrible, all your mascara's smudged. What about the party? Have you taken ill or something?'

I certainly felt ill but it wasn't a physical illness. Reluctantly I sat up in the sofa, drawing my legs up and crossing them. I looked at Fran mournfully, and, pushing the hair back from my face, said, 'Fran, I think I'm in love! And I don't know what to *do* about it!'

Fran let out a gale of laughter. 'Oh, you silly! And is that why you're reduced to a bundle of nerves!' She laughed again and climbed up onto the sofa where she put an arm around me and rocked me. 'Love, that's just fantastic! It's about time too, I always told you it would happen one day! Now come on, you have to tell me everything!'

I pulled away slightly and said, half rising to my feet, 'No, we're late already. Let's go. I'll go and freshen myself up.'

But Fran pulled me down beside her. 'Listen, love, you're not going anywhere until you've told me everything! Who is he? Do I know him? This is so damn sudden! I want to know the whole story and I'm not letting you go until you've told it!'

Finally I told her half the story, and she loved it.

'But then everything's fine,' she exclaimed when I had finished. 'You love each other – he's the one you always wanted. So why the misery? You should be dancing a polka around the room, you silly thing!' She giggled. 'I'll dance it with you, if you like!'

'It's just so strange, so new!'

'Ha! You're just not used to it. You locked yourself out of love, you shut yourself up in your music, but if you're truthful you've got to admit it got a bit lonely in there, didn't it, in your ivory tower? A little lonely and a little sad?'

That's when I had the final meltdown. I grabbed Fran, buried my face in her neck, and blubbered like a baby.

Chapter 37

The weeks until I could see Dean again seem, in retrospect, like a roller-coaster ride that swung me from the deepest despair and doubt to heavenly anticipation and down again. Fran was there through it all, to hold my hand and pull me out of my agonizing bouts of self-chastisement.

'Music and romance just don't go together!' I wailed. 'I'm going to have to choose . . . but I can't! I can't possibly!'

'Nonsense!' said Fran. 'I didn't have to choose, did I?'

'But with you it's different. Julian's a musician. He's just like you. The two of you just sort of . . . merge. Like two rivers flowing into each other.'

'Dean's musical too, if he isn't a musician. It's music that drew him to you, isn't it? It's your soul he loves, and your soul is pure music. You'll see, it'll be all right once you get to be together. You just need to sort things out a bit.'

'Sort what out?'

'Oh, well, you know. Things. Where you'll live. How often you'll meet. That sort of thing.'

'Well, that's just it, it's impossible! Our lives are so different! He's always jetting off to some impossible corner of the world. And you know how much I travel, too. When would we get to see each other?'

'You'll work that out together, Jade. Don't worry about it yet.'

'But I *do* worry, I can't help it! I want to be with him all the time but I want to be with my music too and I'm afraid, so afraid that thinking about him stops me thinking about music! I'm losing my concentration, Fran! My focus! I play so badly these days. My thoughts keep drifting off to him. I play like a bloody amateur. Swirls of emotion – where's the *clarity* I used to have! Oh, I wish I'd never met him again! I wish it was just me and my music, like it used to be! Everything was so clear and so simple in those days!'

'Give it time, Jade darling. It will all sort itself out. You wait.'

Then there were the times when I sailed above the clouds, when my love for Dean seemed to carry me on wings and lend the very clarity and vision to my music that previously, in the days before Dean, I had sought in vain; when loving him was the key to the essence of music I had yearned for and which had constantly hovered just out of my grasp. Now it was mine. Nourished by love, my music was out of this world. If only it could be that way constantly.

Dean rang me whenever he could. From Ecuador and Chile; from New York and San Francisco; from Tokyo and Hong Kong. The one time he came to London in seven weeks I happened to be in Boston. Once we just missed each other by one day, in Paris.

Each time he called he professed an undying love.

'Jyothi,' he said. He still called me that; I was Jyothi, light, to him, he told me, and always would be. 'I love you. My love for you is the one constant in my life. I need you; you're like a beautiful melody at the centre of my life, calling me back to myself and to everything that is precious. Without you I am lost.'

'Calling you back from what?' I would say suspiciously.

I had the disturbing habit of turning over each of his words a hundred times in my head. My imagination did the rest. Sometimes I wished he would not ring me because those calls seemed guaranteed to throw me into a whirlpool of emotion. I wanted to ask him what had happened to Julia but didn't dare; each time I formed the question in my mind my mouth turned dry and I could not speak the words.

'It can't work!' I told Fran with absolute conviction. 'It's not going to work. I feel it in my bones. I'm just a passing fad. Dean likes petite blondes.'

'Here we go again!' Fran said, rolling her eyes. 'Darling, it's just nerves. It's because you'll see him again tomorrow. Now take it from me, a good friend and a married woman besides: it's going to be fine. Just stay calm and be your beautiful self.'

I longed for the cool, confident, sophisticated woman Dean had met the evening after that concert. The successful musician who didn't need a man to make her happy. That was the woman Dean had fallen in love with. But she had disappeared as if she had been nothing more than a passing spirit who had borrowed my body for a few hours. Now I had to face Dean; and I had no idea who I was.

'You're you,' said Fran. 'Just be yourself.'

'He loves Jade. But the girl who loves him is Jyothi,' I said. 'I haven't really changed. He thinks I have but I haven't.'

'One part of you has changed and one part is still the same.

324

The part of you that loves him and always loved him hasn't changed and that's the most important part.'

'Yes, the Jyothi part. But what about *Jade*? The woman he loves?'

'All right. I'll show you where Jade is,' said Fran. We were at her home, at the time, sitting on the couch; she stood up, walked around the couch. She took some time; I knew what she was doing without turning to peek. I heard the click of my violin case behind me as she opened it. She returned with my violin and the bow in her hands; she placed them in mine. 'All right, come on!'

She gestured to me to follow her and I did. Her cello stood in the music room, leaning against the wall. She picked it up, plonked herself down in her chair, and with a commanding twitch of her chin ordered me to prepare myself. We tuned our instruments.

We played.

The moment my bow touched the strings it was there: all the magic and all the majesty. The cloud of doubt and distrust way dispelled by the clarity of the music, like an overcast sky swept clean by a strong wind. This was Jade; this was *me*. This was the Jade who, the very next day, would be meeting Dean at Heathrow airport.

I saw him immediately. He was among the first passengers to come through the sliding doors, a black leather case strapped over one shoulder. I have no idea what he was wearing; something blue, my memory tells me, but I only had eyes for his face; I saw his eager, impatient look as he searched the waiting crowds for me. I waved, and called his name. He saw me, and the smile of recognition that lit his features dispelled at once every last thread of uncertainty. The next minute he was standing in front of me; we were two feet apart, and for less than a second we paused to drink in the other; and then we were in each other's arms.

I had gone through our reunion innumerable times in my mind before this meeting; I had pictured the 'First Time' in shades of glowing gold. And naturally enough my idea of courtship and romance was laced through with music; I knew it was my music which had first captivated Dean. We were the warp and the woof of the very same fabric; and that fabric was music. My music.

I had prepared everything; this day would be perfect. Fran had helped by cooking a wonderful meal for us, one of her mouth-watering risottos which was waiting in the fridge to be reheated whenever we wished to eat; unless we decided to go to a restaurant. After we had eaten I would play for him; the music that had always been his favourite: the Mendelssohn. He would sit on the couch and regard me with soulful eyes, and I would play for him as I had never played before. The Mendelssohn would be an altar before which we would both kneel, our two souls flowing one into the other until there would be just the one, perfect union; out of which would flow a physical union so natural there would be no question, no shyness, no pain. I had gone through the scenario umpteen times in my imagination and now it was only a question of following through with it; I could imagine no alternative. I did not have to choose after all, I reasoned. My two loves would blend: Dean and music would complement each other and there would be not one moment when one was in conflict with the other.

My plan was so firmly fixed in my mind that I was rather put out when, right there at the airport, Dean kissed me. I had planned the first real kiss for later, *after* the Mendelssohn. Before that there would be gentle touches; he would stroke my cheek, perhaps, with fingers so soft they felt like rose petals barely glancing off my skin. We would take time, since we had all the time in the world. We would hold hands, our intertwined fingers the microcosm of our physical union, and each and every moment would be perfect. I already knew the heights my soul was capable of and this day was to be a build-up to a climax beyond imagination; with Dean I would soar into realms of rapture beyond belief.

Everyone said, or at least hinted, that this was the greatest thing on earth. And at last I was called to the feast.

That was the theory. That was the plan.

But Dean had never been one to function according to a plan. He pulled me to him, pressed himself against me and his lips against mine, forcing my mouth open. I was so surprised that I simply complied; I could no more repel him than I could pull back from a long dive into a deep pool. I had coached myself into giving myself body, mind and soul to Dean. My love for him had been festering for years, and actively cultivated for weeks. Now that I was in his arms how could I draw away?

When he was finished he looked at me, laughed, linked his arm through mine, and we walked off towards the car park. The welcoming words I had planned to say to him did not come; all I was capable of was looking at him and wondering if I looked as bashful as I felt.

As we drove home Dean could not take his eyes off me. I felt his gaze, and now and then looked back at him and smiled, but my attention was needed for the traffic and I could not let myself give in to the thrill of being, at long last, the centre of Dean's attention.

I drank in his words though; they were like water for one who has been wandering for years in the desert.

'I love you, Jyothi. I always have. It's a love that's been slumbering in me ever since I first met you.'

327

He'd said it before on the telephone. Hearing the words from his lips gave then a different dimension altogether.

'I love you too, Dean. I always have. I've always known it.'

I hadn't actually planned such intensity at this early moment; I'd wanted to ask him about his work – what he had been doing the last few weeks, what he had photographed, where and when the photos were to be published, and so on. And, of course, he was to ask about *my* work: what pieces I had been playing, and where; what Boston had been like, and where I was going to next. I felt uncomfortable as if Dean had taken the conductor's baton out of my hand and changed not only the tempo of our encounter but the entire repertoire. But I put that unease behind me; the moment was too much of a miracle – Dean, saying he loved me! – to raise objections now.

However, the moment we entered my flat Dean changed the repertoire once again, and this time it was not disquiet that filled me, but downright protest. Dean slammed the front door shut with one hand and grabbed me with the other, pulling me towards him with a passion I was quite unprepared for.

I pulled away, and laughed nervously.

'Dean, please! Not so quickly!'

'Dean, please! Not so quickly!' was to become the catchword for that disastrous weekend.

Nothing went according to the plan. Dean had been expecting Jade, an experienced woman who knew the facts of life; instead he met Jyothi, who was at heart still a child, who longed to shed the outer skin of Jade and return to the delicious innocence of youth; who longed for Dean to show her the way home. But the Dean I longed for, the sensitive, caring Dean of old, had metamorphosed over the last ten years into a man of the world who thought he was meeting his equal in an equally matured Jyothi; in Jade. This was a new Dean. I did not know him.

Jade and the new Dean might have had a chance at survival; but Jade was a fake, and Jyothi could not cope with him.

To his credit, Dean recognized the problem.

'It was the first time for you, wasn't it?' he said, and when I nodded sadly he only laughed, and then sweetly took me in his arms and said, 'Oh Jyothi, I do love you so!'

It was his calling me Jyothi that so disarmed me, for that name summoned up all that was lost and all that was beautiful in me. No one else, these days, called me that except for Jack and Rachel. To hear Dean use the name confused me: how could I be the woman he wanted, when he summoned the woman I wanted to be? It was not possible.

I tried to explain to him; but he did not understand.

'We can't go back, Jyothi!' he said. There it was again, that name from another time. 'Those times are over; I loved you as a sister back then. Now we've both moved on. You're a grown woman, not a little girl with a crush; yes, I know you had a crush on me. I always knew it; don't you think guys notice things like that? I don't want you as a sister; I want you as a woman, at my side. Mature; passionate. Give it time; it'll come.'

That first evening he took me out. We went to a West End night club which, it seemed, was frequented by the crowd he mixed with. And yes, Dean had a crowd. They were intellectuals, artists, writers of experimental novels; a few avant-garde musicians. Jade would have fitted in here perfectly. She would have flung her hair behind her shoulders, worn a ravishing gown, her eyes would have sparkled. She would have told witty stories and everyone would have listened to her and laughed. She would have been caustic and sophisticated, modern and incredibly smart, the centre of attention and basking in the limelight as only she knew how. Jade knew the routine, and would have gone through it with easy elegance. Then Jade would have gone home with Dean and rounded off the evening with a private performance beyond anything she had ever done on stage. Jade would have ensnared him. Jade was invulnerable!

Jyothi couldn't do it. I couldn't help it; Dean brought out the innocent girl in me, and it was she who followed him into the smoky bar where she could hardly breathe. Jyothi could not act to save her life. Her shoulders hunched; words froze on her lips. She felt awkward and out of place, and others, noticing her discomfiture, smiled patronizingly and turned away.

During our taxi ride home Dean was unusually withdrawn and I knew it was on my account. I wanted to break the silence but no words came. That was when I longed for the speech of angels. I longed to be able to speak to him in the only language I mastered! If only he would let me play for him! In music, Jyothi and Jade could merge: in music, Jyothi grew wings and was greater than the sum of her parts; she became Jade, the woman he loved. Jade could not exist without Jyothi – how could I let Dean know! And Jyothi, without Jade, was a pale wisp of a girl, unworthy of his love, the little sister of the past.

On Sunday we both made a renewed effort. I had lain awake for hours, thinking; and in the morning I got out of bed before him, showered and dressed, and woke him with music – nothing soft, nothing romantic, nothing to awaken old memories; instead, I began with Elgar's La Capricieuse, moved on to Wieniawski's Scherzo-tarantelle, and finished up with the impressive Devil's Laughter by Paganini. These three pieces successfully put me in Jade-mode; I managed to hide my nervousness behind my virtuosity and to my relief I saw I had him fooled. He laughed, and pulled me back into

330

bed, carefully removing the violin and the bow from my hands.

Sunday was a lazy day; we read the newspapers, went for a walk, and talked. Dean was chatty, and everything appeared normal. But the talk never went beyond the superficial, and I feared Dean would see the woodenness of my act. Perhaps he did; perhaps I fooled him. He never let on, and as evening came upon us I believed I had saved the relationship, and his love.

Monday came, and I had not once played my Mendelssohn for him. It seemed he was not interested. Next time, I comforted myself; when we are more comfortable with each other, I will speak to him in the true language of my soul. Not now.

I sat on the bed and watched him throw stray pieces of clothing into his suitcase.

'Where are you off to now?' I asked.

'South Africa,' he said casually.

'When's your flight? Shall I drive you to the airport?'

'Oh, don't bother, I'll take the tube.'

'No, I don't mind, really.' I didn't; I still loved him and now that he was leaving I was racked by panic, and horror at my own childish behaviour. My Jade act had been a failure; it had lacked conviction, he must have noticed. He must have felt that all the while I was with him it was Jyothi, not Jade! Why had I been unable to be the woman he wanted?

I stood up and walked over to the bathroom. 'I'll get myself ready.'

'Jyothi, I said, don't bother! Listen, the truth is I have to do some stuff in town. My flight isn't till tonight.'

'But then you can leave the suitcase here. Why lug it with you into town?'

'Oh, I often do that. You know, British Airways lets you

check in at Paddington, and that's what I do usually. It's much more convenient.'

'Oh, I see. Well, I could drop you at Paddington. What've you got to do in London? We could meet for lunch?' Suddenly I could not bear to part with him. I feared I was losing him, and all through my own immature behaviour.

'Just some boring business stuff – and, sorry, I've got to meet this editor for lunch. But hey, don't look so miserable! I'll be back!'

'Yes, but you know what it's like. When I'm here you're not and when you're here, I'm not. Who knows when our paths will cross again?'

'All that means is that we have to keep in touch. And it needn't be in London.'

'Oh, right . . . but somehow I can't see myself giving a concert in the middle of the Tatri mountains. Or you taking photos of the Sydney Opera House. We travel completely different routes.'

'We managed this meeting, didn't we? We'll find a way.'

'Dean, you do love me, don't you?'

'Jyothi! How could you ask! You know I do!'

'You must think me a complete baby.'

Dean stopped his packing then, looked up at me and flashed me the most charming, irresistible grin. It made my heart miss a beat. 'Jyothi, you know what? I'll tell you something. In a way, I think your very innocence is what attracts me to you. It makes you so special; you're like a a pristine mountain that nobody has ever climbed before; you've kept yourself for me and there's nothing more appealing for a man! So it's a difficult peak, but so what! Reaching that summit is all the more of a challenge! You know, when I saw you there on that stage, completely taken up in your music, you were like a goddess, playing on divine strings, so far above us mortals . . . it was out of this world. It was as if something clicked in me, and every other woman seemed to be made of clay. I forgot that behind that exalted, exquisite woman is the sweet and innocent girl . . . I want to show you what love can really be like. And it's worth waiting for.'

'Oh Dean, if you'll wait I promise to do everything in my power . . . I promise to change, for you . . . I promise to be the—'

Dean threw back his head and laughed, and said, 'You silly, of course I'll wait! You don't think that after finding this splendid lonely peak I'm just going to walk away before reaching the summit, do you! Don't worry, I'll be back, and sooner than you think.'

And I had to be satisfied with that.

I hadn't told Dean – he hadn't asked, and the subject never came up – but the next day I was flying to Sydney and the Far East for a string of concerts. As I pushed my loaded trolley towards the British Airways check-in I saw him. His back was turned to me but I recognized the jacket, and the smooth black hair that just touched the collar of his shirt, and the battered suitcase on which one hand rested casually. I also recognized the woman he was with. She was blonde: Julia. Their arms were slung around each other's waists, moulding their bodies together; their faces were in profile, but I did not fear they would see me, for they were gazing at each other; and even from this distance and even in my innocence I recognized the unmistakable aura of passion that enclosed them

Chapter 38

My Far East tour did not go well. I was too worked up to play well; the thought of Dean kept injecting itself into my mind at those crucial times when I needed complete focus. Mr Harvey was not pleased with me; but I could not care less. I was relieved to return to London, to my refuge in Kensington. Yet the moment I walked into my flat and hung up my keys on their hook I was assailed by the memories of Dean. I had to talk to someone, even before sleeping off my travel-weariness.

Fran's answerphone was on. I replaced the receiver and rang again, and again. She was sure to be home but she must have gone to bed. Chances were she was still awake, though, reading one of her beloved mysteries. If she wasn't I'd ring so often I'd wake her up, and if she wouldn't wake up I'd just turn up on her doorstep and press away at the buzzer till she fell out of bed.

I had to talk to her, and her alone. Fran knew about men. She might be living in a perfect relationship now but she had known other, harder times. Fran had been married before, to a banker, of all things. They had had a child, a daughter, who had been killed in a fearful accident when she was five. After the death of the child the marriage had fallen apart, and only then had she sworn that if she ever married again it would be to a man who understood her. She had kept that promise to herself; though I suspect she had not had that much choice. Fran, while not being ugly – her eyes are too beautiful for that – is not the sort of woman men run after in droves. In that she was probably lucky, since the sort of man who runs after that sort of woman would be undeserving of a woman of her calibre. Julian was lucky to have her; and she was lucky to have him. And I was lucky to have a friend in her.

At the fourth call she finally picked up the receiver.

'Fran, thank goodness. Sorry if I woke you up but . . . oh Fran, I need to talk. Can I come over?'

'Jade? Hey, girl, what's the matter? I thought you were in Sydney? What? Now? Why, what's up? All right, all right, of course you can come. You know you can.'

'Fran, you're a saint, I'll have you canonized! I'll be there in half an hour!'

In fact it took me twenty-five minutes as the traffic lights were miraculously all green. Fran and Julian owned a lovely little mews house in Richmond, just two blocks from the river. As I drew up in front of her garage the outside lights flared on and when I got out of the car – *fell* out more like, for I stumbled in my haste – the front door opened; Fran was waiting in her dressing gown. We embraced.

'So darling, this better be good. How dare you drag me out of bed at eleven o'clock, two chapters away from the murderer walking into the noose!'

'Oh Fran, thanks so much for letting me come! I was desperate, I just had to see you!'

Fran peered at me; there was only one lamp on in the sitting room and she turned me around so she could see my face and then said, 'You've been crying, haven't you? Come on, sit down and tell me all about it. Is it Dean? If he's hurt you I'm going to be sharpening my knife . . .'

'Yes, well, not only . . . It's everything, it's my whole life. Dean, and my music. Fran, it's a disaster . . . I can't play any more!'

'Nonsense. Of course you can play. And of course it's Dean. Don't think I didn't notice that I haven't heard one word from you since that ominous visit of his. I take it things went wrong?'

She walked to the window and drew the curtains as if afraid that Dean might be peering in from the garden.

'Where's Julian?'

'In Berlin. He'll be back tomorrow. So we've got all the time in the world. I expect you'll be spending the night?'

'Yes, thanks . . . oh Fran, I've lost everything, I'm a failure, a complete wreck and I don't know what to do!'

The last words came out as a wail. I could no longer contain the misery; it all came pouring out: how Dean had lied to me, and how I had seen him the very next morning in the arms of another.

'The bloody bastard!' Fran fumed when I had finished. Wearing her most fierce frown she pulled me into the kitchen where she filled the kettle and prepared a pot for tea.

'You've got to drop him. Immediately,' she told me as she peeled open a packet of digestives. 'I've been suspecting the worst ever since you didn't ring me so I could meet him, as we'd planned. That could mean only two things, I told Julian – ask him. Either she's up in seventh heaven and has no time for the likes of us, or else she's down in hell and doesn't know how to get out. One look at your face and I can tell which is it. I'm going to kill that bastard.'

'The thing is, he's coming back! He left a message on my answerphone! What shall I do!'

'Well, dear, isn't it obvious?' Fran said. She poured water into the teapot, arranged the pot, cups, biscuits and accompanying paraphernalia on a tray, and led the way back into the sitting room. 'Drop him – like a hot potato!'

'But I can't! It's not as easy as that! You see, it's partly my fault! Listen!' I said. And I told her it from beginning to end, sparing none of the ugly details.

'I love Dean,' I said in conclusion to the long sad story, 'I really do, and I don't want to lose him. But now I've lost him *and* my music. This whole concert tour was a disaster, it all sounds like . . . *Dreck*.' The German word for filth was all that came to my mind. That was how I felt: as if a cloud of filth had settled over me.

'I've lost everything,' I repeated, when Fran said nothing. 'Fran?' I coaxed.

'Just a sec,' she replied. 'I'm just trying to get something straight in my head. Give me a moment.'

I waited, nibbling on a digestive and sipping at my tea.

'OK,' said Fran. 'Just let me run through that again. I couldn't be quite sure I heard right. He spends the weekend with you, gets what he wants, lies to you, and then, when you see him with another woman, you think it's all your fault?'

'Well, it is,' I said. 'If I hadn't been so naïve . . . Oh Fran, I put on this big sophisticated act, to impress him, but only you know it's not true. If I can't maintain it I'm going to lose Dean! And he's the only man I ever wanted. I could never love anyone else!'

'Nonsense,' said Fran. 'Listen to me: if Dean fell in love with your mask are you sure it's him you really want? If he can't love the real you is he worth the trouble?'

'But he does love the real me – it's the me he's always

337

known! We were best friends when I was younger – we were so close, he knew all my secrets! The trouble is, there's a certain type of woman he's attracted to. I've always known that, and I learned to accept it; I thought I could never be like them. But now I've got this whole new me, this Jade-me, and that's my chance! My only chance!'

Fran shook her head. 'Jade, you're a hopeless case. To think that all these years I've been encouraging you to open yourself up to love, not to shut yourself away in your music; and now this. Look here, girl: this fellow sounds like bad news. I don't know him, but I know the type. This airport story tells me everything I need to know about him.'

'No, you don't know him! He's sensitive, tender, funny – and he does care for me, really, he's not as superficial as he sounds! Fran, I know him; I know he's special! Why do you think I waited for him all these years! All I want him to do is to love the real me as a woman, instead of as a child. If he could only feel my love – but I think he does! I think he feels it, but isn't yet aware of it properly. It's as if he thinks he's in love with the Jade-me, but in his heart he knows that it's the real me, Jyothi, he loves. If he could only realize it – if I could just bring him around . . .'

'He's a Don Juan. Believe me, Jade. I can see all the symptoms. All women long to tame such men; but it's not possible. The only way to deal with them is to keep a ten-foot distance, and your wits about you.'

I bit my lip and said nothing. I sensed the mounting anger behind her words and there was very little that drove Fran to anger; she was the personification of calmness. Sarcasm was not her weapon of choice, but now it dripped off her every word; and what was more, the sheer incredulity with which she spelled out my situation made me feel a fool.

Fran was talking again, but I hardly listened. I wanted her

on my side, helping me to find a way to keep Dean; I wanted tips on how to deal with him when he returned. If I could only be happy with Dean, I reasoned, my music would come back.

At the moment I had neither. I wanted both. I could have it all: the man I loved, the music I lived for, and professional success.

'I'm going to see him again,' I decided on the spur of the moment. 'I have to have it out with him. I'll tell him I saw him with that woman; but I'll show understanding. I'll tell him I love him, and I'll tell him I know it's my fault. I had been rushing ahead with my own plans, instead of thinking of pleasing him. I'll admit my naïvety and inexperience with men, and ask him for another chance to be the kind of mature woman he wants. And I'll give *him* another chance. I've made mistakes too.'

'The wise one learns from the mistakes of others. The fool learns from his own,' was all Fran said then, but she opened her arms and I fell into them. 'Perhaps you do have to find out for yourself. Just be careful, Jade. And of course you won't go home now. You must be falling over with exhaustion. Come on, off you go to bed.'

She took my hand and led me up the stairs, pausing at the airing cupboard to take out a pile of sheets and towels which she shoved into my arms. 'Don't let's talk about Dean any more. I want to hear about your tour. We'll have a nice long lazy breakfast tomorrow and I'll tell you all the gossip. Wait till you hear the news about Simone . . .'

We talked again next morning. I told her my deepest fears.

'Fran, he'll always leave me, because I'm frigid.'

Fran was silent, and then she said, 'Jade, you need someone who can understand the incredible warmth and beauty and passion of your soul. Your soul is in your music! Do you think you could play such music if you were frigid? Don't make me laugh! If Dean loves you he must learn to understand you; he should at least be willing to make the effort to understand! If it's your music he loves – as he claims – he should rise up to meet you in your special world, not drag you down into his! That's the kind of partner I wish for you. If you can't find a non-musician who understands, then find a musician, for God's sake! Then we'll see who's frigid. Ha! You've been hung up on Dean for far too long!'

It was as if those words of her tore a curtain from my eyes. And suddenly it no longer seemed impossible to turn away from Dean. It was as if a light went on. Dean's talk of climbing mountains and conquering peaks . . . what had seemed flattering at the time now seemed incredibly insulting. I, a summit he had to climb? The glaring light of insight shone on Dean, as he had been during that awful weekend, and as he had been all through the years, and there seemed to be no difference.

Dean had always been chasing after new peaks. His relationships with women had always been a metaphor for that restless adventurer off to explore the next summit. When there were no physical mountains available women had been the substitute, and I was nothing but the latest, and most inaccessible peak to date. He had said it in so many words.

'You're Chogori in winter,' Dean had told me. 'Ever heard of Chogori? No? Chogori is a local Balti name for K2, the second highest summit in the world. You must have heard of K2. Balti is the language of Baltistan, in the north-eastern extremity of Pakistan, close to the border with Kashmir. Baltistan begins when the Baltoro Glacier ends. Over Baltoro, and everything else in the vicinity, towers K2, or Chogori. People still dream of conquering it in winter. That's you, for me.'

Even as he had spoken the words I had felt a vague shadow

of unease that I had refused to acknowledge; but now Fran's words shone a lamp into those shadows and I saw the ugly cowering shapes they concealed. I had been wearing blinkers; Fran's words ripped them from my eyes.

And then the lamp of Fran's words left the shadows and the unworthy creatures living there, and showed me a door, and I found I could walk through, without even a glance behind me back into the shadows. Tears of relief sprang to my eyes. I felt ready to leave Dean behind, and I told Fran as much. She smiled, and said, 'Jade, you will find out. Music is nothing but the language of love.'

Chapter 39

I won't go into the sordid details.

My plan, of course, ended in disaster. My determination collapsed like a house of cards.

I still could not believe that Dean had changed so much from the boy I had grown up with. I thought that I alone knew the real Dean. I believed I could change him; make him understand that what I had to give him was more that all the blonde sophisticated beauties of the world put together could. I knew I was right about that. I knew it from the bottom of my heart. All I had to do was persuade him. And so, of course I met Dean again. With a mixture of playacting, adoration and suppressed insecurity, I set out to catch him; as Jyothi.

It was a recipe for heartbreak.

Three times in the following year we met. Three times we clashed; three times I met him as Jyothi instead of as Jade; three times Jyothi ended up on the floor. After each romantic disaster Fran scooped me up, brushed the dust off me, gave me a good scolding, embraced me, and shoved me back onto the road running. Music, she convinced me, was my only way out of misery. And so I gritted my teeth and let my Strad speak for me. Fran was right, music kept the thought of Dean at bay.

But only for a while. Sometimes it all burst through the cleverly constructed wall of music like water breaking down a dam. I couldn't help it: it was stronger than I was! And I reasoned with myself: Dean had to get to know me, the real me, Jyothi. I wrote him heartfelt letters, into which I emptied my very soul. He never wrote back; but he did ring me occasionally, and I took comfort from those phone calls. He loved me, he reassured me. He really did. It was just so difficult: the lives we led . . . our different temperaments . . . Yes, we would meet again. Yes, we did meet again, whenever our orbits crossed for a day or a weekend and even, once, a week. And always I found him out. Once it was a photograph, a naked blonde beauty in the Swiss Alps. The second time, a phone call I should not have answered. A postcard, with a loving message I should not have read. Quarrels, justifications, reconciliations. A carousel of ups and downs, a whole year long. And then came the final fiasco.

It happened in New York. I was under great stress, having just completed a major US tour; I had done Boston, Chicago, Los Angeles, Philadelphia and now New York, and longed for the comfort of home. It's hard work staying at the top; to keep an edge on my skill I had been choosing ever more difficult music and I felt drained of all energy. Hardly the right moment for a romantic encounter.

But here, now, was Dean, on his home turf for once in a blue moon. I had let him know I was coming in advance, of course, but there had been no time to meet before the concert. Now it was over, and waiting for me was the usual bunch of red roses, the usual note, and an invitation to dinner. How could I resist?

The very sight of him made my heart lurch, and when he took my elbow to guide me to a taxi his touch, so gallantly gentle, so meaningful, was all it took to melt the last icicles of resistance. This was my Dean, the Dean of old, the Dean I loved.

But who was I? Jyothi, or Jade?

He called me Jyothi, but only Jade could win him; Jyothi, innocent, sincere Jyothi, had failed. He wanted Jade, and Jade I would be. And so with the last remnants of my strength I straightened my shoulders and gave him the dazzling smile of a star, radiating warmth and inner poise. It was a mask, but Dean could not tell. I knew my eyes, at least, spoke to him with a love that was genuine, and deep, and lasting, but that he did not see. The eyes were Jyothi's but all the rest was Jade.

Stay cool, I reminded myself as I squeezed his hand and gazed at him, knowing that I looked a queen, for I was dressed for the stage. Dean was speaking, and though I nodded and smiled at the right places – another practised talent – I hardly listened, for my own thoughts were more pressing. Tonight, I determined, I would prove my love to him, once and for all. I had grown up since our last encounter. I had read women's magazines and books; I knew the role I had to play. I knew I had to captivate him. I had done half the work during the concert, for Dean was always captivated by my music. The musician in me held Dean dangling like a puppet on a string. It was the woman who, till now, had not yet been ripe for him; too much the little girl, mistaking infatuation for love. Tonight I would be Jade.

The taxi set off, and Dean began talking about his last trip.

'Dean,' I interrupted suddenly, 'why don't you call me Jade, like everyone else does?'

'Because I'm not everyone else,' he said, smiling. 'Why? Do you want me to?'

'I think it would be nice,' I said. 'When you call me Jyothi

344

I feel like a little girl, your baby sister. Why, it's almost like incest!'

'If that's what you want, OK,' he said. 'But it'll take some getting used to. And as for you being my little sister . . .' He leaned over, turned my face gently towards his, and kissed me. I responded.

Our lips parted, and in the gloom of the taxi the white of Dean's teeth sparkled as he smiled at me. 'Wow!' he said. 'If that's what calling you Jade means then I'm all for it!'

I grinned back wickedly. 'Little girls grow up,' I said and I tried to put a seductive purr into my voice. To me it felt hollow, false – but Dean seemed to like it, for he folded me into his arms and would have started again if the taxi had not in that moment drawn up outside the hotel.

We had dinner in the restaurant of my hotel, and all went well until the dessert was served. The champagne helped, no doubt; I was witty and lively, flirtatious and elegant all at the same time. Jade, through and through; I had Dean in the palm of my hand. I dipped my spoon into the *crème brûlée* and that's when the waiter sidled up discreetly beside me and murmured a few words. I patted my lips with my napkin, excused myself with a dazzling smile, and, wondering who would be calling me here and now, walked innocently over to the telephone.

'Hello?'

'Is this Jade Keller?' The voice was female; high, excited, fast.

'That's right. And you are?'

'Oh, never mind that. I guess he's with you? He is, isn't he?'

'Could you please tell me –'

'Oh, my, dig that British high-class accent! Very posh! Could you *puh-leeze* . . .'

I wanted to slam down the receiver but found I could not. I

kept calm. I gripped the receiver tightly and felt the sweat on my palms but I kept calm.

'Whom am I speaking to, please?' I asked again.

'I said *never mind*, you bitch! Don't think I don't know what you're up to! I read your letters, see? I know you've been trying to get your dirty fucking claws into him; you think just because you're famous . . . well, listen, honey, I've got news for you. Your *dahlin'* Dean is the biggest skirt-chaser in New York, probably in the world. It's not just you. Chogori in winter, bet he called you that too, did he? Huh? Well, sweetie, there are quite a few Chogoris as far as Dean is concerned. One in each continent, at least; more like one in each country. And if you can't f—' There followed a stream of the vilest language I had ever heard, and that's when I summoned the strength to slam down the receiver.

Dean twisted and turned in the wind, trying to talk himself out of this one. She was Kathy, and she was lying; she was a jealous would-be girlfriend. She was nothing! She was a bitch! An *ugly* bitch! He had never even so much as . . .

I looked at him while he spoke, as from a great distance, and as I watched him, not speaking, the scales slowly fell from my eyes. This was not the Dean I had loved as a child. Perhaps that Dean still existed; perhaps he had gone for ever. Who knows? Perhaps he had been lost on some mountain range; perhaps he had been erased by the Julias and Kathys of this world. I would mourn for that Dean; I would always love him . . . or maybe not. Time would tell. But I would not mistake *this* man for Dean. I could not love this man. I did not know this man. It was over. Fran was right.

My failure with Dean fed into my skill; as if the only revenge I could find for the hurt he caused was to hone my expertise. I practised almost without break and the music that flowed from me was superior to any I had produced in all my life. My fingers danced on the strings with a dexterity they had never before been capable of. A subtle change rippled through me, surfacing as an almost physical need for musical perfection – no longer to scale the heights and explore the depths of feeling produced by music, but to surpass the limits of technical performance. The soulful renderings of Bach, Beethoven and Mendelssohn I once favoured gave way to the skill-demanding works of Paganini. Virtuosity was a fitting channel for my hurt and my anger, and Paganini, both as a composer and as a violinist, and even as a human being, was an ideal musical model in a time of crisis. With music, I would push Dean from me. Music would make me strong. So strong that, should he ever reappear out of the blue, I would never again be susceptible, never again fall, never again be Jyothi, a frail human being with feelings and a heart that longed for love. Paganini would help me in this goal. Paganini, too, had had to struggle with human temptation, and had had to make a clear choice. Paganini was the greatest violinist of all time . . . surely, I could seek no higher ideal! Only time would tell if I could ever arrive at the heights I set for myself, but Monika had always encouraged me to aim for the stars and I refused to set myself a lower goal than this: to be the best, the greatest.

At one Paganini concert, it is said, three hundred people were hospitalised on the official diagnosis of 'over-enchantment.' This snippet of information fascinated and amused me. That was what I wanted to achieve! I imagined it for myself: entire audiences, fanning themselves and swooning from over-enchantment; and an over-enchanted Dean on his knees, broken apart by the magic touch of my bow! Begging for forgiveness! I smiled to myself, over-enchanted by such a gratifying image.

So for my next Asian tour Paganini was my silent mentor, my model and my companion. Jade Keller had turned a page in her life; her star was growing brighter, and at the end of this tour all the world would know it.

As usual, Jack and Rachel were spending the winter months in India, and when I arrived at my hotel suite in Delhi – the culmination of my tour – I found a message saying that they had come to the city for the concert and were staying with Dean's mother. That made me unaccountably angry. I did not like Jack associating with anyone as close to Dean as his mother. It was bad enough for him to be married to Rachel; that I could accept. But did he have to go schmoozing with the bastard's mother? That was an irritation I could well do without. A musician's mind must remain unperturbed in order to give an optimum performance, and now here I was, internally fuming about a matter that had nothing at all to do with music. The next morning I had no time to waste thinking about Dean or his mother – my entire day was planned down to the last minute. I'd been greatly looking forward to this Indian concert – strangely enough the first I had given in the country of my birth – and it was the most important stop on this tour. There were two interviews with the *Times of India* and *India Today* scheduled for the morning, and a TV interview – live – for the afternoon.

The Indian musical elite, it seemed, was as excited as I was. And that excitement went far beyond the musical elite – interest in India for Western classical music is negligible, but I was still a big name among the educated, a source of pride. For I was home-grown, the most famous Indian musician of Western music, and a child of India! The tiny technical detail that I had, in fact, learnt to play my instrument in the West and, had not Destiny intervened, would have ended up a ragged beggar-woman in the streets of Bombay was conveniently overlooked, and I played along by not raising that rather inconvenient detail. No, I was a child of the slums, a rags to riches story – great news copy.

The TV interview went beautifully; I was well prepared. I had spent a relaxing three hours beforehand at the hotel's beauty and hair salon, pampered to the tips of my fingers. I wore an exquisite *salwar kameez* of burgundy silk, and heads turned as I swept into the studio. Studio employees bent over backwards to read my every wish from the batting of my eyes, and the admiration in their own eyes fed into the confidence that was the invisible framework for my self-image: the image of radiant, inviolable, godlike glory. Thus a diva is created, by mutual consent of the devoted and her devotees, a contract to uphold a myth as tenuous as cobweb. How fragile is that contract.

My interviewer, one of those wheat-skinned Indian men of Bollywood charm and beauty, flirted outrageously with me; and I flirted back, gave witty rejoinders to his probing – yet shallow – questions, smiled and laughed at all the right places.

'Tell me, Jade,' he said, leaning forward towards me and gazing into my eyes, 'you have everything any young woman could want – almost. You are successful, brilliant, gifted, rich, well-travelled and beautiful. And yet, you are single! Indian girls are usually married at your age. No wedding plans? Surely out of your myriads of male admirers there must be *one* who meets your approval? Surely you have a favourite?'

His eyes sparkled wickedly, suggestively. I returned the sparkle, smiled mysteriously, and replied with a backward sweep of my hair,

'As everyone knows, I am married to my music. My violin does not leave dirty socks on the floor for me to wash – and will never be unfaithful!'

We both had a good laugh at that, and I returned to the hotel confident that I would once again sweep all before me that evening; I would cast my usual spell and reap the sweet grapes of glory. I basked in the glow of that triumph to come, yesterday's annoyance forgotten.

And then Jack spoilt it all by ringing me.

I had not spoken to or seen him for several months. He and Rachel had been in Rishikesh since early November and would be staying until after Christmas. When Jack first heard I was going to be in Delhi for a concert he had invited me to join them there for a few days ('it will do you and your music good', he had said), but I had politely declined. Not only was my schedule booked up; Rishikesh was the last place on earth I would ever visit. But now here he was, in Delhi, and not particularly welcome.

After we had exchanged the usual preliminaries Jack suggested dinner together afterwards, which is what we usually did in London. And as usual, I agreed, hiding my reluctance.

'Oh, that would be nice. Yes, of course. Shall I book a table, or will you?'

'I'll do it,' said Jack. 'And by the way . . .'

'What?'

'Oh nothing. Hey what's this about your playing Paganini? You never liked him before.'

I smiled to myself. 'Why are you coming if you don't like Paganini?'

'Mostly just to see you in action again, but I'm also curious. And besides . . .'

'What?'

'Oh, here's Rachel wanting to have a word with you. Glance our way, will you? We're on the fifth row, to the left. Bye, honey, and good luck.'

Before I could comment he was gone and Rachel was on the line, telling me about a Labrador puppy she was going to get when they returned to England, to replace Sheba who had died the previous autumn. 'Oh, and by the way,' she said after we had chatted for a while. 'We have a Christmas present for you. It's something you've wanted for a long time. What's your room number? It's a bit big so I'll have it delivered to your room.'

I gave her the room number without enthusiasm for the present, and with little curiosity, less concerned with what it could be than with the fact that I had nothing for them. I would have to go shopping the next morning, a highly unpleasant prospect. I know that some women adore wandering through department stores for hours but I have always hated it, especially in a city like Delhi, which I did not know at all. My memory of shopping in Delhi was indelibly connected with Dean's mother and her white limousine, gliding through the crowded streets to stop outside marble-fronted sari palaces. To make matters worse, Jack and Rachel were impossible to buy gifts for. They had so few desires and lived so simply. I'd buy them some huge, expensive Indian statue to put in their garden, I decided, something nice and spiritual, Krishna or Shiva or something, and have it shipped home. I ticked off that duty mentally. Perhaps I could just send a chauffeur to do it for me. I wondered vaguely what their present was; there was certainly nothing I could think of that I wanted badly. To play on strings divine: that yes. But nothing material. Nothing money could buy.

Nevertheless, Jack's call brought back a little of yesterday's irritation, and cast a slight shadow over the coming evening. I didn't feel like dining with Jack and Rachel. Rahul, the TV interviewer, had hinted he'd be at the concert, and that we might meet afterwards. I was rather looking forward to that. But, I thought, there was nothing to prevent him joining us for dinner, if we were both so inclined. I cheered up.

My first rendition went off without a hitch. The applause

was deafening. There were no hints of anyone falling over due to over-enchantment but that was anyway a far off goal. I was pleased with myself; I smiled with satisfaction and cast my eyes over the applauding audience, looking to see if I could get a glimpse of Jack and Rachel. I did.

But then, at the periphery of my vision, I caught a signal. It may not have been a physical signal. In fact, I am sure it was not. Rather, I felt that my gaze was pulled to the side, to Jack's side, by some magnetism beyond my rational comprehension. I could not have possibly made any logical connection to what I saw. The memories were far too deeply buried to surface in that one split second. And yet that split second was enough.

Eyes. *His* eyes. I would know them anywhere. I could pick them out of a crowd.

Eyes, fixed on me. Eyes that caught my gaze for that fragment of time.

I did not see the face that surrounded those eyes. I saw only the eyes.

Enough to freeze me. Enough to drive every single last note of music out of my mind and to leave nothing but a cold white blank, a cold white desperate blank into which not even the last frayed tendrils of a fractured Paganini strayed, or could be summoned. No memory of any music I had ever played in my life. It was as if I had been born deaf, as if music had never been laid in my soul as the most supreme gift a human could receive; as if what had been once given had been sucked away by a vengeful, wrathful God and left me empty, and bereaved, and humiliated beyond salvation.

I was supposed to play Caprice no. 13, 'Devil's Laughter'. But I could not. I was frozen into silence. As on so many previous occasions the thing that had haunted my music since childhood took hold of me. I became a statue, void of music, void of life. I could not play.

The silence was louder than the music that preceded it had been, louder than the applause had been. As it ticked by it grew louder. I could feel the audience grow nervous. As the silence continued I could sense that uneasiness swell into alarm; I could hear the worried exchange of glances, see the held breath, smell the sweat of anxiety.

In that silence the world I lived in collapsed around me into rubble, and in the rubble another world appeared; the true world, the world that was composed of nothing more substantial than vague memories; memories that could be evoked through a certain smell, or a bar of certain music, or a word; or, as in this case, a pair of eyes; memories that could be summarized with one word. India.

And somewhere at the back of that silence, I heard the devil laugh.

'I'm sorry,' I finally whispered. I turned my back on my audience, and, held head high in a last puny and meaningless show of bravado, walked off the stage.

As I walked on I felt hands reach out for me and heard voices calling my name. I recognised a few faces: Mr Harvey, and this person, and that. I ignored them all. I pushed my violin into a pair of hands reaching imploringly towards me. Whose hands? I have no idea. I continued on my way down the stairwell to the stage door and out into the street. I walked and walked, I had no idea where I was. The streets teemed with people, but they parted as I came as if they knew, as if they guessed, as if avoiding me. I flagged down an empty taxi and returned to Le Meridien. Sailed up to my suite in the glass lift.

As I entered the suite I saw it: a big, long box, placed against the wall, wrapped in cloth, tied with string, a label with my name in large letters. The present. I ignored it and walked into the bathroom. I removed my clothes and make-up. I went to bed. I waited for sleep.

But sleep was as obstinate as music. It would not come.

I lay in deathly silence for half an hour. I was fighting with all my might to keep my mind a blank, not to let a single memory of what had happened penetrate to my consciousness. It was a losing battle. I felt walls crumbling inside me as all that I had worked to build over the years fell apart. It was not just my career that was in shambles. It was my very personality. Who was I, without music? Now that music had died, how could I continue to exist?

I recalled the times it had happened before; few, and far between, but never as serious as now. I had never before fallen from a pinnacle.

That time, years ago, in Rishikesh; again, it had come about through my confrontation with India, and the memories that overflowed from my depths to the surface of my mind, preventing me from playing. There had been other, minor, lapses, mostly during private practice.

But nothing had been of this magnitude. Nothing could compare with the immense void that had descended on me at that crucial moment. It was a void that had still not left me to brood in solitude over my failure, but dug deeper into me with every passing second, and taunted me with the contemptuous words that echoed on in me where once there had been glorious music: *Failure! Little Nobody! Scum of the Streets!*

And again I heard the devil laugh.

Chapter 40

The telephone rang. I did not respond, and it rang again. I knew it would be Jack.

I realised he would not leave me and so I agreed that he should come up. I stood up, wrapped my dressing gown around me, and walked to the door. Jack, and just behind him, Rachel stood there. And just to compound my humiliation, they had brought *him* I refused to acknowledge his presence.

Now Jack was standing in the middle of the room. Rachel seemed to be inspecting the room, but when her eyes fell on the box, still wrapped in the corner, she glanced at me and I knew she had been looking for this. Suddenly it came to me, in a flash of insight; I knew what was in that box. It all figured.

'It won't work,' I said. I was speaking to the figure near the door, but without looking at him. 'You can't do it this way. You can't force me. See, I *chose* the violin, back then. You wanted me to choose, and I chose violin because I am a violinist. I mean, I was a violinist. You can't come back now and ask me to choose again. It's too late. It might have worked then but it won't work now. I don't know what you did to me in the concert. I don't know if you have some sort of hypnotic powers. Maybe you do. But it wasn't right to use them in this way, to drive my music from me.'

I felt a sob rising inside me and choked it back. 'Music was all I had; the violin was all I had. It was my life and if it's gone I don't want anything else.'

'Jyothi, you misunderstand. I never meant for you to choose,' Rabin said. And finally I raised my eyes to meet his.

He walked out of the shadows then. He seemed not to have aged a day, but his hair was longer and his eyes darker and brighter than I remembered. He was not smiling – it was not a time for smiling – and instead of holding out his hand to shake mine, he placed his palms together in a namaste, slightly bowing his head towards me. I did not return his greeting. I was irritated by his words and more so by his presence; in spite of what he had just said I knew that he had come to Delhi just for this: to destroy my life, to seduce me away from the path I had chosen. After wrecking my career, in public view, at the very pinnacle of my talent, he had come to add the finishing touches. He need not do so in words; the very fact that he stood here before me now, that he had found me after so many years, and come all this way to rub my abject failure in my face, was enough.

Jack spoke. 'Jyothi, I think you should listen to what Rabin has to say. We met him at Rishikesh and he told us a little of what happened there so long ago, when you were fifteen. I remembered your telling me, back then, that you wanted to change to the sitar and I remember how I dismissed you offhand. I'm sorry. I should have listened. Maybe it would never have come to this. But, that was then. I would not have understood back then. Now I do. Rabin explained; he was astonished when I told him you had wanted to change from the violin to the sitar back then.'

Rabin said: 'The instrument doesn't matter, Jyothi; it is secondary. What matters is the music. What matters is *you*; that the music flows unstained and in its original pristine beauty from you; it doesn't come from the instrument, but through it. It starts in you.'

'You said I had to choose. You did. I heard you.'

'Yes; but not between instruments! You had to choose how you play. A true musician gives. He doesn't take.'

'What was I taking? What was I doing wrong?' The anguish in me welled up and it came out as a cry of desolation.

'Taking music. Using music. Using it to become a Somebody. Becoming a parasite that feeds on the music. Attempting to own the music. You cannot own music. It just is. You can at best be a channel for it. Then the music is at its most glorious.'

'Jyothi,' Jack interrupted. 'You know I was worried about you. I couldn't put it into words what exactly bothered me but when we met Rabin again after all these years and we spoke of you I was able to understand what it was. You've changed so much. I don't know . . . lost so much. You were becoming so distant. So ambitious. It didn't seem right. You didn't seem right. Most of all, you didn't seem happy.'

I could not look at any of them. I could not speak. Rachel had not said a word till now but as from a great distance I heard her voice.

'Jyothi, what happened tonight is not the end of the world. We spoke to Mr Harvey before coming here; he says . . .'

'Behind my back! You're all talking about me behind my back!'

I turned to Jack; I could not bear to speak to Rachel. I wished she would go. I wished Rabin would go. And Jack too. I could not bear any of them.

357

'No! Jyothi, don't think that way.'

But I was beyond reason. I felt the tears welling in my eyes. I felt the shame and degradation sweeping through me in great waves. My career, my future, in rubble around me, fingers pointing. Rachel smirking. I didn't want their pity. I didn't want their condolences. I could not look into their eyes; I was reduced to nothing, and all I wanted was to be alone. But they would not go.

I heard Jack's voice as from a great distance:

'. . . we think it's not too late, We think it will help you. Because we know you are a true musician.'

Who were they to discuss my life, my music, whisper about me in my absence? What did any of them know? Had any of them ever felt that grandeur, that glory, that power? How could they judge?

'She is,' said Rabin.

There he was, speaking of me in the third person. As if I were invisible. He who had come to bring me down, to pull the earth from beneath my feet.

'How on earth do you know!' I cried, to him. 'Whenever I play in your presence I break down. It's something you do to me. You look at me as if you would destroy me.'

Rabin spoke and at last I looked up to meet his eyes. They were grave, full, too understanding for me to bear. I looked away again. 'Should I take that as an insult or a compliment, that I should have such power? I guarantee you I have done nothing to you.'

'Then why? Why did it happen? Tonight, of all nights! It was so important for me! Why did you come, if not to destroy me? And now I look such a fool.'

'Perhaps . . .'

But I could not listen. I turned away from Rabin. I forced

myself to speak calmly and collectedly and not to let the voice screaming inside me take over.

'Go away,' I said to the room in general. 'I don't care.'

I had to do something with my hands; those poor abandoned things that had been denied the touch of the strings and the bow. They itched, they felt useless, like great flapping appendages without a task to perform. I pulled the waistband of my dressing gown tighter and retied the bow, folded my arms to quieten my hands

'Don't say that!' Jack cried. 'It's not the end. You can't just give up.'

'Please go.' My voice was expressionless and final. Jack knew it.

'Very well. But I think it would be a good idea for you to come with us for a few weeks – to Rishikesh. Rabin's there and . . .'

'Go.'

And I turned my back on them. I went into my bedroom, closed the door, and a few minutes later Jack called out that they were leaving. I did not reply.

The next morning I rang Mr Harvey and told him my career was over. I asked him to cancel all my future engagements.

'But, Jade . . .' But I refused to listen. Inside me was a barricade, behind which resided over the domain 'music' and all things related to it. The wall was insurmountable; to breach it was beyond me. On this side of the bulwark it was unbelievable empty and lonely for I could not imagine a life without music and yet that part of me was as if turned to stone.

I, who had once been so strong, who had sailed so high, reduced to a cringing heap of nothing on the floor. How could it have come to this? I did not know. I did not want to know.

Tears stung my eyes as I said, with as much drama and pathos as I could muster: 'Goodbye. It's over.'

I spent the day in my hotel suite. I had a long luxurious bath and ordered the beautician and hairdresser and a masseuse to come and take care of me. I ordered the most expensive lunch the hotel had to offer. I lounged in bed, watching television. A news programme came on and I saw myself on stage, just before the fall. I switched off the TV. I remembered my own words: 'music will never be unfaithful to me'. And I could imagine tomorrow's headlines: 'Jade Jilted!' I burned with shame. I refused to take telephone calls or see visitors.

I needed to be coddled and spoiled, to fall into the lap of luxury. I can afford this, I told myself. This is what I deserve. This is what I worked for. I am a star; I have been applauded, I am a success! No matter what comes, I am a star! I am!

But I looked into the mirror and saw a different story.

Instead of my own face I saw that of a little girl; a little girl in rags.

I looked away.

No! I told myself. I have escaped that! I am another!

But I knew the truth.

I ordered three bottles of wine and got drunk.

I went to bed and slept. When I woke up it was dark.

So what now? Said that voice, and it was mocking.

Well-housed, well-clothed, well-fed Jade.

Are you also well loved, Jade? Are you satisfied?

Or are you Jyothi?

I was alone with myself, and it was not a self I was acquainted with.

I mentally tried to grab the glitter, to press it to me, to roll my name in it. Jade, Jade, Jade, I said. I am Jade.

But the little voice replied:

Jade is no more. Jade has crumbled into nothing.
You are back where you began.
You are Jyothi.
You are a little girl in rags. Just a little girl in rags.
All else was illusion.
The glitter, the fame, the applause was all illusion. Where is it now? Where are you now?
How does it feel when the glitter and the glory is stripped from you? When you are naked, back where you began?

I dressed myself in a simple cotton *salwaar kameez*, went down to the lobby and walked out into the streets, ignoring the gestures of the waiting taxi drivers. I walked and walked, and before long I found myself where I wanted to be, in a street of high, decaying buildings from which loops of limp, ragged washing hung, the street itself teeming with life. I melted into the crowd, this time inconspicuous, an Indian like any other. The air was thick with a thousand sounds and smells all jumbled together. My senses, assaulted, gasped for breath. I felt stifled; I could not breathe. I escaped into a quieter side street. Here, the pavement was lined with bodies, covered in grimy, tattered cloths; lifeless forms, perhaps sleeping, perhaps dead. Some of the forms were tiny; little children, such as I had once been. I stepped gingerly between them; and I remembered.

I smelt the stench of poverty; I tasted it on my lips. It was a familiar stench, a familiar taste. I was back where I belonged.

Jade is not real! I told myself. This is real! This is where you are from! This is you! This is Jyothi!

'No!' I howled, and ran for my life.

I was lost. I could not find my way back to the hotel. So I summoned Jade. It was Jade who could find a taxi with a snap of her fingers, Jade who, without a penny in her pocket, could order a hotel employee to take care of the driver, please, and place it on the bill. This hotel and all its luxury was all earned by Jade

Defiance leapt within me as I re-entered my suite. I would not let Jade die. I would reclaim her.

I was so alone, so desperately alone. I sat on the bed and stared at the telephone. There were several people I could ring to end the loneliness. Jack would be overflowing with love and understanding; if I called him he would come. He would be there for me, but I could not bear the pity, the 'I-told-you-so' smugness.

I needed to speak to someone who still believed in Jade. Oh, thousands of people did. I had my fans. They had all bent their knee before me, but I could not bear their adoration now. I wanted someone real, someone close, someone beloved. Someone who would remind me of myself, of who I had been, and who would reassure me that I still lived on.

I wanted Dean.

I fumbled in my bag and took out my address book. I dialled Dean's New York number, but without much hope. Dean was very rarely at home. He had a mobile phone but it was usually switched off. For all I knew, Dean was traipsing through the Amazon jungle (highly unlikely; Dean hated jungles) or sliding down a Himalayan glacier right now. I dialled all the same.

Miracles do happen. At the other end, from the other side of the world, I heard Dean's voice.

'Dean! Oh Dean!'

'Jyothi, hey! Great to hear from you. Where are you?'

'Oh Dean! It's always been you!'

There was a moment's silence before he replied, and with a shade less enthusiasm in his voice. 'Jyothi? Is something the matter?'

'I love you Dean. I've always loved you. You love me too, don't you? You do love me?'

Another pause; caution, hesitation. A coolness I chose to ignore.

'Jyothi, you know I do! Of course!'

'Really? Truly? There's no-one else? No Kathy? She really was lying?'

'Jyothi. Something's the matter. Tell me. What's up?'

'I just need to know if you love me. I need someone to love me. I want someone to believe in me.'

'Of course I do, but . . .'

'Then let's get married!'

'Married?' This time there was no pause, no hesitation. But I didn't give him a chance to continue.

'Yes, married, Dean. Can't you see. I'm the one who always loved you, I'm the one who's always waiting for you, at the end of your affairs. You know I am. And I know you love me, deep down inside. You know me. You're the only one who really knows me. And I know you. Deep down inside we belong together, you know it, I know it. Those other women, not one of them really knows you or really cares. Dean, please . . .'

Then I heard it in the background. I have perfect hearing and can pick up sounds others cannot, and there it was: a female voice saying. 'Who is it, Dean? Come on, put an end to it.'

So I put an end to it. I sadly replaced the receiver. Yes, I told myself. Put an end to it all.

I was sobbing, and with my tears all the accumulated despair broke down though barricade and a century of sorrow came pouring out; Jade's sorrow, and Jyothi's, and the sorrow of a million Jyothis and a million Jades.

Jade stood before me. I saw her in my mind's eye, standing before me, a golden effigy. Cool, triumphant, Jade. Smug, bitchy, self-centered Jade. Jade's smile was false, and her gaze was cold. Jade was a façade, a mirage; I had built her out of nothing. I had thought her strong, but she was weak – all shine, no substance. I had thought her rich, but she was poor, as poor as Jyothi. I did not like her. I had clung to her as to life; but she had nothing to give. I had to let her go.

So I let her go, and she imploded back into her creator. Somewhere inside me Jade and Jyothi mingled and became one, and I learnt then that they had never been separate. Jade had always been Jyothi and the misery had always been there, behind the glitter and the glory. Jade had never been more that a mask; a mental construction, born out of my despair at the time of Monika's death, constructed to win Dean's love, a mask to hide behind, to face a taunting world. She was unreal. I had always been Jyothi, the little girl from the back streets of Bombay, and all the fame and all the triumph could never eradicate that. Jade and Jyothi: one as poor and ragged as the other, mirror images of each other, both hungry, desperate, for love.

That's when the telephone rang again, and this time I answered it. It was Jack. He was downstairs in the hotel lobby.

'Oh Dad!' I cried. 'Yes, come up. Please come up!'

Jack became my father once again, and once again I was Jyothi, a devastated little girl whose world had just fallen apart. Jack had done it before: brought me back from the brink. Just like so long ago, he did it with love, and with music.

Together we unpacked the sitar, lying abandoned on the couch all this time.

'One step at a time. One note at a time.' Jack told me. 'Just like then, when you were a little girl in Bombay – remember?

That's what brought you back from the brink so long ago. Try that.'

'Not here,' I said. 'Not in this hotel. Dad – take me back to Rishikesh.'

Chapter 41

It was just Jack and me. No Rachel, no Rabin, and I was grateful. Rishikesh was cool at this time of the year, and the nights were clear, and the stars seemed so close you could touch them. Jack and I spent hours on the roof of our bungalow, embraced by the night and by the music.

I began slowly. I touched one string, and I heard that deep, rich, yearning sound, and it echoed within my soul. After that it was easy. It was enough to listen to one string at a time. The sound resonated through me, resonated with every fibres of my being, balm on the troubled waters of my spirit. Just one tone over and over again echoing in spirals down to the very bottom of my consciousness. Bringing me back home.

I took Jack for a walk the way Rabin and I had gone, to Swami Satyananda's hut. It was a half ruin, deserted, the roof caved in, overgrown with weeds. Tears came to my eyes as I saw that ruin; it was as if something in my past had died; something exquisite. The most perfect morning. I felt I would gladly exchange all the years of triumph for just one moment of that morning. I did not speak. I turned around, signalled to Jack to come with me, and we returned to the ashram.

The past cannot be recalled, I realised. The walls of that hut have crumbled, that morning is over – and yet its spirit is ever present, here and now; in music.

And slowly, I awoke to the mystery of music, of something so ineffable it could never be expressed except as a tingle, a thrall of magic beyond the substance of notes, something embedded in the spirit of music and can never be created by the musician, but is simply given, and can only be revealed. The language of the most exalted part of my soul; the speech of angels; a language yet unknown to me but which I would learn, with time.

I let the idea take root, and grow, a hesitant seedling. I watched it grow; and as it grew so did something else, vague at first, and small, yet radiant with a warmth that seemed to have an independent source in the depths of my being. I stood on the roof, swept by the wind, and spread my arms out wide, and closed my eyes; and it was as if that warmth spread through my being and filled my every cell, and I knew what I had to do.

Rabin came. I was ready for him now. I dared to recall the past again, not just the back streets of Bombay, not just rags and dirt and squalor, but other pasts, other Jyothis; and, at last, music.

We sat on the concrete steps with our feet washed by the Ganges.

'Do you remember when we first met?' Rabin said.

'Of course I do! How could I ever forget that morning?'

'I think you have, you know. It was a different morning.'

I looked at him, puzzled. 'What do you mean?'

'You have forgotten. Of course you have, how could you not forget? How old were you, four? Five?'

'Rabin, what on earth are you talking about?'

'Listen,' said Rabin, and he smiled into my eyes. 'When we met here, in Rishikesh, I had a feeling about you: a certainty. But I didn't go into it. It was only after the second time that I met you that I bothered to follow up on that feeling. By then I knew your name, and a bit about your past. I made investigations. I had my memories. I remembered a sunny white room in our village home; I remember a little girl who came one morning to hear me play. The dhobi's daughter.

'I went back to my home village, and I learned some more. The ladies in my family remembered well, of course. And in the village your family was well known; the dhobi family, with a little girl named Jyothi. You had all gone to Bombay, they said, and had never been heard of since. The dates coincided. And your name. Jyothi. The little girl who loved music.

'I well remember that little girl,' Rabin said. 'I was about twelve at the time but she stayed in my memory the way some irrelevant incidents of the past tend to cling to the mind. When I first saw Jyothi in Rishikesh I knew that we were, in some strange way, connected, but I assumed the connection would be in the future, not in the past. Or if from the past, then from a past life. I did not remember that room.'

I stared at him. Something crept into my mind which was not a memory but a knowledge, and I knew Rabin was right because that's what this knowledge told me.

The little girl who danced in the street. The girl Jack found.

We shared a long silence. Then I said 'What is that future, Rabin?'

'Who knows?' he answered. 'Swami Satyananda died two years ago. Now I myself am a teacher of sitar.'

'Will you teach me?'

'Of course I will. But, you know, you can never replace the violin.'

'I know. I don't want to.'

'Nor do you need to replace Western music with Indian music.'

'I know that, too. But Indian music gives me serenity, It brings me back to myself. It takes me to my source. It makes me whole.'

'And out of that wholeness you will play the violin again. You will play differently, then.'

'I know.'

'But, you know, violin and sitar also go very well together.'

I nodded. 'Yehudi Mehunin and Ravi Shankar. I know.'

'So there are many possibilities.'

I nodded. 'Yes. I can see that.'

He paused. There was a silence between us, a comfortable, easy silence.

'One should not plan too far ahead,' Rabin said then. 'It's better to be open to the moment, and see what happens.'

I nodded again.

'And as for your career . . .'

I shook my head, vigorously. 'I've had that. I need to move on. I've been doing it wrong. First I played for my mother. Then I played for Dean. And then I played for myself. That was the worst. I wanted music to transport me to some exalted heights. I wanted it to glorify me. It was always me, me, me.'

I stopped, and listened to the stream rushing down the hillside, gathering in the pool where Dean and I once played; disappearing into the earth, re-emerging in a burst of crystal clear, sunlit water swirling up around the rock on which we sat.

'But it's the other way round,' I told Rabin. 'This time I need to make music for its own sake. Not for anyone, but for the joy that is inherent in it. To really listen to the music inside me, as it comes. I need to discover music in all its purity; let it come out from the depths, just like that fountain, coming from the earth. I want it to take me with it. Wherever it will. I remember you telling me this, so long ago. But only now I understand.'

'Yes,' said Rabin. 'And as you progress you will find the spontaneity and purity of expression that is so much a part of devotional Indian music will make itself heard.'

'There's a Bach quote – let me think . . .'

Rabin laughed. ' "The goal and final purpose of all music should be for none other than the glory and praise of God." ' That's exactly the Indian way. It will become your way.'

I smiled, because I understood perfectly.

'It could be a long journey,' Rabin teased. He was like that, serious and teasing, never giving instructions but letting me discover for myself. He was going to be a great teacher, the best I had ever had. I could feel it in my bones.

'Yes, well, it could be long,' I conceded. 'But look at this stream here. It's got a long way to go, too, till it gets down to the sea. But it doesn't seem worried. Not in the least. It's so joyful, so playful, here and now.'

'Ah, yes,' he said. 'But, you know, sometimes two streams meet, and flow together.'

I smiled; I understood again.

'And there's something else,' I added quietly, so quietly I thought at first he had not heard. But he had. He turned to look at me, and his eyes were questioning.

'Rabin, I've been lucky. So very lucky. I've come such a long way. I've been lost but I found my way back. And yet there's something missing.'

There was a silence between us as Rabin listened. He did not press me to fill it, so I did not. I was thinking. And slowly, unbidden, the idea took form in my mind. At first it was just an inkling, a vague notion. After a while I tried to put it into words.

'That child in Bombay – the child that was me. She has been given so much.' I said slowly.

'Yes,' was all Rabin said.

'I feel, as a musician, I can give some of that back. And yet . . .'

'It's not enough?' Rabin asked.

'No.'

I was quiet for another moment. In the distance I heard the rush of a stream, and it was soothing, like the constant sruti note in Indian music, calling the mind back to its source.

'I need to do more,' I said. "Give back much more. So many children, like me. Beggar girls. Homeless families. I've had the benefits of a life in the West, education. Most of all, education.'

'Mmmm,' said Rabin, waiting.

'Music was in me all the time. It was inside me. I don't know how it got there, it's as if it was planted there. By God, or something. What if other children have music in them? Other Bombay slum children? Or Delhi children. Or poor country children. And not just music. What if they have other gifts. Dance. Art. Sport? So many gifts, just lying fallow.'

'Until somebody comes along.'

'Yes, like Jack and Monika came along. Passed me by on the street, and my fate was sealed.'

'So?'

'So I'd like to go and have a look. Go back there. With you. And Jack.'

'And then?'

'Oh Rabin, you know what I'm getting at. You know perfectly well!' I pinched his arm fondly, and laughed. I felt a familiar buzz of excitement, the kind of thrill that filled me just before I went on stage. But this was different – on a far higher frequency. And there was none of the nervousness of a pending stage performance. Instead there was enthusiasm, and eagerness. Now that the idea had been nudged awake it seemed to be have grown wings with the speed of light, and those wings seemed to be flapping with greatest urgency.

'Oh Rabin, can't you just see it? It's going to happen!'

'What, exactly?' he asked, and the teasing tone did not escape me.

'If you can't guess I'm not going to tell. I don't even know myself, not exactly. I just know it'll be marvellous!'

I flung out my arms in exhilaration, and, well, I don't know how it happened, but next thing I knew, Rabin was there in them, and laughing with me, and I knew everything was going to be all right.

Epilogue

Jack easily found the place again. The hovels were there; different hovels, and different people in them, but the same cracked pavement, and the same wall, black with the same grime, just thicker. I had been a child, back then; yet how familiar it all was! That old-young woman in rags might have been Ma; that little girl with matted hair could have been me. The smells were the same, and the sounds, it all came back as if it were yesterday. I leaned over and beckoned the little girl with my forefinger. But she was shy, and hid behind her mother's skirt. She was about five.

Rabin held my violin case for me as I opened it. The little girl left her mother's skirts and came nearer to look. There were other children as well, an older girl, and two young boys, an infant in her mother's arms. A few women, curiously eyeing the shining brown instrument as I lifted it from its case.

I played *Salut d'Amour*. I played Beethoven, but I saw their frowns and knew they could not follow. So I played a Spanish dance, lively and lilting. The children stared, and the adults. How they stared! Their faces were solemn, dirt streaked, suspicious, but only at first. Pedestrians stopped to watch and listen, as did a cyclist, and another. Cars slowed as they passed by, the drivers leaned out and turned down their radios. A traffic jam was in the making.

The children drew nearer. One of the little boys began to clap in time. And a second. The older girl smiled. The infant stretched out her arms to me.

The five year old tapped the pavement with her toe, in time to the music.